EXO

A NOVEL

COLIN BRUSH

DIVERSION BOOKS

Diversion Books
A division of Diversion Publishing Corp.
www.diversionbooks.com

For more information, email info@diversionbooks.com

First Diversion Books Edition: November 2025
Trade Paperback ISBN: 979-8-89515-052-8
e-ISBN: 979-8-89515-053-5

Design by Neuwirth & Associates, Inc.
Cover design by Michel Vrana

1 3 5 7 9 10 8 6 4 2

To Col S and Ben, precocious voyagers

ACKNOWLEDGEMENTS

Thank you to the intrepid explorers who survived first contact with *Exo*:

Col L, Pauls S and C, Andy, Mike, Jonny, Ben, Dan, my agents John and Joshua, my editor Toni, Nina, Shannon, and everyone else at Diversion Books, cover artist Michel, and the copyediting team of Henry and Amy.

> "What is the meaning of it, Watson? What object is served by this circle of misery and violence and fear? It must tend to some end, or else our universe is ruled by chance, which is unthinkable"
>
> —Sherlock Holmes,
> "The Adventure of the Cardboard Box"

CONTENTS

DAY ZERO

SEVEN MINUTES INTO THE EXPERIMENT, a slow-motion explosion rips through the lab.

Empty space unfolds and five staff—four scientists and the comms officer—are instantly lost. She's lucky, crawling out on hand and knees. Her left hand presses her left eye, holding in the blinding pain, covering that stippled void.

Behind her, twisting metal groans, concrete percussively cracks, and walls stop being walls. Dimensions uncoil. Space burps and foams. She can't see it, but she feels a shuddering deep in her bones. Registering the cries of the left behind—the three whose disappeared limbs prevented them running with the others who got out ahead of her—she resists any urge to glance back. This is the point of no return.

In the corridor, orange lights flash, indicating a breach. An alarm is ringing. Mercifully, drowning out the screams.

She walks her hands up a wall and rises to her feet.

The lab is between her and the only safe exit, into the compound out the back.

She has no option but to follow the others into the monitoring bay and down the ramp. The survivors are gathered at the huge storm doors as they slide apart. Someone has obviously overridden the security protocols. Out there, certain dissolution. In here, imminent obliteration. Make your choice.

Light spills through the gap. The familiar pebble slope. The haunting gray.

Yawning death.

Red lights flash on the wall. Signs snatch at the gaze of her uncovered eye:

WARNING:
EXPOSURE TO CAUL.
DO NOT PROCEED
WITHOUT AUTHORISATION.
TETHER AND BUDDY
SYSTEM MANDATORY.

Every second of her existence is tormented by the gray waves. They call. They threaten. They cajole. Up and down the shore, colleagues have succumbed. Friends. Rivals. Even lovers. Lost to it, time and again. Count the years. Count the decades. Add up the long centuries before her arrival. Lives uncountable.

The waves batter the beach with a rhythmic thumping that always sounds to her ears like a hungry giant knocking at a door. One day the door will open. *This day?*

By the signs, two large reels hold coiled rope tethers. Weekly safety drills have instilled in them an overwhelming need to obey the signs. *Death is out there.* Sweat prickles the skin of her forehead. But the idea of stopping, of pausing to attach a harness and a sprung rope to help her resist the lure, is for the birds.

The unfolding destruction behind is a more clear and present danger. She can hear it devouring more walls, more building. This bunker, this fortress, this prison. Designed to keep them safe inside. To protect them from what is outside. The threat was never supposed to come from within. (She has always known it lies within.)

The others ahead of her—who also made it out of the lab alive—stumble down the pebbled slope. A hundred metres away the waves roll up the beach. High tide.

Instantly, she feels it. A tingling in her legs. The need swelling inside her.

She forces her feet to slow. They resist, wanting her to let go, to freely run down the slope. To run until there is no more running left. Wouldn't that be wonderful?

The gray—insidious, murderous, ravenous—is singing. *I have been waiting.*

With a lurch in her heart, she sees that the others aren't slowing.

She knows what happens next. Has seen the cam footage too many times. So many lives lost. Fury overrides her legs' urging. Stones scatter as she halts. She calls their names. One after the other. They don't hear, or they hear her too well.

Her feet tremble. A dangerous St. Vitus's dance. One step. Two steps. Getting closer. The rolling gray waves are all she sees. Their roar is all she hears. The gray is all there is. She covers both eyes—the good and the bad—as the rolling and pounding lulls her. She's immediately drifting, almost floating. Caught on an infinite tide. For a moment, she is captured by this immense stillness.

In her left eye the void flickers.

She takes away her hands. She is ten metres further down the beach. The four ahead of her are now three. One is on his knees just metres from the gray. One is up to her ankles in the shallows, and one is sprinting the last few metres.

No more calling, she thinks. It is too late for names.

The one in the shallows has her back to the waves. Tears on her cheeks. She takes several steps backwards, up to her waist and then, just as the sprinter rushes past, she vanishes in an instant. The sprinter turns back, a wild look on his eager, young face. He gives her a crazed grin: triumph and delight. He's made it! He scoops the gray in his cupped hands, throws hands up so the gray splashes down around him. Then, and it is always nauseating to recall later, he seems to shrink, like he falls away in several directions at once. There one second, gone the next.

Her sore eye stings. The stippled void flickers. Shadows in the emptiness. Three of them. I'm seeing the other side, she thinks. Feels repelled. Not more ghosts.

She shakes her head to dismiss them. When she looks again the one on his knees is swaying drunkenly. He will be staring into some far-off place. He has already gone. Nothing else matters. Family. Colleagues. Comrades. Their mission. She calls out anyway.

Suddenly, he lurches to his feet. A moment later, her bad eye glimpses another shadow. Ghosts everywhere she turns. What's one more?

Dazed, she steps forward.

A hand falls heavily on her shoulder. Holding her back.

She turns. The doc. He's made it out. His smile is pained.

"Buddy system," he growls. "Mandatory."

The spell broken, she takes the offered hand. Comfort in the firm grip.

Slowly, one careful step at a time, the two of them turn from the gray and its ghosts. They keep their backs to the building that for so long has been an outpost and a shelter, a research station into which so many hopes have been invested, and which is now tumbling into a vortex that in days will begin drawing down the sky.

And, silently, she wonders: Has it worked?

DAY ONE

MAE WAS OUT checking her traps when she found the girl.

It had been a long, disappointing day. Most of the cages were empty. After consulting her map—three traps left before she was done, each a long walk, close to the Caul—she'd trudged reluctantly towards the shore. Her pack, a couple of meagre marbit carcasses hanging from it, felt heavy. Pebbles rolled under her moccasins, jarring her brittle bones. If you weren't careful, you could turn an ankle. Once, she'd always been in a hurry, careless of how the stones shifted under her feet. Now she didn't give them the chance. Besides, what need had she for hurry?

The persistent wind—some days it blew until your head hurt—gnawed her ears and needled the craggy contours of her face. Another winter on its way. Her thirtieth here. But who was counting? Who wanted to be reminded they were an exile, a prisoner, a ghost? She'd come here to find somebody and turned into a nobody.

Here and there, wiry sparsely leafed bushes grew. Brittle and dry, they survived on frugal falls of rain. Numbers were thinned through uprooting by storms that spilled out of the Caul and by her fellow penitents' kindling-gathering. She stepped over a gray-brown vine growing in a straight line. Its hard, succulent tear-shaped leaves, if eaten, would make you sick for days. These creepers grew in one direction: towards the gray mass to the south.

The distant booming on the shore was like hammer blows on stone.

She passed a rusted hulk sinking into the plain. An exterior door hung open, steps descending into the pebble grave in which the rocket's nose was buried. Wind whistled through gaping plexiglass-scavenged portholes. Networks of alloy pipes clung to the hull like cobwebs. Ribbed burners pointed at the sky like giant clapperless bells.

The first two traps were empty, the second's bait was gone. She scraped away the rust speckling the tripwire with her knife. She popped open a small plastic vial and applied grease sparingly, wishing she could do the same to her own joints. She replaced the lost bait with a succulent green leaf.

She looked up. Had she heard something? In the distance was another wreck. A brown pipe on the horizon. The feeling of being watched was strong. She shook her head. You had to guard against it. The Caul had you imagining all sorts of things. She sniffed the air: dust, time-pounded stone. For others it was metal, plastics, recycled air—the stale reminders of confinement. Hers was the quarried walls of the Mars orphanage and the church's chill benediction. She hated the smell of dust.

The trap was set. Last one and then home.

The rusting hulk was long and thin. It had come down close to the Caul and years of storms had wrought brutal devastation: broken-backed, skin-pitted, holed. She gave the rocket a wide berth.

Hairs rose on the back of her neck. That uneasy feeling of not being as alone as you had thought. She still trusted her senses. Some of her fellow penitents called that a weakness. But in her former profession it had been her strength. Watching, listening, sniffing out evidence. Of course, none of it had helped here. Ghosts left no traces. Pausing, she peered closer at the ship's carcass.

Out of a dark hole in its base a white face stared back at her.

Small, rosy-cheeked. Round, almost boyish, features that despite their paleness reminded Mae of someone. The same someone who'd damned her to this planet.

Neither of them moved for a time.

The face disappeared and a short while later a little girl emerged from behind the ship. She wore a red coat and red boots. The coat toggles were undone. Under the coat was an odd, ankle-length green dress with buttons down the front from collar to hem. The girl had long, straggly, chestnut hair and about her mouth and gray eyes there was a cool blankness. She stood stiffly, arms at her sides, as if chilled. She didn't move, only stared. She appeared to be six- or even seven-years-old, but Mae knew she was younger.

Mae looked around but could see no sign of Magellan, her father. Where was he? The man knew enough not to allow his daughter to stray like this. She bit her lip. And Mae knew enough not to mix herself up in the affairs of other penitents.

She broke eye contact with the girl and continued walking.

After a hundred metres she turned and saw that the girl—her name was Siofra—was following, stumbling over the pebbles. When Mae stopped, so did the girl. They regarded one another for a short time. The girl looked miserable, weary. Mae wanted to shout *Go back to your father,* but didn't trust her voice. They barely knew each other. The child wasn't her responsibility. Siofra had to be made to understand that.

Mae carried on and this time she didn't stop to look back.

○

DRAWING ASIDE THE PLEATED FOLDS OF HER COAT, wizened fingers stiff with cold felt for the leather haft of her knife. Mae drew the blade and placed it on the ground. Next, she sat, an operation that took a degree of bodily coercion. Her lower back protested. She shrugged off her pack and took out a plastic cup, which she screwed firmly into the pebbles.

The wire cage of the final trap lay between her splayed legs. She carefully opened the door and grasped the marbit. In size, shape, and colouring, it resembled a cross between a marmot (front end) and a rabbit (rear). Hence the bland and, to Mae's mind, inaccurate name of marbit. There wasn't much meat on them and that little was stringy and tough. But if she cooked a stew with some of the samphire she cultivated, she could eke out a carcass to provide for five or six days. The bones would make a thin broth. Having a meagre appetite did not stop her stomach grumbling.

Dehydrated and weak, the marbit barely stirred as one hand grasped the animal by the back of its neck and the other took up the knife. A single cut slit its throat. She dropped the knife, took hold of the long back legs and flipped the animal upside down. It kicked, blood squirting and running into the cup.

She could feel the girl's eyes on her back the whole time. What was wrong with the child? She had matched Mae, step for step. Not so hard. She looked over her shoulder as the last, sluggish drops of blood oozed into the cup. The girl sat fifty metres away, watching.

Mae knew she was supposed to feel something, but it had been so long since she'd felt anything but numbness towards anyone, she had no idea what it was she should feel. I am gray inside, she thought. Gray as the Caul, dead as this world.

She shook her head. If Magellan chose not to keep his daughter on a short leash, what business was it of hers? You used to care, she reminded herself. Once, it was your job. You were good at it.

She looked at the sky. Dark clouds promised rain—a promise so rarely kept.

She reset and baited the trap and tied the animal to her pack. She held the warm cup in her hand. She turned at the sound of pebbles moving. The girl was approaching. Mae sighed.

"Where's your father?" she asked.

The girl stopped. Ten metres away.

"You're far from home. Does he know you're out here? It's not safe."

The girl's face was expressionless, almost vacant. Her wary eyes strayed from Mae's face to the cup.

"You want this?"

The girl shook her head.

"Where's your father?" she repeated

The girl opened her mouth, but no sound came out. She held a folded piece of paper in one hand.

"Still not talking," said Mae, wondering when she'd last seen the child. Months ago, at least. Penitents kept themselves to themselves. For who wanted to look into the eyes of another haunted soul? Not when it was a reminder of your own neediness, of the weakness that had driven you here—a humanity which, year by year, you were slowly surrendering.

The cup was warm in her palms. She raised it and sniffed. A hard, iron scent. She drank its contents. "You go home now, Siofra. Back to your father. And tell him if I catch you sniffing round my traps again, there'll be trouble."

○

MAE WAS NOT A BORN TALKER. Whenever she was difficult the sisters would remind her: You never spoke a word until you were five. As if those old nuns knew the whole story.

She'd been found, aged three, crawling around one of the habitat's public areas. Couldn't walk, couldn't talk. Searches were made for her parents. No one came forward and no one was found. Not a single DNA match. You'd have thought it impossible to hide an infant aboard a habitat of a hundred-thousand souls, where resource allocation and orbital mechanics required measurements down to the exact gram.

But not so.

Mae had been birthed and nurtured for three years. And no one had noticed.

Admittedly, *Mae K Jameson* was one of the poorer Jovian habitats. Low employment. Low wage. Low skills. A high percentage of people daydreaming 60/24, lost in their individual ideas of paradise. Whatever you wanted (read: could afford). Cosplay that allowed you to feel mud between your toes, a breeze on your face. The scent of freshly sliced coconut. Flex your muscles in a thousand activities impossible in a cramped, sweaty-socks-smelling wheel orbiting Jupiter.

A surprising number of kids were in Mae's situation, which was difficult to understand. The single child policies, conception costs, habitat restrictions, and overall crappiness of hutch life made having kids the hard option—and that was with full administrative support. Why do it secretly and alone?

Well, some people thought laws were made for breaking, until they found out too late why those laws existed in the first place.

Whether she had not been talked to or refused to talk before she was discovered or had simply given up on talking after being found, Mae left it another two years until she uttered a word.

By then, she'd been moved from one childless foster parent to another, rotated around the habitat like a rent-a-pet for anyone with affection or kindness to spare. That sort of love brought extra rations. Whether Mae saw any of those rations was another matter. She never stayed anywhere long enough to much care.

But that was to fit right in. Jupiter and its near hundred moons were their own miniature system. Teams of engineers shuttled back and forth to mines and refineries. Nothing and no one were ever still. Lives measured in arcs and orbits.

"Round and round and round," one of her kindlier foster parents had laughed as they'd watched a borrowed hamster spinning its wheel.

What were her first words? *Mae K Jameson.*

"Her home!" Sister Joanna had proclaimed in delight and promptly christened the new arrival with her first utterance. An albatross to hang for life around a girl's neck.

○

IT WASN'T LONG AFTER she started back that Mae realized she was going to have to take some sort of direct action to stop the child following her home. "You go the other way. Back to your father."

This and other suggestions were greeted with wide blank eyes and pouting mouth. Mae took to throwing stones, but because she was afraid of actually hitting the child, her shots were unconvincingly short or wide.

"Are you lost? It's that way." She pointed back the way they had come.

Half an hour of this and Mae's patience ran out. She turned and walked up to the child. "What do you want?" she shouted. The girl didn't even flinch, just looked up at her. Mae put her hands on Siofra's shoulders and turned her around, gave her a gentle shove. Siofra took two steps and stopped. She turned and faced Mae. Her gray eyes were cold. She held out the folded piece of paper. Mae swore silently, took it, and opened it.

She saw a crude drawing of a tree, done in pencil, and a string of numbers, in pen. A gust of wind nearly ripped it from her hand. "What's this?" she asked, disgusted. She hated being manipulated.

The girl ignored her.

Mae clutched the paper tight. Was it a message from Magellan? Or did it mean something to the girl? I don't want this, she thought, but for good or ill it was now hers and could not be dismissed.

"Shit," breathed Mae, shaking her head.

It was the wrong direction. It would be dark in under two hours, it would take two just to return here and two more to get home. Perhaps she could talk Magellan into giving her a ride. He'd owe her for this.

It was over three kilos to Magellan's place. She walked ahead, Siofra a few metres behind. The girl seemed reluctant now, lagging back. Perhaps there'd been a row and the girl was in the doghouse. Maybe she'd even run away.

So what was the paper for?

The girl and her father had always seemed close. Unlike so many strained relationships beside the Caul, there appeared to be a silent understanding between the pair. Might something have happened then? "You and your pa fallen out?" she asked.

The girl didn't respond.

"Running away doesn't fix anything," she said. She could hear the Caul booming across the shore. "Just puts at least one of you in a very bad place."

This was her bad place. Purgatory, hell. Call it what you like, Mae was being punished. Punished for having a heart, punished for daring to love someone and not being able to let them go. She looked at the girl, telling herself this was simply a head problem. Straightforward resolution, minimum involvement.

The clouds darkened as the light drained from the sky.

"How old are you?"

Siofra held up four fingers fully and one partially. She smiled.

Mae looked at her. "Well, Siofra Magellan, who is four and a half, this is the longest conversation I've had in months. Even if it is entirely one-sided."

Siofra's eyes returned to their vacant state.

They continued in silence, walking alongside the ridge pushed up by the Caul. Mae liked to keep the gray out of sight, if she could help it. They passed a few gnarled, twisted, deep-rooted bushes. Dead, killed by the slow toxicity of the encroaching Caul. She felt the shifting mass in the pebbles under her feet, the tug of it.

Control in all things. That was the secret. Over the years she had learned to devote her full attention to every action. But there was still that familiar tingling—a sense of being watched—when her back was to it.

She noticed Siofra's gaze kept returning to the dead animals hung from her pack. The girl's eyes narrowed, got a curious look. "Do you like marbit?"

Siofra's mouth twisted in distaste.

Mae smiled. "We have to make do with what we can find. Of course, you and your father don't do so badly."

At the mention of her father, the girl's face fell. Mae said nothing more.

○

MAE SUPPOSED SHE'D BEEN LUCKY those first few years. If it hadn't been for the church, she'd have been passed around one foster parent to another her entire childhood. The church was visiting the habitat on one of their regular recruitment drives. Religions were popular, of course. People emerged from their hutches, peeling off haptsuits or climbing out of dreamtanks, to see what the preachers had to say. Curiosity, or perhaps boredom, brought them. They hung around, however, for the promise of hope.

If you could call such airy promises hope.

Each religion was selling something different. A new start. A return. The fires of damnation. A purgatory to be endured. Mae figured much of their success was down to how they all offered a good story. You just had to choose the one that most suited you.

Aged five, Mae had no choice. The Church of Venerable Light had got money from somewhere and they were splashing it on recruitment. They'd been given a preaching spot on the *Mae K Jameson* in exchange for taking the habitat's orphans (and not mentioning the recent suicide epidemic). The promise of better prospects. Nearer the sun. On a planet. Light and solid ground. The administrators didn't need persuading: They simply saw one less problem on their hands.

At the same time, Sister Joanna once told Mae, parents had queued, begging the church to take their children too. "They'd got it into their silly heads that you orphans were the lucky ones."

Mae was happy to be leaving the habitat. She'd no access to dreamtanks or haptsuits. With no escape into other worlds, she was trapped 60/24 inside station life. No wonder the church wanted orphans. They knew nothing better.

The ship dashed back to the sun, taking them closer to the mass of humanity clustered on the habitats, asteroids, moons, and planets of the inner solar system. Towards the dome-shielded cities and underground citadels of Mars, and Mae's first experience of something approaching solid ground beneath her feet.

Mae K. Jameson had been one of the first outer system explorers. Her namesake was going backwards.

○

IT WAS TWILIGHT when Mae and the child finally reached Magellan's place: a cluster of buildings arranged in a quincunx. Four plastofab cabins at the square's corners and a long metal caravan in the middle. Perimeter lights were on. Strewn across the pebble ground between the cabins were small heaps of stone, some rusting machinery, and rows of sealed plastic crates. There was also a wheeled jeep and a microsat launcher, both of which were weathered and dirty—one from overuse, the other from neglect.

As they approached, the child dropped back. The closer they got the more she slowed. Thirty metres away, she stopped altogether. Despite Mae's encouragements the girl wouldn't take a step further. She sat down on the pebbles, biting her lip.

"What's wrong?"

She would not look in the direction of the cabins and caravan.

"Siofra, is there something I should know about?"

The girl wouldn't even look at her.

Mae sighed. "Okay, you stay here. I'll go find your father."

While the perimeter lights were on, the cabins themselves were dark. She hesitated. She knew Magellan, but there were few worse crimes than trespass. You did not encroach on another penitent's space without loudly announcing your intentions first and then awaiting an invitation. It avoided later misunderstandings. She put down her pack beside the girl. Stiff, wrinkled fingers checked the knife under her coat.

She approached the caravan, loudly calling, "Magellan." A cabin door was banging in the wind. The light was falling rapidly, and she wished she was carrying her torch. Stupid. The wind, punctuated by the banging door, moaned as it tore through the camp. She passed inside the perimeter lights: solars, brightening. A pump beside a cabin hummed, lights flashing red. Touching ancient memory: Red meant a fault, or warning.

Mae's mouth was dry.

She could hear the booming roar of the Caul pounding the nearby shore.

She walked around the caravan. It was larger than her shack. A long, narrow box with smooth, curved corners and an orange-stained, pitted silver skin. Metal, even alloys designed to withstand harsh environments, wasn't proof against the Caul. The caravan was raised on deflated wheels, which had sunk into the pebbles. She remembered the Magellans' arrival, eight years ago. The consternation among the penitents as a pair of Main scientists lived among them—as if they belonged out here and not sealed in a lab inside their concrete bunker. She'd visited a few times over the years but not since his wife had vanished. She avoided coming out this way. She wasn't one for getting involved. She hadn't come here to study the Caul.

She looked back at Siofra, still sitting there. The girl had turned to watch her.

"Magellan," she called. She rapped on the door. Bang, bang, coming from one of the cabins behind. She peered in a window. Saw an empty but made-up bunk. A dining booth covered in papers and some dirty plates and cups. A stove, with pans on it. A keyboard and a couple of blank screens. She pulled at the door. Locked.

Mae paused. She had to lean against the caravan. She felt dizzy, overcome by a sense of dread. The feeling of being watched was now overwhelming. She felt violated. Why was she doing this? She had an urge to walk away, a frightening urge to head straight to the Caul and . . . And *what*? It hadn't been this strong in years. She knew what it was. The stench of death. It was all around her. She should take the girl and go. Get out of here. Come back tomorrow when it was light. She took deep breaths, resting against the caravan's side. Get a grip, old woman, she told herself.

"You stay there, Siofra," she called. "Okay?"

No response, but she hadn't been expecting one.

"Magellan," she shouted, walking towards the cabin to the north. A cube half the size of the caravan. Its walls made of a durable plastic composite that had been patched badly where it had decayed. A window shield was padlocked shut, as was the door.

That other door kept banging, an itchy sound that needed attending to.

She checked the vehicle—empty—and the other two cabins, both padlocked and window-shielded. Magellan clearly security-minded.

The fear of what she would find rose as she turned towards the large cabin. Wind swept the door back and forth. The Caul could blow up suddenly, angrily. It caught you out like that, even after thirty years. Taught you the necessity of respect.

The urge to turn and go was growing near unbearable. Home, the Caul, anywhere but here. Her hands fidgeted; her legs shook. She stopped to gather herself. She checked on the girl. Siofra still sitting there, arms wrapped around her drawn-up legs. Why not leave and come back tomorrow? The fingers of both her hands were entwined, aching.

She caught the door mid-swing and latched it open. The interior was black. She stepped inside and waited for her eyes to slowly adjust. There was a large window but the blinds were down. Tables, chairs. Tables under layer after layer of paper sheets, mostly photographic prints. A couple of terminals and a scabby mass-printer. Under the tables were stones. Books on shelves along with bottles holding liquids. Everything a mess, a jumble. Every few seconds a gust of wind would reach in and toss papers around.

In the corner, she saw him.

A mane of long shaggy gray hair half-covered his face, which was tipped forward, chin pressed into his chest. His tall, narrow body swung gently, slowly rotating, from a length of rope tied to a ceiling strut.

Ah shit, she thought and sat in a chair before her creaking, overused legs dumped her on the floor. What am I going to do with the child now?

Outside, the wind gusted. Behind it, the Caul crashing against the shore.

○

IT WAS EASY TO THINK of the Caul as something else: the sea, an ocean. Huge and indifferent, those gray waves didn't look like they had intentions or wanted to harm. That's how it seduced you.

Some days it was gloopy like oil, transfixing in its languorousness.

The research Mae had done before arriving claimed the gray was made of fluid nanoparticles. (*Fluid particles?* The Caul was an industry in paradoxical terminology.) That was about all scientists had learned after hundreds of years, she discovered. They couldn't yet explain the Caul's hypnotic allure or why it smelled similar but different to everyone, reeking of childhood memory. In Mae's case that turned out to be the dusty stone walls of the church on Mars.

That was how it sneaked into your head, by preying on your weaknesses.

Because the Caul killed.

Or, more precisely, it took life.

Covering a third of the world's surface like a liquid skullcap, the Caul compulsively drew to it every living creature that got too close until they were lost in its gray waves. Some succumbed in just seconds: on arrival, running for all they were worth towards it. Others, after many long, troubled years living by its side, just disappeared one day. And a few chose a very different way to put an end to the battle of wills. The outcome was always the same, however. The Caul got you.

For thirty years, she had been waiting for her turn to come.

○

FROM THE CHAIR, Mae noticed that Magellan's feet in their holed socks only just cleared the floor. Took his boots off, she thought, before he did it.

She moved to close the door. A wall switch turned on an overhead light. She returned to the chair, breathing slowly. If she felt anything it was relief. The uncertainty over. Death she could cope with. Death she at least understood. If Magellan had been sick or mad or missing, she hadn't known what she'd have done. She looked around the room. On the floor were papers and broken glass. Chaotically strewn about. The wind had made hay in here. Or someone had done this, as if in a sudden fit. There was a chair on the floor near the body. On its side.

She had better get it over with. She stood and approached the body. She reached out and touched a hand. It was cold, the skin puffy. She pulled back the hair, looked at the contorted face. The gray eyes were beginning to cloud over. His tongue protruded from his mouth. She tried to bend his fingers, lift his arm, but everything was stiff. It hadn't been that long.

She thought about getting him down. She uprighted the chair, stood on it and examined the rope knotted to the ceiling strut. That wasn't coming down without being cut or the body's weight removed to release the knot. She didn't have the strength or will to manage either. But she didn't want to leave him like this, not with the girl out there. She shrugged. Magellan had left her no choice. She stepped back and looked at the body again. At the mess. The shutter open, but blinds closed. She turned away, resentful. As his discoverer, this was now her responsibility.

She looked at the papers and notebooks. If he had left a note it was lost in the mess. She thought of the girl's piece of paper. Numbers.

On a high shelf she saw a clan-branded bottle, nearly full. She took it, unscrewed the cap. Sniffed. Sipped and winced. Another. Warmth burned inside her.

She turned the light off and closed the door, using the open padlock to hold it closed. Dark now. Siofra was gone. She picked up her pack. Nearly ten kilos to walk home, in the dark and without a torch. She slung the pack over her shoulder and looked at the cluster of buildings and the vehicle. In her hand she held the bottle.

She very nearly set off on her own and had to stop herself.

She checked the cabins and the caravan once more, but all were still locked. She could see if Magellan had a key, but she didn't want to go back into that cabin. The wind whipped at her, snarling through the camp. Dammit, she didn't have time for this. Where might the girl have gone? She heard a faint clunk. She swallowed. Was someone else here? She felt exposed, and, for the first time in a long while, alone. A tightness in her chest. The moon hung in the sky like a watchful eye.

"Siofra!" she called. This was stupid, *she* was stupid. Going senile, she thought.

The perimeter lights rattled in the wind, shadows shifting on the ground. Despite the fire in her belly, it was cold. Her eyes settled on the jeep. She went to the driver's side, tugged the door open and climbed in. Slammed the door shut and was enveloped by a still, cool silence. She sat, staring at the cabins, detached from it all.

The girl was curled up in the passenger seat. Her eyes stared unblinkingly at Mae, who did not know what to say. She sipped the vodka.

Siofra looked at the bottle.

"Thirsty?" She almost passed it over. She stopped herself and took out a plastic bottle from the pack. She opened it and handed it to Siofra.

Siofra drank and made a face.

"Sulphurous? I know. We don't all have access to a filtration plant."

The girl continued to drink noisily.

"Do you know what I found in there?"

The girl looked away.

She tried again. "Have you seen . . ." She wasn't able to say it out loud. She'd always been plain speaking, had once been known for her no-nonsense honesty. But she was out of the habit. "Look, your father . . ." She thought of the man hanging there. Should have got him down. She just couldn't say it. She rested her hands on the steering wheel and stared through the windscreen at the camp. Lifeless now. She looked at the girl. Both parents gone. One had chosen to cross over, and the other . . . The other had made a different choice. An orphan child in a world that no longer had children. Perhaps it was best not to say anything.

"I don't think we should stay here tonight," she said. "I'm going to go home, and I think you should come with me, okay?"

Siofra looked at her but gave no other response.

"I'll take that as an affirmative."

In the back was a blanket. Mae reached over for it. She spread it over the girl. "Now, have you any idea how we are to get there?"

The girl's eyes flickered towards the steering column.

Mae saw a bunch of keys hanging from the ignition socket.

"That, Siofra, is the best idea you've had all day."

YEAR ONE

Day 11, Month 4 (Sol Standard)

Tomorrow, we make planetfall. We crowd the viewing port, staring out at our old new home (Gemma winces at my paradoxes). We are too excited to speak. So few of us have had the privilege of seeing this. Neither Gemma nor I can believe we're here. I think we both expected some last-minute hitch would delay or prevent our arrival.

We've seen the pictures and feeds a million times but seeing it with the naked eye is different. That huge expanse of uniform gray on the daylight side is like a shadow cast. The night side is far stranger: it glows, the noctilucence making it a dim star.

To think that tomorrow we will be down there and *outside*, not cooped up in a tin can or under a dome. We will be breathing fresh—not recycled—air. The sense of impending freedom is almost too much to grasp. My hands shake. Excitement or fear? So much depends on us.

"Down there is where we are meant to be," I told Gemma.

She raised an eyebrow. "Manifest destiny, Carl? We haven't even landed."

"Surely, you feel the weight of responsibility," I replied.

She grimaced. "I'm certainly feeling the gravity."

I could tell she was suffering. She's done remarkably to hide it. I took her hand. Stroked it. "Everything will be okay. Down there a new life awaits. The pain belongs in the past. You'll see."

My wife stared at our shadowed new home. "I see a world in pain," she said.

Day 12, Month 4

First impressions: We are prisoners in all but name.

An ugly, sparsely windowed block of concrete, Facility#241 is an edifice devoted to confinement. A substantial compound—holding farm pods and plastofab buildings—at the rear it's surrounded by a high nanomesh fence. To the north, east and west, lie hundreds of square kilos of empty pebble plain. To the south is the thing none of us can stop thinking of yet about which no one dares speak a word.

We were ushered from the carriers that brought us from the Drop Zone upstairs to a canteen—its south-facing windows shuttered to prevent us catching a glimpse of the Caul—and given a brief, cordial welcome by Director Hastings. We were then led to our rooms—Gemma and I have separate but adjoining ones—and, if you can believe it, locked in.

We were told the doctor would see us soon. After three hours, I was near climbing the walls. My feet itched. I couldn't sit still. The rooms are habitat standard: not what I'd have expected here. A small window looks north. I stared out of my cell at the compound and the pebble plain. I saw no one in all that time.

Dr. Machalek, his large head and face enveloped in shaggy white hair, is a plump polar bear. He's one of the few who were here in the heyday of MainClan's investment—before the infighting between the controlling families led to cutbacks. He looks like a man inured to purgatory. His posture is hunched whether standing or sitting as if he is not so much beaten by life as broken by it. He walks with a stick, swinging his right leg awkwardly and hissing pain-wracked oaths. Gemma noted his shrunken pupils, which she says is indicative of opioid use. I told her she of all people shouldn't condemn a man for alleviating his suffering. "I'm not talking about his leg," she said.

Dr. Machalek apologised for locking us up and suggested he see myself and Gemma together, after our individual medical examinations. Fitting us all into Gemma's room was a squeeze. She appeared none the worse for being probed and prodded with his crude instruments. I sighed in relief. Our little secret was safe.

Satisfied with our physical condition (the journey's fitness regime to build muscle mass was brutal), he asked questions designed to evince how we are being affected by the Caul. Surprisingly, we both seem barely to have noticed anything untoward. He asked about any urges to move around, to escape from our rooms. I laughed, telling him no sane individual could fail to have the urge to break out of these cells. He gave us notebooks, telling us to keep a log of our thoughts. He asked if we'd noticed any unusual smells. I perceived a strong whiff of hot metal when we left the carrier, catching traces of it inside the Facility. It reminds me of my fathers' workshop.

Next, he gave us a talk about Tess, the suppressant we've been taking. I bore the brunt of this lecture, yet it was Gemma who wanted to know exactly what was in it, ingredient by ingredient. "It was in the contract the PA made us sign with MainClan," I reminded her. "Carl, that was the brochure," she said. "Now we're here, I want the truth." Dr. Machalek listed a madhouse's medicine cabinet of neuroinhibitors, antipsychotics, antacids, immunoboosters, antiseizures, contraceptives, vitamins, and I forget what other blunt, inhumane drugs long ago consigned to the medical history books.

"It makes everything foggy," she told him. He nodded sympathetically. "You will find you stop noticing the side effects in time." Gemma's smile was icy. "Doctor, I don't want to stop noticing how stupid your drugs are making me."

Dr. Machalek warned us to be on our guard against unusual thoughts, feelings, or urges. We've lived in orbitals or under sealed domes all our lives. For the first time, we were on a planet with a breathable atmosphere. I asked him, "Weren't unusual urges to be expected?" He scratched his beard. "The Caul is three hundred metres away," he said. "In the air are compounds to which our pheromone-sensitive cells respond, some we are conscious of and others not. It has an electromagnetic field that disrupts both microelectronics and the electrical activity of our nervous system." His smile was pained. "You cannot let your guard down. That's how it gets you."

I was a model patient and took this unpleasant medicine without protest. Dr. Machalek told me I'd have to return to my room, explaining we had to be monitored for forty-eight hours before given permission to roam the building freely. I told him I was here to work not to roam. When would I get a first proper look at Cluster#66? He scratched his beard. His next words chilled me: "Let's see how your first month in here goes." I protested, but Gemma said, disloyally, "Carl, it was in the damned contract."

Day 15, Month 4

Including we seven new arrivals, we number thirty-two in total. This I ascertained at today's townhall meeting in the canteen. Only half of us are scientists undertaking research. The rest, including Director Hastings, are here to help run the Facility.

The scientists are supervised by Dr. Carlyle—tall, stiffly middle-aged in her buttoned-up lab coat—who speaks in clipped sentences and couldn't be less interested in my existence. She introduced herself to Gemma, not even glancing at me. My wife was startled by this interest. Dr. Carlyle had read Gemma's papers, suggesting they had points in common. I don't see how. Dr. Carlyle is a meta-materials physicist. Gemma is a topologist. Their spheres of interest are separated by astronomical units.

Few of our fellow newcomers looked like they'd slept. Some carried sick bags. Caul sickness, explained Hastings, should pass. He didn't say what would happen if it didn't.

Hastings apologised for the state of Facility#241. MainClan built it when they won the contract from the Planetary Authority sixty years ago. On every wall are cracks. And to think this is our home for—well, who can say? Hastings told us he'd lobbied for construction of a new facility away from the Caul, but MainClan—whose shadowy families war over the purse strings—demurred. Over the years, the Caul has steadily encroached until high tide is now within three hundred metres of us. Such proximity requires extra vigilance. We are on the cusp of the zone where the Caul exerts its strongest influence—its Thanatos. He reminded us that "the Caul fries even shielded microelectronics"—hence all implants being surgically removed pre-arrival. "Analogue beats digital, but most signals get drowned in noise. We call it full-spectrum pandemonium."

We are free to wander inside the building, but no one is to go outside yet. When I asked how we were expected to acclimatize to planetary life, he looked puzzled. "This, for most of you, is it. We don't leave the compound. It's too dangerous." He added that there were simulations we could use to experience life out there, though they were rather crude. "Nothing like the dreamtanks or haptsuits you are used to."

Three days, and we've yet to glimpse the ineffable Caul.

Day 16, Month 4

Unlike everyone else here, Gemma and I are not on MainClan's payroll. We were sent here by the Planetary Authority. As such, we are treated not as guests to be indulged but as untrustworthy spies. I feel it in the canteen. Suspicious glances. Conversations that dry up when we appear. A frustrating guardedness. Don't we all want the same thing? We are here because we have a common cause.

Difficult day for Gemma. She was unable to leave her room.

Day 17, Month 4

I have requested a meeting with Director Hastings but he is busy supervising the refitting of Dr. Carlyle's laboratory. It is easy for her. Her work is here, studying the Caul. Ours will be at Cluster#66. I must put an end to this absurd thirty-day lockdown. I am wasting valuable time. Gemma remains bedridden. Dr. Machalek believes it is Caul sickness. Let him think that. Her stoicism is remarkable. Not once has she complained that the hoped-for improvements have yet to materialize. Nevertheless, I feel wretched.

Day 21, Month 4

Gemma complains the suppressant dulls her wits: It takes hours to solve equations that should take minutes. I blame the oppressive atmosphere in the Facility. We'll feel better outside. But I secretly fear she is correct. My concentration is enfeebled. My mind wanders constantly. I take wrong turns, forgetting where I am going. When I read in my room, I prefer my back to the window. When I told Gemma, she pointed out that beyond the door I've been facing lies the Caul.

Day 23, Month 4

Lunched with Hastings. He listened sympathetically to my concerns about site access. I learned that his team is understaffed. "It's Caul fatigue," he admitted. "Centuries of study but we're no closer to figuring out what's going on. We won the research contract from the PA by promising to put more scientists here. What have we to show for it? Missed targets and missing staff. The average survival time here is now just four years. The average length of stay in all facilities is under three." I hadn't heard these numbers. "Defeating the Caul was once our fever dream," he said, then shook his head. "Now the research grants are in Light drives. If we can't save our former home, then it's time to look for another further afield. What scientists worth their salt will risk everything on this hopeless cause? The ones we get tend to be"—he paused, colouring—"ah, out of the ordinary." I told him it explained some of the oddballs I've encountered. "Don't you vet them?" I asked, but he changed the subject.

I find myself looking at my companions and asking, what have they done to end up here? Like we are all malefactors who have committed some unspoken crime.

Gemma worse today. Even stroking her hand was too painful.

"Do you ever feel like you're damned?" she asked me.

"You mean your condition?" I replied.

She wouldn't look at me.

Day 25, Month 4

Before Gemma and I became drawn to it, here's what we knew about the Caul.

The first discovery of the "invader" that rapidly expanded into the Caul came at the end of the half-millennia Climate Wars. Zones of a "gray toxicity" appeared in ocean abyssal plains. The slightest contact with these "dead zones" meant dissolution: disintegration of any living thing and much inert matter, such as plastics or metals. Observations showed that this dissolution had neither chemical nor biological basis. Instead, it occurred at the subatomic level: An alteration in the fundamental state of matter. Only rock seemed immune. These zones spread, rising from the deeps and transforming swathes of our oceans into gray. Instead of fleeing the zones, marine life appeared irresistibly attracted to them. Whales, singly and in pods, willingly swam hundreds of kilos to their destruction.

Over the centuries the enormous losses of water began to affect the hydrological cycle, and our once blue-green world began to turn brown-gray. Researchers raced to figure out what was turning the oceans gray and find a way to stop it. Meanwhile, mass evacuations and an exponential expansion of intrasystem habitats went from inconceivable via impossible to inevitable. Just two centuries after the gray's first discovery, the new Planetary Authority declared an end to the Exodus—a few survivalists hung on before eventually succumbing or dying out—and enforced a strict quarantine lest the contamination get off planet. A number of "Facilities" remained to monitor and research the Caul.

Over the course of several human lifespans, Earth—our home—became poisonous to us. Our population, already halved during five hundred years of climate wars, had halved—and halved again.

Today, the Caul occupies two-thirds of the oceans and half the planet's surface. (Whole-Earth pictures look like mould spreading over an orange.) At its shores, the Caul's depth is measured in metres, but seismographs indicate that in places it penetrates the upper mantle. There are fears it is affecting core convection. Plate tectonics has ceased. An anomalous wobble has been detected in Earth's orbit. So far, the magnetosphere is unaffected.

At its liquid surface, the Caul obeys the basic rules of physics: Tides respond to the sun and the orbit of the moon, while wind and atmospheric conditions create waves and storm surges. The little life still left on Earth (a few plants, animals, and scientists clinging by their fingertips) continues to be irresistibly drawn to it.

These are the basic and incontrovertible facts any habitat child will tell you.

Ask an adult about the Caul, however, and no two answers are ever the same. The facts, like the blue turning gray, become transfigured by belief. Whether it is an alien invasion, God casting us out, the singularity, a gray-goo scenario, a critical mass of pollution, a manifestation of the multiverse (the Clusters are heavily implicated in this), a parasite, or simply the End of Days, the cause of our banishment from Earth is a deeply personal conviction that is the source of division, conflict, anger, and, ultimately, despair.

The prevailing scientific view is that it is extra-terrestrial in origin. But of what provenance no one can agree. Some—I imagine Dr. Carlyle is one—insist optimistically that the Caul is a new kind of matter: When we've uncovered its secrets, physics and the human race will be transformed. Others claim its effect on the behaviour of living things is evidence of emergent properties due to novel molecular arrangements: it is life, but not as we know it. Lastly, I have read papers arguing the Caul's waves display patterning markers, suggesting a rudimentary mathematical intelligence is in operation. The truth is no one knows.

In three hundred years, the Caul has come to mean different things to different people. But no one can deny one fundamental truth: our exile. The human race has been ejected from our home. We have been cast out of Eden for the second time. Most scientists have given up hope of ever discovering what's happening here on Earth.

Three fundamental questions remain as far from being answered as ever:

What is the Caul?

Where did it come from?

And what the hell is it doing?

It is a measure of the Planetary Authority's apparent desperation that Gemma and I, neither physicists nor chemists but a bio-mathematician and a topologist, have been tasked with getting to the bottom of at least one of these questions.

`Day 1, Month 5`

Today, they opened the roof to allow us newcomers our first glimpse of the Caul. We were sent up in pairs, with Hastings and Sarah Blaffer—the head of maintenance, grumpy and gutter-mouthed—to watch us. Gemma is much improved and joined me.

After twenty days of incarceration, fresh air and freedom were a sweet prospect. It is summer. A warm morning, barely a cloud marred the sky. But my first breath had me choking. The air *reeked* of solder; my eyes watered. Hastings insisted I take the nasal plugs I had earlier waved away. They helped, but not much. The back of my throat still feels burnt. It was a minute before I was able to cross the roof to the waist-high wall, where Gemma was already staring out.

I hesitated. Earth has been under strict quarantine for two hundred years. Many who officially come here never leave, while thousands of previously law-abiding citizens commit criminal acts, crossing the solar system to encounter this entity. Now was my moment of truth. Yet I averted my gaze like a shy virgin. I wasn't scared, but I wanted to hold on to this moment of *before*. Only the passage of time will ratify or reject the truth of the matter, yet I was (and remain) convinced that once I looked upon the Caul, I would have crossed a Rubicon. I would be forever altered, everything after would be different.

My eyes fixed on the concrete floor, I stepped over to the wall.

I stood beside Gemma. I put my hand on hers. Together we had sacrificed so much for this. Careers and opportunities, possibly even our lives. I looked up.

Before me, a vast grayness stretched away endlessly. What I saw filled me up. I'd seen oceans of methane on Titan, sulphur lakes on Venus. I'd skimmed through thousand-year-old storms on Jupiter. But this rolling gray liquid, stinking of hot metal, with its waves processing up the slope of the beach and tumbling into a seething white froth that retreated over the pebbles with a volcanic hiss, whose booming and shushing along the huge shore gathered into an echoing roar that to my ears lay somewhere between the angry scramble of white noise and the happy drone of foraging bees, this endless gray, which appeared restlessly unstill all the way to the horizon where it met the cloudless azure of the sky in a sharp and distinct break like the very end of the world, this entity horrified me.

Here be monsters!

It was no Caul but a bubbling Cauldron.

Its whole surface quivered, revealing a million shades and shadows. It seemed to speak of some hidden soul shifting beneath. The waves' roar echoed off the great bowl of the sky.

I quailed before such naked power. My knees shook. And it was all I could do not to vault over the wall, fall to the ground, and drag whatever was left of my sorry carcass over the shore to its edge. I wanted to enter it. I wanted to be inside it. I wanted, more than anything I've ever wanted in my life, to be a part of it. I gripped the wall with both hands, terrified of these urges. Thanatos indeed.

A hand clamped down on my shoulder.

"Awful, isn't it?" hissed Hastings. "You don't know whether to run into it or kill yourself where you stand."

"It's the most beautiful thing I have ever seen," whispered Gemma, whose aesthetic appreciation rarely stretches beyond a finely balanced equation.

"I feel so inconsequential," I said, stupidly.

"Good," said Hastings. "If you felt anything else, I'd lock you up."

I couldn't tear my eyes from it. The Cauldron was gray but a gray that seemed made up of a multitude of different colours. I could see the yellow of the sun, the shadows of clouds, the browns of the beach, the copper in Gemma's hair. The Cauldron was every colour but gray. Gray was its camouflage. There was nothing in the literature about this. Not a word. If you will leave description to physicists and engineers, what do you expect? They have no poetry in their souls.

The word no one uses to describe the Cauldron is sea. They always say liquid or ocean or even lake. But it is a sea. There are still oceans of water on Earth, but an ocean can be divided up, made smaller. The sea cannot. It is utterly singular and always itself. It is primordial. The ooze from which all life emerges. The Cauldron is a sea. Entering it, it seemed to me this morning, would be like returning from whence we came. Why does that idea feel so treacherous?

Day 2, Month 5

I didn't sleep last night. How many times did I get up to check my door was locked? Gemma reported a similarly troubled night. I can't concentrate. I can think of nothing else. At lunch Dr. Machalek said: "All perfectly normal. Give it a day or two." He smiled reassuringly, but his dark, sad eyes remind me he's spent decades here.

Day 3, Month 5

I may have got an hour or two's sleep. I do not feel refreshed. Twice, I've caught myself walking up towards the roof. At least I could work for a few hours today. Gemma is in the throes of a terrible attack. I do what I can to help. She is very low.

Day 6, Month 5

Town hall meeting. Apparently, some staff have been skipping pills. They complain Tess makes them feel unwell. Dr. Machalek was unsympathetic. “Better sick than dead,” he said sternly.

Day 8, Month 5

The published information about the Cauldron is but a drop in the ocean compared to what is held back. After days of badgering, Hastings finally gave me access to the Facility’s restricted library. Some of what I’ve read shocked me.

Since Earth’s quarantine, over ten thousand lives are recorded as being lost. Most are Caulers, who’ve been finding ways to get to Earth illegally. OVER HALF of those who come to study the Caul succumb eventually to its influence. Most walk in before they leave, a few find their way back here illegally, and the rest, sometimes many years later and after thwarted attempts to return, kill themselves.

My hopes about why so much research on the Cauldron remains unpublished have been dashed. I’d long believed the truth was too dangerous for public consumption: that the PA had uncovered an unpalatable secret it was keeping hidden.

But that would imply they’d uncovered something fundamental. In fact, according to the library, no genuine progress has been made regarding the Cauldron’s nature. Such a discovery is no less daunting or dispiriting for being so prosaic.

Main can only speculate on the hows and whys of the Cauldron’s siren lure: chemical and electrical stimulation that leads to imbalances in the endocrinal system. Considerable (and ethically dubious) animal research reveals well-documented physiological effects but no clear causes. The list of measured effects unmatched to any concrete causes runs on and on.

Humankind’s dreams of dominion over nature were shattered by the Climate Wars and eradicated by the arrival of the Caul. It is no wonder the consensus is that it is an alien invader.

No new information on the Clusters.

Day 12, Month 5

We have been here a month. We are allowed onto the roof unsupervised. We may visit the compound at the back to stretch our legs. Also, we have all been allocated menial jobs in addition to our areas of expertise. Most involve the farm pods.

It comes from Dr. Machalek, who is convinced a little husbandry will relieve the stresses caused by our proximity to the Cauldron. I was initially unhappy about this. We are PA representatives, not Main dogsbodies. But after a few hours in my allocated pod—crickets—I find myself enjoying tending to my nymphs' various stages. Daily, I see their transformations as they slough off one shape and adopt another.

I can't complain. Gemma was allocated the stinky Witchetty grubs pod.

Day 13, Month 5

This evening the whole company gathered on the roof for drinks in our honour. We seven newcomers have survived our first month here. Gemma and I have barely socialised with our colleagues, so it was a relief to finally let our hair down.

Yet even in the Facility they think us mad for coming here. I had to explain why two academic mathematicians toiling with abstractions aboard the *D'Arcy Thompson* orbital needed to be on Earth. Why couldn't someone else gather the data we needed?

I told them that only by being in the field could we study actual specimens of ideas that usually only appear in equations. "Carl wants to get his hands dirty," Gemma explained.

Not for the first time did our Main hosts look at us with scepticism. For most of them this is just a highly dangerous, but well-paid, job.

Caul-modeller Abdel Badawi asked what position Gemma held on *D'Arcy*. "Head of research at the Topological Studies Unit."

"Topological studies—what's that?"

"Topology is the study of non-rigid shapes," she explained and talked at length about multiple dimensions, transformations, non-Euclidean geometry, and what we hoped to discover in the Clusters to much confused head scratching.

"Don't let Gemma befuddle you," I said. "My wife is so used to thinking in higher dimensions, she forgets the rest of us are confined to those we can see and feel."

I fared little better explaining biomathematics, however. When I told them I studied morphogenesis, the process by which animal and plant body patterns and structures are formed, they appeared more bewildered than ever.

"But neither the Caul nor the Clusters are alive," they'd say.

"Interesting, isn't it?" I'd reply.

Dr. Carlyle was particularly dismissive. A materials physicist, she's been here for two decades yet, like her forebears, has failed to make a single breakthrough with the Cauldron. Perhaps that explains her brittle demeanour.

"Are you a biologist or a mathematician?" she asked me.

"Both."

"So much for specialisms," she declared.

"I always thought physics was mere messy mathematics," said Gemma tartly.

"Mathematics in the real world," said Dr. Carlyle. "We're far past the idea that a few equations will solve the mystery of the Caul, don't you think?"

"You know as well as I," Gemma said, smiling waspishly, "it's maths all the way down."

The doctor's necklace is a lazy eight: an infinity-symbol-shaped snake lying on its side and eating its own tail. I say it is a lemniscate. Gemma believes it a Moebius band. Such a minor detail, yet we argued and went to bed not speaking.

Day 16, Month 5

A hot acrid wind blowing off the Cauldron. Petitioned Hastings about visiting the site. I was told no new arrivals can leave the Facility until

Dr. Machalek deems it safe. I enviously watch the departing jeeps and carriers visiting the Drop Zone for supplies or to fix glitches.

Day 21, Month 5

Around twenty years after the Exodus ended, the first of the Clusters emerged out of the eroded remnants of Shanghai. For a long time, questions were asked about what was occurring in these semi-submerged ruins. Was Cluster#1 a transfiguration, rebirth, or excrescence? Answers remain frustratingly elusive.

Astonishingly, there proves to be little documented research into the Clusters even in the library. There are over a thousand Clusters now and many occupy spaces where Earth's major coastal settlements once stood: Sao Paulo (#6), New York (#27), London (#89), Mumbai (#165). Ghostly names for changeling cities.

The Clusters *are* a puzzle and the proposed explanations for their existence are almost as weird as the structures themselves, ranging from Cauldron cities to Earth mustering a geological defence against this invader. While such contrary beliefs intoxicate various religions, science has so far had little to contribute to the conversation.

Why?

Investigating them is fraught with difficulties. Yes, the Cauldron has a deserved reputation for killing off those here to study it. Unfortunately, the Clusters' rep is just as bad.

As Gemma frequently reminds me, no one who has entered one has ever returned to tell the tale.

Day 28, Month 5

Gemma is bedridden every other day, the pain as bad as before we arrived. She says she's noticed Dr. Machalek watching her. I think she is being paranoid. Worryingly, she is secretly reducing her dosage of Tess. I found a folded piece of paper in which she is hiding the pills she pretends to have taken. (I have said nothing.)

Day 3, Month 6

This morning Dr. Machalek cornered us at breakfast. “You’ve been concealing Gemma’s condition,” he said bluntly. I was all for dissembling further, but Gemma shushed me. “How did you know?” she asked. “Caul hypersensitivity doesn’t come and go. What is it?” “Nociplastic syndrome,” she admitted. “It’s not in your medical history. How did you pass the fitness assessment?” Gemma smiled. “I’m a good liar.” She explained how she’d suffered from the hypervigilance of her brain’s pain centre for over ten years. The slightest touch is often agony. I saw the horror in his eyes. “But we can’t treat you here.” I swallowed, blurting out: “There are reports of people suffering diseases of the nervous system finding relief beside the Caul.” He huffed. “There’s no medical evidence of that.” Gemma took his hand. “Doctor, my body has turned against me. I will try anything to reverse that.”

Day 9, Month 6

Nothing like the Clusters has been found elsewhere in the solar system. They are not fixed but change from tide to tide. They are a source of infinite fascination and consequently endless exposition. Gemma and I call them Topologies, as Clusters is a poor label for entities in constant flux. Yet for all the Topologies’ fluidity they have a constancy of transformation. Gemma discovered it, her topologist’s mind detecting patterns no one else had seen. It is why the PA offered us this chance. I wanted—needed—to come, but Gemma’s brilliance put us here.

Day 12, Month 6

Finally, Hastings has announced it is safe for us to leave the Facility compound. He added that we should spend no more time outside than is necessary. That is rich. Those who’ve been here a few years regularly fraternise with certain denizens of the shore.

These "wreckers," many of whom have been here for years—even decades—are tolerated. Officially, they don't exist. Not all arrive illegally. Some once worked at the Facility. I want to know how they have resisted the Cauldron for so long without Tess to sustain them.

Day 15, Month 6

Intolerable! We are still confined. Hastings says we need a driver. What he really means is that we require a chaperone to keep an eye on us. He promised it would just be a few more days.

Day 16, Month 6

Finally. Nina Chaperelle, a young woman who I confess I've barely spoken to, is to be our driver. She knocked on our doors this evening and told us we'd be leaving at 6 a.m.! Too excited to sleep.

Day 17, Month 6

A day I shall never forget. It is impossible to assimilate everything: My mind races away on wild seas of thought. I must get it all down, in detail and in order, lest I lose its meaning.

We woke at five (luckily it was one of Gemma's good days) and had eaten, loaded the jeep and left the compound by six. It was a bright, sunny, already warm morning, but we both felt groggy. Gemma blamed Tess. For me it was lack of sleep.

It is only fifty kilos to Cluster#66, but we crawled along at twenty kilos an hour. Our route curved inland away from the Cauldron, so we'd only approach the site when we were directly north of it, adding kilos to the journey. A needless precaution that would curtail our day, I told Chaperelle. "Would you rather stay behind, Prof?" she asked.

It was a three-hour drive through a barren pebblescape. We passed a few pre-Exodus ruins that rose up like spectres—hamlets, towns, an airport. Unable to check the sats for our coordinates or trust a compass for direction, Chaperelle consulted an annotated map, spotting visual clues—huts, derelict rockets, cairns, a fallen bridge—and taking careful note of the odometer. The shell of a cannibalised carrier emblazoned with the logo of the PA was the final marker. Cluster#66, she told us, was directly south. The bottom tip of the continent we once called Africa.

Next, she did something that left us speechless. After carefully facing the jeep south, she took out a length of rope, secured one end to the passenger door, looped it tightly through the steering wheel spokes and tied the other end to her door. Now, she couldn't adjust our direction. We stared at her in astonishment. "Spend enough time out here, you get to know its little tricks," she said.

We drove on, Chaperelle taking careful note of the odometer. I was desperate to get my first glimpse of Cluster#66, but there was only a grayness where the pebbled plain met the sky ahead. The brightness of the advancing day diminished, fading as we were engulfed in a pale mist. Visibility shrank to a hundred metres then almost nothing. We halted, immersed in thick, yellow-tinged fog. The whiff of solder was strong. The Cauldron was close.

"What happens now?" I asked.

"We wait," said Chaperelle boredly. "And hope."

Ten minutes later the fog thinned and we proceeded again. "It comes and goes," said Chaperelle.

The fog seemed to be being blown off the Cauldron. It thickened and we halted again. We proceeded in this stop-start manner for another half hour. Finally, we saw the pebble plain fall away ahead. At the top of this slope, we stopped. Chaperelle told us we weren't getting any closer. "It's about half a kilo away."

I stared into the fog. Nothing.

I tried opening my door and found it locked.

"Just wait," said Chaperelle.

What choice did we have?

I opened my notebook, staring at the blank pages.

Ten minutes later it happened.

The fog began to stream around us. In minutes it had thinned to a patchy mist that allowed us to see quite some distance—up to a few kilos, I estimated.

Through the jeep's windscreen, I caught my first glimpse of what we'd risked all to see. It emerged piecemeal from the mist. Faint geometric shadows across the pale white sky. Tall and rounded shapes. Great gray blocks. They came or went as the mist thinned or thickened. A sinuous cylinder, with a fluted opening at its top and a sleek tubular growth on one side, rose smoothly up into the heavens. With its long open throat and side-projection it resembled a jug. Shell-like conical structures abounded, their helical surfaces spiralling to sharp tips. In front of them, like foothills, were the dome-like tops of squashed spheres and split tori. The fog drifted and this scene vanished before I finished sketching it. Just as it did, Gemma gasped and pointed further east, where another extraordinary tableau had appeared. Trefoil knots. Morin surfaces. Pleated walls. Annuli. And above it all a huge broken yellow ring a hundred metres in diameter hung unsupported in the air. This six-metre-thick curve floated half a kilo above the shore. What was holding up this half halo it was impossible to tell. I itched to get up close.

I don't think we spoke for half an hour. I sketched furiously. Gemma photographed. Chaperelle drummed her fingers on the steering wheel.

"It's low tide now," she said, checking her watch. "Here, the tidal range is big, just over three kilos."

Twice a day Topologie#66 is engulfed by the tide. The yellow fog swallows it whole and then everything changes. It was literally mind-boggling to think that what Gemma and I were photographing and sketching was unique. Within hours it would be swept away, and a subtle transformation would take place. I'd seen pictures. I'd read reports. But being before it, I simply did not believe it. Nothing so vast, so solid, so unalive could be so mercurial, could it?

I rolled down my window and stared through my binoculars. The fog continued to drift around us. The tori and distorted spheres and twisted bands appeared to be made of some kind of pale ceramic.

No one is sure because no one who has ever been inside has returned.

We heard a distant ringing. It was faint but harmonious. Notes floated on the air. Thin, ambient sounds like far-off tolling. I had read about this. The Topologies sing to themselves (or each other). Low-pitch resonances seemed to shift with time. It is believed to be caused by the wind whistling through gaps and holes in the structures. I saw tears in Gemma's eyes.

Late in the day, the fog cleared. We caught our first glimpse of the Cauldron. Its surface was still, almost glassy. By this point, Chaperelle told us, the tide had turned, and the Cauldron would be re-entering the Topologie, sweeping in at incredible speed.

Finally, we were granted a view of the entire Topologie. It stretched deeper into the Cauldron than I could quite believe. It must be two or three kilos squared and seemed to float on the gray like an island. In that moment it appeared fragile, ghostly, a dream fading at the break of day. Diaphanous wisps of mist drifted teasingly between us. Klein bottles. Seifert surfaces. Pentafoil knots. Stellated dodecahedra. Double tori. It was a tumultuous jumble as living as the city it has supplanted. A home built for mathematicians. Topologie#66's mysteries seemed within our grasp if only we'd step a little closer to investigate them.

The longing to be outside the jeep deepened. I had stopped sketching. I think I tried to open the door again, to roll the window down further.

"No, you don't," said Chaperelle, reaching back and grabbing my arm.

We struggled and it was only after a sharp rebuke from Gemma that I came to my senses.

"Is it stronger here than elsewhere?" she asked.

Chaperelle shrugged. "Bad all over for me." She explained she was hypersensitive. For months it had been touch-and-go whether Dr. Machalek would send her back, facing six months' orbital quarantine.

"How do you stand it?"

The woman shrugged. "Got a job to do. Wife and couple of kids back on *John Muir*. Focuses the mind." We stared at her in disbelief. Main's staffing contracts are for a minimum of ten years. Chaperelle will miss her children's childhoods. And I thought Gemma and I had sacrificed much coming here.

We watched the Cauldron invade Topologie#66, rising like a gray flood, fingering through this fifty-year-old structure. A structure that has usurped one of Africa's oldest cities. Millennia of human history bulldozed and mockingly rebuilt and renewed twice a day. The tide came in at great speed, and with it the dry, yellowy fog. It rolled towards us, higher even than the floating ring, like an atmospheric event. Before we were enveloped completely, Chaperelle turned us around and drove slowly north, the steering wheel once more knotted tight with rope, her eyes scanning the horizon for her markers.

I stared out the rear window, a knot in my stomach reminding me that we were leaving behind the greatest opportunity, or biggest mistake, of our lives.

Day 18, Month 6

Chaperelle unavailable. Developed Gemma's photos (a bad day). Many blank, though enough good ones.

Day 19, Month 6

Frustrated. Chaperelle assisting Blaffer. Gemma, suffering, remained locked in her room. I have so many questions but most I dare not speak aloud.

Day 20, Month 6

We approached closer today.

Just Chaperelle and myself. (Gemma is still bad.)

I stared out the windscreen, comparing what I saw with my sketches and the photos I had developed. I shook my head, amazed.

Topologie#66 looked the same, yet nothing was quite as I recalled. The tori, distorted spheres, trefoil knots, Whitney umbrellas, Borromean Rings—they had all transformed. The whole structure appeared reconfigured. Renewed. I sketched, took photographs. I talked about this wonder to Chaperelle, but she said it sickened her. "It's wrong, unnatural." I couldn't agree more and yet I am drawn to it like a moth to a light.

I sketched the new arrangements when the fog permitted. I ticked off the structures I had noted from our first visit. Unique identifiers allowed me to give names to the more recognisable ones: a tall helical cone is the Shell, an elaborate projective plane is the Bulb, the floating half-halo is the Ring. The open-necked cylinder: the Jug.

During one of the periods when the fog relented, we left the jeep for ten minutes. Together we walked towards the Cauldron. I took my binoculars, my sketch pad. I listened to the singing.

My predecessors claimed that either the Cauldron or the yellow fog creates the Topologies. Yet this does not account for the structures changing shape and place at high tide as if they become unmoored and drift about under the yellow fog's cloak. I have seen sat photos and time-lapse footage but nothing that has been able to capture the alteration from one arrangement to another. Whether the fog creates the Topologies or not is unclear, but what is clear is that it is dangerous. Over a hundred individuals have vanished trying to penetrate the fogs. Just as there is no return for those entering the Cauldron, there is no way back from the Topologies.

As I was looking at it, I, who study the patterns made by living things, was struck by a strange idea. The Topologies are regarded as mathematical megastructures. Yet twice daily they transform. They sing harmoniously. Those who enter them never return.

What if they are more biological than mathematical? What if they are alive?

Day 10, Month 7

We lost Senior Tech Jenks today. No one could find him anywhere. A review of cam recordings revealed the tech outside the west wall at one a.m., heading for the Cauldron. Hastings was visibly upset. He wanted to know why no alarms had gone off when an outside door had been opened. Blaffer's been telling anyone that will listen that the alarm on the west door had been disconnected. Child's play for Jenks.

Day 18, Month 7

Gemma and I get out to Topologie#66 twice every ten days.

I grow frustrated by what we have missed. Our maps of the arrangements of the structures are like fragments of a jigsaw where no two pieces lie adjacent to one another. Nothing fits. The layout of Topologie#66 changes twice daily. If we are to make any sense of it, we need an accurate record of every change.

Today, we set up cams to photograph and film the site in our absence. It is but an inadequate solution.

Gemma only takes her pills every three days. Tess, she believes, makes her attacks worse. They also cloud her mind. I am still taking my pills daily, but I, too, feel diminished.

The Facility isn't helping. The hours people keep are erratic. They talk too much or too little, depending on disposition. They take drugs. There is bed-hopping—sex blots out the Cauldron for a few hours, which for Gemma and I have had the joyous result of rekindling our passion—with all the attendant relationship repercussions when multiple liaisons occur in a small, enclosed group.

Day 26, Month 7

Cams retrieved but unresponsive. I showed Blaffer, who laughed humourlessly. "Prof, they're fucking fried." Their shielding was insufficient protection for so long outside. Yet we cannot go out there without Chaperelle and she is monopolised by Hastings.

Day 10, Month 8

Our inability to gather a regular stream of data has become a serious impediment to our work. Gemma explained this to Hastings at dinner. He heard her out, making his usual placatory noises. But she was not to be put off. She demanded action. He poked his food around his plate silently as she spoke. Then he did something I haven't seen him do in our four months here. He lost his temper.

He subjected us to a lecture on the problems bedevilling the Facility. Problems, I confess, neither of us have quite appreciated. Staff are wandering the corridors in their sleep. He has had to instigate night patrols. A quarter of Dr. Carlyle's team are suffering from various degrees of Tess hypersensitivity. He has six names on a list of evacuees to the orbiting quarantine station. Main's new shielding for the lab equipment is proving defective. The list, he said, went on.

Then he pointed angrily outside, where a gale was whipping the waves into a frenzy of tumbling gray froth that attacked the beach. "The Caul has never given up its secrets without a struggle," he growled. "It has already driven us from Earth and each year it assimilates a little more of *our* home. How long before there is nothing left to save? We are in a war against this usurper, and we cannot afford to be distracted."

Topologie#66 was a "damn sideshow." His job was to ensure Dr. Carlyle stayed focused on the Cauldron. It was his view that any exploration of the Clusters was a diversion from the matter at hand. We were as stark an indication as any he'd seen that the PA had lost its way.

We left the canteen with our tails between our legs. I have never felt so unwanted and disheartened. In silence we went to our separate rooms.

Day 12, Month 8

We haven't been to Topologie#66 in ten days.

Day 3, Month 9

We are at the mercy of Facility glitches and failures. Chaperelle travels back and forth to the Drop Zone carrying spares. Hastings won't allow us to take a jeep on our own. The situation is intolerable. Gemma spends hours on the roof watching the Cauldron. I speak to her and sometimes she doesn't respond as if hypnotised. She takes Tess every four days. I daren't follow her lead. The Cauldron fills my head if I am not careful. When I look at it, I see hills and valleys rolling endlessly towards me. Nothing else matters. I feel dizzy and must force myself to look away. I often wake in the night covered in sweat. I no longer dream.

Day 10, Month 9

A cold, clear day. Gemma and I were woken early by Chaperelle. She had a day off and said she'd happily drive us to the Topologie. A good day's study. The mist thinned so much that we approached the edge of the yellow fog bank around the base of the Topologie. It is so thick it is like a wall. One can almost touch the boundary.

Day 18, Month 9

They have brought a copter from the Drop Zone and, astonishingly, Chaperelle is a pilot. Who knew? Well, apparently everyone but me. Chaperelle was driving while waiting for the all-clear from Dr. Machalek and Blaffer. The doctor has judged she's acclimatised to working beside the Cauldron and Blaffer is happy the copter's systems are sufficiently robust not to suffer from Cauldron interference. Chaperelle has promised a trip to Topologie#66 in the next few days. I am not holding my breath.

Day 25, Month 9

Utterly breathtaking. I think we saw more in two hours of flight than we have in five months. From the air we saw that the plain stretches as far as the eye can see, at least eighty kilos in every direction. We saw few traces of our former civilization: ruined towns, a pitted highway snaking north. Instead, we saw rockets, huts, and other signs of recent human activity littered here and there. We saw the temple and, of all the unexpected sights, a prairie house. All post-date the arrival of the Caul. (More surviving human structures—roads, buildings, bridges—from before the Exodus are found further from the stormy, advancing shore.)

Chaperelle did several flybys, revealing the Topologie from multiple, elevated angles. One could see its depth. Instead of plotting the Shell, the Bulb, the Jug, and the Ring in a line on a flat sheet and using their relative elevations to decide which was closer or further away, we were able to chart their positions in three dimensions. If we had this view every day, if the sat photos were more than gray blurs, we'd be taking first steps towards understanding the Topologie.

The tide turned and the Cauldron rushed in at incredible speed. It was a flood, a rout. I can think of nothing else. The Cauldron has invaded me.

`Day 10, Month 10`

The damn copter is a curse. Chaperelle is deploying sensors for Dr. Carlyle along the shore. Dr. Carlyle's team is months behind schedule, and our poor pilot is working round the clock.

`Day 19, Month 10`

We have behaved recklessly and have been punished, yet I am jubilant.

Early this morning, Gemma took a set of keys from Hastings' office. In the compound, I opened the gate and before the few who were up knew what was going on, Gemma had driven a jeep out. I closed the gate, and we didn't look back!

A satisfying day's work. Without our minder we got closer to the Topologie than we've ever approached. We were careful to make sure we always knew where the jeep was parked. One of us was always marking it. We had a couple of hairy moments when the fog thickened and engulfed us. But we didn't panic. We stayed still. Gemma had been marking the jeep and kept her eyes fixed on that spot. The Cauldron sounded frighteningly close as it lapped the shore. But fog amplifies sound. Eventually, it thinned and we saw the jeep again. We thought about turning back but then the Ring came into view. We gazed in wonder.

When we got back to the Facility, Hastings was waiting. He was furious. We'd broken the rules. We'd stolen Main property. We could have been lost. We were a risk to the Facility and he should deport us immediately. Gemma tried to make light of it but that was a mistake. We are not being expelled, but we are confined for an unspecified period.

I'd do it again tomorrow!

Day 29, Month 10

We are still in detention. Chaperelle will "not be available for the immediate future," even though they are no longer using the copter.

Most of the staff are gearing up for the big day when over thirty Facilities turn on their sensor array, which now stretches thousands of kilos along the coast. It does sound impressive. But they have many problems to fix first. The lasers' electronics are not robust, and they are running around madly trying to get everything ready.

Day 6, Month 11

We are in shock. Chaperelle is missing.

Later

Hastings called a meeting. The cams indicate Chaperelle walked out the compound gate early this morning. They don't know where she went. Hastings vetoed any searches. The second disappearance since we arrived and yet this hurts so much more than the first. Chaperelle has a wife waiting for her. Children. Who will pass on the news? What will they say? She's not dead, just disappeared. Had she feared she'd never return to her family?

Is loss of hope the true tragedy of the Cauldron? It has taken our planet. It has cast us out. This alien entity. Until the Caul, humanity used to be so certain of its place in the universe. No more. We are doomed to be wanderers; orphans who desecrated then lost our home. It took our optimism.

No one knows what the Cauldron is or what it wants. No one knows what happens when you enter it. Why are we even here? We have made no progress. Until we do, it will be impossible to get our home back.

The Cauldron makes you doubt yourself.

Day 10, Month 11

Much excited chatter in the canteen over news that MainClan's rival FashClan has been observed testing a Light drive in the outer system. A successful demonstration would put other stars (and their worlds) within our reach. "Don't get your hopes up," said Dr. Carlyle dismissively. "Their quantum engineering is second rate."

"Yup," cackled Blaffer. "Light drives are fifty years away and always will be."

Day 19, Month 11

Gemma has been speaking to Hastings daily about our situation. Finally, he surrendered and gave her the keys to a jeep. "Do what you like," he told her, angrily.

We will!

Day 30, Month 11

Freezing. The pebble plain glittered with frost at dawn. Another good day. We are out every day, from six a.m. to six p.m. We are told to be back by dusk, but that would mean losing data. Most days we record two tides. We have two fixed positions five hundred metres apart from which to observe the Topologie. When the tides are favourable, we make four measurements a day. We have a dozen structures we can identify and track.

Since we spend our days apart, we have agreed not to approach the Topologie.

I have reduced my dosage to a pill every other day. I feel clearer headed already.

Gemma's attacks are both less frequent and less debilitating.

Day 10, Month 12

Jeep wouldn't start when we set out to leave late yesterday. It was dark, the wind getting up. We'd been warned a storm was coming. We had no choice but to sit tight. No food and bitterly cold. We snuggled in the back of the jeep for warmth under an inadequate blanket. I locked the doors. We put the key at the bottom of a bag, just in case.

We soon had to retrieve it. Once the tide and fog had receded, we were back out, photographing and sketching. The jeep lights helped us keep our bearings. The Cauldron's eerie noctilucence is a thin, milky glow, more haze than illumination. Every part of the surface glowed palely, lighting up the undersides of clouds streaming above us. The fog was brilliant, as if electrically charged. Newly emerged structures appeared spectral, to glow like faint phantoms. Behind us, the darkness of the plain was solid. It was the most haunting and magical night of my life.

The Facility didn't send a rescue party until early this morning. They found us back out photographing and mapping the Topologie on the next tide. Badawi and Blaffer were our rescuers. Neither was cross. In fact, both seemed amused. A loose spark plug, Blaffer explained. “If you’d known what you were about, you’d have been up and running in five minutes.”

Gemma and I exchanged a smile. We know exactly what we’re about.

Day 13, Month 1

Spring, and thoroughly sick of the drive. Our top speed, 25 kph, still puts us in the jeep for four valuable hours every day. While they unravel the glitches afflicting the sensor array, the Facility is stifling, oppressive, and gloomy.

Gemma believes MainClan’s motives are questionable. The clan’s controlling families do very well out of the status quo, running countless habitats. If we ever returned to Earth, they’d lose out. Main, she says, isn’t interested in understanding the Caul to stop it spreading. They want to understand it in hopes of exploiting its nature.

Day 19, Month 1

In the improved weather Gemma and I are overnighting by the Topologie. Hastings didn’t even put up a fight when we took an ancient tent from the store. The first couple of nights my sleep was troubled. The roaring of the Cauldron is loud and frightening under nylon. But we will get used to it. We are a versatile species. We can acclimatise to any conditions. Have we not demonstrated this? Besides, it is bracing to be woken by the sight and sound of breaking waves the hue of wet slate.

Day 23, Month 1

I have studied shapes my whole life. My earliest memory is being in the *Kang Tai* orbital’s Earth Memorial Museum and holding an actual whelk shell in my hand and finger-tracing the spiral from its wide-whorled anterior to its pointed posterior, marvelling at how the spire’s spirals grew smaller and smaller until they were beyond discernment. I (incorrectly) imagined that they continued shrinking, retreating further and further back in the whelk's life to the beginning of everything. When I put one finger on the apex—the point of origin, the alpha—and my thumb on the aperture's tip—the Omega Point—I believed I measured a whole world within my brief handspan.

I was a peculiar child. Or so my fathers tell me.

Shapes have sent me across the solar system. I study their origins and relationships; what they tell us about the structure of matter from the subatomic scale up to the filaments of galaxy clusters. Shapes reveal life's true patterns, its history and evolution. They have led Gemma and me to the shores of the devouring Cauldron. If there is any discernible pattern, it is the cold inevitable order of death.

Only we plan to cheat death.

Day 2, Month 2

We've returned from a week away from the Facility. I've never felt so alive.

Day 9, Month 2

In the compound at the back of the Facility there is a rusting metal caravan. I spent the evening looking it over.

Day 15, Month 2

Our long absences mean we notice changes in the behaviour of colleagues on our return. People develop tics and odd mannerisms, and no one bats an eyelid. Rose, in charge of comms, drinks at all hours. Fung reports for duty half-dressed. Nothing is said. People pair off and break up repeatedly. There are cliques and loners. We witnessed a physical altercation. In the compound, altars appear and disappear with curious regularity. Is this a slow slide into madness? They blame the Cauldron as if this makes it acceptable. I am reminded of the parable of the boiling frog: A creature unaware of the gradual deterioration of its environment. Gemma says an asylum is no place for the sane.

Day 29, Month 2

Another glorious week by the Topologie. But we are limited by what we can carry.

Day 6, Month 3

We have parked the caravan five kilos from Topologie#66. (A compromise distance agreed with Hastings.) Blaffer had fixed it up for us and we attached it to the jeep. The journey took half a day. But we are here, and I am writing this in our new home. We have supplies for a month. We will get more.

Day 11, Month 4

We've agreed: This is our home. We are not going back.

DAY TWO

THERE WAS A TREE—an oak, the last on Earth, she'd been told—a day's walk north-east of the Twins' place. Mae used to visit it occasionally. She liked how the tree stood alone on the pebbled plain. Its remaining—truncated, twisted—limbs creaked in the wind. She'd sit and stare at this last of its kind and think about all it had seen over its long life. It was of course dead and had lost its bark. She doubted it was the last of its kind, or even if it was an oak. (Only conifers grew on Mars's thin soils.) Nevertheless, she'd sit and wonder what the tree's leaves had looked like. But she never could picture an oak leaf.

When Mae considered herself—and being of a solitary nature she was obliged to do so frequently—she imagined being like that ancient, gnarled tree. If you were to slice her trunk in cross-section, you'd find the accreted layers of her eighty-one years enclosing the central core of her birth on the habitat she'd been named after. Girdling this centre were faintly discernible rings representing her early life on Mars in the church. Surrounding these were her years in the Service. These were more pronounced, thicker, as she was carried from one densely occupied habitat to another, posting to posting, until fetching back up on Mars in the underground mining city of New Sheffield. These rings were the years that had defined her, when she'd met and fallen for Albert, and they'd built a sort-of-life together. When she'd worked hardest and been happiest. Those thirty years were orderly, each ring a neat circle indistinguishable from the next. Quite unlike the last thirty, spent here on stillborn Mars's dying sibling, Earth. These rings were uneven and broken. Some years were so starved that barely any ring had been recorded. Scarred indentations indicated chunks of monotonous decades mercifully lost and forgotten in her stumbling search for Albert or her troubled existence alone beside the hated and monstrous Caul. In the split and broken outermost layers it was clear the trunk was cracking open, the tree dying. Mae couldn't be more relieved. In thirty years, she hadn't surrendered to the Caul—her adversary—and now, she had convinced herself, she never would.

○

THE GIRL CRIED OUT IN HER SLEEP and Mae paused at the stove. The stew bubbled, filling the shack with an earthy smell. Her stomach rumbled. She watched the girl, her small face contorting briefly, as if in pain. Mae feared her waking. She knew that the moment she did, she'd have to take charge. But the stranger in her home, reluctantly invited, settled, allowing Mae to turn back to her stew. She added a few torn leaves, stirring.

She rubbed her head. It hurt. The two-thirds-full vodka bottle sitting on the shelf reproached her. Most nights she slept fitfully, feeling every one of her eight decades. Last night, thanks to the bottle, she'd been mercifully dead to the world.

Penitents were hoarders by circumstance—you never knew what might be useful—and the air mattress the girl slept on filled the small stretch of floor not jammed with stuff accumulated over decades. The rusted sheet metal walls, bolted and welded together, were hidden by shelves laden with tools, utensils, glass or ceramic bowls, the bleached bones and dried skins of animals, plus other bits and bobs retrieved or scavenged. Mae's bed was along one wall. Near the stove—powered by solar cells on the roof—was a wobbly table around which two could sit. Two bulbs hung from the ceiling but this morning light from the porthole and the ferroglass panel in the slanted flat roof sufficed. It was cramped without a guest, and Mae, not wanting to disturb the girl, didn't dare move from the stove. Over the bubbling of the stew, she could hear the wind turbine. Its whirring nipped at her sore head.

She tasted the brown stew, grimaced: bitter, but she swallowed greedily. She turned and saw the girl sit up, pushing back the covers. She blinked, pouting sleepily. The girl's green dress (actually an adult's sleeve-severed shirt) was wet. Mae smelled it immediately: The urine reek overpowering that of the weak stew.

"You've wet yourself, child," said Mae. The girl bit her lip.

Mae stripped her and the bed, dumping everything outside. Next, she led the girl out and washed her in precious water from the rain tank. The girl screamed as the hose squirted cold water over her bottom and legs.

"Stop fussing. We'll soon have you cleaned up."

She burst into tears.

"Stop that!" snapped Mae. But this only made matters worse. She used a sheet to rub the girl dry. She took two rugs off her bed and wrapped them around the shivering and sobbing creature. She filled a metal bowl with more water, took a stick of greasy soap and went outside and washed the sheets and the girl's dress and knickers. She hung them up to dry on one of her lines. They snapped in the wind.

Back in the shack, she found the girl poking her nose into her things. Mae sat at the stove, the stew had reduced and tasted less bitter, and watched Siofra peering at the shelves, picking up items and examining them with a frown. She wanted to tell her to stop but restrained herself.

The girl paused at a photograph stuck on the wall over Mae's bed. The face of a man stared soberly back. Siofra looked at it for so long that Mae grew uncomfortable. This photograph was all she had left. A bulwark against forgetting. Without it, she knew she'd have lost Albert completely. Yet the image was a damned lie. Over forty years old, it was a fragment out of time. What might he have looked like now? Mae couldn't see him as an old man. She couldn't imagine him diminishing as she herself had diminished.

This tall, skinny creature before her was only four years old. Long, tangled chestnut hair ran down her back. Large gray eyes looked out of a pink face that could appear inattentive, even vacant. Sometimes the girl looked at Mae as though she wasn't there at all, like she was looking right through her at something else. It had Mae turning away. She'd heard the talk, of course. The girl was autistic and, without access to gene-therapy, she'd never been treated. To Mae's knowledge she'd never spoken a word. She'd heard Siofra could shun contact altogether, refusing to respond to any outside stimulus. There were tales of violent tantrums. And then there had been the disappearance of her mother. Looking at Siofra, Mae saw little resemblance to either parent. Silent and sullen, the girl appeared sui generis—nothing less than a child of post-Exodus Earth. Someone to be wary of, to keep at arm's length. Like the Caul.

"Hungry?" she said when the girl caught Mae looking at her.

Was there a trace of her mother around the eyes? Mae had barely known Gemma Magellan, finding her cool and aloof. After the birth of her child, she'd become withdrawn and depressed. She and her husband had argued. Mae wondered if Gemma vanishing had been a relief to him. He'd shown little sign of regret or guilt. Until now, perhaps.

The girl examined the pot suspiciously.

"I'm eating," said Mae. "You can join me or starve. Your choice."

She ladled the stew into plastic bowls.

Mae ate a spoonful. Not bad at all, considering.

The girl sat at the table, unmoving, her eyes hostile.

"You better eat. You won't see any other food till tonight."

The girl dipped her spoon in, touched it to her lips and slurped with a grimace. But the spoon went down again and soon she was lapping it up.

"How are you feeling?" she asked, more out of duty than curiosity.

The girl looked at her and then turned back to her food.

"Siofra, I don't think we properly introduced ourselves, yesterday. I'm Mae."

The girl blinked, carried on eating.

"I know you don't talk but have you got anything you want to tell me? About your father or anything?"

That got her an angry pout and she wished she'd said nothing.

The girl's bowl was empty. She looked over at what was left in the pot.

"Nothing wrong with your appetite, at least."

After they'd eaten, Mae went outside and saw to the marbits she'd collected from her traps. Siofra watched her skin, gut, and cut up the animals.

"I'm guessing your father didn't do this?"

The girl shook her head.

"Clan rations, huh?" She sawed cartilage with a knife in need of sharpening. "The trick is to keep everything. It's all useful. The pelts I mostly use for shoes. Marbit-leather wears out fast on the pebbles. If I've got enough furs and the patience I can make a coat, gloves, or blanket to trade. Bones and guts will do for a broth."

The girl was sitting on the pebbles, watching intently. Occasionally her face took on an empty look as if there was no one inside looking out of those gray eyes. It caused Mae to shiver. What was she going to do with the child? Her thoughts kept returning to Magellan, still hanging in that cabin. She couldn't leave him there. She needed to think.

She went inside and heated some water. She gave the girl a scourer made of wires and told her to wash the pot, utensils, and bowls. The girl held the scourer like it might bite her.

"Young lady," said Mae. "You stay with me, you work."

The girl's mouth moved, like she was about to speak.

Mae waited.

The girl shook her head, stamped a foot, and threw the scourer on the floor.

"There's the door. Your clothes are almost dry. I won't miss you."

The girl's face wobbled, and Mae felt both pain and longing. She squashed it down. She didn't want this child in her life. She hadn't the space or strength or spirit. She hadn't the love that was required. This wasn't her problem.

"Don't worry," she said softly. "You won't be here long. I'll figure something out, but while you're here, you do your bit. And, right now, that means washing up."

The girl started reluctantly but soon went at it with gusto. She did a good job and when she'd finished Mae gave her some other jobs to do while she prepared and stored the meat. She made no further attempts to get the girl to respond to her questions about Magellan. It was none of her business.

Yet Mae had no idea what she was going to do with Siofra. Return her to the Facility? But that would lead to questions and clan interference, and she didn't want that. Damn Magellan. One way or another he and his wife had been an inconvenience ever since they had arrived. Better they had stayed within the Facility they claimed to loathe. She watched Siofra work. She was clumsy but she tried hard. What are you doing, Mae? she asked herself. Treating the girl as a servant? Acting the matriarch?

She laughed aloud and the girl turned and looked at her sharply.

Did the girl even know her father was dead? She didn't seem to be pining, but then she'd communicated very little. She was just a child, and what did Mae know of children? Perhaps it was hysteria, denial of some sort. She had to think back a long way for any real context. In the Service, long before Earth, she'd encountered traumatised kids who'd lost parents. They made poor witnesses. Too caught up in their own worlds. Too unreliable.

That was well before Albert led her here. She'd expected to be long dead by now. Some days—too many—she wished she was. But that would involve doing something about it. Which had always been her problem. It was not that she clung to life—instead it clung to her. She hadn't the strength to fight it off.

She bit her lip, feeling the worry inside. I don't want to feel anything, she thought. That's why I came to Earth. No, she corrected herself. It's why I never wanted to leave.

Magellan was still there. She kept picturing the scene in her mind, like the old days. It was wrong to leave him. What if one of the others found him?

"That's a good job, Siofra. Now, we're going out."

The girl stopped what she was doing, face still.

Outside, she gathered in the dried sheets and clothes. She put the clothes on the bed and left the girl to dress herself. She only needed help with the buttons. They were too stiff for her small hands.

By the time they set off, the day was half gone.

○

THE DAY MAE HAD IDENTIFIED and named the Caul her adversary was the day she'd learned she'd never willingly cross over. For eighteen months, she'd wandered back and forth along the shore. She'd felt the urge to enter it, but she'd resisted. There were others like her. They called themselves penitents and came in two varieties. Firstly, those who'd discovered they couldn't bring themselves to surrender to the Caul, their body unwilling or unable, at the final moment, to take the suicidal last steps that their head had committed to. And, secondly, those like her, who had a reason for resisting the Caul.

But when she at last accepted her reason for resisting—Albert—was long gone, she'd made a decision: to enter the Caul herself.

One evening, she'd walked directly to the shore. Standing within metres of it, she felt the familiar urge in her legs. All she had to do was let them take her in. She'd seen others do it, watching, in horrified fascination. Never once attempting to intervene. It was a personal, deeply private, struggle. But she didn't move. Her feet wanted to—it was downhill, dammit—but something held her back. She wasn't afraid of death. If she could have vanished herself with a thought, she'd have done it. What was stopping her? She'd stood, swaying, knowing that if she stumbled, moved one foot, she'd be on her way. Yet, she was a statue, staring at those foul gray waves processing in. And she realized it was the Caul itself stopping her. Entering it would feel like giving up, like surrendering to the enemy who ultimately had taken Albert from her. It had to be resisted. In that moment the Caul became the adversary.

Out of sheer obstinacy, she turned away from death to scavenge a life.

○

MAE PARKED THE JEEP twenty metres away. It resembled a small shanty town: a dozen shacks of oil-blackened wood and hammered metal sheets arranged in a horseshoe. Tangled webs of wire, nylon, and coloured tape were strung between the shacks and the forest of rusting rods, struts, and poles, acting as anchors and pivots, planted inside the crescent. From the myriad lines were hung bottles, silver discs, shards of mirror, pipe bundles that clicked and chimed in the wind, pots, marbit skulls and pelts, springs and lumps of dead electronics. It was meticulously ordered, childishly crude, wildly paranoid, and clearly the manifestation of an unhinged mind.

Regretting coming here already, she opened the driver's door carefully. The girl, eyes wide, stared at this frightening spidery nest. Mae'd rather leave her in the jeep but from experience knew that the slightest surprise would lead to trouble. "No hiding, Siofra," she said.

The wind gusted, lines shook, causing a loud and unnerving jangling, bonging and ringing of the suspended farrago of flotsam and jetsam.

Siofra stepped closer but Mae put a hand on her shoulder.

"We wait," she said, looking for a sign he was at home. She'd not visited since spring. A long time to allow his sense of neglect to fester.

"He'll get upset if we trespass." He'll be angry at being bothered at all.

"Kozlov!" she called.

It was five minutes before he emerged.

Until Siofra, Kozlov was the only person Mae knew of who'd been born here on Earth. In his forty-something years he'd grown two metres tall with a correspondingly gargantuan girth—some feat in a meat-starved environment—yet had shown no similar intellectual or emotional growth spurts, remaining mentally trapped in infancy. This was not just the fault of the parents who'd abandoned him—presumably for the Caul—in childhood. Mae believed Kozlov's lack of cultivation was the fault of every penitent who had turned a blind eye to this manchild, leaving him at the mercy of urges and appetites he could no more understand than control.

Long black hair and a beard hung greasily and lankly over a large ruddy face from which two small eyes peered out, not with intelligence but with low animal cunning. He stood outside one of his huts in dirty furs that were a crudely stitched patchwork of pelts, and growl-shouted sounds, which the wind scattered.

"Good to see you," Mae lied.

His hands gripped two of his lines, causing their anchoring poles to lean.

"What?" Terse. Like Mae, Kozlov kept away from the others, finding company difficult. Unlike her, he made heavy work of his loneliness.

"I need your help."

He spat, the poles tipping further.

Mae nudged Siofra forward, the girl reluctant now to approach. They stood at the edge of the web and its organic and inorganic carcasses.

Kozlov was staring at the girl. As well he might. He and Siofra had similar origins and now they had orphanhood in common. What else, Mae wondered, might they share if the girl stayed here?

"Busy."

Mae snorted. "This," she said, "is Siofra. Magellan's daughter."

No response.

"She needs your help."

"Said *you* need my help."

"She can't talk. I'm speaking for her."

Kozlov exhibited military-grade levels of stupidity and incomprehension. At times this could be maddening. But it could also be useful, if you knew how. "What she want?"

Siofra tucked herself behind Mae, peering out from behind her legs. A little hand clasped her own, but she shook it off. She needed to concentrate. Kozlov was her best hope, and she needed all her strength of will to get him to do her bidding. He lived like a beast, the human he might have been glimpsed but rarely. You had to coax it out of him slowly and carefully. Even then, it didn't always respond to reason.

"Her father . . ." she said and halted. Was she going to say it? She couldn't.

"Don't like Magellan. He hurt me."

She tilted her head. "When?"

He shrugged. "Told me to stay away."

"Now they need you. Siofra needs your help." The girl squirmed at her legs. "We want you to come with us. Once we're done, I'll bring you back."

"That Magellan's jeep."

"It is."

"Magellan give you?"

"In a manner of speaking."

He shook his head.

She stepped closer. "Why were you hiding, Kozlov?"

He looked at the ground.

"Do you know what happened?"

He looked startled then sly. Shook his head wildly. "What?"

Her heart was beating hard. Had she made a mistake coming here? Maybe they should leave. She could go and talk to one of the others. But she knew where that would lead. She told herself to calm down. This was the right way. She could handle Kozlov. She'd done it before. Between them there was a brittle trust. It just required care.

"I need you to come with us. I need your strength."

The man growled and snarled. He was on the move, pulling at his wires, loosening poles. The web jangling. "Nobody ever come. Only for I do this, I do that. I don't like being told what to do."

He was surprisingly fast, ducking and rushing forward through his tangled lines. The web shook, a cacophony of ringing and thrumming.

"Kozlov," said Mae, "I need the civilised man you're scared of being."

He was nimble, his huge form slipping through the slightest gaps. Fast as a spider scuttling along its web. Siofra gasped, pulling Mae back, but she stepped forward.

"You will help me, because though you live like a beast you are not one. You will help me because you are human inside. We may be isolated and living in the ruins of a dead world, but in our times of need we turn to one another. I need you. Siofra needs you." She paused. "Magellan needs you, one last time."

Ducking and swooping, over and under, he came on. Though the web shook and jangled, he was careful not to damage a single line. He was almost out.

Mae stepped closer to meet him. "You will help us."

"No!" A bear's howl of pain. "Leave me be!"

Her knife flashed, cutting a line. The severed strands pinged apart, and a rope hung with skulls struck the ground.

Kozlov ran on, screeching like he was in pain, like she had plunged the knife into him. Hate in his eyes, and fury. Beyond reason, Mae thought.

She took her knife to another line, heart galloping. "I can keep going, Kozlov. You know I will. Now, or some other time, when you're not here."

He stopped, just the fine blue cord and blade between them. The thinnest lines of silver, of blue. Touching, crossing.

Then he snorted and laughed horribly. His hot breath in her face was sour like spoiled meat. Siofra gripping her other hand painfully.

"Get in the damn jeep," Mae said in a whisper.

○

MAE HAD NEVER BEEN AFRAID of an argument, of conflict, of not doing what was expected. From the moment she'd arrived at the church on Mars, she'd been classified as difficult. Difficult because, aged five, she was barely talking. Difficult because for months she even resisted adjusting to Mars's lower gravity—40pc orbital standard—by wearing a pack of stones on her back. ("You carry unnecessary burdens, child, like others bear grudges," Sister Ursula once remarked.) Used to living in hutches with a single foster parent, she hated the orphanage dormitory she was obliged to share with thirty other kids. Or perhaps she just hated other children.

The sisters (and Mae) agreed it was difficult to tell.

The Church of Venerable Light's headquarters was under the two-kilo-high plastic sky of the misnamed City of Red Glass. Tens of millions packed tight into a two-hundred-square-kilos hemispherical tent. Over-tended parks, reservoir lakes, and sparse woodland offered the scrappy illusion of a sustainable world.

The orphanage occupied three floors of the church's deep basement. A basement quarried to provide the rock for the domed observatory walls. Mae's first discovery about the church was that it had an obsession with stone. A love of ancient things. It was infatuated with something it portentously called "Deep Time."

And hadn't the sisters running the orphanage seemed such old, desiccated hags. Strict too. So many kids should have run rings around them, but these old dears were harsh disciplinarians.

Their days were tightly organised. Rise at dawn. Cleaning and exercise in the yard before breakfast. Then into the church proper for morning prayers. After, lessons until lunch, followed by their daily half hour in the local park. Afternoon lessons, then evening prayers and dining with the astronomer-priests. Washing up, reading time, and then lights out until tomorrow—unless it was an observatory night, in which case they'd be up again at midnight to stargaze.

This, the orphans were informed, was their place. Helping the Church of Venerable Light to realize its dream of quitting our moribund solar system and heading deep into space in search of other worlds. In short, using old light to find a new home.

As orphans, they were a captive audience.

But not difficult Mae. The church had never quite taken root. And Sister Ursula alone had noticed. She was the only one of the orphanage nuns who took any real interest in Mae. That was her Service background: spotting what others missed.

"You have grit, girl," the old woman had said at their first meeting. Six-year-old Mae had stood in the infirmary rubbing her scratched and dirty face, thinking she was being scolded for her slatternliness in addition to fighting with two older boys. Instead, the old nun gave her some advice: "Your tormentors' speciality is violence. You'll lose unless you change the field of play."

For the next ten years Sister Ursula had been her mentor, teaching her all the things the church wouldn't and putting a thousand ideas in her head it would never have countenanced had it known. It had also been Sister Ursula's doing that had put her on a rocket to the Service Academy, where Mae's allegiance had been swiftly and painlessly switched from one suspect belief system to another.

○

MAE UNHOOKED THE PADLOCK. A gust of wind caught the door, slamming it into the wall. A smell—putrid, faecal—made her pause, hand over mouth. Kozlov, behind her, growled impatiently.

She stepped aside, allowing him in first. He ducked, lumbering carelessly into the fetid gloom.

Mae glanced back at the jeep, could see the girl fiddling with a bundle of orange twine. Hopefully, she'd keep herself occupied and stay put.

Mae entered, flipping the wall switch. Hard white light revealed Kozlov in the middle of the room staring at the body: head angled up, nose twitching. Mae, breathing through her mouth, watched. She hadn't told him and though he kept back she noted the indifference of his unblinking stare. The body was just another object to him, like an artefact he might suspend in his web.

She adjusted the blinds and opened the window wide. "I need you to get him down," she said.

He continued, with detached curiosity, to stare at the body. He approached it, stuck his hand out, and gripped Magellan's left hand. "Cold," he said.

"Kozlov, he needs to come down."

He stared up into Magellan's face. A grunt that turned into a giggle. "Hung like a marbit," he said. "To bleed."

"He's a man and we need to get him down."

"Why?"

"Because we can't leave him there."

"Didn't like Magellan. He hard on I. Get himself down." He giggled again. It was high, almost childish. He let go the hand and turned to walk out the door.

Mae blocked his path. "I brought you here to help."

"I not want to come."

"That girl out there has lost her father. Do I have to go out there and explain to her that you won't get him down?"

"Magellan wasn't—"

"I don't care. He's her father. Do it for her."

"Not penitent. Belongs to them."

"He's lived out here for eight years. He's one of us. And he needs our help."

Mae turned away and began clearing the long table in the room's middle.

Kozlov stayed where he was, watching. "He shouted at I."

"Everybody shouts at you. It's the only way to get through to you." She paused, struck by a sudden thought. "Did you come over here, yesterday?"

He took his time to respond, a brief shake of his head. "On own. Magellan shouted at I to leave Baré alone. To stay away."

Mae cocked an eyebrow. "You've been warned before, Kozlov. By me and others. You scare Jean. You keep away from her."

He twisted his fingers together. The corpse reek was dissipating but Kozlov's animal-stink was now asserting itself. She'd driven here with the windows down. "Baré pretty. Like looking at her face."

Mae was not impressed. "That pretty face turns ugly when you're near."

He growled. "I—"

"Get him down, Kozlov. No matter what he did, he can't be left like this."

"Not penitent," Kozlov grumbled. "Outsider."

"He's not one of anybody now. He's dead."

He turned back to the body, staring at it. She wondered what she'd do if he kept refusing. Who could she trust? But after heaving a sigh he raised his arms and hugged Magellan's chest, lifting the corpse. Mae climbed on a chair to cut the rope. It took time and Kozlov was grunting before she'd finished.

When Magellan's neck was freed, his head fell on Kozlov, who staggered to the table. He gently laid the corpse on its back. The dead man looked at peace. His tongue, protruding from his mouth, was black. The eyes were wide and clouded. The ends of his fingers and his chin were blackened where blood had pooled.

"Didn't like Magellan poking around. Not penitent, *other*. Visiting Cluster. Not Magellan's place."

Mae examined the body. The rope had cut a deep groove in the neck. The skin was black, bruised.

"Always interfering. Going where not wanted."

"Like us," she said, lifting an arm.

Rigor mortis had passed. Magellan's limbs were quite pliable now.

"Not. *Other*. One of *them*. Poking Caul. Upsetting it."

She glanced at him. She wished he'd go outside, leave her be, but she knew it was better he was in here, where she could keep an eye on him. Kozlov knew only Earth. He'd never known civilization. He didn't obey rules. Of all the penitents, he was the least fathomable. The last one you'd trust and thus the only one Mae could turn to.

The corpse's feet were swollen—and they were big feet to start with—socks fat and squidgy. Brown trousers, holed and repaired, were damp front and back where bladder and bowels had evacuated. She'd seen the signs before. In New Sheffield death was limitless in its variety, and suicides all-too common. Dozens each day. That was the clans for you. Good for a living, bad for a long life.

Kozlov continued talking. He was like all the penitents. Taciturn at first but soon enough the flood gates opened. The thoughts you were forced to keep to yourself would come gushing out. Listening to it was oppressive. It was one-sided but Kozlov didn't care. He talked about who he'd seen recently, what they were up to, why they'd upset him. Everybody upset Kozlov. Mainly, Mae knew, because everyone avoided him. He scared people. The penitents, no matter how far they'd descended, and some had fallen far, could usually put up a civilized front whenever they encountered one another. It was a pathetic delusion: A mutual protestation of the *we're-not-mad-yet* kind. Kozlov, however, lacked a sense of community. He'd grown up alone, without limits or guidance—only those controls that the penitents, never a reliable or consistent group, attempted to instil in him via rare interventions. If he was anyone's monster, he was theirs. He was also, as far as they had been able to tell, completely immune to the influence of the Caul.

Mae didn't really know why she was examining the body. Only that not to do so felt like doing Magellan a disservice. Neglecting him. She kept coming back to the marks on the neck. They cut deeply into the skin, caused by the hours he'd been hanging. There was no drop and fall to break his neck. Just slow strangulation. The marks made by the rope were coarse but no wider than the rope, suggesting no struggle. As if, in his death throes, he'd hung limp as a . . .

Leave it, a part of her said. She ignored it.

"Baré lived here," said Kozlov. "Didn't like that."

Mae was only partly listening. She'd cupped her hands around Magellan's head, probing with her fingers. His hair greasy, gritty.

"Saw Magellan and Baré. Out in Cluster but also away. Looked happy. Made I sad. Wanted to join but Magellan saw I and sent away. Watched Magellan and Baré later. Laughing. Laughing at I." Mae was vaguely aware that he was pacing about the cabin.

"Someone been visiting I's place. Things missing. Think I won't notice. They wrong." He was picking objects up and putting them down.

Mae's fingers moved intimately over Magellan's scalp. There was a small bruise on the crown. At the rear she found a small scab. She rubbed it with her finger, looked at the fingertip. It was red. She probed further. A bruised spot and then a spongy area, which gave a little under her touch.

A terrible thrill of fear caused her to step away from the body quickly.

Kozlov was behind her, muttering to himself. She turned, put the table and corpse between them. Her mouth was dry. "Where—"

She stopped herself. Heart fluttering. "Where were you, yesterday?"

Kozlov fell silent. He looked at her. Then at the corpse. His face creased into a snarl. "I want to go home. Now. Take I home."

He walked around the table, and she moved too, keeping it between them.

"Home," he demanded.

"Where were you?" she asked.

"Home!" he screeched. He was moving quicker.

"There's the door, you can walk."

He howled. "Helped Mae!"

"I'm staying here. Go, Kozlov!" Her hand had slipped under her coat. She gripped the knife handle, though she knew the weapon wouldn't do her any good against him.

His hands were making fists. He'd stopped. "Home! Now!"

"I can't. Thank you for your help. You need to go now."

"Jeep not yours. Magellan's. I take jeep."

"Don't be absurd," she said. "You can't drive it. It won't let you."

"Let you!"

"It belongs to the Facility. It's one of their things. Not ours."

He shook with anger and uncertainty, tears on his cheeks. He roared and then he stomped out. Mae followed him to the door. He kicked stones, hit a cabin wall but kept walking.

Sometimes, not so often these days, she didn't like herself. These were the times when she thought she deserved to be here, alone. At other times she felt that being here was too good for her. Which was how she felt now.

She looked over at the jeep. The girl had unravelled the bundle of orange string—taken from Kozlov's web—and held it in a knotted tangle in her hands.

Only later did Mae realize the girl had made a cat's cradle.

○

GOD HAD NO FIXED position in the heavens of the Church of Venerable Light.

Deities were neither disavowed nor discouraged. They were simply a matter of personal preference. What was non-negotiable was the eschatology. These were the end of days. Earth was lost. The solar system a cold, airless purgatory. And humankind's only duty was to escape. Thus, the astronomer-priests scanned the heavens for new worlds. They funded Light-drive research and the sending of probes to investigate nearby stars. Their rockets, like those of other churches, crisscrossed the solar system.

God might not be in heaven, but salvation still lay there.

Because, with each passing year, the human population was shrinking. Most chose not to have children because life was difficult enough without cramming yet more of it into overcrowded habitats. The rejectionist religions were vociferous: We'd despoiled Earth and Earth had rejected us, shaking us off like fleas from a dog. We were shipwrecked mariners clinging to the wreckage of our vessel. What the church sought was a glimpse of a safe harbour. It offered a lifeboat to take us into the future.

Even as a child Mae had thought this was but a threadbare comfort blanket. Surely, only the credulous would cling to it. Yet the more she learned (thanks to the church's teachings) the more she was appalled at the short-sightedness of people. They saw their own hopes and fears clearly, but truth only rarely. If they recognized it at all.

The sepulchral gloom of the observatories remained imprinted on her memory. Close her eyes and the words of the sacrament still rose up, unbidden in her mind.

The Church of Venerable Light's vast temples to astronomy had stone pews that froze an orphan's bones when the great dome opened on dust-storm-free nights to allow the astronomer-priests to lecture them on the stars. Never mind that they had to peer myopically through the dirty fluorine-plast shield to see the light of those distant stars. The orphans chanted names and designations, willing the light to send clues that would aid the astronomer-priests in choosing the most promising new home.

Earth Two is a laudable goal, said Sister Ursula, who believed wholeheartedly in the power of hope, but decried the blinkered romanticism that characterized every dream of salvation. What if the world we choose has something wrong that we cannot see? she'd ask the astronomer-priests. What if getting there proves beyond us? she'd goad them. What if we haven't learned the lesson of Earth One? she'd shout as they led her away, her voice echoing off the great open dome as it yawned at the covered sky.

○

IT HAD BEEN A LONG TIME since there had been any real choices in Mae's life. On Earth, you did what was necessary to survive. Choosing otherwise meant death or doing what people came here to do: enter the Caul. The one thing Mae had chosen not to do. And still chose not to do, day after day, year after year. The not-choosing an ongoing choice.

She sat on the chair she'd stood on to cut the rope, the door bolted closed in case the girl tried to come in. She stared at the body, pondering her options.

Magellan hadn't chosen the Caul, either. That and abandoning his daughter had made her suspicious. You didn't hang yourself when the great unanswered questions of your life were right before you. Oblivion or the next place, or whatever you believed it to be, was yours with just a few strides into the gray. A surprising number of arrivals *did* kill themselves rather than enter the Caul. These few couldn't live in its proximity, nor had they the courage to walk in. You saw it after a few months: they grew thin, hunched, distant. On Mars she'd got to recognise those who stood on the edge of something momentous. A wariness in the eyes. A hesitancy to every action. Magellan just wasn't the sort. He believed in himself, in what he was doing and why he was here.

He'd left Mae with an entirely different choice. Or rather *he* hadn't but the person or persons who'd killed him had. Two blows to the head. One at the crown, the other to the base of the skull. Already, she could feel that long dormant part of herself stirring. She had to decide whether to let it awaken.

She stood, squinting under the bright light. Her eyes were no good for close work. Bouts of tinnitus affected her hearing. Her hip was playing up. Bits of her body ached in rotating shifts. Its betrayal felt more complete with each year. On Mars they'd have long ago retired her or stuck her behind a desk where she couldn't cause trouble. What could she do here? Who was she fooling?

But there was Magellan's face. First time in years she'd looked at it so closely. The high forehead and sculpted chin. The demanding brown eyes clouded now. His firm mouth, black tongue protruding slackly. She was startled to be feeling so angry, so alive. Injustice was an ache inside her.

She told herself to calm down. She hadn't decided anything yet. There was no harm in just taking a look. Nobody else knew. She didn't have to do anything. It could be her little secret. Hers, Magellan's, and the others'. She thought of the girl and shivered.

She went through Magellan's clothes. Found two rings of keys, which she pocketed. Systematically, she examined the cabin, picking up sheets of paper—printouts and pages of drawings—and arranging them. It was a confusion of material concerning the Cluster, the weird structures he'd explored, looking to her untutored eye more like an alien city than anything naturally occurring.

After she'd finished, she still had not found any footwear. Magellan always wore a pair of black boots. She'd never seen him without them.

She turned off the light, left the cabin, closed the door.

The girl was playing among the huge and complicated arrangement of ceramic bits and pieces that took up nearly a third of the camp. It resembled a city of towers and spheres and blocks. Siofra was remaking it, seemingly unaware she was being watched. Mae used the keys to open the neighbouring cabin: a storage shed piled high with crates. She cracked a few seals: rations, cold-weather clothing, instruments, all bagged and stowed. Most of it old.

The next was a workshop: a mess of tools and parts. Like the storage cabin, it showed no sign of recent entry. There were tools Mae dearly wanted to take home with her. She shook her head. A scavenger, yes, but not yet a thief.

None of the keys fitted the padlock of the last cabin. It remained a mystery.

She turned back to the girl playing with her ceramics, but she had disappeared. She'd been there seconds ago. She spent five minutes looking for Siofra, calling her name, only to find her exactly where she'd last seen her, as if she'd never moved.

She went over to the caravan. On the door was a small, weathered sign: "Let no one ignorant of geometry enter here." Gemma, she thought. She tried the keys on the lock. The door opened easily, releasing stale air. She latched the door, popped a window. Down one end was a small bed with a few worse-for-wear toys. A kitchen area piled high with days of dirty dishes. A tiny bathroom had Mae staring at the grubby shower and loo with longing. At the other end was a bed-cum-sitting area frozen in mid-transformation. Sheets and cushions were piled around a fold-down table covered in papers, toys, and books. No boots anywhere she could see.

Feeling done in, she sat, examining it all. She picked up toys—plastic, home-printed, bashed about—that were well-loved. Moving some books revealed a pair of plastic handcuffs attached to a bar. One end open, the other hooped on. She nodded. Unsurprising. A number of the penitents' sleeping arrangements involved confinement. Who *did* trust themselves enough not to sleepwalk? Magellan, in his position, couldn't take any risks.

She pottered around the caravan, taking pleasure in snooping on somebody else's life. However, it brought back feelings and memories with which she was uncomfortable. The return of that old existence: impulses, suspicious modes of thinking she'd gladly left behind. Yet she couldn't help herself. Part of her, she appreciated, was coming back to life. She picked up a folded blanket and hugged it tightly.

She heard footsteps and the girl rushed up the steps, halting in the doorway. She stared at Mae, eyes wide and face flushed. Mae momentarily felt guilty at her trespass, then realized the girl wasn't angry but frightened. "What is it?"

Worried eyes flicked outside.

"Is someone there?"

The faintest nod.

"Kozlov?"

Was that a shrug? Mae glanced out the window. "Which direction?"

The girl pointed north without enthusiasm.

"Stay here. Choose some things you want to take," she said. "Not much, mind. I haven't room for clutter."

Outside, the wind had got up. She scanned the pebble plain. The cabins blocked her view. Wouldn't be hard to hide here, she thought as she walked the perimeter. The feeling of being watched was no stronger than usual. But a sense of dread accompanied it. Who might be out there? What did they want?

It wasn't clear to Mae how much she wanted answers to these questions. After ten minutes of seeing no one, she gave up. She was still clutching the blanket. Instead of returning to the caravan she went to the cabin where Magellan lay—it smelled bad already—and spread the blanket over him. That felt better. Sometimes making a small choice helped with the larger one still hanging over you.

She sat down at the terminal, stabbed a button. The screen blinked on. She poked around inside the machine's memory. Long time since she'd done this. A double act of dredging. It was slow. She found out why soon enough. A memory full of nothing, which was odd. She examined directories and took a look at its history. Well then. Overnight, all content had been overwritten. A command executed yesterday had killed its memory. Everything it had contained had been lost. She wondered if it was backed up in the Facility. The little she knew of Magellan suggested not. But it was done by someone who had as much, and likely more, knowledge of comps than she did. Thinking of her fellow penitents, she found this interesting.

Outside again, she examined the sat dish, pointing at the sky. She cracked open the control box. Dead. Probably hadn't worked in years. The girl was still in the caravan.

Mae paused, asking herself what she was doing here. She felt vulnerable all of a sudden. There was a killer out here. Among them. It could have been someone from the Facility, she supposed. For some reason, she felt this was unlikely. There'd been killings before. In those instances, it had been obvious who was responsible. People acting out vendettas. The community enacted its own justice dependent largely on whether the individual concerned was seen as a further threat or not. But usually they didn't need to bother, as the killer's next step meant either absolution or dissolution. Justice too often the Caul's responsibility.

She rejoined the girl in the caravan. She'd filled a blanket with toys. Mae shook her head. "You can take two. The rest needs to be clothes. Where are they?"

She poked around some more. Scavenger feelings had to be resisted. Partly as she was not taking anything that might lead the clan to come visiting later. But also because she'd have felt ashamed doing so in front of the girl. Her conscience kept nagging at Mae around Siofra. It was infuriating.

On a bookshelf behind a cushion, she found a stack of handwritten journals. On each cover was marked a year, one through nine. But there were only eight. One was missing. She flicked through them. Erratic entries, mostly about work. She took the journals with her when they left. She was careful to lock everything. The girl sat in the jeep, still showing no curiosity about her father or what had happened. It worried Mae.

Taking no risks, she locked the body in the cabin.

She knew she'd be back. She couldn't let this go. It was because of the deception. Somebody had gone to the effort of hanging Magellan from a strut. More than likely the same person had also erased his comp. They had tried to hide their part and reasons for murder. It twisted her gut tight. Wound her up like an old watch's coiled mechanism.

The ceramic shapes the girl had been arranging were incredibly intricate. Mae decided not to touch the structure in case she knocked something down. To one side was a pile of blocky yellow pieces. She bent down and picked them up one at a time. Held them in her hand. Some were too heavy to hold easily. She kept at it, until the light was fading from the sky. A crescent-shaped piece fitted snugly in her hand. She examined others until she found one near the top of the pile with a darkened edge.

That was when she knew. She either had to leave this alone now and walk away, or she had to commit to it, like she'd committed to taking the girl in. But she also knew that to do so would cause a lot of trouble. She was old. She didn't rush into things. She would sleep on it, she decided. See what it looked like in the morning.

Before they went, there was one outstanding matter that required attention. She'd realized it last night when she'd dug out the sheet of paper and stared at the tree and the numbers. Magellan's last request. She hoped he'd known what he was doing.

She walked over to the microsat launcher. Sitting in it was a small monitor-and-signal orbiter. It was old and weather-stained, but its display still came on when she touched the keypad. She unfolded the paper.

The light was bad. She had to get her torch to read the numbers. She punched the buttons on the keypad, entering the strings of coordinates. She clicked through displays that meant nothing to her. Fail-safes were easily overridden. Finally, the on-screen countdown started.

She walked back to the jeep and backed it away a few metres. A fussy female voice warned bystanders to keep their distance. The engine started its burn. The tiny rocket shook, then suddenly shot into the darkening sky, streaking up in a concave arc.

"Well," she said to the girl in the passenger seat, "now we've gone and done it."

YEAR TWO

Day 8, Month 6

We haven't seen another soul in two months.

Our camp consists of the caravan—sleeping, cooking—and two plastofab cabins we have erected. In one we store food, fuel, tools, water. The other is our lab-cum-office. Hastings made no objection to our taking some old mass printers, tables, and chairs. Well, Blaffer didn't. Hastings can't object to what he doesn't know.

We lock the jeep and padlock our doors. Blaffer warned us about the wreckers, accusing them of being thieves. She gave us solar lights to mark our perimeter. "Scavengers ought to respect boundaries," she told us, locking the store.

We are forty-five kilos east of the Facility but could be on a different planet we are so alone. Topologie#66 is five kilos further east. One kilo due south lies the Cauldron. Outside Dr. Machalek's zone of dangerous influence, we sleep better, but we lock the caravan door at night. The key is kept in a tin in a high cupboard.

Most days we drive out to the Topologie, but sometimes we rise early and walk. We take photos, sketch, measure, and probe the fog as far as we dare. Between tides, we picnic and observe. Topologie#66 appears like a huge ice island heaving out of the fog.

Later, depending on those tides, we return home and one of us works while the other cooks our evening, or late-night, meal.

I have never been happier in my life.

Day 9, Month 6

I stare at the vast partial ring hanging over the Topologie, unable to fathom what supports it. It is not alone. We have seen at least two other curved structures that appear to float far above the Topologie. One of them is hollow. Neither of us can discern what they are. Gemma has noted a number of prisms that between tides alter from triangular to hexagonal and back again. There are also rhombic dodecahedrons whose shapes range between hexagonal, triangular, and octahedral. When I look at them, I imagine I am only ever glimpsing part of some larger whole.

Not all we observe is strictly topological. There are numerous examples of fractal geometries and activator/inhibitor patterning, creating extravagant shell-like shapes, precise honeycombs, and neat coral branching. Gemma shows only casual interest in those, but their beauty enraptures me.

Day 13, Month 6

We still take Tess. In the camp neither of us feels any serious urges but since we spend at least half our day within a few hundred metres of the Cauldron we both feel it would be reckless to let our guard down. We haven't time for errant thoughts!

Gemma takes her pills every four days, while I dose daily. I plan to cut down, but I fear a contest of wills with the Cauldron. "You don't trust yourself," she tells me bluntly. We've pledged to be honest about our every fear and urge, agreeing to confess unusual thoughts, feelings, or experiences. Are we our own support group? Neither of us has yet reported any urgent need to commune with the Cauldron.

A couple of times, lost in thought, I have caught myself wandering south out of the camp. I haven't troubled Gemma with such minor lapses.

Day 15, Month 6

Today, I found myself reflecting on how we came to be on Earth.

I study forms and growth, mostly biological systems but also physical such as the branching patterns of a delta or the tipping-points of avalanches. Anything that obeys a mathematical rule. When the PA forced Main to release its Cluster data, I was curious, but it was only when I heard certain theories regarding the partial glimpses of strange tori, distorted spheres, floating rings and polyhedra that I looked seriously at it. Those theories, based on sat photos and limited ground reconnaissance, claimed the Clusters were never the same twice and were being built anew with each tide. This sounded inefficient. When I looked at the photos of structures partially emerging through the fog, I saw not new forms but changed ones.

It was Gemma who identified that between tides the structures are transformed in a topological sense. They are homeomorphic (i.e., the same) and change according to Euler's laws. We published a joint paper (our first!), modestly suggesting the Clusters' true appellation should be Topologies.

Within a month the PA had invited us to Earth. Gemma, troubled by the fate of our forerunners, refused. "It's a death sentence. We'll never come back." Reluctantly, I rejected their offer. They offered to put Main's equipment and staff at our full disposal. "Wild horses," said Gemma. Officials came to charm us, to plead and cajole. We were shown confidential information about habitat population decline. Birth rates in free fall. Death rates (particularly suicide and filicide) soaring. Shocking projections of the human population's decline if we couldn't "get back to Earth." Despite my entreaties, Gemma held out: "Statistical blackmail." She didn't trust them. I was desperate to convince her we needed this. Then, in my researches, I came across papers describing how sufferers of certain neurological disorders found their symptoms eased in proximity to the Cauldron. Gemma reread them repeatedly. For the first time I saw hope in her eyes.

Neither of us mentioned what happened to those sufferers in the end.

Why muddy further already muddied waters?

Day 19, Month 6

Gemma sick.

Day 25, Month 6

Some remarks regarding our process.

Lacking regular sat or aerial photos of the site we have had to fall back on our resources (limited) and initiative (boundless!) to chart the Topologie's changes. We each have a base from which to make our observations. They are four hundred metres apart. At each base fixed bearings marked with stones allow us to locate key structures (e.g., Shell, Jug, Bulb). We then photograph, measure, and draw every structure we see. When we return to the camp every evening it is a matter of matching our drawings to the structures observed in previous tides while using both our measurements in a simple act of triangulation as a check. This ensures we correctly identify each structure. We do this once for each tide. This way we now have an accurate history of the changes for the last three months.

None of this helps us identify what happens when the fog bank smothers everything at high tide. To do that we must penetrate the fog and live to tell the tale.

Day 2, Month 7

Sometimes I close my eyes and listen to the haunting airs drifting from the Topologie. Harmonic hymns, ringing resonances, eerie echoes: They float through the fog like whale songs. This constant music is the Topologie singing to itself. I lose myself in it, feeling as though I am drifting free of my body. At other times I find it maddening. Each new tide and alteration in the Topologie subtly alters the songs.

Day 7, Month 7

We had visitors today. We were at the site, but they left a letter inviting us for dinner. It is signed: Sousa and Serpa. Their names are familiar. Hastings calls them the Twins. They live in the extraordinary prairie house ten kilos away. Did they really walk so far, only to discover we were out?

Day 12, Month 7

The Twins' for dinner. Up close, their house—which they call Kansas—is imposing. One of the tallest buildings on the shingle plain, it resembles a two-storey, cross-gabled prairie house and looks so alien and yet familiar that it might have tumbled, spinning, out of the sky. According to the Twins it was built piecemeal over years—wood cut and hauled from dead forests in the hills to the north. When I raised an eyebrow at these slight, elderly women—neither can be under eighty—they cackled and said they used to throw construction parties, inviting their neighbours on the plain. I can well believe it. In just one evening these two well-meaning old ladies have Gemma and me twisted firmly around their wrinkled fingers.

Surrounding the house is a wild garden festooned with sculptures and plants. In the shingle as well as soil-filled metal tubs were many natural (i.e., un-genegro'wn) native species. I saw runner beans, tomatoes, courgettes, pumpkins, tiger lilies, sweet peas, camomile, mint, thyme, foxgloves, carrots, sunflowers, apple and pear trees. Bees from two hives droned around us. Dotted here and there are welded steel plates and carved wooden poles: sculptures worked from whatever had taken the artists' fancy.

Sousa and Serpa were waiting on their porch. Both are thin and stooped, like half-starved children. They have close-cropped hair: Sousa's gray, Serpa's bone white. Networks of fine cracks like sun-parched soil wrinkle nut-brown skin. Rarely apart, they seem to prefer to be treated as a single, inseparable entity. Sisters, lovers, or something deeper, the Twins keep their relationship's true nature to themselves.

The pair are artists and astonishingly they've been here over fifty years, beguiled by the Cauldron. "We're all drawn to it," I responded. "The trick, which surely you've mastered, is not succumbing." "Oh no," said Serpa, "my twin has succumbed." "I was glad to," added Sousa. "But you've not entered it," countered Gemma. They looked offended and then laughed at our confusion. "It is our muse," said Sousa, or was it Serpa? "Is the Topologie then ours?" I asked Gemma. The look she gave me was unfathomable.

The evening was a feast both in dining—I haven't eaten so well since we landed—and conversation. The Twins are stimulating, provocative, and curious, asking many penetrating questions. Their knowledge of Earth is wide-ranging, though they take little scientific interest in the Cauldron or the Topologie (which, curiously, they call the megalith, as if it were a monument). Instead, they are artists responding to an aesthetic stimulus. They told us stories about our neighbours on the plain, our fellow wreckers. Who to talk to, who to avoid. We learned little about them pre-Earth. Hints of a rancorous family dispute that saw them give up everything to come here. Gemma was especially taken by them. We were invited to stay the night, and I think she would have done so gladly if I had not reminded her I'd not missed measuring a single tide in months.

Day 2, Month 8

Here is the problem: Twice a day at high tide when the fog is at its thickest and most impenetrable, the structures in the Topologie transform. During those obscured hours, apparently solid or hollow structures, weighing hundreds of tons, change. Do they alter physically, under the influence of the Cauldron? Or do they dissolve at high tide and re-form? What causes it? Is it triggered by the Cauldron invading the site at high tide? Or is it a consequence of the fog's appearance? Perhaps the fog is merely a result of the reassembling? The structures' lower parts are obscured by the permanent bank of fog that keeps us from the Topologie. We have insufficient information. Our ignorance is legion.

Day 6, Month 8

Gemma and I promised each other we would not approach the Topologie without the other. But I make my readings so quickly—fog permitting—that when I am finished, I grow restless. I run down the slope and explore the ground in front of the fog wall at the Topologie's base. It is low tide, so I am safe. The Cauldron is at least three kilos distant.

Today, I found something which made me re-evaluate how safe it is along the littoral zone. I found a silver pool. I nearly stumbled into it in the damn mist. Flat and still, it resembled a puddle of quicksilver. A stone dropped into it vanished with neither a splash nor a ripple. It frightened me. I read that when it retreats the Cauldron, always a single entity, never leaves any part of itself behind. Another statement undermined by the evidence of my own eyes. What other assumptions here have no basis in fact?

I want to tell Gemma, but I'd have to admit I've broken our pact.

Day 10, Month 8

I was making another excursion into the fog when who should I bump into? Yes, Gemma. We both stared at one another in disbelief. Realization, then anger, flashed in her eyes, mirroring my own. Finally, we both burst out laughing. Each of us has been making these brief forays. Discovery has brought us to our senses. We promised to be honest with each other and have fallen short. I blamed the Cauldron. Gemma said we must own our betrayals. Tomorrow we will manage these excursions together.

Day 18, Month 8

Our forays into the miasma around the Topologie progress slowly. One watches from the shore, calling out regular marks, while the other proceeds cautiously. When you enter the fog bank, sound becomes muffled and visibility drops to metres. Gemma's voice grows distant and directionless. You try to walk in a straight line, but you stray. It is impossible not to get turned around. It plays tricks on you. You think you're going one way but actually it is another. The fog thins and you believe you've found a way through. Then you hear Gemma's voice nearby and discover you're walking out close to where you came in. We can't penetrate the fog bank. Gemma says we are being turned back.

Day 1, Month 9

Message from Hastings: Main want us to return to the Facility. We've postponed our next trip for supplies. Gemma is down to a pill a week.

Day 2, Month 9

The jeep has developed a hiccough. We are loath to return to the Facility to have the engine looked at. Main will never allow us another vehicle. Besides, what if it breaks down on the way? Sousa and Serpa have told us about Hannu, the mechanic. I risked driving to their house. Neither was there but I left a message. Thankfully, the engine, by now making an awful racket and belching smoke from its exhaust, got me home again.

Day 4, Month 9

When we returned this evening, a sort of lorry was waiting outside our perimeter. It was made of such a plethora of mismatched parts it resembled a mobile junkyard. A young man emerged from the bulbous cab. Tall, rangy with a mop of blond hair over a long dirty face, he introduced himself as Hannu. We'd barely shaken hands before he got to work on the jeep.

The Twins told us he may be the only wrecker who has not come here by choice. Most rockets stolen by Caulers are crewless, but Hannu had been repairing a damaged engine when a particularly desperate band had boarded his vessel at Port Olympus. He'd told them they'd never make it. Unfortunately, they'd believed him and forcibly kept him aboard to ensure they did get to Earth. He's been desperate to get away ever since.

Hannu says he can repair the broken part. It will take a couple of days. He accepted dinner. He's only been here a few years. He told us he's visited the Facility on numerous occasions, explaining how he came to be here, but they either don't believe him or see him as a problem they can't resolve.

Day 11, Month 9

This morning, Gemma spotted something floating in the Cauldron, east of the Topologie. It was silver and about the size of a jeep, consisting of an assemblage of giant cubic crystals, not unlike pyrite. This bobbing berg astonished us, and we have no clue what it might be. Had it broken off the Topologie? Or might it be joining with it? Are there others? Could the Topologie be an accumulation of such bergs? As usual, we've too many questions and no proper answers. Half an hour later, it had vanished into the fog.

It is at moments like this that I miss the Facility library. These moments are rare.

Day 20, Month 9

I couldn't write about it yesterday. I went straight to bed when we returned and didn't trust myself to get up this morning. Gemma had to drive to the site on her own. I don't like thinking about it, but I must write it down. Perhaps doing so will help me forget.

It was my turn to probe the fog. I was walking, watching my feet and listening to Gemma calling out—she counts down from fifty. When she gets to zero, I am to turn around and walk back out. We never get to zero before I emerge, however. Whether her counting lulled me, or I started to daydream I don't know, but my mind blanked.

I came to, hearing the lapping of the Cauldron nearby. I froze. I had no idea how much time had passed or how far I'd walked. I called out but the sulphur-tinted fog swallowed my voice. I turned around but the lapping came from every direction. I chose one and walked but I kept coming across the same pewter-surfaced puddle. Somehow, I was going in circles.

I stumbled back and forth, thinking this was it, this was how it got all the others. I was struck by a terrible idea: I would spend eternity blindly wandering through a miasma. I imagined meeting lost predecessors like Cartier. Next, I became convinced I was going to die: I'd step into the Cauldron and slip under the surface, my consciousness brutally subsumed.

I grew more disoriented, as if the space around me was constantly shifting. It is hard to describe but I felt as though I was moving in directions different than the ones my feet were taking me. I felt sick and extremely dizzy. Was something awry with my inner ear? I grew hoarse calling Gemma's name. I saw more little pools of Cauldron, but I was unable to determine if they were new, or ones I'd seen already. I was delirious, but I kept moving. I knew that to stop would be the end of me. Over the hymnlike ringing, I heard the Cauldron, the gentle booming of waves, getting closer. High tide was coming. I was on the foreshore. I was going to die.

I'd never have made it out if not for Gemma. She drove the jeep into the fog as far as she dared. She roped herself to it and walked in. Like me, she got lost wandering back and forth. She is unsure how long for. She was calling me the whole time. I never heard her. I stumbled over the rope. She felt the tug. She retraced her steps until she found me. She said I was staring stupidly at it. She spoke to me, and this is the real horror: I ignored her. She said I glanced up and it was as if she wasn't there. I looked right through her.

She took my hand and led me out. Only when she had me back in the jeep did I seem to come to myself. I don't remember any of that. I remember being in the fog and then shivering uncontrollably in the jeep. Somewhere I lost four hours.

She is furious with me. She made me promise never to do that again. But I don't know what happened out there. I don't know what came over me.

Day 22, Month 9

Gemma in bed. She tearfully confessed she's been hiding bouts of pain, which get worse the closer she gets to the Topologie. Also, a furious urge to enter the Cauldron has come over her. "It's up to you, Carl," she gasped. "You must be our eyes and ears." This is a terrible reverse. Coming here was supposed to save her.

Day 28, Month 9

Why *me*? I have been asking myself this question since before we arrived on Earth.

I am no one special. Born and raised in the outer habitats, my fathers were Saturnites: moon miners plundering supposedly inanimate rock and ice to feed our insatiable requirement for resources.

To live in that teeming ring system is to be awed by orbital mechanics. Moons, asteroids, each lump and grain of ice and rock trapped in Saturn's halo: Everything is locked in an intricate clockwork dance. Gravity is less a force than a choreographer, directing trillions of interlocking parts. Thinking about it boggles the mind. Tracking and predicting the movements of so many pieces taxes our finest arts. Errors creep in. "Blame it on the weather," is a common refrain. A resentful admission of the limits of our control. Gravity is God.

As a child, I was fearful. The trajectories of our fragile habitats are the gossamer threads of a web so easily torn or destabilized by a stray chunk of rock or ice. I felt gravity's intention: An entity with a will of its own. For billions of years, the ring system had been under its sole rule. Then we arrived. Shunting asteroids, stealing chunks of ice. Mining moons, constructing habitats. The intricate clockwork ballet was being altered and adjusted without a thought for the disruption of the dance.

Life is cheap out there. "Blame it on the weather" hides an ugly truth: many, many die in accidents. Miners endure horrendous conditions aboard the deep rigs. Shifts last months at a time. Accidents and suicides claim one in a hundred each year. It adds up. My fathers would return exhausted and wired. They'd sleep for a week. PTSD treatment is mandatory. They argued a lot, especially about me. They hated their work, but they made it clear to me that we were privileged. Clan salaries bought me a clan education. It was also made equally clear to me that this education was to ensure I would not be following them to the rigs. But though I was being groomed for better things, I lived only for my shell and geode collections: My love of those natural forms untainted by human hand.

My fathers split when I was ten. They managed to stay on good terms, mainly, I suspect, for my sake. I was fifteen when Austin died. An ice shelf collapsed on Titan and his rig sank to the bottom of Ligeia Mare. I think the last time I cried was when I was told that no attempt would be made to recover the bodies from the methane lake.

After that I understood why George, my surviving father, wanted to keep me out of Fash's mines. Instead of neglecting my schoolwork in favour of my shells and geodes, I found a way of combining these disciplines. I went from coasting to scholarship potential in six months. Suddenly, the clans were bidding to sponsor me.

That future nearly came to nothing when our habitat was struck by an untracked asteroid whose "orbit had shifted as a result of destabilization processes." In less clan-inflected language: mining. Three hundred people were shifted out of their lives in seconds. Blame the weather.

If you had eyes, you could see the whole thing was unsustainable.

Two hundred years of vagrancy had desensitized the human race to our impact. We'd ravaged the Earth, and instead of learning our lesson we were now pillaging the solar system. We contaminated moons and planets with our spoor but left nary a thought to what native life or natural processes might be affected. It sickened me.

Before I left for the inner planets, I flirted with the Remediators. This atoning movement believes we must earn our right to return to Earth: first admit our guilt, then make amends. Fundamental to their belief is how we'd been custodians or stewards on Earth, not owners or inheritors. They reject the alien usurper theory, saying instead that it is we who must seek forgiveness for our trespasses. (It is rather too self-flagellating to be a popular creed.) Yet among Saturn's rings, I'd seen how we thoughtlessly disrupted fragile, intricate physical processes. Harvesting water from Enceladus's geysers. Mining Titan's cryo-volcanoes for paraffin wax. Draining the liquid hydrocarbons of Kraken Mare. Alien environments whose alien life takes forms we appreciate only for what we can take. Patterns and systems we treat as mindless because we ourselves are too small-minded to see the bigger picture.

Day 10, Month 10

This morning, Hastings arrived unannounced. He told us he was merely checking up on us. He came out to the Topologie and watched us make our observations. You'd never know Gemma had spent the last five days in agony.

At dinner he told us why he'd come. Main is unhappy with the progress of the array. He wants us to help Dr. Carlyle, hinting that he could afterwards direct resources our way: equipment, even staff. I could only be impressed by Main's deviousness.

Hastings was apologetic. "They are furious," he said. "We've lost too many staff already and you are out here. Please come back." When he left, disappointed, Gemma was vexed. "From now on, we are on our own," she said. "We tell them nothing." I stared at her in disbelief. "But he's right," I protested. "This is dangerous."

"We're close, Carl. I know we are."

"Don't let it possess you, Gemma."

"Why not?" she snapped.

She wants me to lower my dosage of Tess.

Day 30, Month 11

Ice on the windows. The walls of our office are covered in drawings and photos of the different shapes taken by various topological structures. Gemma says we have gathered sufficient data that we ought to be seeing patterns. She says she is hampered without comp support. It means we must continue making our observations and I will keep carefully probing the fog. Gemma insists I am always roped. I have come no closer to the Topologie.

Day 2, Month 12

Met another wrecker. Mae Jameson. Her skin is so dark, leathery and wrinkled she seems to predate the Caul, as if her African ancestors never left Earth. According to Gemma, this old woman is reticent. I'd call her terseness rude. Apparently, she rarely comes out this way. She doesn't like the fog, but she was following a marbit that had escaped one of her traps. It was lame. She'd lost it in the fog. Or so Gemma later told me. I could barely get a word out of her. She's been here twenty years (according to the Twins). She's ex-Service. You can tell. She is watchful. I stared back, wondering how she looked before arriving here. I couldn't picture anything else.

Some people are possessed by the Cauldron from the moment they first hear about it. Dr. Carlyle is one: captivated in early childhood, Gemma told me. Others spend half their lives by it and appear utterly unaffected. I am troubled by those like Mae who are unchanged. Is their immutability a refusal to acknowledge the numinous? Before I came here, I'd have called that quality admirable. Now it bothers me.

I am taking three pills a week.

Day 1, Month 1

Last night, a celebration at the Twins' to welcome in the New Year. Wreckers and Facility staff were in attendance. My recollections of the evening are hazy. I remember Gemma and Dr. Carlyle deep in conversation. Gemma tells me Dr. Carlyle has lowered her guard, pronouncing herself "officially intrigued" by Gemma's mathematics. (I call it fishing.) Halfway through the evening, Gemma suffered an attack and had to lie down. Dr. Machalek sat with her for a time. She tells me he has made a suggestion. It will not help with the attacks, but it might improve how she feels about them. He thinks a pain journal will allow her to put the bouts in perspective. To allow her to contain them.

I remember an unsettling conversation with the Twins about the Cauldron. "The Caul is so potent because it combines our two greatest fears, death and the unknown," Serpa told me. "In it, we see our annihilation."

Stunned by her fatalism, I spluttered: "Then you believe it is our nemesis?"

She met my eye. "It is as irresistible as it is inevitable."

I nodded: "Like the truth we artists and scientists are forever seeking."

Sousa raised an eyebrow at her twin. "Hubris comes before, not after, nemesis."

Serpa snorted. "We are but Robinson Crusoes, marooned on our island Earth."

Day 6, Month 1

Gemma refused to let my explorations proceed further without additional tether, so we've borrowed two more coils from the Facility. That gives us over three hundred metres. "But is it enough rope to hang ourselves?" I asked.

Gemma also raided the library, removing hundreds of sat photos. She is mapping and matching structures. When sick, she scribbles incessantly in her pain journal. Writing, she says, distracts from the pain.

In the fog today, passing the point where yesterday I was literally at the end of my tether, I wondered how much progress we'd make if we could enlist others in our work. Markers, rope holders, measurement-takers, freeing up valuable exploration time.

Gemma poured cold water on the idea, reminding me both Cartier and Yishiha had operated with teams of six and ten, respectively. It hadn't done them any good. No one survived Cartier's expedition. The lone woman who returned from Yishiha's later killed herself.

In Norse mythology the outermost part of Hel is called Niflheim: A realm of thick mist in which the dead wander.

We both feel dull-witted. Is the drug making us more stupid over time? I dare not reduce my dosage—two pills a week—further, like Gemma: She's down to one. I catch myself staring in the direction of the Cauldron, as if I am screwing up my courage to do something but I don't know what.

I feel it whenever I leave the camp.

Something is about to happen.

`Day 12, Month 1`

The long rope is a drag on progress. I feel its weight behind me. Gemma says I was two hundred metres in today. We estimate another two hundred to the Topologie. I'd have got further if not for the incoming tide. We have also borrowed some sound pulsers from the Facility. The fog dampens and smears out the sound, yet if I'm facing the right direction—dead ahead—I can hear the synchronous but differently pitched pulses in each ear. I use them as a guide to head in the right direction. Often I lose the pulses, or they blend together, or I get confused with the ringing emanating from the Topologie and then I get turned around. I only know that's happened when I pick up the pulses again and they've switched ears.

Day 14, Month 1

Two hundred and fifty metres, according to the length of rope Gemma spooled out.

Day 17, Month 1

Two hundred and seventy-five metres.

Day 19, Month 1

Three hundred and five metres.

Day 20, Month 1

The song—loud, deep, directionless—feels as if it is inside me or comes from a place I cannot fathom. Sometimes I pause with the strangest feeling: I just need to turn or slide in a certain direction, and I'll find the source of this music. Straining to listen hurts my head, however. Gemma is excited. "It means you're close, Carl." But she has not read Yishiha as closely as I have and doesn't know Cartier at all. I have not told her their descriptions match what I hear. Yishiha speculated the sounds might be a warning, just before she and her team disappeared. Cartier also made mention of being troubled by songs deep in the fog. It was his last entry.

Only three hundred metres today.

Day 22, Month 1

Three hundred and ten metres. My progress has stalled. I don't know if it is the song or some other force holding me back. The song—beautiful, hymnlike—reminds me of Christ's apostles, talking in tongues. I find myself stopping, listening. I forget the pulses and lose all sense of time. Gemma's urgent cries or the Cauldron lapping against the shore awake me from this reverie.

Gemma has made sequences of the shapes of several structures we have been recording, revealing how they transform over time. She showed a prism that changed from being triangular to hexagonal in form and back again. "What we see as a shape altering in our three dimensions," she said, "is actually a higher dimensional object passing through space. It is a hypercube. When it enters our space edge first, we see triangles and then hexagonal forms and when it enters corner first, we see rhombic dodecahedrons." I tried to get my head around this idea. Gemma, however, is excited. "No wonder your head hurts," she said triumphantly. "The fog hides higher dimensions." I am not reassured.

Day 8, Month 2

Gemma revealed she stopped taking her pills a month ago. Seeing her breakthrough with the higher dimensions and my failure to penetrate the fog further than three hundred metres, I have decided to follow. I feel uncertain about the wisdom of this action. I am the one out there, lost on the foggy foreshore, half-hypnotised by the ringing songs of the Topologie.

Day 22, Month 2

I feel no untoward effects—no increase in strange or unwanted thoughts. I feel fine. More than fine. I feel sharper. I don't feel groggy when I wake. We work longer hours. The ghostly hymns seem louder every day. Three hundred and twenty metres.

Day 30, Month 2

Stuck around the three-hundred-metre mark. Sick of seeing the same stones. I feel half-pursued and half-pursuer. The fog is a febrile miasma. It seems to condense at my feet and if I stay still long enough it forms small pools. When I leave, it clings to my clothes, hair, and face. Gemma pushes me ever onwards.

Day 3, Month 3

A brief note. Too excited to write much now. Need to sleep—if I can—to be fresh to return tomorrow.

This morning, I was determined to break the three-hundred-and-fifty-metre mark. I was sure I was close. Conditions were excellent. We made our measurements as usual and drove out to the fog early. We had three hours. I was excited but Gemma cautioned me to keep calm.

I entered the fog with the pulses pinging in each ear and Gemma calling the marks. I made good progress until two hundred metres, when the haunting ringing distracted me. I couldn't place where it came from. At the same time, I had a terrible sense of space opening up around me. I grew dizzy and fell. It was frightening. I looked around me but could see nothing unusual. Just the shore and the fog, and yet I sensed that just out of reach was some vast and unexplored vista. I got to my feet and stumbled about, trying to find a way forward. I was no longer able to hear Gemma or the pingers.

When I saw a loop of rope on the ground, I knew I was in trouble. Somehow, I'd double backed on myself, heading out the way I had come. I sat down, closed my eyes, and tried to compose myself. I'd had such high hopes for today, and now here I sat with no idea where I was, other than the knowledge I'd been here before.

But as I was sitting, staring into the yellow-tinged gray surrounding me, listening to those reverberating intonations, a curious thought struck me. What if the fog is simply the Cauldron? Water can be a solid, a liquid, or a gas. Why not the Cauldron? In which case was I not in some sense *in* the Cauldron? Had I not already entered it? No wonder Cartier and Yishiha never came back.

A thrill of fear rushed through me.

For wasn't I inhaling it? I'd been inhaling the Cauldron for months, nearly a year.

Why hadn't anyone investigated the miasma? Then I remembered it had been studied. Every analysis indicated it was just moisture. Except I couldn't think where exactly I'd read that. Who wrote the study? Who commissioned it? Where was it published? Was this all in my imagination? Was the Cauldron trying to lead me astray? Yet if the fog was the Cauldron, why was I able to leave it? I was determined to think it through. Gases are diffuse liquids, less concentrated. I shook my head. I felt confused.

How long had I been sitting there? I couldn't hear the lapping of the Cauldron, which was the usual sign I'd lost track of time and should leave. I got to my feet in a panic, turning around. Which way? It sounds stupid writing this now. I had the tether. All I had to do was pull on the rope, to follow it back to Gemma. But I could no longer think straight. I feared my own thoughts. I was no longer certain they *were* my own. The ringing was a terrible screeching. My head felt groggy. I was suffocating. I stared into the mustard gray. I wanted to touch something solid, real, another human being. I screamed Gemma's name, but the ringing got louder. I put my hands over my ears. Suddenly I felt an urge in my legs. A desperation to run. I knew what *that* was. I should have been on my guard against it, but I couldn't resist. Anything was better than staying here. I ran, stumbling. I knew, I just did, that I was running south.

I knew, again I don't know how, where the Cauldron was. I was running pell-mell, hell for leather, down the foreshore. I could hear the Cauldron washing and sucking ahead of me. At the same time, I could feel the space around me expanding, swelling, as if it was unfolding and stretching—inflating like a giant balloon.

And suddenly I stopped. I knew. The answer was simple. It had been with me all along. The rope. Tess. The pingers. Even Gemma. I was holding myself back. I didn't trust myself. I thought of Chaperelle and the others who had disappeared. Each of whom had freely left the Facility, on their own. I thought of Cartier and Yishiha, each making their painstaking forays. The Cauldron knew what they were doing, was aware of their trespass. If you wanted to enter the Topologie, which belonged to the Cauldron, you had to enter willingly and completely. You had to surrender to the space.

I had to forget the boundaries of our world.

I did not hesitate. I spared not a single thought for Gemma.

I couldn't unknot the rope. I had to cut it. Of course, I didn't have anything like a knife on me. I knew I couldn't go back and do it. Gemma would stop me. I found two stones the size of my fist and smashed them against one another until one broke in half. I used a sharp edge to cut the rope.

Finally, free of the tether, free of Tess, free of the constraints chaining my mind, I followed the urgings of my feet.

Every step could be my last, but I kept putting one foot in front of the other. I don't think I could have stopped myself if I'd wanted to.

Before I knew it, huge dark shadows were looming around me. I stopped, looking up, craning my neck in wonder and awe. I was still in the fog but rising above me were vast structures I could barely discern. Great shadowy curves and slabs towered overhead.

I still can't describe it even now. It has taken nearly two years. But I've done it. *We've* done it. We are the first. I have entered the Topologie—and, by some miracle, returned.

DAY THREE

DRIVING UNDER A SHROUD OF UNBROKEN CLOUD, Mae, who'd awoken fresh and clear-headed, felt almost giddy. Anticipation bubbled up inside her, bringing to the surface hazy memories of Service raids on Mars. Her hands were jittery on the wheel.

The girl, on the seat beside her, yawned. Her gray eyes were red and teary, like she had found sleep elusive. Mae was worried about her.

Last night, they'd had another one-sided conversation. It wasn't clear how much the girl knew or understood. As best she could, Mae had explained that her father was gone. He'd not crossed over but died. Tomorrow—today—they had to let others living by the Caul know of his passing. The girl had remained silent, only nodding after Mae had asked if she understood. Knowing it was futile, Mae had asked about any visitors they might have had recently. Names provoked no reaction.

The kilos ticked by quickly. Mae ground together teeth that had hurt for so long the persistent, rhythmic throbbing was as familiar as breathing. Like her other chronic aches—hip, ankles, back—it was a kind of vital sign, reminding her she was still alive.

She looked at the girl, her unwitting co-conspirator, and doubts rushed in about the folly or wisdom of what she was doing. Was she endangering the girl? What was she hoping to achieve? She didn't have satisfactory answers, and she feared the questions her fellow penitents were sure to ask.

Kansas appeared as a dark silhouette on the horizon, growing rapidly. Mae parked the jeep at a polite but not standoffish distance, beside the wooden signpost. The girl didn't want to leave the warm interior, but Mae took her hand firmly and together they approached the house. The Twins were in the garden and on seeing them—side by side, smiling, eyes sparkling good humouredly—Mae felt her own years catching up with her.

The Twins were not the only people along the shore who'd been on Earth longer than Mae but they were the only ones she knew of older than her. Not by many years, but enough that the pair—self-sufficient, mostly united, content and proud possessors of a home that was a civilised outpost in a wasteland of human flotsam and jetsam—couldn't help but radiate an air of serene superiority. Or, more likely, Mae allowed herself to admit, she couldn't help but feel a lesser human being when confronted by the pair's rounded wholeness, the entirety of their oneness. Being around them was more painful still because she was reminded of how much she had lost in Albert, of how for thirty years she had been incomplete. The Twins' happiness, Mae felt, was a rebuke to her own fractured existence.

"Mae, you've been a stranger," said Sousa, straightening up.

"But you've brought a friend," said Serpa, "so we forgive you."

"Siofra, how are you, dear?"

"She's keeping up her vow of silence," said Mae.

"Then don't stand out there."

"Come into the garden. Here, silence is golden."

Among the greenery, earthy, mulchy scents got in Mae's nose and drove out the dry, stale scent of stone. For her, visiting Kansas felt like a too real dreamtank vision of life pre-Exodus. Only here at the Twins' did Mae ever feel properly homesick—that umbrella diagnosis for humanity's post-Exodus discontent. Reason enough, perhaps, for staying away.

"You'll have to take us as you find us, I'm afraid," said Sousa. "Work to do out here. Only a small storm, but it hit us hard."

"Siofra, where's your father?"

"That," said Mae quietly, "is why we're here."

The girl had pulled away and was peering into one of the huge oblong planters. Apple and pear trees, fruit-picked and leaf-browning, formed a canopy.

"Is Carl okay?" asked Sousa.

Serpa bent down with a faint gasp to attach a bay tree to a stake. She called the girl over and asked her to hold the trunk straight while she tied it up.

Sousa stared at the girl, then back to Mae.

"He, uh, he's no longer with us."

Both women exchanged a glance Mae was unable to interpret.

"Could you be more specific, Mae. In which particular sense do you mean?"

"I've seen . . ." Now that she was here it was difficult to say it.

"We understand," said Serpa. She coughed suddenly, doubling over. Sousa looked at her with concern.

"I think you should sit, dear."

"I'm okay."

"Dear, I said sit."

Serpa rubbed her chest. She gave Sousa a filthy look, then took the girl's hand and walked to the veranda and sat on a bench. She whispered to Siofra. The girl's eyes widened, her mouth dropping open, as she listened.

"When did it happen?"

Mae and Sousa were walking slowly around the house, threading their way among planters, beds of earth, and the plate and pole sculptures.

"A couple of days ago. I found Siofra by the shore. He was in one of his cabins, hanging by a rope."

Sousa furrowed her brow. "Suicide? I can't imagine Carl . . ."

"We don't imagine anyone will kill themselves until they go ahead and do it." Or so we tell ourselves after, she thought.

Mae was careful to say nothing more, but it was hard. If there were any two people among the penitents whom she ought to trust it was the Twins. They had been good to her. They were good to everyone: sharing their bounty liberally, throwing parties, never turning anyone away. She should come more often, but, these days, it was a long walk, and she felt like an imposition. She also felt homesick and out of place here. She had little to say for herself, while they had so much to say about everything. They lived in the world, excitedly, acted as if they were an essential part of it. They were aware, noticing and relishing the smallest details. To them Earth wasn't a dying world, being slowly consumed by the Caul. They saw each new change as part of the daily struggle between the old and the new. Around the Twins, Mae felt like a fraud, like she didn't deserve her life because she didn't live every moment to the full.

"How's the child taken it?"

"Hard to tell."

"And Jean? Where is she?"

"Jean Baré? What about her?"

"Ah. Well, then. Not my place to say."

Mae peered at her. "When did you last see Carl?"

Sousa raised a thin eyebrow. "Questions, Mae? Really? Is there something we should know?"

She looked away, realizing how clumsy it had sounded. She hadn't meant it like that. They'd completed a circuit of the house.

"I don't remember when we last saw Carl."

"It was a couple of months ago." Serpa joined them, leaving the girl playing on the veranda with some stones. "He and Siofra came over. Carl wasn't happy. He was missing Jean. Is she okay?"

"Jean? What's she got to do with it?"

"Mae, do keep up."

"She used to look after Siofra."

"And warm Carl's bed."

"Cold now."

"Indeed."

"Any other reason he was unhappy?" Mae asked.

"He was bothered about his Topologie. Main were interfering."

"On the whole, Carl was as happy as a pig in shit," declared Serpa, looking sharply at Mae, after she'd heard the details. "I simply won't believe he'd kill himself."

"Mae says you can never tell who will or won't."

"I disagree," said Serpa. "You can see it in the eyes. A carelessness. They've lost the fear of death."

They were a curious pair, never discussing their pre-Earth past, as if they'd just arrived here as they appeared: wizened shamans. Over the decades Mae—ever the policewoman—had stitched a few remarks and mentions into a patchwork of facts. The pair belonged to an old, wealthy family. Groomed for roles in a firm caught in a clan's clutches. A terrible ruction, leading to a break with the family. It was the only source of conflict between them, she'd noticed. Sousa: *We chose solitude, withdrew from up there to be down here.* Serpa: *We fled a family feud, we were betrayed, marooned.* Mae had once asked if they missed anyone. Sousa had said, "You never had kin. You don't know what it's like. Bound by blood. Here, we've lives of our own." Serpa kept her council.

Mae suspected the Twins of secretly enjoying how their silence, sowing doubt and confusion, deepened their air of mystery. As a result, rumours about them ran the full gamut from escaped felons, via spies covertly watching the Facility for the PA or a rival clan, to being the last descendants of refuseniks who had never left Earth.

Serpa started coughing again and was soon doubled over.

"Dear, you've got to sit down," said Sousa. "Rest. I warned you about getting excitable."

"I'm sorry," said Mae. "I shouldn't have come. Are you okay?"

"Mae . . . don't be an ass. I'm fine."

"She's a stubborn old girl," said Sousa. "Never one for listening."

"Look who's talking."

Serpa was worryingly frail. They both were. Yet they were always welcoming, glad of the company. They showed off, but who cared when it was so much fun. Why did she hesitate? Why didn't she trust them with the truth? Did acting the stranger make it easier? She should just tell them of her suspicions. But she knew she wouldn't. That would only cause trouble. More trouble than she was about to cause.

"Always liked Carl," Serpa said as she straightened.

"But you liked Gemma even more, didn't you?"

"Ssh. I liked her before and after she went strange. Mae, did you know Carl was a patron of the arts?"

"He bought your sculptures?"

"Paid well too."

"An atmo-pump. Latrine composter."

Mae reached out and touched one of the wooden logs. Lines had been carved into its surface, forming geometric shapes. Other logs and a few rocks were similarly patterned, showing distorted spheres and cubes.

"Carl got interested in my abstracts."

"What excited him about them?" Mae asked.

"Mae, you are asking questions like an officer of the law," said Sousa, giving her a severe look.

"You can take the girl out of the Service," said Serpa.

Sousa put a hand on her arm. Her grip was surprisingly strong. "Mae, I know he lived out here, but Carl never belonged to us. They won't tolerate interference."

Serpa clucked, shook her head. "You did a good thing, Mae. Siofra needs someone. But my worse half is right. They will be upset."

Mae shook her head. "He lived among us. They don't even know."

"Perhaps. But he is theirs. You must tell them, allow his kind to decide."

She shook her again. "He needs taken care of."

The Twins exchanged troubled looks. "Mae," said Sousa, "you do that and you're claiming him."

"Yes." She didn't want there to be any doubt.

"They won't like that. And few round here will either. It will lead to trouble."

"I found him. This is my duty."

Serpa coughed, doubling over.

Mae tried to go to her, but Sousa maintained her grip.

"The funeral will be the day after tomorrow," she said, finally.

Sousa seemed about to speak but Serpa said, "Then he's in good hands. If anyone takes her duty seriously, Mae, it's you."

"Too seriously, sometimes," said Sousa. "You take care of Siofra. She needs love."

"It's Jean *I'm* worried about," said Serpa.

"Yes. Go to her next, Mae. She loves that girl like she's her own."

Mae nodded, not wanting to leave. "Will you—"

"We'll be there."

"We're not dead yet."

"Ignore her. She's a morbid moo at times."

As they were leaving, Sousa called out, "Come to us, Mae, if you need help. You walk a lonely path. Now is not the time to be a stranger."

Mae, disturbed by what she meant by that, could only nod in reply.

○

AROUND AGE TEN, Mae had grown aware of her place in the scheme of things. Despite living inside the cloistered environment of the church—busy with chores and learning, assisting in the search for signs of the future in the light of the past—she had never understood and barely even wondered what was wanted of her.

Yes, the daily rituals of church life—lens polishing, astronomy lessons, starlit prayers—drilled into the orphans a sense of humanity's manifest destiny. Our species was not to be confined to one planet or solar system. New worlds beckoned—and the church and its servants had vital roles to play in that destiny.

In classes two floors below the observatory, they calculated the sizes of suns and the scales of galaxies. Measuring out the universe one piece at a time. At midnight masses they stared up at so many pinpricks in the black cloth of the firmament. Stars uncountable, with their invisible revolving worlds. Stars arranged in spirals, like milk stirred in coffee, or bright blobs, resembling eyes peering from the distant heavens. Stars, they were taught, spinning around huge voids at a galaxy's heart over hundreds of millions of years. Galaxies colliding, merging, subject to great astral tides. Ebbing and flowing. Keep measuring the spiral coiling, count back the universal aeons. Help the astronomer-priests calculate, tabulate, assemble a timeline, a vision, a religion of the future.

Give the church its due: It never doubted what it was seeking. And an ignorant orphan like Mae had her role to play. Even Sister Ursula agreed: "Like it or loathe it, the church offers believers a sense of moral purpose."

She remembered days polishing ancient telescopes too myopic to see very far back in time. These were symbols of the astronomer-priests' quest: looking back to see forward. The future was written in the past. She had spent many thousands of hours listening to choirs sing and chant, filling huge, enclosed spaces with voices reaching for the sanctity of the heavens. Their need all consuming.

They scanned starlight for signs of suitable Earth Twos by the nightly blessing of the astronomer priests: "*When you know what you're looking for, given sufficient time, you are bound to find it.*" Sister Ursula called it a curse: "Knowing what you want and getting it are different matters that every religion tragically confuses."

And wasn't that true in Mae's case? She not only knew what she wanted but also knew she'd never find it. An orphan's deepest desire can't ever be satisfied because what you are—your very orphanhood—precludes what you most yearn for.

Thus, Mae had learned she'd no true place in the scheme of things.

○

THE JEEP WAS STILL ROLLING towards the shack when the girl got the door open and ran.

Jean Baré—small and slight, wind whipping long, fair hair across a white face—was standing in the open doorway. She swept the girl up in her arms and held her tight. Over the girl's shoulder, Baré frowned as the jeep ground to a halt.

Mae cut the engine. The shack was, like Mae's, small, but, unlike Mae's, homely. Neatly symmetrical, it had two round windows either side of a door under a slanted roof. It was well-maintained, looking quaint as a cottage. Pots and tubs held fading flowers and crop remains. The generosity of the Twins was in evidence. Baré liked company. Though she'd walked out of the Facility, she'd not taken to solitude. She was no penitent. Not yet.

Baré spoke quietly to the girl, eyes trained on the jeep.

Mae popped the door. Got out slowly.

When she saw who it was—or wasn't—Baré's face wobbled, scrunching up. She shook her head and took a step backwards. Her eyes wide and disbelieving. Turning, she vanished inside the shack.

She was still carrying the girl.

○

JEAN BARÉ WAS YOUNG, no more than twenty-five, and spoke hesitantly, almost haltingly, like a walker who has found themselves on uncertain ground, testing the firmness of each step. The penetrating gaze of her sharp blue eyes, however, belied any irresolution on her part. This was a woman, Mae thought, who knew what she wanted and would patiently find a way of getting it.

Mae poured tea from a metal jug. It was bright and warm inside the shack, the walls insulated by sheets of creamy plastofab. Window coverings and pictures were neatly hung. Three years ago, this shack had been a derelict ruin.

Baré sat on her bed, arms around the girl. Her eyes were red, face tear-streaked. Balled in her hand was a cloth. She spoke softly.

"He sent me away a year ago. We had a row, and he told me to pack. I wasn't allowed to say anything to Siofra. I did, of course. There was no need for us both to be heartless about it. He insisted on driving me. Wouldn't talk the whole way." There was a croakiness to her voice.

Baré stroked the girl's hair absently. A faint smile touched the girl's lips, her eyes closed. She'd drifted off to sleep. She trusted Baré, that much was clear.

They drank their tea in silence.

"How long were you there?"

"About nine months. Not all the time. Sometimes I'd come back here for a few days—usually Siofra would come with me. It gave him space to work."

"You miss her."

"Miss both of them."

She wants to talk, Mae thought. She'd only been out here three years, spending four in total on Earth. Not trusted by a few. They were suspicious, thought her a spy. Mae didn't think so. She was too artless to be entirely fake. Mae had encountered Main's spies before. They always thought too much of themselves to hide their origins successfully. They liked to show off. But then she'd been wrong before about people, hadn't she? Appearances *were* deceptive.

Baré rested her chin on the sleeping girl's head. "I don't believe he killed himself," she said.

Mae was careful. "It's not unusual. The Caul upsets people. You were in the Facility. How many have they lost over the years?"

"He wasn't the sort. When the Caul has got a hold of someone, you know it. They behave differently."

Mae swallowed. Not always, she thought. "He didn't choose the Caul."

"He wouldn't. Not after Gemma. He was devoted to Siofra and his work." She swallowed. "He didn't need anything else."

Mae saw a picture of the three of them on the wall. They were messing about, Magellan laughing. Someone had taken that photograph, she thought.

"You look happy," said Mae, indicating the picture. "What happened?"

Baré looked at the ceiling, biting back tears. "He never said. He barely spoke after he told me to go. At one point, I thought he was sending Siofra away with me, but then he seemed to change his mind. He was clearly upset. I felt it was . . . something I'd done. He'd been spending a lot of time in the Topologie and studying in his cabin. He'd grown far away."

"Did you love him?"

Baré flinched, disturbing the girl.

Mae smiled. "Sorry, I'm just trying to understand. You really don't know why Magellan ended it?"

Baré shrugged, tight-lipped now.

"Did you get many visitors?"

"A few. Why?"

"Just a few?" Baré welcomed guests and often called on others. Not Mae.

"They were a distraction for Carl. Once, the Twins came over, and we went to their place a few times. Hannu stopped by to fix things. *Why?*"

She was out of practice. She'd made Baré suspicious. Suspicious of what, exactly? she asked herself. You're not investigating this. Leave it to Main. She was cross with herself but wasn't sure why.

"There'll be a funeral," she said. "Day after tomorrow. Noon. Usual place."

Baré looked aghast. "Mae, you can't."

"I don't see why not."

"Main won't like it."

She shrugged carelessly to indicate what she thought about that. She got slowly to her feet.

"You're leaving already?" Baré clutched the girl tighter.

"I need to tell the others."

She nodded. Then she said, "You don't think he killed himself."

Mae licked dry lips. "Why do you say that?"

"You ask too many questions. I'm a scientist. I can tell the difference between curiosity and inquisitiveness."

Mae stared at her. What was there to say? She was already sick of the deceit. It brought back too many bad memories.

"Who would want to . . ." Baré shook her head. She shivered.

Mae leaned forward and gave the girl's shoulder a shake.

"You could leave her here, with me." Baré smiled tentatively. "It can't be good for her, hearing you tell everyone about Carl."

There was a need in the woman's eyes that made Mae wary. "No, I think she should stay with me."

No anger, only disappointment. "You think she knows who . . . was responsible?"

"Hard to say." She had been trying not to think about it. This is not my problem, she kept telling herself. Then why make it your problem? she wondered.

"You think she's safer with you?"

Awakened, the girl was resistant, clinging to Baré's waist. Mae tugged at her as they all stood at the door. She peeled an arm off, got the door open.

"Why won't you let me help?" asked Baré desperately.

Mae paused. Baré was right about the girl. Having Siofra at her side was a risky strategy if she encountered Magellan's killer. More importantly, Baré was also right about something else. This wasn't good for the girl.

Siofra was wailing. Nothing wrong with her tongue. She wanted to be with Baré, clearly much more than she wanted to be with Mae.

Mae stood in the doorway. The empty jeep beckoned.

○

THE TEMPLE WAS VISIBLE for several kilos in every direction, dwarfing Sousa and Serpa's prairie house and rivalling the Facility in its brute ugliness. But more impressive than the structure itself was the story of its construction. The hulls of four cylindrical rockets had been hauled here, broken up and reassembled to form a cone towering into the sky. Long ago it had been painted black with a white cap—resembling a pre-Exodus picture Mae had once seen of a lighthouse—but the surface was now thickly scabbed and streaked with rust. In the time she'd been on Earth it hadn't seen a lick of paint.

Around the tower's base stood a few long shacks, dormitories for the worshippers who'd once gathered here. Like the structure they were huddled against, each was in a wretched state, even by the standards of the penitents. It looked long abandoned and forgotten, which it was. Almost.

She left the jeep some distance away. The vehicle only raised questions she didn't want to have to answer. Not with the temple's occupant.

She crossed the shingle bed to the temple doors. One appeared rusted shut, the other, its base partially buried, was open. She called his name.

Inside, the reassembled rockets formed a large hollow spire webbed with steel struts. The floor was a circle of bare metal plates, supporting ringed rows of steel pews, and an altar at the centre. The altar was a gray slab of stone with a carved undulating top suggestive of the choppy Caul on a windy day.

On his knees before the slab was Rawat. He wore a loincloth, never anything else no matter the season, revealing dark skin stretched across thin bones. Long, black hair in a knotted tail ran down his short back. He didn't turn, continuing to chant quietly. Mae took a seat and waited, listening. The Ten was part of the liturgy of the Caulers. It could last minutes or hours.

Not everyone hated the Caul. For those like Rawat it was God: their north, south, east, and west. They'd once fled the habitats in their thousands, defying laws of property, traffic, and migration to come, worship, and, finally, sacrifice themselves to this entity. And there lay Rawat's tragedy. To be the only one of his kind marooned on Earth. To be waiting for rockets that had stopped coming. Watching for worshippers no longer able to avoid or prepared to risk persecution by the authorities in their attempts to get here. Desperate for someone to relieve him from his post so that he might enter the Caul with a cleansed soul. So, while he waited, he roamed the shore, watching, preaching, and generally making a nuisance of himself. Rawat had thought he had been given a great honour but as the years passed that honour had weighed heavier and heavier on him, until now he seemed to stoop under its terrible burden. You could see the dilemma in his tortured face. Was he really the last of his kind? In which case could he legitimately and honestly enter the Caul? Or would he be damning himself in God's eyes?

After a time, she cleared her throat.

He shifted, accusing eyes flashing. She smiled. He continued to chant—loudly now—for another few minutes, but his heart was no longer in it, and he kept glancing her way. He stood, bowed to the altar, made the sign of the Caulers: A flat hand, rising and falling, moved left to right before the face.

"You are trespassing," he said, turning but not approaching.

"I thought the temple welcomed all."

"All believers."

"It's nice to see you too, Rawat."

He glared at her.

"I come with news."

He stepped forward, eyes lighting up. "Has there been a rocket? I knew it. They wouldn't leave me. I have been tried but I have stood firm. Hallelujah! I've proved my worthiness. How many have come? Where is it?"

She saw tears of relief in his eyes and was sorry now she'd not come right out with it. "No, Rawat," she said. "There is no rocket. It's just us. Though we are fewer now. Magellan is dead."

Like a lamp smashed by a thrown stone, the light of salvation died in his eyes. He staggered and grasped a pew for support.

She watched him closely, as she'd watched the others. She didn't know why, but she couldn't prevent long-unused mental muscles from twitching. She wished they'd stop. "Hanged himself," she said.

He nodded. "He never listened. I told him, but he never listened."

"What did you tell him?"

He came forward, eyes gleaming fervidly. "To stay away."

"From you?"

"The Caul. He was interfering."

"He wasn't interested in the Caul."

"He visited the Cluster. He removed sacred material he should not have dared touch. His entry was an act of desecration. He claimed it was his duty to discover the Cluster's secrets. Those secrets belong to the Caul." His raised voice echoed above. "I warned him of hubris, it is a sickness. He has paid the price for not listening. I warned him!"

She wanted to go, had heard enough of his poison. But he had a right to know. He was, no matter how much she might not like it, one of them. Being obnoxious did not negate your rights as a fellow penitent and human being.

Rawat and the other worshippers had lived a life of poverty—in most ways that mattered—yet had lorded it over everyone else, as if there was something inherently noble in suffering. Now he was the last of his kind and the doubt was plain on his face. The One abandoned, forgotten. Left behind.

There was always One. It was their duty to wait for and instruct those who came next. Under the tutelage of the One, new arrivals spent a year devoted to the Caul: living a pure ascetic life, absolving themselves of all sin, preparing for their immersion. Then the One would lead them all over—all except for the newly anointed One. Rawat was the last One.

Once, it had been an honour, not a curse.

For there had been no rockets in ten years. No new Caulers to lead. This had unhinged Rawat, Mae supposed. She had found him once by the shore, weeping. He'd pleaded with her to push him in. His reasoning, if she'd understood him correctly, was that if he involuntarily went in, then the Caul wouldn't be angry with him for deserting his post. He'd been desperate, torn between desire and duty. She had little sympathy for him. The Caulers were a cult, pure and simple. Those they led were brainwashed into coming here—she'd broken up Cauler groups on Mars, arrested their leaders. Half those who came in the Cauler-hijacked ships vanished before the year was out. Vulnerable and terrified and lost, they were never able to resist the Caul's lure for long.

Under his breath, Rawat was reciting the Ten: The origin myth that had once drawn thousands from across the system. It was a curious melange of old-time religion and twisted post-Exodus scientific speculation, attempting to shoehorn two competing belief systems into the same small box. Salvation of the species via redemption of a chosen few. The Caul a liquid heaven: a molecule-scrambling quantum foam. By some weird alchemy it managed to sound even crazier than the sum of its parts.

She stood up. "There'll be a funeral day after tomorrow," she said.

"They're sending him over?" he snarled in outrage.

"*We are*," she said.

He peered at her suspiciously. He shook his head. "This is not wise," he said with a note of panic. "This is a mistake. They will not like it."

"He's one of us."

"No, no. We must leave him well alone. They will come. In numbers. They will be angry. They will—"

"Rawat, they don't care. No one cares about us. We don't matter."

His mouth hung open and he stared at her in utter disbelief. He seemed to shrink before her and once again she found herself feeling sorry for him.

"You are welcome at the funeral, if you can behave yourself," she said.

He nodded, looking at his feet. "I'll be there," he promised quietly.

She looked up into the dark-strutted gloom above. Bars of light from the portholed hulls crisscrossed the space. The impressive thing about the temple was that it had been built by human hands alone. So many of them.

But that story, like all stories told here, would soon be forgotten.

○

WHEN SHE WAS TWELVE, Sister Ursula had taken Mae on a series of virtual tours of Earth's great religious spaces. These haunting reconstructions, filmed in the original buildings, had been polished to recapture the magnificence and awe their medieval builders had sought to instil in their flocks. The urge to fall on her knees had been unexpectedly irresistible.

As they'd walked around one unreal vaulted space, rafts of lit candles causing painted pillars to shimmer out of the darkness, stone flags trembling under a hushed chorus of male voices, Mae had dared ask Sister Ursula if this was why she'd left the Service to join the church. Here, it seemed to her young mind, was a force so much vaster than anything she'd ever conceived.

"I lost faith in the Service's ability to do good," the Sister had said. "Since the Exodus our lives have become so small, confined and grubby. Yet the church wants us to believe in a bigger picture. It has a mission. Look about you. Do you not feel awed?"

"But you call the sisters cranks misguidedly obsessed with the past!" she'd whispered, thrilled at repeating such transgressive words.

"They are," Sister Ursula had admitted. "But they seek a better future. They took *you* in. And now here I am, showing you what humankind once built."

She'd stamped her foot. "But it's just a replica of an old, dead church. It's not even real."

The Sister had shrugged and smiled ruefully. "It was once." Then she'd touched Mae's forehead. "And before it was real it only existed in the minds of its creators."

○

"A LOT OF RUST DOWN HERE." His voice, coming from under the jeep, was muffled. "I told him, you gotta take care of it or one day it'll just fall apart on you."

"Hannu, have you listened to a word I've said?"

"A few days' work at least to make it roadworthy."

All she could see of him were the holed soles of his oil-stained moccasins. Time, she acknowledged, to make him a new pair. Favours for favours. "You seen any roads recently?"

"You're funny."

"And you're not paying attention. Come out from under there."

Mae sat on a rusted engine block, the least uncomfortable looking "seat" she could find. Low hills of parts surrounded her. Heaps of metal, rubber, plastic. The guts ripped from rockets the length of the shore. As well as whole ground and air vehicles abandoned by the clans, scavenged and broken up. Two of the larger mounds were actually half-buried workshops. Under the overhang of one lay a cot. Stacked here and there were piles of coiled wire and jars of decanted oil. On close inspection, it was surprisingly orderly for a scrap heap. It reeked, like Hannu always did, of oil and fuel.

Hannu worked hard. He worked for himself and he worked for others. Mae had never seen him not working, tinkering, fiddling, ripping apart and putting back together again, or assembling from spare parts tools and vehicles that might work "if only I can convince 'em to believe in me like I believe in them." More often than not, his belief went unrequited. However, this rarely seemed to dampen Hannu's spirits or enthusiasm for his projects. He'd simply take it to pieces and start all over again. He'd already built himself a solar-powered lorry and an unreliable hoverbike. The big prize, though, the real honest-to-goodness life-saver was going to be his rocket. This lay in several large pieces around his yard. He'd been building it for ten years by Mae's reckoning. "Gonna get outta here 'fore it kills me," he'd say. And Mae believed him. More than anyone among the penitents, Hannu didn't belong here. He hadn't come here searching for something or someone. He'd been brought here against his will. If anyone deserved to get away, it was Hannu. He'd worked too hard not to.

Hannu shuffled out from under the jeep. Under his long tangle of blond hair, his dirt-smeared face offered her a pained look. An oil-blackened hand held a spanner. "He's not looked after it," he complained.

"Perhaps," she said patiently, "he had other things on his mind."

"Keep telling him. Number of times he shows up here, asking for help. Not got the right mindset, you know? Still thinking he's in that concrete box: *If it breaks just order up a replacement from Main*." He popped the hood, revealing the engine: oily metal, cracked rubber and brittle thermoplast. No smooth plastic circuit box. Just honest Caul-incorruptible chemistry and mechanics.

"Is that so?" Mae resigned herself to waiting for the penny to drop.

"Out here with us now, ain't he? Got to be careful. Understands but doesn't quite get it, follow me?"

"Not really but carry on." The wind turbines fixed to the top of each mound whirred noisily. Behind her, generators hummed like hives of bees.

He went at the engine with his tools. She sighed, letting him. "On our own out here. Something wears out, you don't just replace it. Sure, I got plenty parts but they're for other things. Got to modify 'em, hand tool 'em. It's all jury-rigged. Gotta live by our wits. Extemporise. Far from easy, see?"

"I do, but Hannu—"

"But he don't. Been telling and *telling* him." He forced a metal plate out with a grunt. Next, he poked the screwdriver in and hit its handle hard, like it was a chisel. He kept on hitting it, face red and just about snarling with effort.

Good, she thought, some part of him had been listening.

She looked at the pieces of the small rocket he'd been slowly assembling. He talked brightly about leaving Earth, but Mae wondered how deeply being stuck here festered inside. Like all of the penitents, she worried about him. What the hell would they all do if he decided to make the attempt, and succeeded or died trying? It wasn't worth thinking about. Mae didn't know if he simply couldn't get his rocket to work or if he kept it in pieces for some other reason she couldn't figure out.

Hannu had stopped, bits of engine stacked on both fenders. He rubbed his brow with a dirty finger. "Why'd he go and do a fool thing like that?"

Mae shook her head sadly. "That's the question."

"Got a damn daughter."

"I know."

"Where is she?"

"Safe."

"Facility?"

"Hannu, she's safe, okay."

He shrugged, staring helplessly at the butchered engine as if unsure how it came to be in this state.

"Now, will you put this jeep back together? I got other places to be."

○

AS A TEEN, Mae had learned the pivotal role religion played post-Exodus.

The more trusted orphans accompanied astronomer-priests on their tours to other Mars settlements as well as to orbital habitats. It was the orphans' job to persuade the crowds who'd gathered to sign up or part with donations. "The church's patter of a deep past offering clues to a deeper future appeal to the romantic inside each of us," argued Sister Ursula.

On Mae's first preaching tour with the Church of Venerable Light she discovered just how competitively religions fought to expand their congregations. These faiths were as contradictory as they could be at variance from reality. And the wilder they got, the stronger their believers' convictions appeared to be and more bad-tempered were the exchanges between the competing congregations whenever they met.

These faiths came in a variety of flavours, but nearly all were born, or reborn, after the Exodus.

The purgatorial religions damned humankind for committing a crime, resulting in banishment from the Earth for an unspecified period. As such, Christianity had a second flourishing after reframing the Bible's Garden of Eden story, turning metaphorical myth into prophecy. Similarly, "told you so" enviro sects claimed we'd failed in our stewardship of the Earth, which had cast us out. Atonement creeds declared any return was dependent on us accepting our role in the ravaging, preaching humility. Faiths of healing imagined Earth in recovery. Eschatologists argued we had to leave the womb of the world prior to escaping the solar system. While believers in the singularity insisted the Caul was a step, a levelling up, we as a species were too scared to take. Such doctrines of the Caul insisted it was a manifestation of God. Cluster religions demurred: Interdimensional shapes were God themselves revealing their true form. Dissenters called them changeling cities.

Whatever they preached, the post-Exodus faiths offered hope, despair, comfort, joy, love, solidarity, purpose, esoteric knowledge. Anything their believers wanted. Or as Sister Ursula put it, "Everything but a healthy dose of reality."

○

MAE NEVER MADE IT TO THE FACILITY. Halfway there, a large copter intercepted her, circled the jeep twice, and set down directly in its path. Mae halted sharply.

A tall, thin-faced woman in gray overalls and still wearing her flight helmet and visor climbed down and approached rapidly. Mae got out and met her halfway.

"This is Carl Magellan's jeep," said Facility Director Dr. Jane Carlyle.

Mae, who'd planned to park a distance from the Facility, was immediately lost for words.

Tall and slim, Dr. Carlyle moved and spoke with a clipped severity, suggestive of an unwillingness to dwell on distractions. She'd been here for a quarter century and Mae had been told she pursued the Caul with a single-mindedness that went beyond obsession into some as yet unmapped psychological territory. In Mae's few encounters with the director, she'd seen it in the sharp blue eyes that coldly discriminated between the important and the irrelevant. (The visor at least spared her that, but as a penitent, Mae already knew to which category she belonged.) Dr. Carlyle vaguely reminded Mae of marbits she'd seen racing over the pebbled plain in the vicinity of the Caul. Their gaze locked ahead, haunted or possessed by the terrible thing they rushed towards.

"Well?" said Dr. Carlyle crisply. "Where is he?"

Mae felt a twinge of dismay. Speaking to Main's representatives wasn't going to go how she'd hoped. It would be difficult, just like the others had said.

"Carl's dead."

Dr. Carlyle took a small step back. "Dead?" The word a whisper.

"I found his body day before yesterday."

"What happened?"

Mae had trusted Hastings, would have told him everything. Dr. Carlyle, on the other hand, she was less certain about. Honesty had consequences. "He'd been killed," she said, "though someone tried to make it look like suicide."

"Killed?" Dr. Carlyle shook her head. Denying it. "Mae, you're being fanciful."

She didn't dignify that with an answer.

"What about"—she cleared her throat—"his daughter?"

"She's safe. I've been looking after her."

"Where is she?"

"She's safe."

"Does she know what happened?"

"She doesn't talk."

"I know *that*," Dr. Carlyle snapped. "Day before yesterday?"

"That's what I said."

She frowned. "What makes you sure it was murder?"

"I worked homicide in the Service."

"Mae, that was thirty years ago."

"Murder changed, has it?"

Dr. Carlyle took a step closer. Mae imagined the eyes behind the visor calculating, assessing her. "You were coming to tell us?"

"I thought you should know."

Dr. Carlyle indicated the empty jeep. "Where's the girl? How is she?"

"Jean Baré has her. It's hard to tell how the girl is."

"*Is* she safe?" queried Dr. Carlyle.

"If you want her, you know where she is."

Dr. Carlyle angled her head as if considering this. "The Facility is not a good place for a child. If it is acceptable with you and Jean, the girl should stay with you, until you hear otherwise."

"And Carl?"

"What about Carl?" Impatient.

Mae's mouth twitched, almost betraying her. "He was killed."

"So you keep saying, Mae. Until Main can get a team out there to verify that claim, I suggest you stay away from Carl's camp. If what you say is true, then it is a crime scene. Tampering with—"

Mae wasn't listening to this. "I didn't come to debate it. There is a killer. They might be out here on the shore, or in the Facility with you."

Dr. Carlyle shook her head at Mae. "You said it looked like suicide. Occam's razor. Isn't the simplest explanation the best? He wouldn't be the first. From what I hear he had good reason—"

"What did you hear?"

"Mae, Mae . . ." Dr. Carlyle fiddled with the figure-of-eight pendant hanging round her neck before replying. "You left the Service long ago. You're a nobody and you're nowhere. I don't mean this rudely. Be glad of it. Poking your nose in our affairs is interfering in Main business. They won't take kindly to that. You'll find yourself becoming a somebody. You don't want that."

Mae nodded at the copter. "Where were you headed?" she asked.

"Is there anything else?" asked Dr. Carlyle firmly.

"There'll be a funeral day after tomorrow," Mae said.

"Mae, I told you, I think it is best if you stay—"

"Corpses rot. We have to dispose of it."

"Main won't like that. They'll want the body—"

"There's a place we—"

"I know all about it."

"It would be proper to have some of his people there."

"That will be impossible. It's difficult right now."

Mae looked at her, contempt and pity bundled together.

"Hard all over," she said, turning away.

"Mae?"

She turned back. "Yes?"

"You leave it alone, you hear. Main will investigate. You don't want to get in their way."

Dr. Carlyle's visor stared at her a moment longer and then she strode back to the copter.

○

A TWIST OF HER WRISTS—joints throbbing—and the marbit's neck cracked. The girl turned away, burying her head in Baré's chest.

"Don't be squeamish, child. We've three to feed, tonight."

And, she wondered, for how long after?

Baré held the girl, staring uncertainly at the marbit hanging limply in Mae's hand.

"Not you too?" She kneeled to bait and reset the trap. Twilight now and she found it hard to see what she was doing. But she wasn't getting her torch out in front of them.

"I was thinking," said Baré.

"Yes?"

"Are we doing the right thing?"

It was baited but the trip wouldn't slide in. "For whom?"

"You know."

"I told you." There. It slid home with a click. "It's not a good place for her."

"You never said why Dr. Carlyle wouldn't—"

"I can't be more specific right *now*, Jean."

The woman bit her lip. "Later, you need to—"

"We'll see."

Baré pouted sullenly. Mae wondered what it was had made her leave the Facility. She looked uneasy out here, frequently glancing over her shoulder at nothing. It was how new arrivals acted. An itch at the back of the neck. The overwhelming sense of being watched. A twitchiness that eventually settled into wariness.

"We have to be careful."

Baré's eyes were hard, urgent with her need to know. She'd abandoned friends and colleagues but there were still threads of connection. Her presence complicated everything. Mae wondered if she'd made the right decision. The girl was certainly happier with Baré around. She no longer looked scared and haunted. Once or twice, she'd worn the ghost of a smile. "We'll see, okay?"

Mae got stiffly to her feet. She couldn't see the other trap in the gloom.

"Siofra is welcome at mine. Then you'd be free to . . ."

She gave Baré a silencing look. She'd been in a bad mood since meeting Dr. Carlyle. She felt boxed in by other people's expectations and did not want to talk about it. "We stay together."

Reluctantly, she dug through her furs for the torch.

"Why?"

"Don't be obtuse." She shone the light ahead, walking slowly.

Baré followed, with the girl. "You don't trust me," she said.

Mae saw the trap, fifty metres off. She saw movement. Whatever was in it was big. "Right now, the only person I trust is myself."

"Mae, I don't want this."

She kept walking. "That's okay. I'll take you home. Siofra and I will do just fine."

"That's not true."

She was standing over the illuminated trap. The marbit nearly filled the cage. It sat there, panting but calm. She sighed, noting the signs. Dammit, she thought.

"Mae, what can you achieve on your own? Even if you find out the truth, what will happen? There's no law here, no justice . . ."

She bent down. The marbit blinked at her. It was near full term, dehydrated. She opened the cage. It didn't move. She removed her pack and took out the three leaves she was going to use as bait. She placed them outside the small cage. She removed a metal plate, filled it with water from her bottle.

She stood and stepped back.

The animal looked around, then lolloped out of the cage. It sniffed a leaf, drank some water. "We're going to be hungry, tonight," she said.

The girl, hesitantly, came forward.

"You can stroke it," said Mae. "It's not going to run."

The girl crouched and tentatively rubbed the animal's back. It didn't react.

"Never seen one this far gone out here," said Baré.

"They're rare. I think they maybe follow their mate."

"Hmm. I read that the Caul repels the gravid. Whatever it is normally draws the living toward it works in reverse." Baré was down on her haunches. "The same with juveniles, they try to get as far away as they can. If she followed her mate, it would be an uncommonly strong bond."

Mae stared at the feeding doe. "I once found a litter of pups, a few days old. Mother nowhere to be seen. I looked for a couple of hours, hoping she'd gone to find food. I found no sign. The noise of their cries . . ."

"She'd have gone over. Tests have shown, the hormones cut—"

"They were starving. I had nothing to feed them. The pups were screeching and screeching. It hurt my ears." She swallowed, watching the girl pat the doe.

"Mae, I don't think—"

"I had to do something. Their suffering. I couldn't stand it. How long had the mother been gone? I was kilos from anywhere. They needed her milk. Nothing I could do. Twelve of them, crying. Had to take a stone—"

"Mae!"

She looked at Baré then down at the girl, stroking the doe. Shook her head. She returned her knife to its sheath. "You forget how precious life is."

They drove back in the dark. The meal took time to prepare and when they ate the girl was falling asleep in her food. Afterwards, there was a lot of fussing and bickering to fit everyone in comfortably. In the end Baré insisted on sharing with the girl. Reluctantly, Mae surrendered her bed. Baré asked for a light to stay on so the girl wouldn't be frightened. "Sometimes Siofra wets the bed."

Finally, a welcome silence settled on the full shack. Mae lay on a mattress on the floor, wracked with doubt. Everyone had told her to leave Magellan alone. They were all scared of upsetting Main. Well, she wasn't. She was fed up with being told what to do and she didn't like the distinctions being made about who belonged here and who didn't. We're all human beings, she thought, and though we've all found our way home it's no longer safe. We must look out for one another. Which meant taking responsibility for what happened here.

Baré, she suspected, knew she wasn't going to be able to leave this alone and the woman wouldn't be happy about it. Well, Mae had given her a choice. The truth was more complicated, of course. Mae had realized she couldn't do this without Baré's help. She also wanted Baré where she could keep an eye on her. Was she really going after Magellan's killer? Albert would have admonished her for playing a dangerous game, but he'd also have told her she was doing the right thing by Magellan.

She picked up Magellan's journals. Last night, she'd begun at Year One. The man wrote frequently but irregularly about his work—there were many diagrams and maps—and his day-to-day life with Gemma. There were cross-outs and pages torn out. Much of it was quotidian or technical, which she skimmed or skipped altogether. She was trying to get a sense of the man he saw himself as when he arrived, not the neighbour she had avoided getting to know. She resisted the temptation to jump to the final journal and recent entries. What hurry was there? No one was demanding results. She had all the time in the world to get there.

One thing she'd noticed immediately. The launch numbers on the sheet of paper the girl had given her were not written in the same hand as the journals. Someone else wrote those numbers.

By the time she finished Year Three, the words had turned blurry and misshapen. She had a headache. Some combination of the dim light and the scrawled, hard-to-read writing. That would be it. Not her failing sight.

She lay back, closing sore eyes. She could still feel the bulb shining. Burning into her. She got out of bed, glanced at Baré and the child, sleeping.

She switched off the light.

YEAR THREE

Day 16, Month 5

Let me describe Topologie#66.

It sits on a gently sloping fog-shrouded peninsula made of rock. Ceramic shards cover the ground, cracking and crunching with every step. As you enter, the fog thickens and it's clear that the gray miasma is as much a part of the Topologie's fabric as its solid structures. It drifts, thickening and thinning, obscuring and revealing. Sometimes I can see for tens of metres. At other times it hides my feet.

From every direction comes the ringing, whistling, or moaning. The air hums with feverish song. Caused by breezes passing through gaps in multiple structures, it is mellifluously musical, and I am reminded of the hypnotic harmonics of singing bowls. I frequently stop and listen, beguiled by this living instrument.

Shadows loom over me. I glimpse tubular beams sprouting from amorphous blobs like insectile limbs. Many are kinked at unthinkable angles. I pass under curved planar ceilings whose elegant symmetries Gemma claims adhere to hyperdimensional rules. They trouble my eye, as do the slithering sinuous structures that seem to spill from nowhere. Saddles and polyhedra must be scaled and paradromic rings passed through. Tilted surfaces see-saw depending on the angle from which they are viewed. I round corners that appear to turn one way but actually send me in other directions. Such confused geometries are disorienting. I stumble through a landscape of oddly slanting walls and weird angles, a chaos of broken curves and distorted lines. I pass depthless holes that might be voids into other dimensions. Always towering above me are vast cylindrical shafts and floating curves that stretch into an infinity I cannot grasp. I stare about me, beholding a structure whose cosmic vastness I feel too unworthy to comprehend.

(Not so Gemma. She examines my sketches and photos, dismissively labelling them: degenerate polyhedra, double-holed torus, projective plane, pentafoil knot, Seifert surface, orientable three-manifold, Klein bottle, tesseract. Technical terms to reduce an alien entity into mere geometry.)

Distantly, I can hear the shree and shush of waves rolling ashore and retreating. The Cauldron following its diurnal patterns. This is comforting. Yet occasionally the waves sound like voices. A sort of babble as if many individuals are talking at once.

Gemma pushes me to record every angle, every face, edge, and vertex. My head fills with numbers whose values grow meaningless through sheer repetition.

The still disturbing aspect—even months later—is that every time I go back to the site the structures have *changed*. Nothing is quite as I remember it being. I stumble through the yellow-gray miasma, the shards crunching under my feet, expecting to see what I saw last time or the time before, and once again I am caught off guard. Where yesterday there was a sphere, today it'll be a dome or the sphere somehow pinched like a deflated football, or I'll find it deformed into a saddle. As Gemma forever reminds me, these are homeomorphs—stretched or bent (never cut or tunnelled) transformations of the same geometrical object. No matter how often I am told this, my mind refuses to grasp it.

Twice a day, this megastructure is reborn. Every structure is made of fine yellow ceramic, as if kiln-fired.

It is very, very easy to get lost. Several times I've spent half an hour walking in increasingly desperate circles, retracing my route, trying to find my way back to a point I recognise, hearing the tide coming in, knowing the Cauldron is refilling.

In two months, I've found it hard to penetrate any great distance. The structures are tightly packed, and I am forever lost in a maze of curves that fold back on themselves. Frequently, I see shadows of structures that are not even there.

Today, I came across a towering spiral structure (Gemma shows no interest in anything exhibiting biomathematical geometries) and found an entrance. I climbed a spiral slope as far as I could go. I found a gap and looked out.

The vista I saw from thirty metres up haunts me still. On every side, freakish shapes floated on the formless gray fog, like a fleet of ships on a still sea. Below, lost in the gray, I glimpsed the curved structures I have been trapped among—sea monsters inhabiting the deep.

I have no sense of the Topologie's true form or purpose. It is a chaotic jumble as though the Cauldron daily spews out outlandish shapes and structures according to some complex but moronic algorithm. Nothing is clear. "Garbage," counters Gemma. "Then what is it for?" I ask. "What are you for? What am I for?" she asks. "Are you saying it is alive?" I wonder. "I am saying that just because its form, structure, or order is obscure to us, it does not mean it is chaotic. I see hints of subtle orientations."

Gemma has tried to enter the Topologie with me, but her sensitivity is such that she is soon incapacitated with pain. Every foray ends in tears of agony. I feel her pain.

Day 20, Month 5

Another stimulating evening with the Twins. Though Gemma and I had agreed not to discuss our progress—we don't want Hastings interfering—I could hardly duck a direct question or lie to these perceptive old women. Besides, I have been bursting to tell someone and so inevitably out came the truth. They tried to disguise it, but I think they were both impressed—if a little bamboozled—by Gemma's talk of hyperspace and lateral dimensions.

Before we knew it, we were drawing sketches on the table with chalk. Sousa and Serpa stared at it all, wide-eyed. "Such extraordinary cleverness," said Serpa. "And right on our doorstep," added Sousa. I beamed at them until Gemma said, "Carl, they mean the Topologie."

Gemma grew restless as the evening wore on. She wanted us home so I could get out early to catch the morning tide.

Day 25, Month 5

Relieved. Gemma has been driving me hard and today I reached the Jug. I had little time to take measurements before beating the tide back. The Jug is a Klein bottle, which, topologically speaking, is essentially a sphere: one surface, no edge. It cannot be fully expressed in three dimensions. Nevertheless, there are several here. The Jug is two hundred metres tall, sinuously curved and with a thick tubular handle rising fluidly from its base and entering its side near the mouth, it really does resemble a jug. Sat photos suggest this tubular handle becomes the mouth, giving this impossible structure an ouroboron slant. I am reminded of a whale, some vast oceanic leviathan flicking its tail as it breaches the surface dividing two very different worlds.

Day 4, Month 6

Gemma says I am too slow collecting data she needs to create a picture of the changing structures. I am just one man, I tell her. I can't measure everything. Sketching complicated trefoil knots takes time as does calculating Euler Numbers. I have to make choices. Of course, the further I travel into the Topologie (and it is still little more than a few hundred metres) the less time I have for measurements. If she could join me, we could double the data gathered.

Unfortunately, Gemma turns pale just as we reach the Topologie in the jeep. Frustrated, she often leaves without saying goodbye.

Day 23, Month 6

Dr. Carlyle also dined at the Twins' tonight. We try not to be specific about our work with Main's representatives. Unfortunately, Dr. Carlyle provokes Gemma. She was discussing the Cauldron's resistance to her probing. Gemma told her to stop acting as if it is a dumb material. "It is a mathematical entity," she said. "Don't prod it, talk to it." Dr. Carlyle scoffed. "To hear you *talk* it is made of ones and zeroes."

"Why not?" said Gemma. "The Caul exhibits mathematical properties at multiple scales. Mathematics is our common language."

Dr. Carlyle remained dismissive: "Mathematics is everywhere. It's solipsistic. Go looking for it, you are bound to find it."

Gemma then delightedly explained how I had entered the Topologie and how the measurements I'd gathered indicated structures were orientating around some central point. "Jane," she said, "it is information, and our purest understanding of information is mathematical." I glimpsed curiosity in Dr. Carlyle's eyes, but she was uncowed: "Even if that is the case, it is alien information. You should be careful." Gemma laughed. "With your background, I'd have thought you'd welcome that. Are you a scientist, Jane, or a priest clutching her frock?"

Dr. Carlyle grew angry and left soon after.

Day 25, Month 6

A few remarks on the origins of the Caul.

Dr. Carlyle is following the scientific consensus by treating the Cauldron as a dangerous alien entity. If the Cauldron escapes Earth and infiltrates our habitats, Sol system's other planets or moons, most believe it will be game over for humanity. Hence the quarantine, a commonsense response to prevent further contamination.

Fears of such a breakout were sky-high during the Exodus, and to this day monitoring continues right across the solar system.

Why? Because the primary suspect in our search for the source of the Cauldron is our own backyard. Most scientists believe it is native to our system, having somehow hitched a ride on a returning ship or probe or on a falling meteorite to end up on Earth. Perhaps it came from the less-well-studied outer solar system. For example, certain convection roll patterns thought unique to the Cauldron have also been detected in the supercritical fluids of Neptune's lower atmosphere. Nothing can be ruled out. Even today, centuries after we started extensively mining the asteroid belt, we are finding novel materials and structures. Comets are objects of speculation. The Oort cloud holds many and samples confirm they are riddled with alien material. In Earth's four-and-a-half billion-year history many thousands, possibly millions, of comets have struck our planet or left long gassy tails for it to pass through. At any point an alien passenger could have settled here without our knowledge. (And let us not forget panspermia theories regarding our species' own origins.)

But the solar system as Caul seed is just one idea, albeit with numerous potential expressions.

For those of us drawn to mathematics and physics there is intrusion theory. This has the advantage of explaining the explicitly alien nature of the Cauldron, such as how living matter appears to be destroyed on contact, almost as if it is a kind of anti-life. An intrusion from another universe (or dimension we cannot access) has the advantage of easily incorporating our multidimensional Topologies. For adherents, intrusion theory also explains why living matter is both attracted to, and nullified on contact with, the Cauldron.

Is it an alien intelligence? A messenger? An invasion force? A visitation from a nearby solar system? Has Earth been colonised? Conspiracy theorists insist the Cauldron is an attack, that it is either an alien lifeform or weapon (both?!) designed to eject us from Earth. Surprisingly, credence has been lent to such beliefs via coevolution studies. It turns out we cannot dismiss such fears. Is the Earth being transformed into a suitable environment for some alien species? A literal Earth hack? What might that species be like? Some think the Topologies are changeling cities, noting how so many of them have emerged where our own once stood. My question: Who is being fooled by them, and why?

Others reject the idea of intelligence, claiming instead the Cauldron is just dumb gray goo. Perhaps it is alien, perhaps it is caused by us—a kind of paperclip maximiser operating at the nanoscale level, gradually turning everything it encounters into itself. This is my favourite conspiracy theory because it is a catch-all, allowing believers to blame everyone from governments to clans, aliens to tech, ourselves to life itself, for unleashing it. And like all good conspiracies it is impossible to refute. Of course, if it IS dumb alien gray goo that is fascinating (and alarming!) from a scientific perspective. Just where *did* the goo come from?

Lastly, there is Singularity Syndrome, which comes in two flavours: pre- and posthuman. Posthumanists argue the Cauldron is the trans-human Singularity and our species' duty is to enter it. This is indistinguishable from most Cauler religions. The pre-human version is more interesting and states that the Cauldron has always been here, waiting to be discovered. Some varieties claim it is responsible for all life on Earth. It is an oddball theory, which Gemma, in her darker moments, has some time for.

`Day 3, Month 7`

While I enter the Topologie Gemma travels its shapes in her mind's eye, lost in hyperspace. She hardly sleeps, up before me and in bed long after me. Her exhaustion brings on more frequent attacks. When I return from the Topologie she barely says a word until she sees what I've brought back. If she is satisfied, she smiles. If I have failed, I am admonished by her unbroken silence. We cannot carry on like this.

Day 18, Month 7

Gemma forced herself to join me in the Topologie.

Entry was difficult. Whether it is the fog, the Cauldron's proximity or the strangeness of the space, she was severely disoriented in addition to the pain. Twice, she lay on the ground, curled in a ball, too agonised to move. But her eyes drank in everything they saw.

She was transfixed by each fog-shrouded structure. She stroked their umber-yellow ceramic surfaces. (Identifying the ceramic would require access to Dr. Carlyle's lab, which would mean officially announcing that we have entered the Topologie. Main may *know*, but they mustn't be told officially.)

It was heartbreaking watching Gemma struggle among structures that were her heart's desire, her life's work, yet that made every step an agony. She clung to me resentfully like an invalid. We brought back a bag of shards and, the attack passing almost as soon as we left, she is now poring over them and the photographs I took. I joke that I am no more than her assistant, her eyes and ears. Sometimes it is no joke.

Day 2, Month 8

Low supplies sent us to the Facility. The mood there was sombre—there have been disappearances. In one of the storage cabins outside I found dozens of microsat launchers, most decades old. I took four. No one waved us off when we left.

Day 6, Month 8

Launched three of the microsats. Together, they will allow Gemma to produce accurate 3D models of the topological structures. This will free me to explore deeper into the Topologie.

Day 19, Month 8

Saw some dozen or so bergs in the Cauldron about three kilos out. They floated by and were soon lost in the mist. I was reminded of footage I've watched repeatedly of a pod of right whales in the open ocean. It was as if the bergs were like the whales, on their way somewhere. I shouldn't anthropomorphise by ascribing purpose, but Gemma says I mustn't dismiss my own feelings. It is unliving matter, I replied. She asked: "When have such distinctions ever been helpful?"

Day 9, Month 10

Some days I travel for hundreds of metres. Others, like today, I get trapped in a maze of structures and barely manage a hundred. The problem, I fear, is me. Despite my growing sense of hidden space around me (Gemma's hyperspace), it is more hindrance than help. I am easily disoriented. Lost, I stumble around in unknown territory only to realize I am seeing familiar shapes and structures.

Gemma's disappointment in my Topologie progress plagues me. There are three of us in our marriage.

Sometimes I think about breaking into one of the structures, climbing up to the top, out of the reach of the Cauldron at high tide, and just waiting.

What happens at high tide?

What would happen to me?

Why am I too much of a coward to find out?

Day 20, Month 10

A difficult visit to the Twins. Gemma has been pushing me hard, and I wanted a break, to forget the Topologie. Unfortunately, the Twins asked about our progress and Gemma indulged them. She talked of Mobius bands and Flatland, explaining how higher dimensions intersect with our three by exploring 1D and 2D worlds. The Twins were particularly taken with Flatland, a two-dimensional world populated by triangles and squares that Gemma drew on their tabletop. A teapot stood in for a 3D sphere passing through this flat plane, appearing as a circle that grows and shrinks as it crosses this realm. We discussed bending or rolling up Flatland and how its inhabitants wouldn't notice and what they would experience if lifted out of it by 3D beings such as ourselves. Gemma even demonstrated how a creature on a Mobius band would be reversed as it journeyed along this twisted single-surface loop.

"And this is true?" Sousa asked sceptically.

"Mathematically accurate," confirmed Gemma.

"Some higher dimensional creature could just pluck us from our world?" wondered Serpa. "We couldn't hide from it?"

"There is nowhere to hide. Just as we look down and see every part of Flatland, inside every square and triangle, so they see our 3D world as a schematic. If they looked at us, they'd see inside us. They could pluck out our heart or lungs and we'd only know when our bodies failed."

"They see inside us?" said Sousa, aghast. "Carl, how do you stand it?"

"I'm not surprised you've kept this to yourselves," said Serpa, eyes shining. "Who knows what wild ideas this might give Main."

Sousa shook her head. "I wouldn't sleep safe knowing they could see through walls or pluck me out of my bed without the bother of entering the house."

Our theories seemed to have put them both out of sorts.

Day 1, Month 11

Huge row. Gemma accused me of not pulling my weight. She needs more data. She is close to pinning down the attractor, she told me. "What attractor?" I asked. She wouldn't explain. I need a break. I don't know how much sleep Gemma is getting.

Day 15, Month 11

Gemma finally explained her theory. She believes the structures in the Topologie are oriented around an attractor. However, it is fuzzy and elusive, partly, she thinks, because it is not located within our 3D realm and partly because it is not still. The more data I gather the closer she gets to pinpointing it. The problem is the data I collect, and we receive from the microsats is always for the last tide. At the next tide the attractor has moved. We are always one tide behind. I pleaded with her to get more sleep. “When we have found it,” she said.

Day 5, Month 12

Returning from the Topologie, I found Gemma wandering deliriously in the fog. It is a miracle I spotted her. She was raving about locating the attractor, convinced it was nearby. I feared this. I managed to get her back to the camp and into bed. I gave her some pills and she is sleeping. This has got to stop.

Day 7, Month 12

Gemma is staying at the Twins. When I told them about her, they offered to take her in. Somehow, I persuaded Gemma it was for the best. I dropped her over there early this morning. “We’ll take good care of her,” Sousa told me, squeezing my hand so gently that I felt tears in my eyes. Gemma was nowhere to be seen when I left.

Day 8, Month 12

On the *D’Arcy Thompson* campus, I wasn’t aware of Gemma until she introduced herself to me with the immortal words, “I noticed an error in your last paper.” I was staggered. No one ever cares enough to read colleagues’ papers. She showed me my mistake, and I was grateful—unlike most, who respond to Gemma’s pursuit of truth with silent fury or spluttering hostility, damning it as interference or even sabotage.

I didn't see her again for weeks. She was in the throes of one of her first attacks.

When she'd recovered, I invited her on a spacewalk. As we clambered over the station's skin, bathed in the light of a hundred billion stars, I talked morphometrics and Turing Patterns, describing the stippled arrangements of galactic clusters and filaments.

I said, "I am beguiled by surfaces, by appearances."

She took my hand and placed it over her heart. "I seek deeper truths. That's why I study topology."

I gabbled something about humankind losing its place in the universe. She stamped her foot on the hull. "This is just a tin can and we're insects that fell off the ball of mud we once called home. We are an irrelevance." I gazed at her as she looked up into the heavens. "When I'm with you," I told her, "I feel noticed."

She looked down. "I just want to fuck your mind," she said.

Six months later, we were married.

I wish I had not lied to Gemma about Earth. I was so sure coming here would save both of us.

Day 10, Month 12

Yet another betrayal.

I have been flicking through Gemma's pain journal. It is difficult to read as I can see her affliction in every word. Instead of her usual free-flowing and looping hand, it is all tiny, cramped capitals. A blocky minimalism that apes her own short, sharp statements: Aphorisms in which are bundled whole worlds of thought. The slightest movement is agony, so I can only imagine the pain each line has cost her. It is like seeing someone who is drowning surface to take a great gasp of air before they sink out of sight again.

Gemma was drawn to mathematics because it cannot lie. No inconsistency can be honestly ignored or hidden. Even as a child she thought logically. It makes her direct, though long experience taught her it is rarely appreciated. People think her blunt, rude, in your face. But that is to misunderstand her project. Gemma is a truth seeker.

And she doesn't spare humanity in her journal:

THE DISPLACED PEOPLES ACT AND THE EXODUS SETTLEMENT WERE DECEPTIONS.

Or me:

I HATE NO ONE MORE THAN CARL—INCLUDING MYSELF.

Or herself:

MY BODY AND I ARE AT WAR.

Sometimes Gemma's thinking lapses unexpectedly. She writes of Gaia and the Weltgeist. Both these Earth-as-organism theories have been hijacked by eco-religions blaming humanity's neglect of our planet for causing it to be too weakened to fight off the alien Caul. Gemma, normally contemptuous of such claptrap, asks:

WHAT IF WE MISTAKE OURSELVES FOR THE WORLD?

Day 12, Month 12

Freed from my daily measuring, I have been exploring. I have a well-marked route (important in the fog) that takes the jeep half a kilo into the Topologie. Today, I encountered an enormous new Klein bottle. This one, unlike the Jug, lies on its side. It is three hundred metres in length (but being on its side remains submerged in the fog), with its mouth a dark and gaping hole that is as inviting as it is terrifying. Leviathan indeed.

Day 18, Month 12

Visited Gemma and the Twins. Gemma was glad to see me and didn't once ask about my explorations. I told her about Leviathan and how I've spent the last few days carefully mapping it. I showed her photos. "Be careful," she warned. "It is a point of intersection." I told her not to worry, but not about my plans to enter it.

day 5 month 1

nauseous difficult

food down

yesterday entered leviathan

lost

disorient

terror turned round

breach crawled out

found jeep

headache vomiting

day ? month 1

handwriting headache can't read

vomiting water down

caravan back front

entered hyper changed

day ? month 1

weak food not stay down

day ? month 1

die on own not my earth

reverse dimension

find leviathan return
need gemma
tricked her no cure
I lied
where this earth gemma?

day 13 month 1

miracle gemma came!
tried explain gone help
machalek examine

day 15 month 1

gemma: write
I write
left handed
look at pen right hand
no Carl your left words reversed
confessed from mirror earth not my gemma
exchanged places
gemma : dont be a berk
you got turned around.
how am I to fix this?
gemma cross
my gemma.

Day 25, Month 1

She saved my life. Eight days ago, Gemma drove me into the Topologie. Using my maps, she found Leviathan and hauled me into its black maw. How long were we in there? Thankfully, I have no memory of it, and she won't talk about it. We went in and we came out. She looked like death, but she settled me and made me eat. I could hardly move but the dizziness and disorientation were gone. Then she told me she had to go back. I was aghast. "Carl, when you went in," she said, "you got reversed. Flipped into your mirror image. The only way to flip you back was to pass back through Leviathan. Now I'm reversed. I need to go back." I couldn't stop her. I waited, hearing the approaching tide. After the longest hour of my life, she crawled out, white-faced. She passed out and I drove us home. We've been recovering ever since. I've been eating to build up my strength and she is trying to move again. Gemma says we have both overdosed on higher dimensions. Inside Leviathan we were turned around like those 2D creatures traversing a Mobius loop that get flipped over by the twist. I became my mirror image. Which, thanks to chirality, was proving fatal. Our bodies' amino acids are levorotatory (left-handed) and the sugars we need to survive are dextrorotatory (right-handed)—chirality, or handedness, allows the acids and sugars to interact. When I was reversed, they couldn't, which meant I was slowly starving. Doc Machalek confirmed Gemma's fears. I look back at my scribblings when I was reversed and shudder.

Our unexpected journey inside Leviathan has had one fortuitous result, however. Gemma believes she sees how to find the attractor.

DAY FOUR

THE JEEP ROLLED AND RATTLED and bumped over the plain.

"It goes a little faster, Mae, if you put your foot down."

"I'm old and brittle, Jean. I break easily."

"The shocks—"

"This is the fastest I've travelled in decades. Let me enjoy it."

Baré nodded and shut up. The three of them sat up front. The girl was dozing. She'd been yawning all morning as if she'd barely slept. Mae had awakened to find that the girl was not in the shack. She'd immediately woken Baré.

They'd found Siofra outside, creating an elaborate assemblage out of cutlery, stones, plates, tools, bowls, cups, books, pegs, pans, bottles, batteries, and dozens of other items she'd scavenged. The arrangement was patterned and complicated and Mae was too bewildered by what she saw to be upset. It must have taken hours. She did not know what to make of it. Much more disturbingly, she did not know how Siofra was on the outside of a door locked from the inside.

They'd eaten the remains of last night's stew but afterwards Mae was troubled. Though neither of her guests said anything, she saw the hunger in their eyes: There wasn't enough to go around. She worried over how they were going to get by on the meagre pickings from her traps. There were options, but those also concerned her. Mae hated being beholden to anyone. Here the survivalist creed ran deep.

"What are we looking for?" asked Baré.

"I'm not sure yet," said Mae, staring ahead at the featureless plain. Visibility was hazy. On clearer days you saw that the plain's flatness was entirely illusory, how it was criss-crossed by faint ridges and valleys, some extending for kilos. These shallow dips and rises were no bother on foot. At the jeep's speed, however, you could careen into a gulley if you weren't careful.

"You've been twice already," said Baré.

"And I'll keep going back. Can you jump in the same river twice? Am I the same person who visited Magellan's camp today as I was two days ago? Three?" She felt ratty, despite a long night's sleep. "I've learned a few things since. I've a new perspective."

"I'm not sure it's safe to keep going back."

Baré's questioning vexed Mae. She was unused to having her decisions challenged. We lack patience with one another out here, she thought. We glimpse ourselves in those who have also chosen to stay, and we don't like what we see. That is why we live like hermits. She wondered if Baré wasn't right. Perhaps she should go alone, leaving the pair of them at the Twins'. The girl would be safe there. But that gave rise to another vexing question: Safe from whom?

The ground ahead dropped away and Mae slowed. Thirty metres away she could see a fresh channel several metres wide cut in the plain. It was filled by a gray river. She halted. It cut right across their path, the gray flowing lazily inland. Occasionally, you saw rivers of Caul in the plain, but this was a big one. She had Baré keep an eye on the distance separating the jeep from the river as she drove parallel to it. After two kilos the river vanished suddenly into the ground as if it had never been there. They encountered two more such rivers emerging from and disappearing into the ground.

"Is that smoke?"

Mae raised her eyes from the plain and saw it dead ahead. A distinct dark smudge slanting across the sky. "Oh hell," she said. "We're too late."

"Mae, wh—"

She put her foot down. The jeep lurched forward, bumping and heaving over the pebbles. Baré strapped the girl and then herself in.

How long, Mae wondered, has it been burning? Too damn slow. We should have been up and out earlier. I shouldn't have waited.

The hidden rises and dips came much too quickly for Mae to slow down or steer around in time so that the jeep lurched and slid and bucked. She didn't care about any damn gray rivers now.

"Mae, slow up. We need to get there in one piece."

She reduced speed a little. They were still a few kilos away. She gripped the wheel with her aching fingers. This is my fault, she thought. I did this.

"What's that?" Baré pointed out the driver's side window.

Mae couldn't see anything.

"Something moving out there. Fast." Baré paused, frowned. "Hard to say which way it's going."

Mae spotted a faint plume of dust. "It's heading there too."

"We'll get there first. Just."

Getting closer, they saw that the whole camp was ablaze: all four cabins and the caravan. Three cabins were burning fitfully, but the fourth as well as the caravan were engulfed in flames, responsible for two black snakes of smoke coiling around each other as they chimneyed into the sky. Someone, Mae thought, did this without bothering to conceal their intentions.

She braked to a stop fifty metres shy of the camp. She got out, hurrying towards it, forgetting the others. She was furious with herself. She should have anticipated this. Now she'd lost everything.

At ten metres away the heat seared her face. She slowed, one hand wrapped around Magellan's keys in her pocket. There was water in the camp, she knew, and there would be extinguishers. But she couldn't move. She inhaled black smoke that made her want to retch.

Baré ran past her, carrying the fire extinguisher from the jeep. She applied it to the small fire struggling up one side of the locked cabin.

"No," said Mae, voice dry and croaky, "that one." She pointed at the cabin holding Magellan's body. It was burning like a pyre. A screeching and roaring conflagration.

Baré shouted, "It's too big." She thumbed the extinguisher and a whitish mixture of foam, powder, and gas shot out, smothering the flames.

A hot wind whipped through the camp. Heat scorched Mae's face: the burning caravan on one side and the flaming cabin on the other. There were two big water tanks beside one of the storage cabins. She needed a bucket.

She was tugging the keys from her pocket when she heard a roar behind her. She turned as Hannu raced into the camp on a hovering contraption powered by four rotating horizontal fans. His vehicle came to a shuddering halt in a spray of shingle, before it crashed to the ground. Hannu jumped off and ran straight to the pump unit attached to the tanks.

"Mae," he said, "can you get that door open?"

Mae stared at him, stunned for a moment. Then she got hold of herself. She flicked through the keys until she found the right one and unlocked the door.

"What am I looking for?" she called.

"There's a length of red hose. Magellan uses it for emptying the caravan's toilet. It has a wide bore."

She peered inside, her eyes taking an age to adjust to the dark. She saw coils and lifted a heavy hose from its hook on the wall. She struggled to the door where Hannu took it from her. Hurriedly he attached one end to the pump unit. Mae removed the ties that held the coils loosely together.

Hannu located the other end and put his foot on it. "Stand back," he said and flicked a lever on the pump.

Nothing happened.

"Dammit!" He bent over the unit and pulled open a hatch. He pressed a couple of buttons and the hose suddenly leaped up like a roused snake. Water sprayed out the unsecured head, which was whipping back and forth across the ground. Hannu, on hands and knees, managed to grab it and turned it on the cabin next door.

"No," said Mae, "the other one. The body's—"

"Keeps the fuel in here," he explained. In moments the flames were out.

Hannu then turned the hose on the fire-shrouded cabin, a jet of water arcing on to its walls and roof. The spray of water extinguished flames wherever it hit them, but they swiftly returned when it moved elsewhere. Baré and Mae found fire blankets and extinguishers in the two saved cabins they could get into. The three of them struggled to fight the fire but it had taken hold and wouldn't relinquish its feverish grip. The roof fell in. Hannu continued to jet water on the flames, but the tanks were rapidly emptying. "I can't save it," he yelled.

"Concentrate the water on the doorway," called Baré. The door of the cabin was gone, burnt away or fallen in with the roof. She had picked up the last of the fire extinguishers and was prising at the seal on its neck with the edge of a ceramic shard.

As water rained down ahead of her, Baré approached the cabin.

"You can't go in," called Mae urgently. The heat from where she was standing felt like it was blistering her skin.

"Stay back," said Baré. She was sawing at the seal of the small green cylinder with the shard. She stopped and examined the neck and then gave Hannu a nod. "On the count of three," she said.

Baré spoke quietly to herself, looking scared. She stepped closer and closer to the flames until she was within a couple of metres.

Mae couldn't watch. "Jean, you'll hurt yourself!" she called, knowing it was too late, knowing nothing would have survived this conflagration.

Baré hurled the extinguisher through the doorway and threw herself to the ground. A half second after it had fallen inside there was a huge woomph! The flames within the walls vanished completely, while around the cabin was suspended a cool nimbus of white particulates. After a few seconds the flames returned but they were subdued now and in a couple of minutes, just prior to the pump gurgling and the hose running dry, the cabin fire was out.

Mae, soot-blackened and expectorating black muck from her dry mouth, stumbled around the camp in a daze of strained, overstimulated senses. The caravan, she saw, had burnt itself out and was now a smoking husk.

Yet she could think only of Magellan—of the man's body, hopelessly lost now, and of a crime for which there were neither witnesses nor evidence.

○

YOU DIDN'T CHOOSE THE SERVICE, you were called. And in Mae's case the calling was made by Sister Ursula. She, as all the orphans knew, had once been Service and never tired of using the situations she'd encountered in "decades of habitat hopping" to enliven her teachings. The Sisterhood frowned on this as they did much else about Sister Ursula because they worried it would give the children ideas. That was Sister Ursula's intention, and she nurtured any child in which her ideas took root.

Mae had appreciated Sister's Ursula's rebellious nature from their first meeting, but, only when she was old enough to leave the orphanage, did she see how close the old woman's behaviour was to outright sedition. Like all the bright kids, Mae was selected to take orders and enter into the astronomer-priesthood. But hours after receiving this honour, Sister Ursula pulled her aside. "You are too young for the observatory," the old woman had said, gripping Mae's arm fiercely. This had upset Mae, who was desperately looking forward to the prospect—not in becoming an aspirant trained in the ways of the church, but in being sent away. She was eager to embark on some habitat-hopping of her own.

"How dare they choose your future?" Sister Ursula had growled. "I won't allow it." Weeks later the summons from the Service arrived, causing high dudgeon in the Sisterhood. They didn't like having their will subverted but could hardly refuse a request from an institution that did much to protect their observatories and into which they poured considerable funds. Unable to prevent Mae from going, they could at least punish Sister Ursula for her intervention. She happily accepted yet another confinement, using the time to write a long treatise about the Service, which she presented to Mae on the day of her departure.

Aged sixteen, Mae arrived at the Service Academy on the *Jonas Jones* habitat, out by Saturn. Her training lasted eight years. She'd messaged Sister Ursula often and once a month received a long paper letter in return. This disjointed correspondence amused her fellow students. Messages passed across the system in a matter of hours, but Sister Ursula insisted on keeping her side of their correspondence private by writing by hand. The months between a letter being written and received reminded Mae of the vast gulfs of space separating her from the only woman she had ever dreamed of calling mother.

According to Sister Ursula's treatise, the Service trained its staff "to act as both guardians and representatives of the moral complexity of the post-Exodus settlement." It had taken fully eight years of study for Mae to understand her meaning.

In short, the Service sustained the system under the aegis of the clan-controlled Planetary Authority. But the Service was not the true law of the system. That was clan law—the law of profit and loss. Yet profits require stability and for that you needed rules and someone to enforce those rules. Hence the Service, funded by the clans via some complicated revenue equation that all sides were clear was not a tax. The Service operated in the spaces between the clans—in the gaps, the cracks, down which those without bonds or contracts would fall if it wasn't there to catch them. It was also the oil greasing any high-friction spots where clans rubbed up against one another. With three areas of operation—health, education, law enforcement—the Service had to be careful. It was at the mercy of clan politics, easily crushed or pushed aside if it was convenient. Funding could be cut. Departments closed. Positions lost. Yet the clans needed a fig leaf to pretend the rules were not entirely rigged in their favour. Someone else had to be there to take the blame whenever anything went wrong.

In truth, the Service was morally compromised from the get-go.

"Think of it," Sister Ursula had written, "like original sin. We are born bad, but we aspire to goodness."

By then it was too late. Mae was one of them. The Service—its strengths and its weaknesses—had entered her blood.

MAE WANDERED AMONG smoking ruins reeking of burnt plastofab sharp enough to make her gag. It brought back memories of New Sheffield on Mars: In the sealed atmosphere of that underground city, it was the smell of poison, of death. She observed the others. Hannu, slump-shouldered, carrying a bucket and dowsing recidivist flames. Baré sat on a crate, coughing, her face soot-blackened, staring at the caravan's burnt shell. The girl was painstakingly adjusting the pebbles and ceramic shards of her huge arrangement that had been scattered as they'd fought the fire.

Against a cabin's scorched wall was a blackened pile of debris, which Mae nudged with her foot. Wincing, she crouched to examine it: a melted plastic container.

Footsteps crunched behind her, coming to a halt.

"We're lucky you came along when you did," said Mae.

"Heading out this way," said Hannu. "Saw the smoke. Can't ignore fire."

"This one was set on the outside," she said.

"They all were, except perhaps for the caravan and that one." He indicated the destroyed cabin in which Magellan's body had been lying. The cabins had been locked, she recalled, but had she also locked the caravan?

She slowly got to her feet. "I thought plastofab was incombustible."

"Not with the right fuel," said Hannu.

Mae looked up at him. Etched on his long face, under that mop of blond hair, was a look of puzzled bafflement. There was a weariness around his eyes.

"Petrol?" said Mae, as they walked over to Baré and the girl.

He shook his head. "Not hot enough."

"More like kerosene," said Baré.

Mae nodded. "Where do you get kerosene round here?"

"The Facility," said Baré. She rubbed her sooty chin. "Whoever did this was here very recently."

"We didn't see anyone."

"We weren't exactly looking."

"You mean they might still be here?" said Hannu quietly.

Baré shrugged. They looked around the camp. Loud ticks and pops of cooling material filled the silence. The girl squatted, continuing to carefully rebuild the shard structures between the cabins. "Keep an eye on her," Mae told Baré. The girl's habit of disappearing or passing through locked doors was getting to her.

She approached Magellan's office. The roof and one of its sides had fallen in. She could see several black mounds, melted chairs. Moving around the cabin she saw that the table in the middle was upright and intact. She moved closer in, though the heat was still terrific.

"What's up?" called Hannu.

"The body's gone."

"What?"

"It was on the table."

"Be in there somewhere." Hannu came over and put down his bucket.

"You're not going—"

"Be alright," he said and stepped through the open doorway. He was nimble on his feet, not keeping a foot in one spot for more than a second at a time. He was agile, his whole body shifting and twisting as he darted here and there, briefly examining corners and floor. Twenty seconds later he was back out. The soles of his boots smoked. "No body in there," he declared.

Mae nodded, catching a stale whiff of dust on the breeze.

"They must have taken it," he said.

"They?"

"It's a body. Hard to move on your own."

Mae's hand clutched the keys to the other cabins. She approached the one Hannu had said contained the fuel: the workshop. Its door was closed but its padlock lay on the ground. She picked it up. It was broken, the hook having been forced. Inside, she could spot nothing unusual or unexpected. Were some of the tools missing? She looked at the fuel drums but couldn't tell if any had been tampered with.

She crossed to the storage cabin she'd examined the day before yesterday. This one had also had its padlock broken off. She paused. Why set fire to the outsides of these cabins if you had access to their insides? Were they in a hurry or did they want to make it look like the fire had spread?

"Hannu," she called.

The man came over. "Yeah?"

"Just be here a moment," she said.

She pulled the door open and there, lying on the floor, was Magellan's body.

"Well, shit . . ." said Hannu, turning away at the sight or smell.

Mae held her breath, leaning over the bloated corpse. Hannu retched behind her. She crouched and took a strand of Magellan's long hair between her fingers: It was singed. She eased herself onto her knees—her lower body hurting—and put her nose to his coat sleeve. She sniffed: Over the stench of decay were distinct threads of smokiness.

The door had been closed, she thought, plus she could see no signs that the small fire outside had penetrated the walls.

She heard footsteps and then a cry. Mae turned, seeing Baré, her hand clamped over her mouth. "Get away, Jean. You don't want to see this."

Baré allowed Hannu to pull her away.

Mae stood painfully and stepped inside the cabin, pulling the door closed. She breathed through her mouth as her eyes adjusted to gloom. From half a metre beyond the door, irregularly spaced crates and tubs, stacked up to the ceiling, packed the cabin. She could barely move, the corpse occupying the small stretch of empty space. Mae peered at the crates. Were they less tidily arranged than two days ago?

Cool and silent. She shivered, glancing at Magellan's body. I should cover it up, she thought. She remained still, the pain in her legs gradually abating. She held her breath, the silence enveloping her. Outside: The crunching of either Hannu or Baré moving about. She closed her eyes, straining to pick sounds out of the silence. It was neither entirely still nor properly silent in here.

She could feel another presence.

"Come out," she said quietly.

Her heart beat loud in her chest.

"Come on now. I can hear you." She couldn't, of course, but the twitchy sense she couldn't put a name to told her she wasn't alone. It wasn't far removed from the niggle she experienced whenever she ventured too close to the Caul. It was the troubling feeling that you were being scrutinized.

Sounds came from behind the stack of crates. She retreated a step, her back against the cabin door.

He emerged from one of the wider crevices between crates, his bony body sliding through the gap with ease. His face was set, defiant even, but she saw that his eyes were wide and fearful. He said, defensively, "It is written in the Ten that—"

"Oh, give it a rest, Rawat," she told him.

The door swung open. Hannu stood there, staring stupidly for a moment. "Strewth. Rawat. Where'n hell you spring from?"

At first, he wouldn't leave the cabin, sitting on the floor next to Magellan's corpse. He claimed he alone had charge of the body now. "I saved him," he said over and over. In the end Hannu had to physically remove Rawat, gently easing him to his feet and over the body, then out the door. In the daylight, the preacher blinked at the destruction, soothing himself with whispered prayers.

Mae hadn't the patience for the man's schtick at the best of times. "What are you doing here, Rawat?"

He stared at her like she was stupid. "I was called," he said. "To save—"

"He's dead," said Mae. "You didn't do any saving."

"Save his physical form, from the fire."

Hannu, who'd been sitting on a drum, stood up suddenly. "Did you do this?" he shouted. His anger caught Mae by surprise.

"I was called," said Rawat.

"You're being evasive," said Baré.

"Why did you come here?" asked Mae.

Rawat retreated a little from the three of them. He rubbed his nose thoughtfully. "I had to see for myself," he admitted. "I came last night."

"What were you looking for?"

"A sign, of course. The Caul always leaves a sign."

"What sort of sign?" asked Baré.

"If I knew that, I wouldn't have needed to come looking for it."

"That didn't answer her question," said Mae.

He gave her a sullen look. "I did not realize I had to."

"You've been here since last night," said Mae. "When did you light the fires?"

"I lit no fire."

Hannu smiled, shaking his head. "Don't see anyone else round here."

"I spent the night in the caravan."

"It was unlocked?"

He reddened. "I had to open it."

"So you slept here, then what?" asked Mae.

"I was awoken by a great thunder outside. I . . . I feared discovery—you wouldn't understand—and hid in the caravan."

"Who was out there?"

"I never saw them."

"*Them*?" barked Hannu. "How many were there?"

He shrugged. "I do not know. One, perhaps two. Doors were being opened and closed."

"How long did you hide for?"

He shook his head. "Until I smelled smoke. The caravan was burning! When I got out, I saw that the cabin with Magellan inside was also on fire. The roaring of the flames was terrible!"

"You didn't try and put them out?" said Hannu.

"The caravan and the cabin burned righteously. Then I knew what I had to do. I'd been called here to rescue Magellan from the flames."

Mae shook her head. "You got him out on your own?"

He nodded. "The Caul would protect me from the flames. But I heard thunder. I feared whoever had done this was returning."

"Thunder? You mean vehicles?"

He looked puzzled by the question. "I got Magellan into the cabin," he said.

"It was also on fire," reminded Baré.

"I did not want to be discovered."

"You could have just run."

"Where? Concealing myself was the only option. It was God's will."

"You carried the body on your own?" asked Mae.

"Dragged," he said, shame faced.

She looked sceptically at his skinny trunk and limbs. His loincloth was so filthy, Mae couldn't tell if it was singed or not. She didn't know what to believe. "What does God want with Magellan's body?"

Rawat shrugged. "I am but the vessel for God's work. I await further revelation."

"What were you going to do with him, you bastard?" demanded Baré.

Rawat refused to meet their eyes. "Beware the temptation of our quarantine," he said quietly and nodded to himself.

"We need to move Magellan," said Mae. "He can't stay here now. Rawat and Hannu, can you please carry the body to the jeep? Jean, can you keep Siofra out the way. I'll find some covering."

Rawat started at mention of the girl's name. He got to his feet, turning like a marbit with a scent and only stopping when he caught sight of Siofra.

Baré put a hand out. "No, you don't," she told him. "You keep away."

They wrapped the body in a tarpaulin Mae found inside a crate. Hannu's anger had dissipated and he was more his congenial self as he and Rawat together carried Magellan. Rawat threw glances in Siofra's direction, but Baré had taken her over to the other side of the camp. The girl was busily sorting shards Magellan had brought back from the Cluster into small piles. Baré had her back to the camp, staring into the wind.

Mae joined Baré. It was some time before they spoke.

"You expected this," said Baré.

Mae sucked her teeth, caught out by the younger woman's perspicacity. "Not exactly."

"Yesterday, you were out telling everyone about Magellan. You were testing the waters, trying to get a response."

Mae said nothing.

"And the funeral. There's no need to hold a funeral at all, let alone tomorrow. You should leave it to the Facility. But it's another test, isn't it? Get everyone together in one place, is that it? See who lets something slip?"

Mae ground her teeth together. "I found him, I choose how he leaves here."

"What is this? You think you're his guardian angel? You're as bad as Rawat. Carl's gone. What are you trying to prove? You'll stir up trouble."

"Don't get in my way, Jean."

"Think about Siofra. Your crusade won't help her."

Mae stormed off. The accusation she was a troublemaker made her angry but only because Baré was right. It *was* a crusade. Here was a problem, a man's death, she could sink her teeth into. She could exercise her mind, tax her intellect on the moral puzzle of it—for she was sure this was no random or motiveless act. Someone had decided this broken world would be better without Magellan in it. Contemplating this heinous decision thrilled Mae. She felt alive for the first time in years. She couldn't give this up. Besides, didn't they owe it to Magellan to find out the truth? And if there was a murderer out here, didn't they owe it to themselves to discover who it was?

Mae stiffly walked a slow circuit of the camp.

At the back of her mind was a nagging doubt. It was one of the reasons she'd come back here. They did need to collect the body for tomorrow's funeral, but she'd also wanted another look at the camp after what she'd read in Magellan's journals. She felt like she knew the place now. However, the dwellings—caravan, office—she'd wanted to examine were burnt out. Someone had attempted to finish the job begun with the murder of Magellan. First the man and now his work had been destroyed.

Hannu and Baré talked together while the girl was constructing a spiral out of flat irregularly shaped shards. It was nearly as tall as she was. Nothing else mattered to her. Rawat was sitting away from them, watching the girl as intently as she worked.

Mae continued to pace around the camp. She couldn't figure out what was bothering her. Baré's words still stung. What had Albert used to say? "It's not that you have to be right, Mae, more that you're terrified of being wrong."

What else had he used to tell her? *You have an overdeveloped sense of justice.* But what justice was there here? There was no one to uphold Planetary Authority laws. By coming here they'd all broken enough of those. No, she thought, we have no laws here, only duties. And if she had any duty at all it was to protect the girl until assistance arrived. Yet, if she didn't discover the truth of Magellan's death, could she ensure the girl's safety? To neglect the father was to put the daughter at risk.

That, she thought with a bitter smile, is the Service talking.

For thirty years her sense of right and wrong had been buried. Ever since she'd lost Albert and boarded the Cauler rocket to come here. Was this what it was all about? Yes, she thought about Albert every day. That never went away. But the depth of feeling, the pain of his loss, had eased, as it must. Why had Magellan's death brought it all back? It had reopened that hole in her which had never been filled in, only covered over. All those half-answered questions. Why, Albert? Why did you run? What was waiting here? Why did you abandon me? She shook her head. What, she asked, am I hoping to achieve now?

She halted beside the fourth cabin. She didn't know why. It was still locked, she noticed. It was the one she couldn't find the key for. The padlock was larger than the others, heavy-duty. Was that why it hadn't been broken into?

She called Hannu over. "Can you get this open?" she asked.

Hannu looked at her. "You've got the keys."

"Not for this."

He examined it. "Alloy," he said at last. "Ain't nothing going to break or cut that open."

"I want it open, Hannu. Now."

He shrugged and disappeared into the tool shed. Baré had come over.

"What'd Magellan keep in here?"

"That he wouldn't tell me. He kept it locked."

Mae nodded.

Hannu came back with some kind of rock cutter. "Step back," he said.

"I thought you said—"

"The Gordian Knot couldn't be untangled. This padlock can't be broken. Ways and means, old woman. Ways and means. I said get back."

In moments their ears were assaulted by hideous grinding sounds. Hannu's body shielded what he was doing. After five minutes he stepped back. There was a clunk as a chunk of the door and frame to which the padlock was attached fell to the ground.

"Call me Hannu the Great," he announced grandly.

"Just open the damn door," said Mae.

○

IT WAS NO SURPRISE that Mae was selected by the Service Academy for law enforcement training. Sister Ursula had predicted it. "You've a moral nose. And like me, you don't care where you stick it," said the old woman in another letter light on congratulations and long on advice. But no advice could prepare Mae for what came next.

Five years of being shuttled from habitat to habitat at six-month intervals. Sometimes working security: port surveillance, patrols, dreamtank confinements. Other times an investigator: sabotage, smuggling, trafficking, fraud. Whatever was needed. There were just enough of them to keep a lid on trouble: To stop the clans from complaining. "Are we just protecting their bottom line?" she'd exhaustedly asked one captain. Days later she was shipped elsewhere.

Orbital policing was dull. Tanked people committed few dirty crimes. Mostly it was deskwork overseeing arts uncovering data anomalies and issuing fines for fraud. Instead, Mae gravitated to moon and planetary habitats, where people got out and about. Rubbed up against each other. Friction created excitement. She, it turned out, liked that. It was how she ended up working homicide. Few wanted it. The dirtiest of dirty crimes. Death was messy. But Mae was drawn to wreckage. Shattered lives. A life taken deliberately or accidentally required explanation. Every case a puzzle. Mostly, the solutions were boring, repetitive. But occasionally they asked Mae to be a bloodhound. It took ten years for her to realize she was content. That she'd found a kind of peace making a life in death.

A placement in New Sheffield on Mars and a stopover in the City of Red Glass meant she could visit Sister Ursula. She hadn't seen the nun in a decade though the letters still followed her around the system. It was not a happy reunion. She was led to the infirmary to discover Sister Ursula dying: For years a treatment-resistant cancer had been devouring her by increments. The disease had not been mentioned in the letters.

Mae was cross but stoic. "You made me," she'd told the old woman in the bed.

The reply a hoarse whisper: "My nurture, your nature."

She held a delicate, bony hand, thinking: Every death diminishes those left behind.

Months later, she received a final letter. It was in Sister Ursula's hand, informing Mae of her own death. Written pre-mortem, dispatched post-mortem.

The nun damned if she wasn't going to have the last word.

○

MAE, HER BACK TO MAGELLAN'S CAMP, heard the distant boom of waves pounding the shore. She felt each sonorous concussion in her bones. It had a rhythm as regular and familiar as the beating of her heart. She lived alongside the Caul and yet it had let her be. Like the other penitents she could resist the irresistible lure that caused everyone else to enter it. Many times, she'd wondered what finally possessed those who went willingly into the Caul. At other times, like now, she wondered what was lacking in those like herself who were left behind.

The wind, having got up, whirled about her. Coming from the south it was pungent with the Caul's cold-stone spoor. Mae breathed it in gratefully. The reek of burning hadn't driven her out of the camp, but the acrid air was an unsparing reminder of her miscalculation.

Yes, she inhaled the Caul's scent with every breath. Yes, the Caul was in her thoughts from the moment she awoke. Even sleep brought only a partial respite, for her dreams were often of drowning, or wandering a bleak, endless shore. And, yes, if sleep eluded her, she lay awake half the night wondering how long she had before she too felt the gentle but insistent tug. But unlike some of her fellow penitents, who believed the reason they had managed to coexist beside the Caul for so long was because a piece of it had somehow entered themselves, she knew it was no part of her. The Caul was and would always be distinctly other. The adversary.

It was her enemy for it had stolen the only man she had ever loved.

It was why, she knew, she'd never felt a serious urge to cross over.

Yet it had always felt to Mae like the Caul had known her from the day of her arrival. Maybe it had known her even before then and been waiting for her to fetch up on its shore. In coming to Earth, she felt as though she had surrendered to, and, in some manner, she could never properly explain, now belonged to the Caul. After all, hadn't it more claim to Earth now than all the penitents and clan entities along its shore? Didn't the Caul cover the world, and didn't it feel like the world belonged to it rather than the other way around? Wasn't the Caul the puzzle everyone came to solve? In the Service she'd wondered why we're always more interested in the murderer than the victim.

Mae heard the rasp of approaching footsteps. She turned to face Baré. The young woman looked tired but her eyes remained piercingly bright. "Rawat's gone," she said with relief. "He looks rattled."

"Probably trying hard to fit what he saw in the cabin into his faith. He'll survive. Caulers are good at slotting square objects into round holes."

"Did you see his face? He looked utterly repulsed. He wouldn't look at it."

"Religion demands the universe be orderly and comprehensible."

Baré raised an eyebrow. "Even the Caul?"

"Especially the Caul. Caulers come precisely because they believe the Caul is divine and orderly. If they doubted that they'd run *away* from it, screaming. For Rawat the disorder is an affront, like dinosaur bones and fossil fish up mountains. It is the big trick God plays on you scientists." She smiled wanly. "I rather like their attitude, if not their logic."

Baré snorted. "What do you think he was doing here?"

Mae considered the question. "Rawat has spent too long alone. His thoughts have turned primitive. Perhaps he came to dance on his enemy's grave."

"So you think he did burn the camp?"

Mae shook her head. "It is the sort of damn fool thing he would try only if he thought it would help him."

"*Help him*, how?"

"Bringing him closer to his beloved God. But to my mind Rawat is not yet as deranged as he would like to be."

Baré rubbed her chin. "Why'd he hide the body?"

"He shouldn't have been here, and he was scared. Perhaps in his Cauler-twisted mind he believed he was rescuing Magellan."

"What for?"

Mae shrugged. "There'd be precious point in holding the funeral without a body. The ritual would be rather hard to work. He respects that at least."

"I wanted to ask you about that."

Mae exhaled slowly. "Go on."

"It's a curious way . . . I mean he still worked for the PA . . . Shouldn't we . . ." Baré seemed unsure of herself, her bright eyes unable to meet Mae's.

"I found him, Jean. He stayed when he might have retreated to the Facility. His life was out here. I don't care what they think. He was one of us."

"But he was also—"

"He didn't think of himself as clan any more than you do."

In silence they listened to the distant booming of the waves.

"Hannu's leaving, if he can get his bike going. Says he damaged the motor racing to get here. He seems rather pleased with himself."

Mae smiled. Trust Hannu to ignore what was going on around him and focus on the performance of one of his machines.

"Bit of a coincidence he got here right after we did," continued Baré.

"The smoke was visible for kilos."

"He could easily have left here, ridden a loop and returned behind us."

Mae frowned at her. "Suspicious, aren't you?"

"Paranoid. And getting more so."

Mae nodded, thinking: You're upset about Magellan. And the bright eyes. Baré was angry. This had briefly been her home. She had been happy here. Now she'd witnessed its destruction and seen her lover's corpse. It had been worse than thoughtless of Mae to bring her and Siofra back to the camp. There was nothing for them here but pain.

"How's the girl?" she asked.

Baré grimaced. "Busy rebuilding. I told him to keep her away from . . ."

"Jean, you really didn't know about that thing inside the cabin?"

"I told you. He kept it locked." Baré's face suddenly crumpled. "He told me never to ask him about it. I thought it might be about Gemma."

"Gemma?"

"A shrine or something." She sniffed.

"Are you okay?"

Baré wiped the corner of an eye with the back of a thumb. "I'll be fine," she said, turning away.

Mae followed her back to the camp to be greeted by the sickening stench of burnt plastic. She thought it best to keep Baré occupied and told her to get the girl away from the cabin. "I don't think she should be anywhere near it. She has a fascination for shapes that's, well, unhealthy."

The damned locked door, she thought. She couldn't make it make any sense.

Hannu was on his knees inspecting his vehicle. He was bent over the left rear fan, spinning it manually, with one ear pressed against the rim shield and his eyes closed. His mouth moved silently as though he were counting.

Mae stood watching. Her legs were aching, and she wanted to sit beside him but just imagining the palaver and discomfort of getting on the ground and then, worse, getting back up again kept her on her feet.

"One of the blades is twisted but as long as it don't touch the shielding I can make it home," he said, eyes still closed.

Mae nodded. She was staring at what he was wearing on his feet. "Where'd you get the boots, Hannu?"

He opened his eyes, glancing from her to the boots and back.

"Magellan," he said, sitting up. "In exchange for fixing the water plant."

Mae nodded. "You got the better deal, I think."

"Called me out here six times last month to fix the filter I'd made him." Hannu smiled ruefully.

He flipped a switch and the four fans began spinning with a rising whine. He straddled the bike as the noise escalated to a roar. The air swirled around them and the whirring fans drowned out all other sound. The hoverbike lifted off the ground unsteadily.

"Need 'em," shouted Hannu, pointing at his feet, "to ride this!" He lowered a pair of goggles over his eyes. The bike swung away, swaying as it sped past the cabins. Hannu made one complete circuit of the camp, waving at them, and then shot away north in a straightening curve.

It was some minutes before Mae's ears recovered sufficiently to pick out the booming of the distant waves. She was still looking in the direction in which Hannu had vanished. "If I had boots like that," she said to no one in particular, "I'd wear them all day, every day."

She turned to see that Baré was now helping the girl rebuild the fallen structures filling much of the space between the cabins. The arrangement looked vaguely familiar but she couldn't place it. Baré glanced up pointedly. Mae nodded. She held up her left hand, fingers splayed. Five minutes, she mouthed.

Mae was uncertain what she hoped to discover and did not trust her own motives for returning to the cabin. It was hard to stop thinking about it, she had to admit, irresistible even. Just one last look, she told herself.

She opened the cabin door and stepped inside, careful to avoid looking in the corner where it lay. She was confronted with more stacks of boxes and crates stamped with Main's gray puddle-like logo, some she had looked through half-heartedly.

She was careful not to breathe through her nose. The mustiness of the air—of the thing—was quite overpowering. From dust to dust . . .

The more I discover the less I understand, she thought. I feel lost, out of my depth. Why can't I make any sense of this? She considered just handing over what she knew to Dr. Carlyle in the Facility. Then she could go back to her shack and forget all about it. But that would solve nothing. They wouldn't investigate, the truth would remain hidden and there'd be no justice for Magellan. She'd claimed him as one of their own and now she had a duty to see this through to the end, even if someone—a person, she now suspected, she must have spoken to yesterday—was trying to cover their tracks.

Even as she was standing there with her back to the corner, she was aware of a presence behind her. There was a prickling at the back of her neck. She felt watched, under scrutiny. Normally it was only out in the open air that unsettling feelings of never being quite alone got to you. Inside, enclosed by four walls and a roof, you usually felt less exposed, safer. But not in here.

She felt a twinge in her legs and had a sudden urge to walk right out of the cabin. She had to force her legs to keep still. She put a hand on the door frame, gripping it as if clinging on for dear life. She shook her head, caught by a touch of vertigo. She held herself still, breathing raggedly. She'd not felt an uncontrollable urge this strong in years. It was deeper than any longing for sex, more acute than any hunger. It was a sudden physical tug, as if her body was being drawn away by another force. She felt violated, betrayed. She didn't move, tentatively checking she still had full control of this creaking old shell she inhabited, making sure her body was still her own.

Slowly, she turned to look down at the source of the trouble. She no longer wondered why Magellan had hidden this thing in here.

The man had clearly known the risks he was taking bringing it into his camp. She had a horrible suspicion she knew exactly where he had found it. Yet it was big and heavy-looking and would require a couple of people to carry it—how had he managed it? His jeep, perhaps? But that still left unanswered the question of why he'd brought it out at all. She shook her head. He was smart, but smart people were not immune from doing stupid things.

She stared at the object. Multiple, nested polyhedral shapes. Like, but unlike, crystals. Silvery, metallic surfaces. They were joined together at their base, like they'd sprouted or thrust out of a central point. The shapes were strange, reminding her of the Cluster. They appeared solid but up close they weren't. Edges were faintly blurry, her eyes quite unable to focus on them. Surfaces rippled as if they weren't solid. They had a faint smokiness as if slightly shadowed. It was one of the bergs Magellan discussed in his journals and which in recent years you saw increasingly out on the Caul. Somehow, he'd managed to fish one out. Get it back to the camp.

What it was, however, was not why it was so troubling. That was down to what it did.

Before she knew quite what she was doing, Mae had once again got down on her hands and knees to get a closer look. She barely winced as her body protested at this cavalier treatment.

Mae wobbled inside as she leaned closer. The silvery surfaces shifted before her. It was like watching flames or uncoiling fractals, hard to tear your gaze away. Glints and glimmers. She felt a faint stirring of memory as she caught momentary glimpses of shapes or patterns she knew. Nothing concrete. Nothing definite. Just the briefest of suggestions. Serrations that reminded her of the jagged leaves of the succulent they'd kept on their kitchen table in New Sheffield. A stippled pattern that was a spit of the herringbone weave of Albert's second-best suit. Curling gray wisps that had her thinking of the hair on the crown of his head. Oh, it hurt to look at this, but at the same time she was flooded by feelings of longing and belonging she'd not felt in decades. A sadness and a joy, a memory of what once was and what might have been.

The urge to reach out and touch the silvery surfaces grew stronger the longer she looked. But that would be stupid. This was Caul stuff. She balled her hands into fists, pushed the fists hard into her hips. She felt her aching bones and joints. She felt tears running down her face. What was it doing to her? Yet she couldn't turn away.

Only when she heard footsteps outside did she find the will to turn. Irritated, embarrassed, she wiped her face and turned to see the girl with Baré at her back.

Baré was angry and accusing. "I wish you'd never opened it," she said.

Mae nodded, flustered. She felt like she'd been caught doing something shameful, revealing a stain on her soul.

The girl, her eyes wide, came over and sat by Mae.

"Don't touch it," said Mae.

"Siofra . . ." said Baré.

The girl leant forward and stared at it but not quite like Mae had done. She seemed to be watching it, leaning in, something Mae had been careful not to do.

"Did the girl ever enter . . ."

"Not that I saw."

Something strange was happening to the berg. Shadows were rippling over the faces of the shapes. Like clouds streaming across a sky. Mae put her hand on the girl's shoulder to draw her back. But she was too late. Before Mae could stop her, the girl poked a finger into one of the silvery polyhedrons. Less a poke than a piercing.

"No," moaned Baré.

Mae tried to yank the girl's arm back, but the arm wouldn't move, as if the finger was stuck in the berg. She stared stupefied as the shadows skimming on the faces were distorted by ripples spilling out from where the girl's finger penetrated the polyhedron.

The girl appeared unharmed. She was smiling, delighted.

Mae was frozen. She stared from the girl to the berg. Angles and lines shivered. Surfaces flickered: light and shade. There was the faintest crackle of electricity. The hairs on Mae's skin stood on end. The girl's reflection—pin-sharp, shard-like—stared out of every one of the crystalline surfaces. The girl in myriad pieces.

This, Mae decided much later, was the moment she got scared.

YEAR FOUR

[Pages torn out]

Day 19, Month 9

Every day I visit Janus. I have not much time. Once I've driven as far as the Topologie allows I've lost an hour. I negotiate bent and brutalised geometries for two hours, measuring angles in the hope of pinpointing and locating the damn attractor, around which, Gemma believes, the entire Topologie is oriented. Neither of us has a clue what it might look like. Add on the return time and I have under an hour to commune with Janus, to fight its urging with all my being. If Gemma knew, she'd be furious.

Day 20, Month 9

Every night I dream of Leviathan. Its huge maw wide, its self-inserted tubular end a thrashing tail. I fall into that dark mouth, a terrified Jonah, twisting and turning until I'm back to front and inside out. I wake covered in sweat and gasping. Gemma cannot know how the Topologie terrifies me. Yet every day I must enter it alone.

Day 24, Month 9

Sat link down. No microsat data for Gemma's equations to locate this tide's attractor. I went anyway. I took no measurements, instead visiting Janus. How long did I stare into its multifarious glinting faces? The Topologie scares me, yet when I look at Janus all anxieties melt away.

[Page torn out]

I fear for Gemma, alone all day with nothing but the impossible equations of hyperspace. She claims happiness but looks haggard. I've suggested we take a break. We could visit the hills. Stay at the Twins'. "We must finish our work," she chides me. Every day I do not tell her what I've found feels a deeper betrayal.

Day 27, Month 9

Dinner at the Twins'. We were joined by Mae Jameson, taciturn as ever, despite Sousa's efforts to draw her out of her shell. Service to her core, I'd say. The extraordinary lengths Jameson took to follow her missing husband received Gemma's sympathy. But it was refused. "Albert was married to me," said Jameson. "I had a right to know why he'd left." "Are you sure he came here?" I asked. Gemma shot me an exasperated look. "I am Service," said Jameson. "So was he. He left evidence . . ." "For you to find?" asked Gemma. Jameson shrugged. "I loved the man I lived with on Mars. The man who came here I never knew."

She spoke of a tree a day's walk from the Twins' that she says recalls Albert to her. She spoke as if it were a shrine. Gemma said she'd like to see it.

Day 3, Month 10

I am speechless! Gemma insists she is pregnant. We should seek confirmation but neither of us wants anyone to know. The moment Main hears this news, they will be apoplectic. We have violated the terms of the PA contract.

How could we have let this happen?

Day 4, Month 10

The smell—liquid copper, white-hot steel—of molten metal and furnace heat draws me. My fathers. My childhood. I want to climb into Janus. I remember Leviathan, those hideously wrapped-up dimensions. Janus—Roman guardian of doors—stares back at me, silver and pure. Only the thought of Gemma stops me. I must tell her, but I can't.

Day 5, Month 10

Frustrating. Gemma's coordinates for this afternoon's tide lost me in an impenetrable maze of tangled geometry. Gemma and I are avoiding talking about you know what.

Day 6, Month 10

> *[Missing. The following pages, to Day 23, Month 10, torn out but present as if removed and reinserted.]*

—I returned tonight; Gemma had made dinner. "Carl," she said, "we can't bring up a child here." I nodded glumly. Everything is my fault. "However," she continued, "I think pregnancy makes me glow. I've been walking along the shore. I've had no attacks in weeks. I feel properly myself for the first time in three and a half years." She smiled. "I wonder if I can help in the Topologie. We have a little time until I need to visit Dr. Machalek."

I looked at my wife, at the light shining in her eyes. A bright mischievousness that beguiled me on the day we met. Why does it trouble me now?

Day 9, Month 10

Dropped Gemma off, spent an hour taking readings, then raced to Janus. I knelt before those many faces, ready for my daily rapture. But something was wrong. I could not concentrate. I kept looking over my shoulder, half-expecting to find Gemma watching me. I felt . . . guilt, as if I were committing a sin. I could not concentrate. I did not trust myself to resist it. I gave up, fled. Out of sorts, I collected a jubilant Gemma. Is her presence a distraction?

Day 10, Month 10

I cannot concentrate with Gemma in the Topologie. I feel her nearby, a constant distraction. It makes it impossible to navigate Janus's hypnotic surfaces. I dare not lose myself in those forests of angles for fear of not returning. Those familiar shapes that days ago triggered cascades of beloved memories are now treacherously irresistible.

Day 14, Month 10

What if I moved Janus out of the Topologie?

Day 15, Month 10

I climbed the Shell today, staring gloomily out of a hole at the stormy Caul. Huge wind-driven, white-crested gray mounds roared into shore. Some were big as barns, moving faster than any jeep. Sometimes they collided, tossing themselves into the air with fearless abandon. I spotted bergs out there. Half a dozen together. I want to call them pods. Gemma asks why she records more measurements than I do.

Day 16, Month 10

Frustrating day. Gemma accused me of neglecting our work. Couldn't go anywhere near Janus. I miss its haunting reflections.

Day 17, Month 10

I see my life in Janus, those myriad glinting prisms. Am I looking into my past? Or just into myself? The patterns in the silver faces are achingly familiar. I see myself growing, forming, emerging. It is the Caul times a hundred. I wonder how much it weighs.

It is not the same, but I still cannot resist it. I came close today, within a whisker of not returning. Thankfully, booming waves awoke me from my reverie with Janus. I shook free of it to find the tide was within metres. I ran to the jeep, my heart in my throat. A minute later and it would have caught me. I found Gemma, walking out. She was furious with me. I almost told her in my remorse.

Day 18, Month 10

Dropped off Gemma (she's barely talking to me). Parked. Unpacked the chains. Wrapping them around it was easy. Dragging it was exhausting. Just five metres progress over a single tide. I've forty to go.

Day 19, Month 10

Fifteen metres, both tides. It is exhausting. I sleep better at night. No dreams.

Day 20, Month 10

Twenty metres. Gemma sees how tired, how broken I am, when I pick her up. She's stopped asking for my measurements.

Day 21, Month 10

I can hardly write. I had us up early, following the receding tide into the Topologie. "Why the hurry?" asked Gemma as I dropped her off.

Drove like the devil. It took two hours to drag Janus the final five metres to the jeep. I assembled a tripod pulley over it, attached the chains, raised and swung Janus inside. I turned and found Gemma watching silently.

"Carl, what is this?" she asked. "Is this what's been possessing you?"

I could see the concern on her face.

"Don't come any nearer," I told her.

"What is it?"

"Janus!" I cried.

"Janus?" She shook her head, concerned. She stepped closer. Her eyes lit up in understanding. "Carl, you've found a berg. That's astonishing."

"Stay back! Don't look! It's dangerous." I tried to explain. I told her how I'd been feeling since Leviathan. My visions, my dreams, the creeping terror. Every night feeling myself turned inside out. Only by staring into my past daily was I able to prove I was still me. "It's a battle of wills," I said. "It wants me to surrender but I won't."

"Why didn't you tell me?"

"I . . . I was ashamed. I brought us here. Your suffering meant you couldn't go in. Without this, there's nothing." I confessed my terror of the Topologie, that I'd have given anything to leave. "What is it? What's it doing to us?" I wept for us both.

I expected censure from Gemma but instead she hugged me and said, "Let us go home."

"What about Janus?"

"It's a berg, Carl. And it's coming with us."

Day 23, Month 10

Today, Gemma examined the berg. I daren't go near it, standing back as she removed the tarp.

She circled it, keeping her distance. Closing in, examining each polyhedron from different directions. "Note the Maraldi angles," she said, making further technical observations. I held my breath, waiting to see if it would affect her like me.

As I'd expected, Gemma's attention was drawn to certain faces and edges. "This fuzziness . . . It's . . . I see . . . patterns remind me . . . It's as if they are not quite there."

"It appears to be a blend of solid, liquid, and gas," I said. "That suggests Caul stuff to me. The transition—"

"There is no *stuff*," she said. "Only energy states and their interactions."

I remember looking into these faces and being hypnotized by the patterns. Each a suggestion out of my past, triggering feelings I could no more resist than deny. Sensing my fathers, as if they were sitting either side of me. Our family whole. Familiar, comforting. I gazed at a mirror into my soul.

"It's hyperdimensional . . ." she said.

She seemed unaffected. Untouched.

"What do you think it is?" I asked. Could she help me see the berg anew?

"The most obvious answer is a transitional stage between Caul and Topologie. If the bergs are the means by which the Topologies form and grow, then, QED, the Topologies are second stage Caul."

"Doesn't its persistence inside #66 suggest the opposite?" I asked. "It has resisted assimilation into the ceramic mass."

Gemma turned to me, cocked her head. "Sharp rebuttal."

We both laughed, relaxing a little. Two scientists at work.

"Why did you want to remove it?" she asked.

I winced, reminded of how I'd sinned. "I wanted to have it close, so I could visit it any time I wanted." I could see now how she was right. I had become possessed by it. "I was going to hide it."

"Why? What do you see?"

"It responds to me. Just like the Caul smells of our childhood memories, the berg offers a glimpse into my own past. I can't resist. It looks into my soul."

She nodded, turned back to the berg, examining it again. "I see familiar patterns too. But, Carl, I don't *feel* them."

I watched my wife. So calm and clear-eyed. The berg had not touched her like it had me. Janus—why had I called it that? It was outside me and yet it looked inside too. Once again, I felt a fool and apologised, but she hushed me.

"I have a theory," she said. "I think the Topologies are the Caul transitioning, novel expressions of its form. That's why they've supplanted our cities. Geometry is imitating life."

I know the berg is still dangerous. But Gemma has helped me see it for what it is—Janus is not my nemesis—though I remain careful not to approach it. I marvel at her resistance.

Finally, she turned away from the berg, as if it was just an ordinary lump of rock and not a part of the forces that have driven humanity from our home. She said to me, "I want to keep the baby. I think it would be good for both of us."

I was stunned. "But the quarantine . . . What kind of life . . . ?"

She took my hand. "Carl, how many lives have been lost on Earth already? My heart would break if we were responsible for the loss of another."

Day 18, Month 1

Visited Facility for supplies. Gemma's condition obvious but no one said anything. We lunched in the canteen and Dr. Carlyle joined us. She was determined to air her theory that the Topologie is merely an emergent property of the Caul's self-organisation. Gemma nodded but initially refused the bait. Dr. Carlyle kept fishing. Gemma finally lost patience and demolished this argument by invoking higher dimensional intersections. "Where are these higher dimensions?" demanded Dr. Carlyle. "We are not equipped to see them," sighed Gemma. I gave her a warning look. "Pure speculation," said Dr. Carlyle, a self-satisfied smile on her face. "We are slaves to the prejudices of our own dimension," shrugged Gemma. "One day," she smiled, "I'll take you for a turn inside Leviathan." Far from appeasing Dr. Carlyle, Gemma is provoking her. Hastings apologized for his head of science. Apparently, she's learning to fly. It is not going well.

Day 7, Month 2

Hastings and Machalek visited. I heard their carrier's approach and was able to lock the cabin before they arrived. However, they weren't interested in the Topologie. They wanted to see Gemma.

They tried to persuade us to return to the Facility, where they can keep an eye on her. They fear a birth on Earth, but if it has to happen, they desire control. That is the last thing we want. Returning to the Facility would mean allowing Main to oversee us.

Gemma consented for Machalek to examine her. I half-expected him to pronounce the pregnancy dangerous, a sly move to get us back there. It was therefore a double relief to be told that everything is fine. Gemma and the baby are healthy. I no longer feel quite so anxious about its arrival.

Day 8, Month 2

Gemma tires easily and no longer accompanies me into the Topologie. She has tasked me with finding the attractor before the baby comes. I rush about measuring Trefoil knots and Morin surfaces. I examine self-intersections and count rotations. She takes my data and creates maps at each tide, trying to pin down this moving point, around which everything is organised. Every few days I unlock the cabin and stare into the berg. For a few minutes, I feel my fathers beside me, I am wrapped in their love. At night, I sleep dreamlessly.

[Days 10–23, Month 2 missing, torn out.]

Day 9, Month 3

Hastings and Machalek came, pleading with Gemma to return with them. When she refused, I feared them telling us Main had ordered our forcible removal. Instead, they merely looked relieved: They had done all they could. Before they left, Machalek told us about recent disappearances at the Facility. Crude psychological pressure to make us fear for our unborn child? Or a warning to keep away? The man appeared depressed. Gemma told me that after examining her, he'd said: "The most salient fact of life is our inevitable death."

Day 11, Month 3

After making my measurements I wandered directionless through the sulphurous fog. The visit two days ago has left me shaken. When our child comes, everything will change. It will be seen by others—the PA, the Service, rival clans—as an indication that Main has lost control on Earth. They will no longer let us be. They will watch us, unable to help themselves. We will scare them. Our existence will be a threat to their survival. And what will that mean for our research? We're close to a breakthrough. I can feel it.

I find myself thinking of Hannu and Kozlov. Neither asked to be here, but they have come to an accommodation with Earth and the Cauldron. One has a purpose in helping his fellow wreckers while he seeks a way off here. The other, raised largely by himself beside the Cauldron, is a giant feral manchild suspicious of everyone. I ask myself whether love is strong enough to overcome fear. And then I find myself thinking inexplicably of Dr. Carlyle and her own determination to root out the truth.

DAY FIVE

THE JEEP'S WHEELS made a thunderous rumble on the loose stones of the plain. Wipers clumped back and forth rhythmically, removing faint spits of rain from the windscreen. Mae gripped the steering wheel with both hands, driving slowly. Very slowly.

"At a funeral pace," Baré had muttered with evident frustration a kilo back.

The three of them were sitting up front and Magellan's corpse was stretched out on the back seat, legs awkwardly folded, under the tarpaulin. Mae looked in the mirror, unable to shake the sense of a presence behind. She was sick to death of feeling haunted.

Goodbyes were hardly ever said. Every parting could be the final time you saw a neighbour. And funerals were a rarity. When was the last one? she wondered. She'd no recollection, which surprised her. A funeral was the one time the penitents on this part of the shore gathered together. The only time they were united about anything.

Mae glanced over at Siofra, who hadn't once looked at her father's body in the back. She wondered if the girl understood what was happening. She was still troubled by the weird berg from the locked cabin. The description in Magellan's journal hadn't helped her understand it any. What he had removed sounded much bigger than what lay in the cabin. She shivered, remembering the way the silvery surfaces had reacted to the girl's presence. What did it mean? She tapped the steering wheel irritably. If two scientists hadn't been able to make head nor tail of it, what hope had she?

The closer they got to the site of the Drowning Stone the more Mae's thoughts were crowded by memories of the day they'd held a memorial for Albert, twenty years ago. The idea, naturally, had come from the Twins, the only others in attendance. Without a body, they'd bundled up spare bits of pipe and ceramic panels, wrapped it in a precious cotton sheet, and placed it on the Drowning Stone. "No expense spared," Serpa had joked. "This is for your own good, Mae," they'd solemnly told her as they swayed in the teeth of a gale. "You need to let go." She'd felt stupid standing there as Sousa read out some poetry she had spent hours preparing. She had barely heard a single word. They had waited in silence for Mae to speak but nothing had come, not even tears. Sousa and Serpa had looked embarrassed. What was there to say anyway? Albert had come and she'd followed, arriving too late. He'd gone on without her. That was the whole tragic story. Despite her neighbours' efforts and best intentions, the memorial had failed. It had backfired really. For she'd found herself missing Albert more than ever and resenting the Twins. The pain rawer than it had ever been.

The Caul was suddenly visible. It was the first time she'd properly seen it up close in a long time. Normally she avoided it, didn't like looking at it. She didn't trust herself near the shore. She watched the waves slowly rolling in. It looked so innocent at times, like water. Other times it had the thick and sloppy consistency of oil or the sticky viscosity of treacle. Then it seemed truly alien, more like the enemy she wanted it to be. Her fellow penitents told her that was just her imagination. Comforting claims, she thought. It was always what it was. The adversary.

The Caul's dimpled surface was the colour of death, of ghostly gray shadows. She frowned, not quite trusting her eyes. You never saw the true Caul, she thought, only what it allowed you to see. It was deceitful, concealing itself in its cloak of gray.

But these weren't the true reasons Mae avoided the shore. She didn't like it because to look at the Caul was to feel the eyes of all those who had crossed over staring back at her. She'd never told anyone this. She knew they'd think her mad. But she did feel watched. Uncountable pairs of eyes looking out at her. All those who'd succumbed: the tens of thousands who'd come here and the millions more who'd never left Earth. They knew all her sins, judging her for not having the courage to join them. It was an ocean of ghosts, a sea of tumbling spectres. The dead's role is to haunt the living.

And into this soup of shades she was about to cast Magellan.

There were dozens of bergs out there, she saw. Some, far out, were huge. Big as islands. What did they signify? she wondered.

She parked the jeep next to an unlikely looking vehicle clearly patched together from the salvaged pieces of several other vehicles of evidently incompatible sizes and shapes. It had six wheels of varying sizes, a cab that hung over the front and sides and a covered-over flatbed at the rear. Every unused centimetre of the vehicle's shell was covered in solar cells. This contraption was Hannu's pride and joy.

Mae ignored it, however, and stared out the windscreen at the view.

The Drowning Stone was situated in a small inlet cutting into the pebble plain. It was formed of a circular platform of flat sandstone that was exposed at low tide and covered over at high. Sitting near the centre of the circle was a large oval boulder whose top had been flattened into a table or altar. This was the Drowning Stone, a name Mae had always thought of as being entirely appropriate while being completely misleading.

The others were already waiting, gathered around the stone. Hannu was sitting between Sousa and Serpa, who he'd presumably brought in his vehicle. The old women were wearing black cotton dresses. Rawat stood with his back to everyone, looking out into the Caul and hunched over like a sulking adolescent. Kozlov was off to one side, keeping his distance but glancing suspiciously at the jeep now and again. She recognised Valentina Tereshkova and

Shipton. Tereshkova wore a brown jumpsuit, her bald head as severe as the scowl on her face. Shipton's gray beard was wispy. A pipe was stuck in his mouth, though he never had anything to smoke. She hadn't seen these two in a while. They both lived over twenty kilos away. She wondered who had told them and how well they had known Magellan. They'd trekked a long way. But a gathering was a gathering. Not everyone was like her. Now and again, they needed human contact. She felt bad that she hadn't told them herself.

She'd had her reasons.

Mae noted shovels, bundles of wood, and some coils of wire. The penitents had come prepared for every eventuality. More prepared than her.

Her gaze returned to the Drowning Stone, upon which Magellan's corpse was to be placed. The flattened oval top resembled, more than anything else, a platter. Mae had on occasion reflected that what was placed on it felt rather like an offering to placate cruel gods. The penitents had among them created something unnecessarily religious about this spot. But was that not in the nature of death? You had to make the goodbye permanent. You had to have a ritual. And the Drowning Stone was all they had.

Hannu, Rawat, and Kozlov came over. Baré got out and the four of them carried the tarp-draped body down the pebble slope and across the rocky platform. They managed it in one go with barely a stumble. Mae and Siofra stood beside the jeep and watched in silence. Mae's hand gripped Siofra's shoulder reassuringly.

Sousa waved and Mae and Siofra approached the Twins. When they were near, Siofra ran over to Serpa. The old woman leaned close, whispering in her ear. Mae found herself standing alone, hanging back and watching. She'd organised this. It was her doing, so why was she so reluctant to take part? What was stopping her?

When the body, still under its tarp, was stretched out on the Drowning Stone, everyone turned to Mae. They waited. She'd yet to speak to anyone and she realized she had no idea what she was going to say.

She stepped gingerly across the rocky platform. Her hip ached badly.

Sousa and Serpa each got to their feet and hugged her one after the other.

"This is a good thing you are doing, Mae."

Was it? She was filled with doubts. She knew how her mind worked, how easily she undermined herself.

"So, Mae, what's it to be?" asked Hannu, coming over.

They all looked at her expectantly.

She looked away, glancing at Siofra. "I don't think we'll need the shovels."

"We never do," said Sousa.

"Wait till it's your turn," said Serpa.

"Dear! Show some decorum."

"And I think we've seen enough flames." She saw Rawat turn away.

"Tide it is," said Hannu. He looked at his watch and then at the shoreline. "That gives us an hour, I'd say. Kozlov, let's get building."

Hannu, with enthusiasm, and Kozlov, without, began lining pieces of wood up in a row on the platform.

"Is no one coming from the Facility?" asked Serpa.

Mae shrugged. "I told them. They know how we do things."

"Do we even have the right?" asked Rawat.

Silence. Mae could feel the tension, everyone worrying he'd make a scene.

"He's not one of us," he added.

"He lived among us," said Sousa.

"That makes him one of us," said Serpa.

"I do not agree. He is theirs." He pointed vaguely in the direction of the Facility.

"Are you saying we can't legally do this?" asked Hannu, lining up wood.

"Morally," sighed Mae. "He's talking morally."

They looked at her.

"I've spoken to them. The Facility knows of our intentions. They have not objected." Not entirely true.

"I'd feel happier if there was someone here," said Hannu, pausing as he lashed the wood together with lengths of wire. "What if this provokes them? Since Hastings went, they've been quiet."

Shipton cleared his throat. "They have their own problems right now," he said.

Mae could see he was about to carry on in his tiresomely laboured manner. She hadn't time for distractions. She reminded them, "We are here to say goodbye to Carl."

"Don't like it," said Kozlov, on his knees beside Hannu. "Should leave to them."

Mae looked at Sousa and Serpa, who smiled sympathetically. "Mae believes this is the right thing to do," said Serpa, but then she had to sit down as a fit of coughing took her. Sousa found some water and fussed over her.

"It is our responsibility," said Mae. "My responsibility. I found him. He left no note or instructions. The Cluster in the Caul was where he worked. It was his life. It is fitting, I think, that he goes over. He chose to live out here among us. We should decide."

"I can't see anything to argue you with there," said Sousa.

Rawat shook his head. "Magellan disliked the Caul. It was his opponent. He came here to overcome it. He would not want to go into it, and it would not want him."

Sousa rolled her eyes. "Rubbish, Rawat. He respected the Caul."

The preacher nodded his head. "As should we. We do not want to upset it."

"Much as I hate to say it, he has a point," said Serpa.

"Has he?" Hannu looked incredulous.

"What about Gemma?" said Shipton, silencing everyone.

"What about her?" asked Serpa, finally.

"Well," the old man's hand gripped the pipe in his mouth, as if to hide from their scrutiny. "Would Carl not want to be with his wife?"

Which it turned out no one could argue with and allowed Mae to get her way.

○

THE RESIDENTS OF New Sheffield called it Hades with good reason. One of several cities sunk into the mineral-rich flanks of extinct volcano Olympus Mons, it descended over three kilos beneath Mars's surface in a series of linked and pressurised shafts, tunnels, chambers, and natural caverns. Fifteen million inhabitants were crammed into everything from rock mansions to plastofab slums. Fusion power gave them heat and light. Surface hydro-harvesters piped down water. Solar-sims and low-g ensured genegro'wn plants and bugs were both prodigious and bounteous. Vertical farming and core mining to feed a ravenous system. It was cramped, dangerous, frantic, noisy, smelly, hot, weird, dirty, and the Service had their work cut out keeping any kind of order. Mae had loved it.

Five years after she'd arrived, she met the person who would alter her life more fundamentally than even Sister Ursula and the church.

Thirty miners had died from asphyxiation after an atmo-monitor had failed. She was investigating to ascertain whether FashClan bore responsibility for the accident. The fault lay in some bug-ridden code. She needed to prove that Fash had skimped on the code to get the miners' families a bigger payout. It was political because New Sheffield's Service funding was being renegotiated and Fash were pushing for steep cuts. Mae was under pressure to get it off her desk quickly, but making any case stick was always a slow, painstaking process.

She was about to mark the case unproven when Albert showed up. He was also investigating the coding unit after uncovering similar incidents in neighbouring cities.

Albert was a journalist, working for a citizen-access news feed. Dressed in a crumpled, ill-fitting suit, he looked like a man late for a funeral. ("My own," he'd joked later.) Slight, with watery brown eyes, he was both unfailingly cordial and maddeningly persistent. Instead of getting rid of him as she should, Mae found herself telling him things she shouldn't. When she later looked him up, she discovered he'd undertaken several investigations in other cities that led to campaigns forcing the clans to admit liability. And he was still alive. Mae had never met anyone like him.

If it hadn't been for Albert, she wouldn't have got the evidence fingering the head of the art coding unit, who'd cut out testing after budget cuts.

They'd celebrated after the PA was moved to reprimand Fash and the families received hefty payouts. It was just the two of them in a bar in Conchtown—a spiralling ductway with no curfew. They'd talked through one shift and long into the next. They had absences in common—family, friends—and each was driven to fill that emptiness. He didn't trust the Service. She granted him that but argued that you had to work with the available structures. He wanted to "burn it all down and start again." She laughed, called him a romantic and said, "Exo *is* our new start." He shrugged, replying, "On Earth we had rights. When we left, they took them away. No countries, no governments, no Earth laws. We are slaves who don't know we're slaves." She had wanted to kiss him then and wondered what had come over her. Instead, she'd ordered another drink.

A month later they were looking for a hutch together in Hades.

○

"LIKE SO MANY OF US, Carl came here to make sense of something he didn't understand." Mae spoke loudly, clearly, to the Caul. "He was joined by his late wife, Gemma. They were hoping, they said, to uncover the true nature of the Topologie. And while I don't know whether they succeeded, their commitment was unquestionable. In the end they gave their lives to it. Sadly, we said farewell to Gemma three years ago. Now we must say goodbye to Carl."

They were gathered around the body, which lay upon the raft of sticks assembled by Hannu and Kozlov, which lay in turn upon the flattened oval surface of the Drowning Stone. The small congregation was standing on either side of the body, while Mae led it at the head, facing the Caul as it flooded slowly towards them.

There were more of them now. Just before they'd started, a copter had landed and doctors Carlyle and Machalek had climbed out apprehensively. Mae was unsure if it was the Caul they feared, lacking the protection of fences and tethers, or the gathering of unrepentant "wreckers" who outnumbered them. The wreckers themselves—staring unpenitentially at the new arrivals—were hardly welcoming.

"It wasn't long after Carl and Gemma came to Earth that they chose to live out here, among us," Mae continued. "A risk taken to be closer to the truth they sought. They were good neighbours, keeping themselves to themselves but friendly and generous when encountered. After Gemma . . . left us, if Carl and Siofra retreated a little, it was only to be expected. Loss afflicts all who come here, and we each must find our own way to make peace with the hole in our lives. Carl devoted himself to his work and he would not be distracted from what he saw as his mission." She paused, clearing her dry throat, and threw the cat among the pigeons. "Whatever happened to Carl, this was not his choice."

Mae allowed her eyes to pass over those before her. She could feel Baré's glare of fury boring into her. She ignored it, too far gone to stop now.

"Life on Earth is hard, but Carl showed a tenacity we could all learn from. He had a task to do, and he saw it through no matter how difficult matters became. His journals are full of his thoughts, ideas, and speculations. He never stopped thinking and writing about the Topologie and the Caul and us, his neighbours."

Mae paused. She looked at those before her, one after the other, letting them see she was watching them. Some, suddenly uncomfortable, shifted their feet. Others were visibly unmoved. Baré shook her head in silent disgust.

"Above all of this, however, Carl was a devoted father," she resumed. "He loved his daughter Siofra and would do anything to protect her. Forced to bring her up on his own, he never once forgot his duties. He kept her close by his side wherever he went."

Baré's hands were fidgeting at her sides.

"Does anyone else have something to say before we commend Carl Magellan to the mercy of the Caul?"

There was a silence filled only by the wind whistling over the heaped stones and the gentle hush and shree of the Caul unhesitatingly invading the shore.

○

THEY LEFT THE DROWNING STONE, climbing the pebbled slope to stand on the edge of the plain beside the vehicles. By then the Caul was rapidly advancing across the rocky platform. They stood in small groups, talking and picking at a few cakes and muffins, which Sousa and Serpa had cooked and placed on a plastic folding table Hannu had taken from his vehicle. The Caul's musty stink was too much for Mae. She had no appetite.

The distant platform vanished quickly, and they watched the waves lap against the stone, rising rapidly up its sides. The bergs, Mae noticed, never approached the shore.

The Twins hugged Mae, thanking her for her words. Baré, however, whispered angrily at her: "How could you, Mae? This was his funeral. Siofra is . . ."

Mae put a hand on the young woman's shoulder. "You've answered your own question, Jean," she said gently, seeking to calm and restrain.

In a difficult silence they watched Siofra eat a muffin, sitting on her own. In her other hand she clutched a small, curved shard. She stared ahead as if captivated by something out there, either her father's body on the Drowning Stone or the Caul itself. Mae wondered which. Did the girl blame the Caul for taking her parents? What did she see out there? Juvenile animals weren't drawn to the Caul. Did it have no effect on them at all? Or was it so altogether different that its influence was impossible to spot?

The silence among her, Baré, and the Twins was awkward, but no one seemed prepared to be the first to break it.

"*Mercy of the Caul*?" said Baré suddenly.

"Whether we like it or not we all live by its mercy," said Serpa. "Fine words."

Baré huffed.

"Someone had to take responsibility," chided Sousa gently.

"Someone was looking to make trouble," hissed Baré, glancing at Dr. Carlyle.

Mae excused herself before she went and said something they'd all regret.

Seething, she stood at the table and tidied up, rearranging the cakes. Her hands continued to shake. Her heart palpitated in her chest. She glanced around fretfully, in case someone had noticed her distress. It had been a long while since she had been surrounded by this many people. Familiar and not-so-familiar faces. Her overstimulated senses were a hot wire into her brain. She had a strong urge to walk away, to be on her own. She took deep breaths to quell her unruly faculties. She blamed the Caul.

By now the tide was close to covering the top of the Drowning Stone. Just a few minutes left. She had brought everyone together, but she wasn't sure what, if anything, she had accomplished.

Kozlov and Rawat, the only penitents perhaps more unsociable than Mae, were not natural comrades yet they were standing together away from the others. For once Mae sympathised with their isolation. They noticed her watching them and joined her at the table. Kozlov quickly began filling his face with muffins.

"A curious oration," said Rawat. "Not what I would have said."

"Magellan wasn't one of your flock."

"You've nevertheless sent him into the Caul."

"Magellan hated Caul," growled Kozlov. "Angry with it."

"Oh," said Mae. "Why?"

"Hurt him. Wife gone. Work lost. Hated it." Like everything Kozlov said, it was spoken with a broken finality that was hard to argue with.

"He never feared it, though, did he?" said Hannu, who had come over.

Rawat was staring at Siofra just like yesterday, with a longing that disturbed Mae.

"Perhaps he should have feared it," she said. "It holds so many ghosts."

"Do you believe in ghosts?" asked Hannu.

Mae thought of Albert. "I think they exist inside us."

"That," said Rawat, "is the only reality there is."

Hannu shook his head and moved away. Shipton and Tereshkova joined them. "Mae, you visited the Facility?" asked Shipton, chewing a muffin.

She shook her head, explained about encountering Dr. Carlyle.

"Something's happened to it," he said quietly. "It's . . ." He opened and closed his mouth, unable to find the words. "It's not the Facility."

Tereshkova frowned. "Have they done something?"

"It's like it erupted," Shipton added, shaking his head.

Mae looked around to where Dr. Machalek and Dr. Carlyle were talking to Sousa a few metres away. She beckoned them over. Dr. Carlyle deliberately turned away but after a moment Dr. Machalek hobbled over. He was wearing a thick coat, but the left sleeve was folded and pinned to the shoulder. "Well, Mae," he said. "Been a long time."

She nodded. Shipton and Tereshkova had stepped back, as if Dr. Machalek might have something infectious. "Fine words for Carl . . ."

Mae hadn't time for his platitudes. "Shipton"—she nodded his way—"says something has happened to the Facility."

Dr. Machalek looked from her to Shipton. He rubbed his beard, glanced at Dr. Carlyle, still talking to Sousa. He lowered his voice. "There was an accident. We had some deaths."

"What do you mean accident?" asked Shipton.

Some deaths, thought Mae. How many was some?

Dr. Machalek blinked. "The experiment. Look, I'm sorry. We can't talk about it. It's a tragedy."

"When did it happen?" asked Mae.

He hesitated. "Five days ago." The day before Magellan was killed.

Dr. Machalek's black eyes were wet-looking as if he were on the verge of tears, or in pain. "I really can't say any more," he said. "Dr. Carlyle asks that you stay away from Magellan's camp."

Mae wanted to ask about the deaths but before she could he hobbled back to Dr. Carlyle, the upper half of his body moving stiffly. The two of them conferred and Dr. Carlyle's dark sunglasses briefly gazed their way. A moment later Dr. Machalek was following her to the copter. Five minutes after, they were in the air.

"Mark my words, they have been making trouble," said Shipton. It was a standard complaint. "No wonder the Caul is restless."

"Restless, how?" she asked, thinking of the river they'd encountered on the way here. The detour had taken several minutes. But he didn't elaborate.

Tereshkova looked unhappy. "Do you know Cluster is incandescent?"

"Incandescent?" asked Mae.

"Glows, day and night."

"Teresh, you're imagining things," said Shipton.

She bristled. "Have you been there, recently?"

He bit down on his pipe.

"Takes my breath." She spoke wide-eyed with memory. "I go. Up close."

"You be careful! The fog confuses—"

"No fog. Fog all gone. Inside, see tiny stars swarming."

Waves were sloshing over the Drowning Stone. They fell silent as the small raft Hannu and Kozlov had built began to move, lifted, and then floated on the Caul's surface. In a minute the Drowning Stone had vanished and the raft bearing Magellan's body was drifting free on the undulating gray.

It was unclear how or why the Caul understood the difference between the living and the dead, but it did so. A living being entering the Caul would submerge or be gone almost instantaneously. Yet the little raft, made of lashed-together wooden sticks, which on water would not have buoyancy enough to support Magellan's weight, floated high on the Caul's choppy surface. Mae looked at the seething, wild gray. You'd never imagine its tides were regular as clockwork. Why do we try to bring order to our short lives, she wondered, when we know we're doomed to dissolution? The Caul is the natural disorder of things.

For a moment it appeared as if the Caul was going to sweep the raft back to the shore: To reject their offering. But this never happened. Already the body was rising on a large counter swell and within moments it was drifting further away. The raft was slowly spinning as if performing some kind of farewell salute.

Mae looked at Siofra. The girl was sitting in Baré's lap, the two of them sandwiched by Sousa and Serpa. She had her eyes open, looking into that unreachable middle distance, some faraway elsewhere.

Magellan was borne out further into the Caul, rising and falling, there and then not there, as if passed from wave to wave. In a minute he was a hundred metres out.

Thirty seconds later he was gone, forever.

WAS IT ANY DIFFERENT to death off Earth? Mae found herself wondering later. That was a matter of recycling. Bodies were sealed in hot tubes where bacteria quickly got to work. After a month the resulting slurry was pumped into pressurised vats to mature into a rich, stinky compost. As if the Caul obliterating all evidence of humanity's existence from the surface of the Earth was, crudely put, a matter of digestion.

She and Albert had attended too many funerals in New Sheffield. Roof collapses, decompressions, cancers, suicides, witherings. Mae never got over the suicides. They came in waves which were often seasonal. It felt like a mood of despair swept through the citizens as if en masse they'd decided enough was enough. Albert deplored it, asking: "How does a collective awakening lead to the big sleep?" Mae had no answers, was too busy fending off the clans who used the soaring death rate as an excuse to lay into the Service. Politics ate into her investigation time. It was win-win for the clans.

Yet she never understood Albert's desire to make a nuisance of himself.

He'd get beaten up regularly. Sometimes it was paid thugs. Usually, it was the people he was trying to help, angry that exposing lax safety protocols led to unpaid shutdowns. The clans flung dirt to discredit Albert, and the Service was leant on to follow up. Mae being Service didn't stop the raids. Mostly the officers came round late at night, made a lot of noise outside for the benefit of neighbours and then sat around drinking tea and gossiping with her and Albert. Occasionally, a newly arrived officer would make trouble until Mae explained the situation. Mae didn't get it. He saved lives. He spoke truth to power. He should've been a hero. Yet half the citizens thought him a kind of fifth columnist. Being a pariah would have exhausted her. Albert thrived on it.

They married in part because it was another layer of protection. Husbands and wives had rights that cohabitees did not. Both knew that if Mae lost her position in the Service, they'd be in trouble. But they were a good team. Citizens told Albert things they'd never tell a Service officer. He had contacts all over Mars. He was able to fill in gaps in her investigations. His reporting on her cases lent them a moral weight she believed they rarely deserved. Sometimes it felt like the whole city was watching. His fellow journalists, who took swipes at the Service for being the clans' catspaw, were told, "She's my muse." And what's more he meant it.

She'd wondered about that a great deal in the thirty years since he'd left her.

○

MAE WOKE and the dream of empty, cavernous spaces broke into fragments that eluded her grasp. She lay on the floor and stared at the ceiling, lit by the faint illumination coming from the shaded lamp Baré had placed on the floor for Siofra. She listened to her own breathing and the faint snores of Baré. Otherwise, there was silence.

She wondered what had woken her. The vodka. For the first time since she'd acquired the bottle, she'd not reached for it before bed. Baré's mood hadn't improved by the evening. Why give her further reason to voice disapproval?

So it was back to the restless nights. No alcohol-laced oblivion that left her feeling calmer the next morning. She moved and discovered Magellan's journals scattered over her chest. She'd fallen asleep reading about the loss of his wife.

She turned on her side and noticed the covers had been thrown back on the bed. Baré was sleeping but there was no Siofra.

Mae sat up. She looked around in the gloom.

Stiffly, she sat and pulled the shade off the light.

"Hell," she said.

Baré blinked awake.

"What is it, Mae?"

"Siofra's gone."

Mae pushed at the door. It didn't open. The padlock she'd put on it as a precaution was still in place. At the foot of the door was Siofra's nightdress. "How in hell did she get out—"

"Shit," said Baré, sitting up. "It's okay. I'll go. I'm used to this."

"We'll both go."

They hurriedly dressed in silence.

When Mae opened the door, she stepped into thick fog. The moon was but a faint white glow across the southern sky. Their torches illuminated just a few metres. She checked the jeep, but it was empty.

"Which way?"

"Your guess is as good as mine, Mae."

"Caulwards?"

Baré nodded. "I'll head southwest, you go southeast. When we get to the shore we walk towards each other."

They set off on their separate routes, feet loudly grinding pebbles. It was a good two kilos to the shore. How much of a head start had the girl? Mae's clock had said it was just before one a.m. She'd been asleep for a couple of hours. A long time. Her thoughts, however, kept returning to what it was that had awoken her.

The fog thickened the further she went. Visibility dropped. The torch light was scattered by the soupy air. She could hear Baré calling the girl's name, distantly.

The air had a sulphurous tinge to it, even in the dark. It came off the Caul. She avoided the fog because she didn't like the idea of breathing it.

Soon she could hear the Caul's steady roar as it raked the shore. Light up ahead. It was close, only a couple of hundred metres away.

The damp air pressed in, its cold penetrating her clothes. The stench of dust was suffocating. "*Siofra.*" Baré's calls were distant, barely audible.

The girl hadn't gone after her father, had she? Could she have wandered into the Caul, desperate to find him or her mother? Had Mae made a terrible mistake in holding the funeral, giving the girl ideas?

I've been stupid, she thought. This is my fault. I should have listened to Baré. The girl shouldn't have come. The funeral must have been wretched for her. Saying goodbye, seeing the body whisked away, strangers talking of crossing over. What was I thinking? Her family is gone, and she watched us send her father into the Caul, the thing we all fear. Only Siofra showed no fear of it. She was a child, not yet drawn to the Caul. It held no terrors for her.

Mae picked up the pace, abandoning stealth. What a fool she had been! Her hip hurt as she raced over the pebbles. "Siofra!" she called. "It's Mae. Where are you?"

The fog, growing denser, seemed to swallow her voice. It was bright, bearing a diffuse but piercing luminescence. It moved thickly around her, in serpentine whorls.

She abruptly stumbled down a pebbled slope. At the bottom she saw a deep and palely glowing white surface running along the shore. The luminescent Caul washing against the beach. It was right in front of her, lighting up the fog dazzlingly. She paused, unable to see more than a few metres.

She heard a sound to the west. Was it Baré? She walked towards it along the sloped shore. After a few minutes she could hear the woman calling, "Siofra!"

She was furious with herself. What had she done? She'd been so careless, so obsessed with doing right by Magellan she'd ignored the one person she could help. Baré was right. She'd treated the girl as a secondary concern. A means to learn who had killed Magellan, rather than a victim in her own right. Siofra had arguably been more harmed than anyone. She was still alive. She needed help. She, at least, could be saved. Baré understood this, but Mae, in her urge to uncover the truth, had not.

She'd as good as pushed Siofra away. Just like the day she'd found the girl lost and alone. She'd refused her responsibilities.

The fog around her was brilliant ink, blinding her and confusing everything. She was careful where she put her feet as she scanned the slope for any sign of the girl. What if she wasn't here?

She could hear Baré approaching. There was still no sign of the girl. "Siofra!" came the faint cry. In despair, Mae almost sank to her knees. She stared at the lit-up waves coming in. I'll never forgive myself, she thought.

She stood, trembling. A movement caught her eyes, and she saw a shadow rise up out in the bright, undulating gray. Out there, dead ahead. She peered at it. Something was out in the Caul, twenty metres away. She watched it for a few seconds. It was coming closer.

"Jean!" she called.

Mae took a step forward and when she looked again, whatever it was had gone.

There was a hard lump in her throat.

A moment later it was back. A shadowy shape, sticking up like a post. The fog and gray seemed to swirl and flow around it, like it was really there. In another moment it was gone again. There. Then not there. Coming and going. Still approaching.

What was it?

"Jean?" she called uncertainly.

The damn fog. She found herself stepping forward to see better, then getting a grip on herself. Stop.

The thing wasn't there anymore.

She looked out there, scanning left and right, and saw it again. It was closer now. Just a few metres away. A dark shape in a luminous swirl of gray vapour.

She gasped. It was moving towards her. A figure walking? Or something else?

Her heart beat hard in her chest.

She took a step forward.

She knew. She knew who it was. She recognised the movement. The walk.

"Ah . . ." she gasped, faltering.

Coming closer.

She stepped forward.

"Mae!" Baré's call was close and urgent. "Mae, stop!"

The figure—it was a figure, surely?—seemed to dissolve and then reform, further over to the west, like it was winking in and out of existence.

She stepped to her left, following it. Too small, she thought, but a part of her was soaring. Her heart clamouring in her chest. It had to be him. He'd come back to her.

"Mae!"

"Stay back, Jean," she hissed. She wasn't going to lose him again. He was hers.

The figure, utterly shrouded in the fog, was within metres of the beach.

Mae stepped closer. She could see the pale-glowing gray, less than a metre from her feet. Tears ran down her cheeks. She'd waited and he'd come. Finally.

The mass of gray vapours was so close she could reach out and touch it. They brightened and she had to shield her eyes. She stepped back involuntarily.

"You found her! Thank heaven, you found her."

Blinking, she looked wildly around. Baré was rushing towards her.

And there, standing not a metre from Mae, was Siofra, naked as the day she was born.

She looked up at Mae with that blank, inscrutable face.

No one else was there. Only Siofra.

Who a moment ago—Mae knew, as certainly as she'd known anything in her long life—had just emerged from the Caul.

YEAR SIX

Day 16, Month 5

Siofra is one! We threw a party. It was supposed to be a small affair: the Twins, Hannu, Hastings, Doc Machalek, a couple of other wreckers I'd dutifully asked but not expected to show up. In the end we had a dozen from the Facility. Jameson and Rawat also came. The celebrations went on long into the evening.

Siofra, of course, was the centre of attention. It's not as if we've hidden her away. She often accompanies us to the Facility. The remarks about how big she's grown were tiresome. She's already the size of most two-year-olds—but Doc Machalek insists she's within the ninety-ninth percentile. (Which is unexpected, he told Gemma unnecessarily, for a baby who weaned herself at three months.)

I was proud of Gemma. She hadn't wanted the party, but so many people kept asking how we were going to celebrate Siofra's birthday that it would have been rude not to do so. (I hope the curiosity surrounding our child will abate now. She's not *so* remarkable if you consider *where* we are.) Gemma chatted carelessly, showing none of the warning signs that tell me we're going to need to ask everyone to leave. She has been better this last month, and I'm optimistic we're through the worst. Doc Machalek said he hoped so.

Siofra's shift from a helpless, hungry, and demanding baby to an independent toddler has been difficult. For six months she would not let her mother out of her sight without howling. Is it any wonder Gemma now feels abandoned when our child barely looks up from her shards when spoken to or wanders off at every opportunity? I'm sympathetic but considering Gemma's periods of coolness and even indifference towards Siofra, I'd have thought she would welcome time on her own. Unfortunately, it has only deepened her depression.

Siofra's love of stones and shards and the staggering arrangements she makes were on display. Typically, she took no interest in her guests. They, on the other hand, cooed in captivation, beguiled by the complex patterns of the structures she was building. She worked for hours, barely pausing to blow out the candle on the Twins' cake. There were numerous comments praising her. (Doc Machalek says her fine motor skills are remarkable.) Only one, Jean Baré, a recent arrival at the Facility, noted the arrangement's resemblance to the Topologie. (I saw Gemma staring at Siofra a couple of times with a troubled frown, and I worried she might kick everything over again. Thankfully, she kept her impulses under control. Perhaps the doc's drugs are working—assuming she's taking them.)

I've tried talking to Siofra about her arrangements. She listens and sometimes she nods. It is impossible to know what she's thinking since she still refuses to speak. We have only the exhilarating geometrical patterns of the shards to indicate what is going on inside her head. I wish they'd remained a source of fascination for Gemma instead of adding to her anxieties. It seems half a lifetime ago when she speculated about whether Siofra might be a mathematical prodigy. "Then she's clearly got more of you in her than me," I remember responding, only to receive a sharp rebuke.

Hastings and Dr. Carlyle (who acts as if Siofra doesn't exist) used the visit as an opportunity to snoop, but I was prepared. Everything important was locked inside cabin three. I ducked the usual questions. They know I'm in the Topologie, just not how far or what I've discovered. Hastings asked me to take him there and despite Dr.

Carlyle's alarmed look I promised him I would (though I said nothing about when).

What would either say if they knew the truth?

Day 9, Month 6

One of Gemma's sick days, unable to get out of bed. Forced to stay and attend to Siofra, I thought she'd be happy playing with her shards, but she was out of sorts too. I couldn't work so we visited the Twins.

Startled by our arrival, they welcomed us all the same. Serpa and Siofra played in their garden while I discussed Gemma with Sousa over tea. I don't know what I'd have done without her advice. She's taught me patience and fortitude. What she cannot help me with is the guilt, a burden I cannot share. It comes in debilitating waves and some days I struggle for breath, feeling like I am drowning.

Day 13, Month 6

This evening, I noticed the padlock on cabin three hanging open. I asked Gemma about it but received a careless shrug. The key was secure in its hiding place in the caravan. Can I even trust Gemma to keep an eye on things in my absence?

Day 16, Month 6

Returned from the Topologie to find the camp in turmoil. Siofra's shards, which I'd left her assembling at lunch, lay in ruins and she stomped around kicking things over and howling. (Our daughter may not talk but makes her feelings clear when she needs to.) Gemma was in the caravan with the door closed. I was patient, waiting until she was ready. Finally, she told me. She'd done something unforgivable.

Busy building, Siofra had again refused to eat, ignoring Gemma completely. Gemma had snapped—it was the fourth day of such refusals in a row—and she'd dragged Siofra to the Cauldron and abandoned her on the shore. She told me she does not know what she intended. The moment she returned to the camp, she came to her senses and ran back. She spent an hour searching before finally finding Siofra, creating a new arrangement out of pebbles behind the ridge. Siofra hadn't wanted to leave and so Gemma, full of remorse, had waited for her to finish. But she would not, even as the light faded from the sky. In the end Gemma had had to carry her back home, screaming.

Siofra, in a rage, had destroyed her earlier arrangement of shards.

Day 18, Month 6

I tried to discuss leaving with Gemma. She laughed: "We can't, Carl." We could blackmail Main: We have our results. "Incomplete. We cannot locate the attractor." I winced at mention of my betrayal. We also have Siofra, I said. Gemma made a face. If word of Siofra got out that would hurt them, I continued. "They won't let it." Gemma insists we must finish our work. What work? I asked. Gemma hasn't looked at my measurements in months. They pile up on her desk. She flew into a rage. Siofra came running to see what was wrong. Gemma pushed her daughter away. I saw that look again: the revulsion. I closed my eyes. I am the cause. When I opened them, Gemma had gone. She has taken to walking by the shore again. She wants me to discover the key to higher dimensions. But giving it to her would destroy everything.

Day 25, Month 6

Unfortunate visit to the Facility. Dr. Carlyle's array has failed once more. Apparently in a reflective mood, she's barely been speaking to her staff. However, she cooked us lunch in the canteen and—instead of her usual needling over the undiscovered attractor—she talked excitedly about Siofra. She watched our child with an interest hitherto unseen. Gemma rarely responds to others' fascination with Siofra, but she smiled and chatted with Dr. Carlyle. I was pleased for Gemma, anything to stop her brooding on her attacks or on Siofra.

I took myself for a wander, ending up by the farming pods. I recalled Gemma's joy when she spotted her Witchetty grubs pupating. For a week she recorded the rates of cocoon formation, noting individual metamorphoses, measured the imagoes emerging from their tunnels. Most of all, I remember Hastings's upset when he found out she'd allowed the edible larvae to transform into inedible moths. Gemma, unrepentant, told him: "Aren't we here to learn how one thing becomes another?"

`Day 2, Month 7`

Doc Machalek came to check up on Siofra and Gemma. He said everything was fine, but before he left, he took me aside. He didn't want to alarm us but thought I should know that Siofra displayed several key indicators of autism. "I'd like to test her." I thanked him for his diagnosis but refused. Heaven knows how Gemma might react.

`Day 19, Month 7`

The return of the attacks of nociplastic pain shortly after Siofra's birth devastated Gemma. They are less frequent but more intense than before, lasting days. Unable to approach the Topologie, which she insists is a trigger, she tells me she feels impaired.

Curiously, the only relief she finds is by visiting our berg—and this worries me. She spends hours at a time in there, neglecting Siofra. She is lost in the berg much as I once was. Yet, it does appear to improve her mood—unfortunately, not for long.

Today, on my return from the Topologie, she was smiling, glad to see me. Talkative, interested in my work, mentioning picking up where she left off with her own. My old Gemma. But over the next few hours, a mask crept over her face. The spark in her eyes went out, the smile drooped, and I knew I'd lost her again.

After the brief rise, the fall is precipitous.

I try to talk to her about it, but she tells me I will never understand. When I ask about Siofra, she tells me to stop rubbing in her failures.

But she has that wrong. They are my failures, not hers.

Day 3, Month 8

Siofra accompanied me into the Topologie. Once we'd entered the fog and were inside the site's tangled geometry, her eyes were big as dinner plates. Outside the jeep I held her hand tightly. I could feel her trying to pull away to follow her own path. I tried to keep her under control, but she would not listen. I was frightened. Sometimes she scares me, and it is then I perhaps glimpse what Gemma sees. I thought about taking Siofra to the attractor. But I didn't have the courage, feeling like a wretch contemplating a return to the scene of his crime.

Day 16, Month 8

Gemma returned from two days being observed at the Facility. Doc Machalek has raised her dosage. Sadly, he can't print the pills he'd like to prescribe and he daren't order them for fear of Main's response. He mentioned something called Capgras delusion in relation to Siofra, but I was too distracted to listen properly.

At dinner, Siofra smiled happily, pleased like I am, that the three of us are back together. As I cleared up, Gemma asked, "Why does she keep staring at me like that?" Like what? I asked. "Like I'm some kind of curiosity." "She has missed her mother," I replied. Gemma swore. "No wonder I hate myself."

Day 28, Month 8

Returning early, I saw a jeep leaving the camp. Gemma—red-faced, perspiring—came out of the caravan. She smiled hesitantly. "Who was that?" I asked. "I got rid of it," she said. I felt cold inside. I walked over to cabin three, yanking the unsecured door open. They hadn't taken the whole thing. A piece of the berg had been left. Gemma glared defiantly and, before I could speak, said: "Don't, Carl. It was a price I was willing to pay to be rid of it. I can't resist it. It had to go." But why give it to Dr. Carlyle? "Because we're supposed to be scientists." I swallowed, chagrined. Why did you keep some? I asked. She frowned. "Siofra got upset. We had to put a piece of it back." She gave me the key and told me to keep hold of it. But Siofra . . . I began. Gemma shook her head at me and said something I still don't understand: "When did doors ever stop Siofra?"

Day 3, Month 9

Siofra came with me again. I daren't leave her alone with Gemma. I do not know what might happen. Gemma is often not there when we return. Since giving Main the berg, she goes on long walks alone. When I ask where she goes, she replies: "Far away."

Day 17, Month 9

A terrible row. Gemma told me Siofra repulsed her. I felt sick. Sick at her and sick at myself for the coward I am. I listened, trying to be sympathetic. I think of her side. I think of what I did, why, and how it has to be like this.

"I'm sorry it is hard," I said and brought up leaving again. She said I was delusional. "Carl, we are trapped here." I wanted to tell her the truth but how can I when I know she'll never understand? She said a lot of cruel things, then returned to the subject of Siofra. I lost my temper and told her I didn't think she was a terrible mother but wasn't this exactly how one would behave? She had a duty to her child. I don't remember the rest of what we said to one another. I don't want to. Two people who love one another would never say those things. It means there's nothing left between them, nothing good. Yet there's Siofra. I cling to her.

I only wanted to fix one bad thing, so how is it I've wrecked everything?

Day 23, Month 10

Returning from the Topologie this afternoon, I spotted a figure in the yellow fog. We stopped—I feared it was Gemma. The drifting fog cleared. The silhouetted figure—clearly not my wife—was looking back at us. I waved but the gray thickened and our fellow venturer disappeared as if they had never been there.

Day 4, Month 1

A fire in the caravan. I was working in my cabin when I heard Gemma's shouts. She was standing outside, watching flames flicker in the window. I grabbed an extinguisher and ran in, spraying foam wildly. The cooker's flames were soon out. Coughing, I opened windows to clear the smoke. On our bed I saw a lump: Siofra, curled up, her face hidden in her hands. When I carried her outside, Gemma was nowhere to be seen.

Day 6, Month 1

I no longer trust Gemma with Siofra. She knows this. I see it in her eyes whenever I leave them together. This evening, she told me she couldn't carry on. She did not believe Siofra was her daughter. She said she had known this from the day of her birth. They had "no connection." She accused me of knowing the truth all along and concealing it from her. I was taken aback, and I did not know what to say. She pushed me up against the wall and said, "I can't take any more." I nodded, dumbly. "I am going mad. Something isn't right. It's the Caul or being a mother or my sickness or you. I feel a wrongness around me, but I don't know what it is. I think you know, Carl. I really think you do but you're too scared to tell me. Is that right?" She was sobbing. "Why won't you tell me? It's killing me." I wanted to tell her the truth but right now she'd never understand. First, I need to get it straight in my head. I will find a way to make her see. She will love Siofra as I do. Tomorrow, she'll be in a more receptive mood. I'll tell her then.

Day 12, Month 1

This evening, I found Gemma by the shore, staring into the Cauldron. "I can't live in this shell anymore," she said. "I can't keep living in a body that has turned against me. Speaking hurts, even breathing." I wanted to hug her, but just my touch is agony. We sat in silence, a gap between us, listening to the eternal whisperings of these desolate shores.

Day 18, Month 2

Meet lone death on the drear ocean's waste . . .

It has ended like I always feared it would end. Of course, it's all my fault. I never told her the truth and she has paid for my deception.

This morning, I went to the Facility to collect supplies. Gemma has been brighter these last days and seemed pleased when I suggested she keep an eye on Siofra. I should have noticed something was amiss when she accepted so readily. Our hopes too easily deceive us.

The Facility proved a distraction, and I returned late. It was dark. The perimeter lights were on, but I knew immediately nobody was in the camp. A cold fear clutched my insides. I headed straight for the Cauldron, driving back and forth along the shore for two hours. I saw no one. Eventually, I abandoned the jeep. Between the moonlight and the eerily still Cauldron's noctilucence, I could see for hundreds of metres.

An hour later, I found Siofra. I stopped, unable to move. She was straight ahead, several metres out from the shore, waist-deep in the gray. She faced away from me, out towards the endless horizon. I didn't dare speak. I thought I'd already lost her. Was she going in or coming out? I stepped closer, trying not to make a sound.

I could see no sign of Gemma.

Finally, I called Siofra and she turned. She waved. Questions raced through my mind: Why hadn't she disappeared? I had heard stories of those who entered the Cauldron, even been shown footage as a warning. Anyone who stepped into it just disappeared, vanishing as if whipped away. But Siofra could have been emerging from water after a swim. She remained in the gray for half an hour. When she eventually waded out—liquid Caul beading off her like water off duck feathers—I rushed forward and hugged her more tightly than I've ever held anyone in my life.

I sat back and, gripping her shoulders, asked: "Where's your mother?" She pouted, then gave me a small smile and pointed.

My eyes followed the line of her finger, out into the endless, luciferous gray.

Day 25, Month 2

I've visited every wrecker within a hundred kilos. No one has seen hide nor hair of Gemma. She left no parting note.

DAY SIX

MAE AWOKE TO THE AROMA of cooking food. A pot was bubbling noisily on the stove. She inhaled deeply and her insides growled with a fierce hunger she hadn't known in years. Raising her head, she glanced around in the dim light. No Siofra, no Baré. Even their bedding had been tidied away. She hauled herself from the floor onto her bare bed, wondering how late she'd slept.

The door scraped open and Baré looked in. "You're awake," she said with a tight smile. She stirred the pot. "We'll eat soon." In response to Mae's enquiring frown: "Siofra's outside. We didn't want to disturb you."

Baré had used the last of their meat in the stew. That meant they would have to check the traps, later. Mae was already feeling guilty about neglecting them. It made plain how much of her routine had slipped. She was losing sight of the only thing that ought to matter: the fundamentals of their continued survival.

Before she went back outside, Baré dipped a cup in the pot, wiped its side, and held it out. A peace offering.

Mae took the cup, its heat burning her fingers. She inhaled the steaming broth and smiled gratefully. Both for the drink and for a cessation of yesterday's hostilities. First the funeral and then Siofra's disappearance and reappearance in the night, each demanding an explanation that the other refused to or could not adequately provide. Mae knew that she and Baré couldn't carry on like this any longer.

She ought to get up, but she lacked the will to move. Instead, she lay in her bed, feeling sore, tired, vulnerable, and now cross with herself. She looked around her shack. Baré had been tidying. Things weren't in their rightful places. She sighed. She closed her eyes, wanting only to be left alone.

She brooded over last night. She was unable to make any sense of it. It had clearly affected her for she'd slept badly, repeatedly waking from dreams of Albert. So many in quick succession. She couldn't remember a time when he'd appeared to her like this. In the dark she'd looked resentfully at the sleeping girl, unsure what any of it meant. No wonder she'd finally reached for the bottle on the shelf and a taste of oblivion.

The cup of broth cooled in her hands.

Her thoughts went in circles. She shuddered, recalling how close she had come to walking after Albert's ghost. But it hadn't been him, just her imagination. Or the Caul. One of the two. What about Siofra? She knew what she had seen. Or at least she knew what she'd thought she had seen. In the cold light of day, she was no longer sure of anything. Did she seriously believe the girl had entered and then returned from the Caul? (On the day he lost his wife Magellan claimed to have found Siofra in the Caul.) Baré had told her she must have been mistaken, confused even. Which begged the question: Who did Mae trust, herself or Baré? She remembered that last night Baré had wanted to go after the girl on her own. Had she expected this? How did the girl get through a locked door? What else was Baré not telling her about Siofra?

She put down the cup and lay back, closing her eyes. Her limbs were heavy. She felt a great weight pressing upon her, keeping her in bed. She knew she had done wrong yesterday. It had been for the right reasons, but Baré was correct to criticize her actions. She'd put the girl under a lot of pressure, and for what? The faces at the funeral had been as inscrutable as they ever were.

Baré came in quietly, rooted around, then went back out.

She was sleepwalking and you saved her, Mae. Yet she couldn't forget what she'd seen. Or thought she'd seen. Hadn't she been convinced it was Albert? Was it the Caul? Perhaps it was her eighty-one-year-old brain. What did she trust more?

She decided it was the hope—the dashed hope—that had her lying here, unable to get up. Hadn't she always wished for this, for the Caul to give him back? Then she wondered: What madness is this? The Caul takes, it never gives. That is its nature.

She shook her head. She was going soft. Age was catching up with her.

Mae dug Magellan's journals out from under her bed and lay back. She continued working her way through Year Seven, reading, skipping, skimming, pausing, flipping back, rereading, assessing the man's movements and relationships. Something had happened in the missing journal, Year Five. He was careful not to refer to it directly, or, she suspected, if he had done so he'd later cut or torn any reference out. Had he destroyed Year Five? Perhaps he had hidden it elsewhere. She should return to the camp to look for it.

Baré came back in. She looked flustered, ignoring Mae, rooting among her things.

"Jean," she said. Baré paused. "About yesterday. You were right. I was reckless at the funeral. I'm sorry."

Baré nodded stiffly. "That's okay. I was just worried about Siofra, that's all."

"We all are."

The woman gave her a tight smile, took her bag, and went back out, calling, "Siofra, I thought I said . . ." The door slammed shut in a gust of wind.

Mae went back to reading. The lack of light tired her eyes. She ended up holding the journal at arm's length the better to read it. Baré came and went a couple more times. It was hard to concentrate. She felt irritable and excluded. She wondered if this was how Baré had felt with Magellan, who laboured under a burden of secrets he was unable to share with anyone after the loss of his wife. She found it curious he had trusted Baré with Siofra but not around his work. Had he just been using her? She considered her own reasons for inviting Baré in. She'd hoped her apology to Baré would ease the tension between them, but Baré seemed more closed than ever. Baré's refusal to be open with her was becoming a problem. She wondered now if she had made a serious mistake inviting Baré here—was it the same error Magellan had made?

The stew smelled delicious. They would eat soon. Then she would get up.

Mae's thoughts continued in tight circles, asking herself the same questions she'd been pondering for days: Why hadn't the killer disposed of Magellan's body in the Caul? Why make murder look like suicide when a cursory examination would reveal the truth? There was one obvious answer: Something had gone wrong. Either the murder had been unplanned, or something had occurred to change plans. Hence the later burning of the camp. Alternatively, the killer had not expected an examination of the corpse. Magellan had been heavy. How had his body been lifted on to the hook? An associate? Two of them. She considered Baré and shook her head.

She stared at the wall and then it came to her. Things weren't just not in their usual places. Some of them weren't anywhere. They were missing. One of her pots. The spare burner. Bed clothes. Baré's bag. Hell. She sat up. She pulled on her smoky clothes. She yanked open the door.

She stopped in her tracks.

The jeep was half filled with Mae's gear. Siofra was standing up in the passenger seat and Baré was dragging a large plastic bottle of water over the pebbles. She stopped on seeing Mae.

"When did you decide to run?"

Baré stood upright, bit her lip.

"Is this about what I saw last night? How did she get out? The door was locked."

"Mae, you won't understand—"

"More evasions, Jean?"

Baré closed her eyes, shook her head ever so slightly.

Mae was standing between her and the jeep. Would Baré force the issue? She couldn't be sure. "Where were you going to go?"

Baré shrugged. "Away. They'll come—"

"Who?"

Baré said nothing.

Mae came to a decision.

She closed the open passenger door on Siofra firmly. Baré quickly followed Mae around the back of the jeep. "You don't know what you're doing. You're putting her in danger. Mae!" Calculation turning to desperation, thought Mae—but hers or mine?

She opened the driver's door, seeing her trap maps on the seat. Baré had planned to rob her of everything. To leave her with nothing to live on. The depths of the betrayal felt like a blow to the gut. She turned on the woman, but no words came. She felt a fool, a gull. How had she let this happen? Instead, she shook her head and got in.

She expected Baré to grab the door and there to be a horrible confrontation. But all the fight seemed to have left the younger woman now she was discovered and the lie was there between them. Siofra sat in frightened, wide-eyed silence. Less an accomplice and more a reluctant witness, or so Mae kept telling herself.

She started the engine and set off slowly. She looked back in her mirrors and saw Baré standing by the shack. Then, after a few seconds, she was running after them, arms wildly flailing like a wind-turbine's sails spinning in a gale.

Mae accelerated and fixed her gaze on the horizon ahead.

○

GROWING UP, Mae had learned you couldn't trust anyone to tell the truth. The church might explain to its orphans they were empty vessels to be filled with knowledge, but the sisterhood was careful not to teach anything that challenged the church's dream of a second, interstellar Exodus. ("Such as the laws of physics," complained Sister Ursula.) Even she, ever suspicious of others' motives, would not be drawn on her reasons for joining the church. ("Life is made of unexpected decisions," she'd respond dismissively.)

But it was living with Albert on Mars which taught Mae that the biggest lie of them all could be a person's declaration of honesty.

From the moment they started living together, Albert made it clear that it would be mostly impossible to talk about his work. His investigations were numerous, lasting from months to years. Dozens were ongoing at any one time, yet Mae could barely keep up with the few he told her about. The ones he shared were on a need-to-know basis: stories about to break, requests for Service help or threats made. If he was deep into an investigation of the Service, however, she knew because a distance grew between them. Often, the first she heard about a story were the headlines or messages clogging up her feeds: a few supportive, some angry, most concerned at the trouble being caused.

Did she mind that the greater part of his life was unknown to her? Both were fighting the good fight. In it together: his way and her way. What did it matter that each struggled alone? They had each other to hold at home. Wasn't justice supposed to be blind? (Sister Ursula: "Blindness is ignorance, pure and simple.") But Mae had convinced herself it was a matter of trust. Faith in your husband. He was trying to protect her. Just like they were each trying to protect the citizens of New Sheffield—of Mars, of the Exodus—from those who'd exploit them.

But it was Albert's weakness for conspiracies which truly tested her faith in him. Secret cabals. Religious sects. Shadowy elites. Ancient bloodlines. He never claimed to believe them, but he pored over every kind of crazy like it was today's news. Aliens who'd driven us off Earth. Death squads in the Service. Church suicide cults. Clans enslaving citizens. The ruling families of the New Order. The Exodus Lie. Light-drive breakthroughs. It was a reporter's job to question everything, but Albert took such blatant fictions seriously. "A conspiracy is a secular religion," he'd said, "a lie that tells an important truth about its believers." Yes, she'd agree, our deepest fears and desires. And Earth, Exodus, and the Caul were often bundled together as "The Big Lie"—one vast mega-conspiracy. Someone, he insisted, had to pay attention to the truths in The Big Lie.

If only Mae had done so. Then she might have stopped him running out on her.

○

MAE FLED WITH THE GIRL under an overcast sky. Last night's fog had been blown away by a stiff breeze, giving the jeep a free run across the pebbled plain. She rolled the window down, hoping a blast of air would help clear her fuzzy head. Her thoughts were a churning jumble, but she clung to just one: An explanation existed somewhere out here.

Baré's attempted betrayal had stirred up a lot of hurt and self-hatred Mae had believed long settled. What was it about her that drove people away? Albert had once accused her of being ruthlessly single-minded, then felt it necessary to add, "That's not a compliment." She'd taken too easily to the solitary life on Earth, preferring to be left alone to figure out the puzzle of her great loss. Perhaps she'd even welcomed the simplicity of her existence here. No one had been demanding swift results.

It wasn't long, however, before she got to wondering why Baré had waited until now to make her move. She could have run with Siofra any time. There had been plenty of opportunities. Why wait until this morning? The answer, obviously, was last night.

Mae was still haunted by what she'd seen in the mist. The girl had emerged from the Caul. She'd never heard of anybody coming back. Once you'd crossed over, you were gone. This immediately led to further thoughts: If Siofra'd been in and survived without losing her integrity, then there could be others in the Caul. And if she'd come back then why couldn't anyone else? Other long-dormant feelings were stirring. Everything on Earth led her back, no matter how circuitously, to Albert. Mae was desperate to find out the truth, but Siofra didn't speak. How could she possibly explain? How could a child even understand the importance of this question? Mae still wanted to ask the girl, but another factor was silencing her. She'd been adrift and alone so long she feared the answer.

They parked some distance away. Mae stared at the giant cone of split and fused rockets through the windscreen. The temple reminded her of a bulb she'd been told about in natural history class: It lay dormant for untold years, waiting for exactly the right conditions in which to flower. She remembered wondering, how long was too long?

She hadn't wanted to come back here, but Rawat's behaviour first at the fire set at Magellan's and then later at the funeral had been too suggestive.

If Baré wouldn't and Siofra couldn't tell Mae what she had seen last night in the mist by the shore, then perhaps the one person who worshipped the Caul could.

○

MAE AND SIOFRA APPROACHED the temple hand in hand. The cone was forbidding, looking like an aborted and long-abandoned attempt to blast off on a journey into the unknown. Siofra, however, stared in wide-eyed wonder at the split angles of its gimcrack geometry.

They found him inside, praying on his knees. Mae wondered if this was all he ever did. Behind the dormitories, an overgrown garden sufficed for Rawat's meagre needs—he trusted in his god's providence. She let go of Siofra's tugging hand, allowing the girl to disappear among the empty pews. Her quick steps echoed in the cavernous space.

The supplicant, who had fallen silent, raised his head. His eyes glittered. Ignoring Mae, he got slowly to his feet, his gaze following Siofra's skipping circuits of the walls.

"I've been waiting," he said, prayers forgotten.

All you do is wait, thought Mae, but said nothing.

"It was just a matter of time. Though I confess I never imagined it would be you."

"Who did you expect?" Mae asked carefully.

He smiled. "You brought Siofra to me, that is all that matters."

Mae couldn't fathom this disconcerting claim to have been expecting them. She'd only resolved to come here after she had left Baré. She wasn't even sure why she thought Rawat held any answers. Just because he was fixated on the girl, it didn't mean he had any true insight into her behaviour. He was a Cauler, believing all he wanted to believe. She asked herself what any of this had to do with finding Magellan's killer. The answer, she was beginning to think, lay with Siofra. Not just that she was a witness of some sort, but also that she might be part of the reason he was dead. She did not know why she thought this. Since last night she was no longer sure about her own motives here. Siofra had survived the Caul. This one fact changed everything. The Caul was not the universal destroyer Main's sober scientists claimed it to be. There had to be another explanation.

Which meant taking some of the irrational things spoken by Rawat seriously. (She imagined Albert raising an eyebrow at her.)

The man had turned, eyes back on Siofra as she stood by his altar, staring up in awe at the dark and crooked apex above.

"You're more than taken with her, aren't you?" said Mae quietly.

Rawat's eyes narrowed.

"I watched you the other day, at Magellan's camp. And looking at you now. You're afraid of her."

"The child is none of your business."

"So why is she yours?"

He said nothing.

"I was a church orphan," she continued. "Services three, sometimes four times, a day. We were taught that the heavens, the stars, were our refuge. Only there could humanity be saved. A second Exodus. I remember how the astronomer-priests looked up at the skies on Mars. It is the way you look at Siofra. The same reverence and fear."

"Then your astronomer-priests understood something you never will."

The temple creaked in the wind.

"I thought Magellan died because of his work. I thought that maybe he had made a breakthrough and there had been . . . consternation." She was amazed at herself, for talking to Rawat like this. Was she hoping that by confessing her failures he'd be moved to help her? Just like Albert and his conspiracies, she thought uncomfortably: Being wrong didn't mean you weren't also partly right. "But that's not what happened. Or at least I don't think that's why people were interested in him. I think Magellan died because of Siofra."

"Be careful of your trespasses, Mae," he said in a whisper.

She was silent, hoping to encourage him to elaborate.

"Magellan came to me, one day," he said slyly. "He was asking about the church. He pretended to be interested. But I saw through him. He wanted to know if I spoke to anyone off Earth."

"Off Earth?"

"Later, I learned he was talking to others on the shore. About leaving. He didn't want Main to know. He planned to take her away!"

"I don't believe you," she said, though she did.

"You don't believe anything of consequence. You won't allow yourself to believe and so you will never truly see."

Siofra suddenly took off, running around the rim of the temple, her feet pounding on the steel floor, the walls echoing.

"See what, Rawat?"

He was slowly rotating, intently following the girl's progress.

"Tell me about Siofra."

The girl ran out the open door. Mae resisted the urge to follow. The echoes of her small feet still reverberated off the walls.

Rawat turned to Mae. "How can I describe colour to a blind woman?" He shook his head sadly. "We each must discover Siofra for ourselves. Feel her in our hearts."

"Rawat . . ."

"That is your tragedy and the tragedy of all those like you." His mouth was an ugly sneer. "You are blind to the truth, yet you will never allow others to see for you."

Revelation and faith. The symbiotic mechanism underlying all religions with real longevity. A few were granted a vision of the truth, and others must believe in them unquestioningly. Everyone else could go to hell. She knew now that she had made a mistake coming here. He would never help her understand. He guarded his faith too jealously. It was who he was.

A cry broke the silence outside. Siofra. Rawat gave Mae a startled, revealing look.

Fool that I am, she thought as she moved as swiftly as she could to the door. No wonder he had been happy to let the girl go. He had been distracting Mae.

Outside, she found the girl dangling two metres off the ground. Kozlov held her aloft in one bearish paw. Siofra was now bawling in distress. The giant glared guiltily at Mae.

Rawat's bare feet ground the pebbles behind her. Slow, steady, in charge. She had an idea what was going on here, but she had made the mistake of coming alone. She'd have to be very careful. She did not approach. "Put her down, Kozlov," she said. "Don't make me cross with you."

He shook his head. The girl's legs kicked wildly as he held her up by the back of her fastened red coat. Was he hurting her?

"Kozlov, I mean it."

He glanced at Rawat. "Where Baré?"

"You should not have interfered in the natural order of things," said the Cauler to Mae. He spoke clearly and precisely, like he had been rehearsing these words. "Magellan is gone. Now she is at last free to fulfil her destiny. It is time."

"What are you talking about?" She moved so that she could keep both Rawat and Kozlov in her line of sight. She put her hand in a pocket, grasped the handle of her short knife.

"I thought I had been alone all these years," said Rawat darkly. "I believed I had been sacrificed, that as the last shepherd I had been forsaken. But I was wrong. I was being tested. Siofra is my reward. It is all in the liturgy. The Caul has been changing. It is a sign that we are living in the end of days. Siofra has come to lead over the last of the faithful. And you, Mae, you have brought her to us."

A gust of wind hit them and slammed into the temple, which cracked loudly.

"Where Baré?" asked Kozlov again.

"Jean's not here," said Mae. "She's not coming. She's staying away, Kozlov."

"Said Baré be here."

"Kozlov!" said Rawat, eyes wide in sudden exasperation. He stepped closer but so did Mae, almost reaching out to grasp Siofra. "Baré is not one of us. She isn't even one of them. She's a spy. Even Magellan didn't trust her. I should have told you—"

The bear howled in anger, raising the girl higher and for a horrible moment Mae thought he might dash her to the ground.

"Siofra has come to lead us over," repeated Rawat. But Mae was only half-listening, wondering how in the world to get Siofra down. "She does not belong out here on the shore," he continued. "She must return home. Isn't that right, Kozlov? It is her destiny to lead us."

"Destiny," echoed the bear hollowly.

Mae didn't like the sound of this. She remembered Magellan hanging in his cabin. Two people, she'd thought, needed to get his corpse up there. How long had Kozlov been under Rawat's spell? How had she not seen it at the funeral?

Rawat smiled again, his eyes sparking with triumph. "I have seen her. She and her father visiting the Cluster. I have seen them together and I have seen her . . . alone. In the night. She passes into the Cluster at high tide. She does not return for hours. *I have seen this.*"

A prickle of fear on the back of Mae's neck. She glanced around. She had never felt more alone. She'd walked into a trap with her eyes tightly closed. Ignorant old woman. How long had she been blind to these patterns on the shore?

"She will show us the way."

Siofra cried out.

Mae stepped closer to Kozlov, who eyed her suspiciously. But it was Rawat who held the bear's leash. He was the one to whom she must appeal.

"She's a frightened little girl," said Mae. "Whatever you imagine—"

"I do not imagine, I observe . . . I have seen it!"

"Rawat," said Mae wearily, eyes on him as she spoke. "You fast regularly. I've found you delirious and wandering the shore. You didn't know who you were. I've taken you home, cleaned you up, fed you, and put you to bed. Don't you think your recollections might be unreliable?"

The little man's eyes were tiny black beads as they glared his fury at her.

"She belongs to the Caul." He stamped his foot. "She must lead us!"

Siofra was snuffling and blubbering above their heads. Suddenly there was a crack like a sail snapping in a breeze. Mae looked up. The girl was a blur of movement in Kozlov's hand. Further shocks of displaced air, one after the other. Siofra flipped this way and that. Cracks and snaps like a bird beating its wings. Kozlov grunted. The girl seemed to flicker now, as if she were there and then not there. All of a sudden, she was falling to the ground. Her empty, still-buttoned coat and shirtdress hung limply in Kozlov's hand.

Half-naked, Siofra got to her feet and ran to Mae, clinging hard to her legs. Mae stared open-mouthed at the two men. Everyone lost for words. What had they just seen?

Kozlov had dropped the coat and was sucking at his hand like he had been bitten. His face was a mask of confusion and pain. A bear with a sore paw.

"See! She came from the Caul, and she must go back to it," gasped Rawat. "This is her destiny," he snarled, glaring threateningly.

Mae shuffled back, Siofra still clinging to her. "She is a child," she whispered doubtfully, "not an instrument of your faith."

Kozlov, still sucking his hand, was backing away. He was looking at Siofra with a kind of fascinated horror. Then he turned and ran from them with heavy footfalls.

"Kozlov!" yelled Rawat, taking several steps after him. But the bear didn't turn, didn't slow. Rawat swung around desperately. Mae looked at him and shook her head silently. The knife had come out of her pocket. She picked up the girl's clothes, helped her into them, grasped her hand, and, just as they'd arrived at the temple not half an hour ago, they left hand in hand. Neither looked back at the man on his knees, sobbing.

○

WHEN THEY WERE HALFWAY to the jeep, Mae emerged from the turmoil of thoughts concerning all she had just seen and heard to guiltily ask, "Did he hurt you?"

The girl, who was staring into the distance, shook her head.

After a minute Mae found herself also asking, "Do you go into the Caul often?"

Siofra looked at her, then shook her head.

"Was last night your first time?"

She shook her head again.

"Did your father know you went in?"

The pebbles crunched beneath their feet. Siofra nodded her head faintly.

They trudged on. Mae swallowed.

"Were you visiting your father and mother, last night?" she asked as they reached the jeep. The girl gave her a curious, inscrutable look. Mae opened the door and they both got in. She glanced at the temple one last time and started the engine.

"I want to tell you about someone," she said. "Someone I loved very much who may or may not have also gone into the Caul."

○

ALBERT NOT COMING HOME was not unusual. He'd get a message to her if he could but, very occasionally, days might pass until she got word, or he returned. He told her to sit tight, do nothing. He dealt with criminals and gangs. A Service officer making enquiries would do neither of them any favours. He was good at talking his way out of trouble and his editors were briefed on his plans. If Mae was worried, she was to talk to them.

After three days, Mae did just that. They told her to sit tight. Twelve hours later they got back to her. They had no idea of his whereabouts or even what story he had been chasing. There was a project he wasn't yet ready to discuss that he'd claimed he had a new lead to follow up. That was the last they had heard from him.

This was the moment when Mae knew. Not just where he'd gone but why. Yet she tried to convince herself it wasn't true, dutifully exploring all the other options first.

The Service had no record of his arrest or of anybody, alive or dead, matching his description being admitted to a medical facility. They asked if she wanted to list Albert as a missing person. Not yet, she said, taking a week's leave. She pulled strings, making her own enquiries. She talked to administrators, fellow officers, bonded and unbonded citizens, councillors—anyone he'd investigated who might hold a grudge. While a few suggested Albert had it coming, none betrayed the slightest culpability. With her leave over, she'd no choice but to report him missing. His disappearance didn't even make the evening feeds.

She hadn't expected to hear anything. He was too good at what he did. It had been building up to this, she realized now. His hunt for the truth behind his damned Big Lie: Earth, Exodus, the Caul. Or Main, Main, Main, as he'd taken to putting it, convinced that the shadowy dynastic families running the clan were up to their necks in blood and money. And no doubt his obsessions had triangulated all this activity back to Earth. Quarantined Earth. If Albert had gone there, he was never coming back.

Suspecting the truth didn't lessen her grief. They'd been together nearly twenty years. She was on the cusp of fifty. Unlike some couples, they'd never been a single entity. Yet Mae found making decisions alone terrifying. She looked into relocating, considered quitting the Service, even pondered following Sister Ursula back into the church. Who was she on her own? Not the better person she'd believed herself to be with Albert by her side.

Then a message dropped of a possible sighting. Some blurry orbital port footage of a fundamentalist Cauler sect stealing a rocket. She recognized him as the last to climb aboard. The ship had effortlessly evaded Service patrol vessels. By the time tracking had lost it four days later, it was still accelerating at 1G towards Earth.

Taking her husband of twenty years to discover if any truth lay in his Big Lie.

○

ON THEIR RETURN, they encountered yet more gray rivers and even a few silver ponds, which Mae had to navigate around. Rawat was right about one thing. The Caul was changing. She wasn't sure what it meant, only that Earth was evolving in ways she did not comprehend. She kept an eye on the fuel gauge, down to a quarter now. It had been full when she'd taken the jeep. Herself, she was running on empty.

As she drove Mae picked over all she'd seen and heard at the temple.

Siofra, sitting beside her, wore the same closed frown she'd had since they'd left. It was impossible to tell how what had happened was affecting her. Mae wondered, not for the first time, whether her dumbness was a choice. She wondered whether it was a kind of performance or deception. Her paranoid imaginings had Siofra talking to Magellan and Baré when no one else was around. She stared at the girl, who had come out of the Caul last night and, according to Magellan, also on the day her mother disappeared. How many other times had she done it? When had she started? Why had the berg reacted to Siofra like it had? Why had Gemma feared her daughter? Why did Magellan believe he'd betrayed his wife after Siofra was born? Where was the journal covering the birth? Did Magellan destroy Year Five or had someone taken it? And what had Siofra done to free herself from Kozlov?

Questions, questions—and to how many did Baré hold the answers?

Rawat had said Magellan had been trying to get Siofra off Earth without Main knowing. Was that even possible? If anyone could help it'd be the cash-rich churches. He must have been desperate. But what could he offer them, other than Siofra?

"I've been reading your father's notes," she said. "He spent so much time out in the Topologie. You did, too, I think. Like a second home." The girl didn't respond. "Your father talked about a place called the attractor. Do you know what he found there?"

The girl glanced at Mae and faintly shook her head.

"Never mind. You met Jean out there, didn't you?"

The girl didn't respond.

"Siofra, Jean isn't . . ." Mae began but did not know how to continue.

The girl was looking at her expectantly. It was a look that reminded Mae of a stray cat she and Albert had once taken in. This emaciated, sick animal was sitting by their hutch one morning. When they'd opened the door, it had cautiously come in. They'd fed it and given it a corner to sleep. They had made enquiries of their neighbours, but no one knew anything about the animal. Pets were rare on Mars. So rare you hung on to them. They had found a vet and paid money to have her checked out. The vet had found an abscess in her mouth and removed a tooth. He gave them a course of pills which they had had to go to great lengths to get down her throat. They had grumbled at first but as the cat recovered and became less docile and more affectionate, they had enjoyed having the animal around. Their work meant that each often came home to an empty hutch. Now there was always someone to greet them. Someone who wanted food and stroking, a warm lap to sit on. They had a collar made. They gave her a name. And then Mae got in one day, two weeks after the cat had first appeared at their door, and she was gone. There was no sign of her. They had no idea how she had got out. They had taken her in, mended her and then she'd disappeared from their lives forever.

"Jean knows, doesn't she," said Mae, trying again. "About you and the Caul?"

The girl was staring out the windscreen, that closed frown on her face.

The light, Mae noticed, was fleeing the sky. "Be dark soon," she said.

Rawat had called Baré a spy. She'd almost missed it in all the drama. Magellan had had his suspicions, hadn't he? She knew Main had agents here. Or at least she believed they had. She'd never have suspected Baré until this morning. Could Main have been involved in Magellan's death? What did they know about Siofra? Where had Baré planned to take the girl, this morning? To what end was all this leading?

When Mae had started this, she'd only been interested in identifying Magellan's killer. Somehow, however, everything seemed to turn on knowing the truth about Siofra. Was the girl really the key to everything?

If so, that was going to make what she had to do next all the harder.

○

BARÉ EMERGED FROM MAE'S SHACK before they'd even parked.

"Thought I'd never see you again," she said to Mae, her eyes wet and accusing. She was hugging Siofra as tightly as a mother reunited with a lost daughter. If this was an act, it was pretty damn convincing.

"We need to talk," said Mae.

"About last night?"

"About everything you haven't told me."

Mae read contrition and fear in Baré's face. The younger woman nodded, still clutching Siofra.

"You should eat."

"Siofra and I visited the traps. Let's make it a feast. I'm starved."

They removed the marbits from the back of the jeep that Mae and Siofra had recovered from the traps. "I'll skin and gut two of these now," said Baré.

Siofra and Baré disappeared round the back and Mae, her bones aching from all the activity, retreated inside the shack. She sat on her bed, ready to lie down. Could she trust Baré with the girl? She hadn't the strength to care. The days and nights were tiring her out. The stew sat cold and untouched on the burner.

She stood up and reached for the bottle. She took a long swig but did not return it to its place. It no longer burned her throat. Was she simply getting used to it or had Baré watered it down? It was the kind of thing Albert had done back on Mars. Worried about her drinking. Thinking of you, he'd said. We're a team. We need to look out for each other. She hadn't thought that at the time. She'd thought of it as the most insidious form of betrayal. Someone taking responsibility for you. An intervention, for god's sake. He'd made her feel ashamed to be herself. She'd never forgiven him for that.

She took another big swig, contemplating what was coming next. Once they'd eaten, she'd have the strength to deal with Baré. First, asking her a lot of questions and then, depending on her answers, perhaps forcing the woman to go. It was risky. Baré would be unlikely to leave quietly without Siofra. She'd have to prepare herself. But she wasn't going to do what Baré had tried to do to her. There would be no deceit. She would look the woman in the eye when she'd made her decision.

She took another drink. She felt dog tired. She had to haul herself off her bed. On her feet she felt almost ready to pass out. She shook her head to clear it. I should have eaten, she told herself. I have to be ready for every eventuality.

The floor was suddenly rising up towards her. It hit, hard. Pain lanced through her body. She was sprawled, leaning against her bed. Why was it so dark in here? Everything looked hazy.

She could see under her bed. The journals weren't there. That's where she'd left them. Baré. She'd been reading the journals in their absence. Her heart beat in her chest but it seemed so far away. She felt old. Broken. When she tried to get up, she found she couldn't. Darkness in the corners of her eyes. A terrible weight descended on her chest.

The door opened. She tried to look up but couldn't. She saw a pair of legs. They stood in the door. They approached slowly. She heard her name being called from a long way away. A hand held her chin. She saw Baré's distant face, like it was at the end of a tunnel, eyes peering down at her like she was some kind of specimen.

And then all was dark.

YEAR SEVEN

Day 13, Month 4

Their intentions are well-meaning, but I tire of this steady stream of minders. It is not only my former Facility colleagues who come every other day to cook or tidy or entertain Siofra or otherwise make a nuisance of themselves. My fellow wreckers also do not trust me to be left to my own devices. Sometimes I sneak away. I stand on the ridge and watch the Cauldron waves roll in, pounding the shore like a legion of hammers. The roaring of these assaults echoes off the great bowl of the sky. I stare into eternity and wonder why it is so gray. Eventually, they come to find me and draw me away, in case I am so grief-stricken I will be compelled to follow the last journey of my wife. (Dr. Carlyle calls it "Gemma's great sacrifice." That says more about her than my wife.) They tell me I must not blame myself for what happened. They know nothing.

Day 16, Month 5

Siofra's second birthday. To avoid unwanted visitors, we rose early and headed into the Topologie. I remember the days when I couldn't enter it, being roped to Gemma. And, once inside, the endless measurements she demanded, searching for the attractor. Now I hunt for other structures, ones with features unrelated to higher dimensions. Structures like the Shell, which exhibit activator/inhibitor characteristics. I explore structural phyllotaxis (Fibonacci is everywhere!) and indulge my love of shear mapping. The Topologie is no longer a mystery, at least not one I care to solve.

Siofra had fun, I think. I had no immediate objective, so we simply enjoyed our visit, climbing the Shell and picnicking on Leviathan. We looked out over the fog, structures sticking out like peaks emerging through clouds. We were climbers, on top of the world.

On the way home, Siofra pointed at something and for a second I thought I glimpsed someone in the fog. If it is not a phantom of my imagination, who can it be?

[Pages cut out]

Day 19, Month 6

Siofra spent an hour in the attractor alone. I wish she could tell me what draws her down there. Doc Machalek claims to be "reasonably unconcerned" by her refusal to talk and yet when he looks at her, he frowns. Every time she enters the attractor I worry, however. I fear she may not come back out again. *[Rest cut.]*

Day 30, Month 6

Finally, we know the identity of our mysterious figure. Jean Baré, one of Dr. Carlyle's scientists, who walked out of the Facility a year ago. She lives on the other side of the Topologie.

She was walking in the fog along one of my tracks to the site when we nearly ran her down. I was shocked at first, calling her a damn fool. However, Jean was apologetic: admitting she had trespassed. She is very young—in her mid-twenties—too young to be lost on Earth. She told me it had taken nearly a year to penetrate the fog. I asked her why she was here: "Exploring, discovering. No one knows anything about this place," she said, adding with a shy smile,

"Only you." I laughed. "What makes you think I know anything?" "Because I've seen you enter its heart." She fixed me with her gaze: "What's it like?" I ducked the question, asking whether the Topologie disturbed her. She shrugged. "No more than anything else here." We would have talked more but Siofra, normally rather coy around strangers, was restless, excited by this new diversion. We drove away, everyone enthusiastically waving.

Day 7, Month 7

Met Baré again. She keeps to (or is kept to) the edge of the Topologie. I told her it is the best place for her, but she snorted at my "presumption." I asked how it was she had time for explorations (most wreckers spend their days subsisting: farming, hunting, repairing). She leaned close and whispered, as though someone other than the stones might overhear, that an associate in the Facility took pity on her and left supplies.

She is curious, fascinated by the Topologie yet untroubled by the Cauldron. Doesn't she fear it? She shrugged, telling me she was careful but if she did enter it then so what? Either she'd be dead and it didn't matter, or she'd find out exactly where her predecessors had gone. "Have you heard of Peter Pan?" she asked. I nodded but warned: The Cauldron is no Neverland. She shook her head. "You misunderstand. Peter thought death an awfully big adventure."

Siofra was delighted to see Baré, and we were delayed by an hour.

Day 19, Month 7

Arrived home to find Dr. Carlyle waiting. We have barely spoken since Gemma's passing. I asked what she wanted. She told me I ought to be careful in the Topologie. I said I'd been careful for six long years. "Forgive me, Carl, but alone you're blundering," she said. "I warned Gemma of the dangers and now I'm warning you."

Of course, this upset me. You know nothing of what we found in there, I told her. No one does.

"You don't appreciate the stakes here," she said. "Main doesn't care about saving Earth. It's a lost cause. Even if we could banish the Caul, it'd be thousands of years before Earth was habitable again. This planet is dead, but the Caul is a speculative opportunity Main cannot resist."

Opportunity for what? I asked, disgusted.

She looked at me, a finger looped through her damned infinity necklace. "The Caul is pure matter transformation. Whoever figures out how to control it controls the future."

Day 12, Month 8

A curious conversation with Baré. We were discussing the Topologie, as much as I dare since she keeps links to the Facility. I mentioned how Siofra's roaming slows progress—I daren't let her out of my sight—when out of the blue Baré, surprising us both I think, offered to watch over Siofra. I was taken aback. I asked her why and she said: "I enjoy her company, and I'd like to go deeper into the Topologie." Unsure of the wisdom of either, I explained I worried how Baré would react to the spatial distortions deeper inside. She glanced at Siofra, then back at me. "Your daughter seems fine, and I've got two decades on her," she said. Laughing, I told her I'd think about it.

Day 19, Month 8

Lost Siofra for an hour today. I was furious and this upset her. Why the hell can't she talk? It would make matters so much simpler. Doc Machalek has twice brought up the subject of "her autism" recently. Einstein didn't speak until he was five, I reminded him. "That is not the consolation you believe it to be," he replied.

Day 24, Month 8

Saw Baré. We discussed her accompanying Siofra and I on our visits. She was guarded at first—has my initial reluctance put her off?—but she agreed to give it a try. We'll begin tomorrow.

Day 3, Month 9

Jean is a godsend. She and Siofra disappear for hours, exploring and playing games in the Topologie while I work, untroubled. I've covered a remarkable amount of ground in the last few days alone, confirming and correcting notes that, in places, are now half a decade old. One thing I have made clear to both Jean and Siofra is that they must not try to enter the heart of the Topologie—even if I go there. It is out of bounds.

Day 18, Month 9

Invited Jean for dinner. She is an interested listener, asking pointed questions which require thought before I answer. (I am reminded of my initial encounters with Gemma, refusing to accept simple explanations, demanding details before making a judgement: nullius in verba.) However, I am careful, couching certain discoveries as speculations.

Siofra slept in the back of the jeep when I drove Jean home. She has a tiny place, half the size of the caravan. It looked cosy.

I want to sleep but my brain fizzes with unexpected thoughts.

Day 30, Month 9

Hannu came to repair the broken pump on the rain tank. He was nonplussed to find Jean visiting the camp. He stayed for lunch and asked Jean a lot of questions about the Facility. He is down on Hastings, complaining the director hasn't pushed his case with Main. Hannu is good at hiding it but there is a haunted look in his eyes.

Most of the wreckers have it. Sousa blames the Cauldron. "It hollows us out," she says. Sometimes I look out from the Shell at the Topologie in the early evening, yellowing in the setting sun, and I too feel an emptiness behind my eyes.

Day 3, Month 10

Waited an hour for Jean in our agreed spot. She did not turn up. Siofra was upset. Eventually we drove into the Topologie on our own. I got little done.

Day 4, Month 10

No Jean again. This is no good. She knows I rely on her.

Day 5, Month 10

Another no show.

Day 6, Month 10

I feel terrible. Jean has been ill. When she didn't come again, we drove to her place. She was in her bed, barely conscious with a fever. I carried her to the jeep and drove straight to the Facility. Doc Machalek examined Jean and said a small cut on her arm had become infected. She is also run-down. She hasn't been getting sufficient vitamins from her diet. He wanted to keep her in the infirmary, but Jean refused. She was angry with me for taking her to the Facility. She's sleeping in the caravan, after taking some soup. She already has colour in her cheeks.

Day 10, Month 10

Returned Jean to her “cottage.” Siofra restless on the way home and I couldn’t think of anything to say to calm her. The camp feels empty without Jean.

Day 11, Month 10

I asked Jean if she’d occasionally like to stay over at the camp. I’d clear a space for her. I said I was worried about her living alone. She was unsure at first but said she was happy to give it a go if it would make things easier.

Day 12, Month 10

We cleared out one of the storage cabins. I put the spare cot I’d slept in while Jean was ill inside it. Jean has brought some things and made it homely. We had a meal, and I found a bottle I’d saved to celebrate.

Day 18, Month 10

Jean has moved her things out of the cabin and into the caravan.

Day 20, Month 10

I don’t think I’ve ever seen Siofra so delighted. She wakes us by snuggling into bed between us, her face so joyful I feel sure she’ll burst if she doesn’t speak. I asked Jean if there was anything she needed. “Everything I want is here,” she told me.

And I have my freedom to work.

Day 8, Month 1

The Twins had the three of us over for a celebratory dinner. We talked long into the night. Serpa was full of questions about us: how, when, where, even *why*! The Twins are as pleased about how matters have worked out as we are. However, Serpa told us to be wary of Main while Sousa discreetly warned me: “Jean is very young. For you, this is a happy arrangement, as much for Siofra’s sake as for your own.” I am lucky to count such perspicacious women among my friends.

The work remains paramount: It takes up all my time. If I can finish writing up our findings and present the implications to Main and the PA, we may yet find a way to rescind the quarantine. I must be circumspect. It would be easy to lose control of the situation. Serpa is right. Once Main has any inkling of the truth, I am done for.

I wonder what Gemma would say. I suspect she’d be thoroughly exasperated.

Day 11, Month 1

Suffered an extraordinary visit. About midday, I heard my name being yelled stridently. I left my cabin to find Rawat, stalking back and forth outside the caravan. Jean and Siofra, having locked themselves inside, watched him fearfully. When he saw me, Rawat grew fierce, walked around me in circles, denouncing my trespasses on the Topologie. He accused me of “interfering.” Said I was no better than the “curs in the Abomination” (the Facility). He said I was a “despoiler of all that was holy.” He denounced me for “humanising the Caul.” How dare we seek to understand it. To do so was to reduce it. To see it in our limited terms. “It is bigger than all of us. It is the embodiment of God!” He turned on Jean, calling her the whore of Babylon. She responded with gales of laughter. Rawat screamed profanities until she opened the caravan door. Siofra followed. And that is when the very odd thing happened. Rawat fell silent. He approached Siofra and fell down on his knees at her feet, unable to look at her. It was an act of worship.

By now I'd had quite enough. I dragged Rawat to his feet and sent him packing. He was slow about it, unable to tear his eyes off my daughter. I told Jean to take Siofra back to the caravan. She continued to find the whole thing very funny. I did not, and I told her to be quiet.

Day 13, Month 2

Too often, I sicken myself. I betrayed my wife and now I fear I will betray Jean. Is that why I am thinking suspicious thoughts?

This morning, realizing I'd left my notebook, I returned to camp. Arriving, I saw the door to my cabin was open. I always shut it before I leave, so I was disconcerted. I opened my storage cabinet to retrieve the notebook and found this journal sitting on top instead of filed below. Normally, the storage cabinet is locked. It would have been had I remembered the notebook. Someone had been here.

Outside, Jean and Siofra were playing with the shards. I was going to say something until I saw Jean's face. There was not the slightest look of guilt on it. Anyone else would have exhibited some embarrassment. But Jean acted as if nothing were amiss. I don't always take the key with me. She could have been reading my notes and journals any time I was not around. She could have been secretly uncovering my discoveries for months. The remark I was going to make suddenly took on the significance of a challenge to our entire relationship. One from which I retreated.

Jean was only in the Facility for a couple of years before she walked out. She'd been living on the shore more than a year before I found her. I have heard stories of spies on Earth: in the Facility, among the wreckers. People sent by the Service or Main (a clan of bitterly divided families), watching us. Spies observing spies in a circle of suspicion.

Day 18, Month 2

This morning, I stood at the shore looking out into the endless wave-tossed gray. The high tide seemed to mutter mournful words to itself. The waves to wallow. I had brought a small bundle of flowers cut from the Twins' planters, but I could not bring myself to cast them in. Instead, I drove to Jameson's tree. Her shrine. I looked up at the gnarled, wind-scoured trunk and branches. Long dead, yes. But somehow intact. Unbowed, Gemma said, when she first set eyes on it. I lay the flowers at its base.

DAY SEVEN

MAE DIDN'T KNOW HOW LONG SHE'D BEEN AWAKE. She drifted in and out of odd, uncertain dreams in which shadowy forms came and went, like ghostly visitors. The transition between unconsciousness and consciousness was a fuzzy border crossed and recrossed. Eventually, bodily sensations—pounding temples, aching back and legs, a mouth dry as sand—grew too wretched to ignore. She wondered if she were dying.

At last, she surfaced, blinking at four familiar dark walls. The porthole window, through which light streamed, glared like an eye outside staring in. She lay on her bed, alone. On the floor beside her was a cup of water.

She reached out unsteadily to grasp the cup. She had no strength to raise herself to a sitting position. She held the cup over her mouth and tipped it, not caring that half the icy water soaked her.

She waited for the pain in her head to recede then slowly raised herself to a sitting position. She hunched forward, leaning on her aching thighs. The vodka bottle lay beside the bed. The cabin was still and empty-looking.

She got to her feet, stumbled across the floor, and shoved open the door. She fell and retched violently. When she'd finished, she felt wrung out. Her pulse tolled in her skull like a bell repeatedly struck.

A bleak, windswept day. The jeep was gone, of course. She was alone and felt sicker than she'd ever felt in her life. She retreated inside, back to bed. Lying there, she tried to sleep but her thoughts whirled in bitter and self-recriminatory circles. She drank more water, sparingly.

Finally, she got up.

She examined the vodka bottle. Unscrewing the cap, she sniffed, wincing at the acrid spirit reek. It would mask the taste, of course. Smart of Baré. She wondered how many sleeping pills were used. She hadn't drunk that much. Then she asked herself whether Baré had tried to do more than knock her out for a few hours.

She decided not to think about that for the moment.

Her stomach, so rarely hungry, growled. She needed sustenance. Yet she could barely move. She hurt everywhere. Ached so she wished she were dead. It wasn't the deep soreness of old age. She felt neither used up nor worn out, but like she'd been utterly smashed. Broken on a wheel.

She imagined dying, staring at the junk she'd gathered around herself over the second half of her life. Soon she'd be gone and it'd be scavenged. Her life's remains broken up, dispersed, and reused. Not long after, she would survive only fleetingly in the memories of those who'd known her, just like Albert only now survived in her fractured mind. A trace, the fading ghost of a person. When those who remembered her also died so too would fade any sense she'd ever existed. She'd vanish completely. Until recently, such bleak thoughts had been a relief: Nothing more was expected of her. Now, however, they bothered her. No lover would mourn her passing. No enemy would dance triumphantly on her grave. She was wrong to think that soon she would cease existing. It had already happened, long ago. She had simply forgotten how to live.

Only once had she felt more deeply betrayed and abandoned. But she didn't want to think about Albert, the hurt around which feelings of upset and loss tended to accrete. Was this the pattern of her life? Bitter loneliness haunted by companions who'd drifted in, then rapidly out of, her life. Everyone moved on. Only she was stuck here, paralysed. Waiting for death, for rebirth, for she did not know what. Thirty years she'd survived, subsisted, but with Magellan's death, with his lost little girl, she'd found purpose for a brief few days.

Now it was gone.

She beat herself up over her stupidity. No one was to blame for this outcome but herself. She'd as good as shoved Baré and Siofra out the damn door. In making it clear to Baré that she wasn't trusted, Mae had forced the woman to act to protect herself.

She stared longingly at the bottle and the oblivion—possibly permanent—it contained. She reached for it. Stepping outside, she unscrewed the cap. She stared at the liquid's clear promise. Such apparent purity. She tipped the bottle up and poured the poison over the stones.

Stiffly, she stripped off her clothes and washed, using the tank's icy water. It was getting low. Well, there'd been three of them. When had it last rained? she wondered. Until recently she'd have known. Survival depended on such important facts and there'd been little else in her life to think about.

Still angry with herself, she tidied the shack, appalled by the gaps, by just how much Baré had taken from her. The ache inside was worse than her sore limbs. She wanted to hate Baré but couldn't manage it. The scientist, this alleged spy, was likely just following orders in taking Siofra, and Mae had unknowingly helped her. Loss and regret throbbed in her chest like another heartbeat.

She looked for Magellan's journals, thinking she might find clues as to where they'd gone. But the journals were missing. Some detail about them from last night nagged at her but she couldn't properly recall it. Why had Baré taken them? What did she not want Mae to know? Could there be another reason why she'd run? Mae's tired, foggy mind struggled to provide any answers.

Baré had left one of the marbits Mae and Siofra had found in the traps yesterday. She chopped up some leaves and made herself a tasteless stew, which she nevertheless wolfed down. Food did her no end of good.

As she ate, she pondered what to do, though she wished only to curl up and sleep. The more she considered Baré's actions and possible reasons the more worried she grew. If Baré had acted impulsively to get herself and Siofra away from Mae, then what she'd done was reckless and stupid. Who knew what trouble they'd get into? How would she deal with other penitents, like Kozlov or Rawat? Or the Facility? Baré's life out here wasn't even self-sufficient. If, on the other hand, Baré had some plan or goal in mind that involved taking Siofra then Mae couldn't simply abandon the girl to her.

Besides, Mae had promised herself she'd keep the girl safe.

If Baré had a plan there was little Mae could do until she divined exactly what that might be. And if Baré were responsible for Magellan's death . . . well, Mae didn't want to think about that right now either. It was too painful. Instead, she tried putting herself in the head of a lonely and vulnerable woman who feared Mae's reaction to what she had seen by the shore the other night. Baré had obviously been scared of Mae and decided running was her best option. Perhaps she wanted only to protect Siofra. She knew a killer was out here and, like Mae, had reasoned they were after Siofra now. If Baré and Siofra were going to run they'd need a refuge. Somewhere safer than here.

Mae just had to figure out where that was.

It was already afternoon. She went outside, looking in every direction like a dog sniffing for a scent. She examined the pebbles for marks left by the departing jeep. Nothing clear. She'd no way of being certain which way they had gone. She could head in any direction and most likely it would be wrong. It was hopeless.

But I have to try, she thought.

Wind buffeted her, musty smelling. The air tasted of dankness and age. The stew in her stomach sat like a stone. Baré's home lay in one direction, the Facility in another. Baré wouldn't go to either place for very long. There was a third possibility, but it was some distance. She didn't think she could make that, not this late in the day.

Back inside, Mae filled her pack with what she needed. A container held the remains of her stew. She was so stiff it hurt bending over to put on her moccasins. She closed her door and set off, heading west at a slow but steady pace.

○

QUITTING WAS ALIEN TO MAE. She was an orphan. She'd started with nothing, not even a name, and slowly she'd assembled a life: career, home, husband. There'd even been an (illegal) pet for a time. She'd worked too hard to walk out on anything. But then, as her fiftieth year approached, Mae had seen all she'd acquired slipping from her grasp. First the cat. Then her husband. Alone, she couldn't afford the rent. A month after Albert had gone, she was forced to move to a single hutch. Her life was shrinking around her.

At the time, she hadn't noticed. On learning that Albert had gone to Earth with the Terran Church of the Second Resurrection, she'd started her own investigation. The church was a fervent believer in a second Eden: Earth, they said, was being reborn. The barren, denuded surface was the rind of a cocoon inside of which this new Eden grew. Followers were sent ahead to lay the groundwork for their flock. They'd enter the Caul as new apostles: Nobodies transformed into somebodies.

Six months before he vanished, Albert had begun attending church services. According to the adherents she'd spoken to, he'd quickly become one of the devout. He'd been a capable organizer, improving recruitment and retention. His donations had helped pay for members' flight training. She knew Albert's methods. This was infiltration. Within months he was essential to the leadership. In aiding the church, he'd committed two big crimes. The donations were significant, and she traced them back to dormant accounts linked to a recent fraud story—details he'd kept secret from the Service. Secondly, he'd used Mae's Service ID to secure a ship disembarkation permit. Explaining that gave her no end of trouble.

Mae now knew the how of Albert's disappearance, but the why still eluded her. Yes, conspiracies were his weakness. His Big Lie had three strands. One: Exodus was a con to get humanity off planet. Two: Earth was not dead but instead a paradise regained, a bountiful playground for the elite. Three: The truth about the Caul was both known and concealed. Where the conspiracies agreed, they complimented one another. Where they contradicted, they encouraged fevered speculation. The key player, in Albert's view, was Main: profiting from orbital life, running Earth's research stations, investigating the Caul. But Main's controlling and competing families had long resisted reporters' attempts to penetrate the clan's structural opacity: It was a black box. Had Albert concluded that to settle it all one way or another, he had no choice but to visit Earth and see for himself? Mae still couldn't believe he'd sacrificed everything—her, foremostly!—over such blatant fictions. Why do it? Why now?

Why? Why? Why? Not knowing ate her up.

She was at a crossroads. Forget Albert, and move on with her life, or follow him.

The decision was never consciously taken. In her investigations Mae had found other churches desperate to get to Earth. She'd joined a congregation, telling herself it was to understand. But she kept coming back. Their services' constancy and regularity were comforting, reminding her of childhood. Then came an opportunity. She raised her hand. Helped acquire another permit. Every day she expected to be caught. Most illegal flights were foiled. But within months, Mae, who'd never walked out on anything, had left the remains of her life behind and was on her way to Earth.

○

MAE WALKED WITH A PURPOSE she hadn't felt in years. It was all the fault of Magellan and Siofra. Others, you were told, provided meaning to life: Living for somebody else was a distraction from your own emptiness. It wasn't always true. She'd pursued Albert to Earth, waiting decades by the Caul for a glimpse of his ghost, but in the end, she'd been the one haunting the shore. Siofra, by contrast, was a defenceless orphan she barely knew. Yet responsibility for the child burned in Mae like a cold flame.

Mae's original pace had slowed markedly and after only an hour she knew she'd never make it before nightfall. She should turn back, get a good night's sleep, and set out again tomorrow. However, worry and urgency kept her going. What if she missed them?

Fearing the Caul's influence, she kept checking she was heading the right way. It always got you when you weren't thinking straight. When you weren't entirely yourself.

She encountered Caul streams, some she stepped over, others she had to follow until they vanished into the ground. She rounded a silver pond reflecting the sky like a polished mirror and stumbled in a place where the pebbles under her feet lay in gray pools. The Caul was growing alarmingly restless in a manner she had never seen before. For the first time its activity was making her fearful.

Wind whipped and snarled. She passed dead and rusted rocket ships lying on their sides like beached whales, remembering seeing Siofra hiding in one. She thought about the girl and the Caul, no longer sure what she understood. It was another reason for going after the pair. Who or what was Siofra? She had to know.

Increasingly tired, she pushed herself until, two hours after she'd left her shack, she found she hadn't the legs to go any further. Sinking to the ground, she cursed herself for ever setting out. She'd been in no state for this desperate expedition.

She drank water and ate the remains of her tasteless stew, already missing Baré's cooking. A few minutes later, she tried getting to her feet but didn't have the strength.

Fretful, she checked her kit. If she weighed down her tarpaulin, she could shelter under it for the night. But she'd get no sleep. Maybe she should keep going. However, a cloudy sky meant no stars to navigate by. She could easily go wrong. And she feared stumbling blindly into one of these Caul intrusions. In the end she decided to keep walking while there was still light. Returning to her shack was not even considered.

She hadn't gone more than half a kilo before she heard a rumbling behind her. Turning, she saw Hannu's ugly hodgepodge of a lorry crossing the plain. She waved but he must have already seen her for its course had altered.

The lorry rolled to a stop. He climbed down from the cab. "Hey! I didn't know you had traps out here."

Mae smiled at him. "I don't."

"Jeep broken down?"

She shook her head. "Jean took it."

"She took Siofra too?"

Mae nodded. "What are you doing?"

He hugged himself against the wind. "Spot of scavenging."

"Here?" These rockets had been stripped decades ago.

"Always more to find. But the ground's got way too soft out this way."

"Can I ask a favour, Hannu?"

"Anything, Mae. You know that."

"Can we get out of the wind?"

Once ensconced in his cab she gave a simplified account of what had happened.

"Sounds like we need to move quickly," he said.

She nodded.

"Which way do you think they went?"

She pointed west.

The electric engine hummed loudly as they set off. Mae's seat was hard—she felt every bump and dip—and the cab interior, cannibalised from many different vehicles, was a Frankenstein's monster of mismatched pieces disinclined to fit together properly. Everything rattled and creaked as if the lorry might shake itself apart at any moment. She got the impression that all that was holding it together was spit and an engineer's dogged belief in his own construction. Indeed, Hannu, normally so chatty, was silent and looking intently ahead as if sunk in concentration.

It was clear to everyone that Hannu preferred machines to people. He liked, he said, things he could dismantle and put back together again: "I hate not knowing what makes stuff tick." Mae imagined he was disappointed you couldn't take apart people to figure them out. She was not above feeling the same.

"Do you never get sick of us?" she asked to break the silence. "You're like an old-time doctor, regularly called out to help keep us penitents going."

Hannu laughed. "No chance, I'd die of loneliness."

Mae didn't believe that. There were times when he was so intent on one of his machines you couldn't get him to listen to you let alone come out and take a look at a busted turbine. Once she'd found him brooding in his junkyard and he'd ignored her like she wasn't even there. She'd left him what she'd come to trade and a couple of days later he'd shown up out of the blue, carrying his tools. She'd been told that a couple of times Hannu had parked his lorry half a kilo from the Facility and stayed there for days. No one knew if this was a protest or an attempt to elicit sympathy as by then Director Hastings had forbidden anyone from speaking to him. Sometimes Hannu's desperation to get off Earth could get the better of him.

The lorry slowed: A twisting gray torrent ahead cut them off. "Something's happened," he muttered, forced now to drive alongside the new river.

"Rawat says the Caul's in its last days," said Mae.

He grunted. "Been fasting again, has he?"

"Talking himself into crossing over."

"The Caul is a physical system. If it has changed, then something is making it change. Simple as that. No driver, no change."

She looked at the river, three metres wide now, a snaking and roiling gray mass cutting angrily through the plain. "How long has it been now, Hannu?" she asked him.

"Fifteen years. Sister'll be thirty now. My older brother . . ." He sighed.

She'd once asked him how he'd ended up working off Mars when he missed his family so much. You know what hellholes the mines are, he'd replied. She did. Main worked the miners half to death to meet impossible quotas. Hannu's grandparents had been among the first to settle New Antelope. A ten-year contract became a life sentence the moment they had kids. Hannu's parents had signed with Main on their sixteenth birthdays, the choice being work or starvation. They had met in the deep core mines, comparing art-neuralink scars. Soon enough they'd had three children. They had also conceived a plan to escape. One child had to get out and earn enough off-world to buy passage for the others. His parents had bet everything on Hannu. They bought him a ship engineer's education, paid for by his father working the extra shifts that finally killed him. Ship work was dangerous, but well paid. They'd calculated twelve years to lift the whole family out. He was nine years in when he'd fetched up here.

"I'd just like to know they're okay," he said. "No word in fifteen years. Those Main bastards. Screw you any way they can. Number of times I visited the Facility after I got here." He shook his head. "Months before they'd even talk to me. Once they'd listened to my story it was more waiting. I offered my help. I could have been useful. Hastings was tempted, I could tell. I'd survived out here, alone. Told him about my family. I wasn't asking for much. If I could just work, send the pay to my brother. He claimed it would have to be cleared first. Of course, they said no. I figured they could at least let us exchange messages. Another no from Main security. They hadn't even told my family I was still alive, and they never would. Wreckers don't officially exist."

He'd got worked up now and she was half sorry she'd said anything. "The Caul's influence is far and wide," she admitted.

"You think the Caul's to blame?"

"Don't you?"

"The Caul's a flaming excuse. Like the quotas on Mars. An opportunity to squeeze dry those caught in your trap."

"Hannu . . ."

He snorted. "Take Magellan. I don't wanna speak ill of the dead, but he was happy for me to fix his stuff, not so ready to put in a good word to his masters."

"Do you know that?"

"Some things you just know. Facility's full of his sort. Gotta think pretty highly of yourself to choose coming here. Have to imagine you're pretty special."

She glanced down into the footwell. "Gave you his boots," she said.

The river they were driving alongside entered a small silver lake sitting in the plain. *A lake on the plain.* Mae had never seen a lake here before. The gray was invading the land. Hannu had called the plain soft. Even the ground was turning uncertain.

"It's odd," she found herself saying. "You and I have been trading fixes for moccasins for years. But just days after Magellan dies without his boots on, I find you're wearing them."

The loud rolling of the lorry wheels couldn't quite fill the silence in the cab.

"You can see why I might be curious, can't you?"

Hannu was staring ahead. Mae rubbed her hands stiffly. She'd crossed a line. He'd rescued her, saved her from her own stupidity, and she was repaying his kindness with a rotten insinuation. But the question of the boots had been bothering her. It was obvious Magellan hadn't given them to Hannu. They'd been scavenged. The question was when. "I thought I was first to discover Magellan's body. Now I'm not so sure."

The lorry had accelerated ever so slightly.

"I wanted to tell you," he said quietly. "When you came over. But I felt bad. You were doing what I should have done. I found him and I panicked. I thought if anyone knew I'd been there the Facility would think I had something to do with him dying. I made sure he was dead, he was still warm, and then I got the hell out. I swear."

"The boots," she said.

"I . . ." He shook his head, rubbed an eye. "He had no more use of them. They'd only go to waste. I'm not proud of myself, Mae. I was scared. Main are . . ."

"You didn't see—"

"I saw no one. I was hardly there five minutes." He paused. "I-I didn't even look for Siofra. I wasn't thinking straight."

They were silent for a time. Mae was trying to fit what he'd said into what she knew, but she kept getting distracted by the ruptured pebblescape of rivers and ponds.

"I thought they'd run," she said eventually.

"Run?"

"From me."

"Why?"

"Baré thinks I don't trust her."

They were moving at quite a clip. Much faster than Mae would have liked.

"Do you?"

"I don't know." She said nothing for a while. "But I don't think they've run."

A silence in which she could almost hear the grinding of Hannu's thoughts. "If they haven't run—"

"They've gone somewhere safe."

"Safe?"

She nodded.

"From . . . what?"

"Me, among other things."

"Um. So where've they gone?"

"Come on, Hannu. Think about it."

The look he gave her was baffled and vacant.

"Sanctuary," she said. "They've gone seeking sanctuary."

"Ah," he said, giving her a lopsided but knowing smile.

She smiled back, wishing she believed him about the boots.

○

KANSAS ROSE OUT of the pebbled plain like a Gothic cathedral in a medieval landscape. Less a stark promise of salvation, thought Mae, than a hymn to a lost world. Above, the sky glowered. Rain lashed down. Winds tore back and forth. But the ground was solid: The erupting Caul had not yet extended this far inland.

For which Mae offered a silent prayer of thanks as they approached.

It wasn't till Hannu's lorry was two hundred metres away that Mae knew for sure they were too late, or she'd called it wrong. The jeep was nowhere to be seen.

The Twins were out in the garden, tying trees and sheltering pots. Neither paused in their work when Hannu and Mae joined them. For a while they all toiled to secure plants as best they could in the teeth of the gale.

"You missed them by an hour," yelled Sousa.

"But well done for getting here so quickly," added Serpa. "We weren't expecting you until tomorrow."

"We tried to get them to stay." Sousa was holding a stake as Hannu hammered it in. "But Jean's scared. She wouldn't say where they were going."

Mae nodded, an ache of frustrated disappointment in her gut. Too old, too slow.

"Forgive me, Mae, but you look terrible. Jean said you'd had a disagreement."

Did poisoning count as a disagreement? she wondered, saying nothing.

Serpa spoke again but the wind took her words.

"She thinks it's time we went in for some tea," said Sousa. "Good idea, dear."

The world might have gone to hell, but you could still be civilized.

○

THEY'D BEEN WARNED that arrival on Earth would be a shock. Naively, Mae had assumed they meant psychological: the dying Earth, the Caul's presence, ecophobic anxiety. But no, the trauma was physical. Despite building muscle and bone strength via an intense pre-departure course of genegro and centrifuge training, as well as ship-board bursts of 1.5G acceleration and deceleration, the tripling of Mars' gravity was soon unbearable.

Her fellow penitents had packs carrying enough kit for a month's survival. Few could lift them. Not that it mattered. Within a week, they'd all entered the Caul.

They'd landed several kilos away. A supposed safe zone. Mae watched as, one by one, they got a look in their eye that she recognized with mounting horror meant they'd be gone by tomorrow. They'd been instructed to band together, keeping close, to complete the month of purification rituals the church mandated before crossing over. It did no good. They were sly, betraying the group first chance they got. Walking, crawling.

Only Mae and Fukuoka, their leader, resisted. He meditated or slept, barely moving, eating, or drinking, in their six days together. He grew increasingly restless until one morning he was gone.

Mae was terrified at how it seemed to possess them. She felt it too, a tugging, a presence in her mind. She waited for it to overcome her. Yet it never grew stronger than a persistent nagging. An urge, an itch. But then she hadn't come to enter the Caul. She was here to find Albert. She spent her first two weeks devouring rations and taking steadily longer walks as her genegro-modded body slowly adjusted to its new weight.

They had landed on the Strip. A three-hundred kilo stretch of shore littered with rockets and buildings both temporary and permanent. Most illegal rockets landed there. It was the southern tip of the triangular continent that had once been dubbed the cradle of civilization. The church said Africa was chosen because it was blessed. (And in Mae's case, her genes argued she'd originated here.) But really it was because it was the terminus of the only public nav-plan for ships without navigators.

Mae might have been the last from her ship, but she wasn't alone.

There were others like her, those who resisted the Caul. Some came to scavenge. Others to barter. Some sought companionship or to recruit her. A few were hunting for prey. Mae offered food, water, power, tools, shelter. Bribing, befriending, asking her questions. She felt at home playing detective, but it was reckless, dangerous.

She'd doubted anyone would remember or care about the comings and goings of new arrivals, but it turned out that the penitents, as they called themselves, had long memories. Some even had maps of the ships coming down, or kept records. Older scavengers had a keen nose for the comings and goings along the Strip.

Within a month Mae knew where Albert's ship had landed. Three weeks later she had found it and interrogated everyone living within ten kilos of the wreck. But of Albert there proved to be not the slightest sign. As if he'd never come here at all.

○

They sat in the reception room, bathed in the warm glow of solar lights, drinking bitter tea out of mismatched china cups. Like everything in Kansas, Mae found tea-drinking agreeably convivial. Penitents and even Facility staff sought out the Twins because Kansas was a tiny oasis of civilization, a reminder that Earth had once been alive. Before they passed over, many gave their treasured possessions to the Twins, leaving a little piece of themselves for posterity. How could the Twins ever refuse such donations?

Outside it was twilight. Gritty gusts of wind scratched at the clapboard walls of the house, investigating weaknesses, looking for ways inside. Rain battered windows.

Sousa and Serpa had insisted neither of them could go back out in this weather. This prompted Hannu to regretfully announce that in any case they were stuck until tomorrow since the lorry's lights were malfunctioning.

"Then we are an impromptu party," said Sousa with an easy smile. "Damn the gloom."

"This is all so strange," Mae said distractedly. "I never imagined . . ."

"Death always unhinges us," said Serpa, never scared of a delicate topic. "It serves to wake us up."

"Are you saying we're sleepwalkers?" said Sousa sceptically. "Because I don't agree."

"I do," said Mae. "Ever since I came here, I feel I've been dreaming. Like I'm waiting for something that will never come."

"If this is a dream, what does that make the Caul?" asked Sousa.

They drank their tea. It had a slight salty aftertaste, hinting at its samphire origins.

The Twins explained that Baré had been agitated, insisting from the moment she and the girl got here that they couldn't stay long. "We begged them not to go," said Sousa.

Mae shook her head. "Jean would know I'd head here first."

Sousa nodded. "She left—"

"So where've they gone?" interrupted Hannu.

"That," said Serpa, "she would not say."

"The Facility, obviously," he said. "The one place she's safe from us."

"But Siofra's not safe there," said Mae. "Besides Dr. Machalek said . . ."

A thunderous gust struck the house, which shook, and they heard a heavy crash outside. Hannu got to his feet. Sousa, alarmed, rose too. "I'll go," said Serpa, joining Hannu. The front door slammed on Sousa's cry of "Be careful."

The house timbers creaked, straining against the force of the wind.

"Jean said you suspected her, Mae. Is that true?" asked Sousa.

Mae glanced at the ceiling and shrugged. "I think you were right," she said. "I should have left this alone. Siofra is what matters here."

The older woman nodded sympathetically, then refilled their cups. When she sat down, she looked suddenly ill at ease. "Mae . . ."

"Yes?" Mae wondered if this was the Talk. She had been expecting an intervention of some sort. She wondered what else Baré had told them. The Twins would not have approved of Mae's recent behaviour.

"Serpa told me something the other day," she said after a moment. "It was after the funeral. That wasn't one of her better days.

She was quite sick. The pain . . . Well, she's very good at hiding it. It can take over. Almost like a drug. Sometimes she doesn't know what she is saying. I don't know where these recollections come from, but she seems to believe them. It's not like she's delirious. They're consistent, if you know what I mean. They make sense. Anyway. I don't think she was entirely lucid the other day. I don't think she remembers what she told me." Sousa paused, glancing down at her ashen wrinkled fingers, which were fidgeting in her lap. "I'm sorry, I'm not making sense." She looked back up at Mae, eyes moist. "You see, Serpa told me she met Albert."

Mae put her cup down slowly. She opened her mouth but not finding anything to say closed it again. Sousa, her fingers white and her voice wobbling, plunged on as if fearful Mae might stop her.

"This was a long time ago. Just before you arrived." She cleared her throat self-consciously. "Serpa was out scavenging on her own, as we once did, and she found a man walking alone. He was tall, well-dressed. Thick, knotted hair. Unlike others you tended to encounter at that time, who usually avoided any contact, he actually approached Serpa. She said he was polite and friendly. He told her he was looking for somebody. He said he belonged to the Service and had been sent here to find a man to learn what he knew."

Mae's mind, which had been frozen in a state of shock, began to work all of a sudden, trying to make sense of this. "He said he was Service?"

"That's what he said. She couldn't help him. He said he'd just arrived. It was in the days when rockets were landing monthly. You'd often stumble on people out here, wandering, lost. Or making camps. People you might see once or twice and then never again. You must remember how it was. Before they got serious about stopping them coming. Anyway. She never saw him again. It probably isn't . . . There were so many, weren't there? You remember what it was like. I can still picture so many of those faces. Like strangers at a port. Wide-eyed people waiting for the call to go somewhere else, even if they weren't sure where they were going." Her white fingers twisted her skirt, and she looked into Mae's eyes. "I'm sorry, I shouldn't have—"

"Tall?"

Sousa nodded.

"Locks?" Her hands shook.

Sousa looked blank.

She felt like someone had just walked over her grave.

Sousa put a hand on her arm. "I really don't know whether I ought to have told you, but I felt on balance it would be worse not to. I thought that perhaps you'd want to know. If it was him, you were right to come. He was here."

"He was looking for someone?"

Sousa nodded.

"If he said he was Service he must have been working. He did that sometimes."

"I don't know, Mae."

"But that means . . ." It meant a lot of things, she realized, and it required a great deal of thinking. Her mind was racing now, trying to put this new information into the context of what she already knew. But it didn't fit. Which meant that something was wrong. She would have to do some mental rearranging of what she knew about Albert.

"I'm sorry," said Sousa. "I've left you with more questions than answers."

"It's not that." Her mind was reeling. She could feel her thoughts all backed up. Everything felt disordered. Albert. It was confirmation. He'd not run away. He'd come here for a reason. "W-why did she never say before?"

Sousa shrugged. "She's come out with all sorts of things recently. Stories she's never told me. I don't believe all of them, Mae. That's a fact. She forgets she's told me."

Mae nodded.

Sousa gazed at her with loving, sympathetic eyes. "It will be okay, Mae."

"I know," she said. But she wasn't sure.

"Can I ask that you don't mention it to Serpa? It will just upset her."

Mae, still in shock, nodded.

Sousa went into the kitchen, but Mae glimpsed the look of pity on her tired and lined face. She'd been an object of sympathy since her arrival—chasing the lover who'd walked out on her all the way to Earth but not taking the final plunge by resisting the lure of the Caul. If she'd ever imagined her life as a tragedy, a cautionary tale of doomed romance with a haunted heroine at its heart, then Serpa's story turned it all upside down. Albert had not betrayed her. He'd simply followed a story that led him to Earth and the inevitable. He'd been the victim, not Mae. The tragedy was his, not hers.

What else, she wondered, will everyone think I've got wrong? They must think her a fool in her attempts to uncover Magellan's killer and protect Siofra. A dangerous fool.

She heard Sousa fussing loudly in the kitchen. She stood up, stretching her sore back. She moved about the room. Picked up a jar on the side table. Analgesics. Main logo. Dr. Machalek? Of course, he'd visit. She looked at the furnishings. The painted walls. The even floor. All this wood. Glass windows! The raw materials acquired or traded, all of it assembled by the Twins. She suspected the Facility had been tapped too. Yet for all that, did any of it belong here? The Twins, like the house, were an anachronism. Like all of us, she thought. She remembered Albert reading to her about colonialists clinging to countries that had rejected them. But we're the natives, she told herself. We've come home.

So why have I never felt like I belong here?

She could hardly blame the Twins. They always acted with clear intentions. How many times had they extended the hand of friendship to Mae only for her to reject it? Up and down the shore they were regarded as the best of the penitents. They were a reminder of what civilization looked like. And how could Mae argue? They built a house. They made a home. They came to a dead world and brought a part of it back to life. They invited everyone here to celebrate that small achievement. Yet Mae had always held back, was always reluctant to cross the threshold. The truth was she feared the Twins. It seemed to her that Sousa and Serpa could see deep into your soul, seeing what you had concealed even from yourself. Mae shook her head in self-disgust. Every time she came here her respect for the Twins grew a little more. None of us, she thought ambiguously, deserve them.

There was a rush of air as Serpa and Hannu returned from outside. They were in the midst of an argument.

"All I'm saying," said Hannu, "is the Caul has no right to act like this."

"Does it know anything of rights?" asked Serpa. The door banged closed.

"Live and let live!" insisted Hannu. "We were here first!"

"Some argue the Caul was here all along, biding its time."

"Well, it has no business invading the flaming shore. That's ours!"

They were both soaking but neither seemed to mind as they sat down. "We once thought all Earth was ours. We were wrong. Perhaps it only tolerates us as long as we don't bother it."

"It suffers us," said Mae.

"Well, we each have rights," said Sousa.

"Does Main also think so?" she asked. "Magellan thought he had a right to live here but someone disagreed." Hannu, who'd been about to speak, closed his mouth firmly." Any rights we have depend on others upholding those rights," she continued.

"Well said," said Sousa, returning from the kitchen. She was carrying a stack of writing books. Mae almost gasped in recognition. Magellan's journals. Sousa put the pile on the table beside her. "Jean left these for you."

Mae counted the journals, then recounted them. "But why?"

"She said the truth was in here."

Mae was wide-eyed. "Have you read them?"

"Of course not. She left them for you."

"But I've read nearly everything. There are gaps. Bits missing. Much of it is technical." She was picking the journals up one at a time and quickly flicking through them, reminding herself. There were only eight she was disappointed to see. Year Five was still missing. She'd hoped Baré would hand it over.

"And what have you learned?"

"Magellan stopped trusting Jean. It's in here."

Serpa was frowning. "Jean was never entirely who she claims to be."

"She has torn loyalties," said Sousa.

"Is she a Main spy?"

"That we couldn't say."

"What would she want with Siofra?"

The old women exchanged a glance. Hannu, catching it, looked at Mae. "What's going on?"

"Mae thinks Magellan died because of Siofra, is that right?" asked Sousa.

Mae didn't say anything.

"You can't think Jean had anything to do with it?" Serpa replied, astonished.

"Who is she?" Mae asked, lifting a journal and staring at it. "She worked at the Facility, but not for long. She got into the Topologie alone and lived to tell the tale, which no one but the Magellans managed. Carl didn't trust her. He sent her away. She drugged me to take Siofra."

Sousa sat down heavily. "I admit it doesn't look good. But, Mae, she loves that child."

"Perhaps Siofra is her only chance off here?"

They were silent as they contemplated this.

"I need to find them," said Mae, staring at the battered old journals.

"We know you do, dear."

"But how?"

"Hannu will take you. Won't you?"

He started. "Of course. But where? Where would she take the girl?"

Mae looked at the notebook she was holding. Year Eight was written on the front. The period when Magellan had sent Baré away. She opened it.

YEAR EIGHT

[Many pages and prior entries cut out.]

Day 7, Month 6

This morning, Jean complained about my "unreasonableness." She told me I'd spent fourteen hours "in there" yesterday. I disputed this, though my recollection is hazy. She read out from a notebook my times of departure and return. I laughed, saying the day must have run away from me. She then read out the times of my "going in" and "coming out" over the past month. I stopped laughing. She's recording my movements. "What's in there?" she asked. My work, I told her. That didn't satisfy her. We had another row. Siofra ran and hid, and it took an hour to coax her out from under the caravan. She is too big for this. And I am too old to argue about how I spend my time.

Day 2, Month 7

Hastings arrived out of the blue at breakfast. It's over a year since his last visit and I'd hoped he had lost interest in us. Alas, no. First of all, he reminded me of the offer he'd once made. They'd welcome me back in the Facility. I have only to share my research. When I declined, he told me Main are worried. The PA are troubled by Main's lack of progress as well as the cost, in money and lives. "They're threatening to pull the plug." I told him that wasn't my concern. "What will you do when we are gone?" he asked.

Next, he claimed I'd made breakthroughs I was keeping to myself. I asked him why he thought that. "Word gets around, Carl," he said. "You've been seen deep inside the Topologie." Only the margins. "We've seen your lights!" For a second, I felt a dreadful thrill of fear and wondered who he had been talking to, who'd been watching me. Then I got a grip on myself. He was simply trying to smoke me out. I kept my cool, which seemed to disappoint him.

Outside, Siofra's shard arrangements caught his attention. They are becoming more elaborate. She spends hours on them. Jean says that some days she cannot get her to do anything else. They take up larger and larger parts of the camp and I regularly have to bring more shards back from the Topologie. Hastings spent time studying them. It is unmistakable what they represent. "You take Siofra with you?" he asked. I shrugged. "Rarely." He watched her disassembling and rebuilding and asked what she was doing. Not wishing to reveal the truth, I was temporarily lost for words. Jean's quick thinking saved us. She told him that Siofra studied sat photos of the Topologie every night and next day re-created them. He nodded, accepting this explanation. (It makes better sense than the truth.) He asked if he could take a photograph and I could hardly say no without reaffirming his suspicions. I am worried. If he sends it to Main they may grow interested in Siofra. Perhaps they already are. What if Hastings didn't come to talk about my work at all? What if he came to see Siofra?

Day 9, Month 7

Yesterday was another indistinct day in the Topologie. What did I do in there?

Day 14, Month 7

Tonight, Siofra wouldn't come out from under the caravan, so I crawled in after her. She has made a cosy nest for herself. Eventually, I coaxed her out. In the nest, I found an assortment of things: plastic toys, a scarf of Jean's, pens. And Gemma's pain journal. I opened it. There were the agonies she'd suffered year after year, written out in short, clear entries. Matter-of-fact descriptions. Like they were happening to someone else. Not for the first time did I think that her relationship with pain had been the most intimate of her life. But there was something else. Between the bare descriptions of her body's treachery lay page after page of mathematics and speculations in Gemma's hand. I put this missive from beyond the grave into my shirt pocket, where it presses against my heart.

Day 18, Month 7

Jean accuses me of hiding away, of giving her the cold shoulder. When I rise to her barbs, it upsets Siofra, which further angers Jean. It is a vicious circle.

Gemma's pain journal is filled with theories about the attractor. They taunt my stasis. Sometimes I spend the night at my desk, having fallen asleep. I dream of Gemma and I inside the attractor, wrapped in the enfolded spaces, no more secrets between us.

Day 12, Month 8

Jean has moved out of the caravan and back into the spare cabin. She said it would be easier for everyone. Just another move in our silent war of attrition. Siofra appeared confused. Of course, she does not understand. She is all that is keeping Jean here.

Day 19, Month 8

Returned from the Topologie this afternoon to find Jean in tears. Siofra had kicked her models down. Months of gradual evolution destroyed in a few minutes' fury. When I was told what happened I, too, was incensed. I drove to Rawat's temple. I found him hiding inside. Kozlov was nowhere to be seen. I told Rawat that if he ever visited my camp again, I would kill him. If he ever threatened Jean again, I would kill him. If he ever came near Siofra again, I would kill him. The little zealot was uncowed by my threats, protesting he'd only come to see Siofra. I told him he was trespassing, and he was scaring them. He said it was only when Jean began throwing things at Kozlov that matters turned sour. What's your interest in Siofra? I demanded to know. He gave me a sly look. "You can't hide the truth forever," he said. Then he spoke words that chilled my heart. "She has the loveliest gray eyes." I ran from him, but he called after me: "She isn't yours to keep!"

Day 30, Month 8

On my way to the Topologie, I saw a couple of carriers parked a kilo from the site. The copter circled overhead. I watched as they surveyed the Topologie, like Gemma and I had done once. When I told Jean, she said Main's problems were not our problems. I wish that were true.

Day 12, Month 9

To the Facility for supplies. There was a townhall meeting and since I wanted a word with Hastings, I attended. Once, we numbered in the thirties. Today, I counted sixteen staff, recognising but a handful. When Dr. Carlyle and Hastings arrived, they conferred and I was asked to leave. Sensitive Main research, they informed me. Were they making a point? On my way out I took an opportunity to snoop. I went straight to the labs. In five minutes, I had seen all I needed. The berg they had stolen has been broken up. Lumps of it were scattered about the lab—under microscopes, in vacuum chambers, baths, ovens, and centrifuges. All the kit for studying the Cauldron has been repurposed to look at my berg sample. No wonder they didn't want me there. From Caul to berg to Topologie: It is a natural progression. Dr. Carlyle is close on my heels. But without the attractor it is meaningless.

Day 16, Month 9

It is over. I'd known it was going to end eventually, but not like this. After my trip to the Topologie, I unlocked my storage cabinet to get an old notebook and discovered that Year Five of my journals was missing. I do not know when I last saw it, but I do know it should have been here. My heart sank.

I invited Jean into the office, and I asked her straight out if she had taken it.

She took a deep breath. "Before I answer," she told me, "I want you to answer a question." About? "What's in cabin three? You spend all day in there!" I was taken aback. What are you talking about? I said. It's been locked for years. "Carl, you pack the jeep and then you stare at the cabin. Two times out of three, you shake your head and leave for the Topologie. But that third time you go to the cabin, block the door, and don't come out till dark. When you do, you're a sleepwalker. I have to put you to bed." The moment I heard her words I knew they were true. Whole days were vanishing as I got lost in the berg's depths. Jean looked scared but also defiant. I thought of the lies she and Gemma had forced me to tell. I no longer know who I am anymore. I felt fear and anger swelling in me at my impossible situation. Jean said, "I've tried to talk to . . ."

I lost my temper. Told Jean not to change the subject. I demanded she hand the journal back. She told me I had no business making accusations when I was lying to her. I told her she was leaving. I went into her cabin and took her things out and put them in the jeep. I emptied the place. I stripped and turned the bed but there was no journal. I demanded to know where she had hidden it. "I have nothing of yours." I told her to get in the jeep. I bundled Siofra in the back, and we drove in silence to Jean's cottage. When we got there, I removed her things. Siofra was in a state of high distress. I had to pull her away from Jean—my girl, at three years old is as big as a six-year-old, and as strong—and locked her in the jeep. I gave Jean one last chance. Return the journal and we can go back to normal. "Normal?" she laughed bitterly. I attempted to reason with her but was distracted by Siofra, who somehow had got out of the locked vehicle and attached herself to Jean's leg. She howled all the way home.

Day 17, Month 9

Disposed of the key to cabin three. Heaven help me if that isn't enough.

Day 20, Month 9

Driving to the Topologie this morning I saw a carrier parked a kilo away. It was still there when I left. I turned towards it, but it moved away rapidly. Did not give chase.

Day 2, Month 10

I don't feel like I have any other choice. I drove over to the Facility and left a message for Hastings. I've invited him over early tomorrow.

Day 3, Month 10

Drove Hastings into the Topologie. His mouth kept opening and closing like a fish gasping in air. He'd brought a camera and snapped away, when he remembered it. So much for him to record, to make sense of. My answers to his questions were terse. I didn't want him to understand. I wanted him to see and feel, to drink deeply of the last seven years of my life.

By the time we left the jeep and set out on foot through the knotted geometry of structures—fog so thick it seemed to settle in our lungs—he held my arm in terror lest he lose me. Near the cenote, he stared in awed wonder at the ring emerging out of the yellow fog above. I think he was glad just to be out in an open space. I felt sorry for him. His narrow horizons were being ripped wide open.

I almost didn't take him inside the attractor, fearing for his sanity. But he had to understand the Topologie as I saw it. He whimpered as I led him down. He would have retreated had I not taken his hand and dragged him after me. The disorientation and sickness were intense. It has been a long time, and I could hardly bear it myself. We lost ourselves down there, simultaneously awed and cowed. Somehow, I got us back out. We shouldn't have gone in. Outside, he fell to the ground gasping. "What is *it*?" I explained Gemma's theories about this being an intersectional point, a depthless unravelling of space. Just enough so he'd understand that Dr. Carlyle's experiments with the berg risked dangerously loosening barriers between dimensions.

Hastings was silent all the way back. I do not know how much of what I showed him penetrated. As he was leaving, I told him he needed to watch Dr. Carlyle, not us. His eyes, already overwhelmed by all they'd seen, clouded further. "Watching you?" he said, then added three words that frightened the hell out of me. "But we're not."

I promised to share my research if he would direct Dr. Carlyle's away from the berg. He agreed it was dangerous and said he'd be in touch.

Hastings is a good man, I think. But goodness counts for nothing here. Main is too adept at persuading its staff where their obligations lie. Where I see a threat, they see an opportunity.

More troublingly: If Main is not watching me, who is?

Day 15, Month 10

In my dreams gray masses roll towards me, crowned with steep ridges of foam, their tremulous cadence swelling in my ears. Sometimes I hear Gemma crying my name. I've taken to shackling myself to the bed at night. I fear a loss of control. I fear cabin three. I am haunted by every bad thing I ever did. Why do we feel our crimes more deeply as we age? They gnaw at the soul daily.

Still no word from Hastings.

Day 11, Month 11

I have been maudlin, feeling blue. I laid bare my heart and now I feel spurned. Gemma, Jean, Siofra, and Hastings revolve in my mind. Four points on a compass. I see how I've made a mess of everything. If I hadn't been so pig-headed, if only I had listened to Gemma, who never wanted to come here in the first place—but then there would be no Siofra.

Yesterday, we visited the Twins. They helped, as they always do. I needed to talk to friends who, even if I couldn't tell them the whole truth, would be sympathetic. I drank far too much of their hooch. I remember singing Hastings's praises as well as damning him to hell, knowing I'd put him in an impossible situation. Choices are never simple here.

One part of our conversation I do recall clearly. I was lamenting the impossibility of getting off Earth when Serpa interrupted: "Of course, there's a way off, Carl. There's always been a way off." This perplexed me. What? How? Serpa smiled. "Main. Do a deal with them." This took me back. But they don't trust me, and I don't trust them, I said. "Dear," said Sousa, telling Serpa off for her suggestion. Serpa shushed her, eyes bright. "Your enemy in getting off here is not Main but the Planetary Authority and the quarantine. Main just need to be offered something they can't resist."

I glanced at my daughter. Is this the choice I face?

Day 3, Month 12

Dr. Machalek came by earlier. He told me Hastings disappeared a week ago. They found his jeep abandoned on the plain, yesterday. There was no sign of him. He'd been heading this way.

Dr. Carlyle is temporary Facility Director.

DAY EIGHT

UNDER ANOTHER DARKLY LEADEN GRAY SKY, Hannu's wind-buffeted lorry rolled unsteadily onwards. Here, silvery rivers. There, radiant lakes. As if the pebble plain were sinking. The Caul's night-shining now day-shining—dilucent. Mae regarded these unexpected changes suspiciously. Material omens for someone who did not believe in omens.

Hannu grumbled every time he had to drive around one. She suspected he'd have turned for home if the Twins hadn't firmly told him to stay with her until she'd caught up with Baré and Siofra. "What else am I gonna do?" he'd asked with a callow smile. "Get distracted," Sousa had said. "As usual," added Serpa.

Nevertheless, Mae was uneasy at being alone with him. He'd lied to her, and she couldn't think of a good reason why. She'd not mentioned these fears, so allowing the Twins to talk them both into this was all on her. But she also needed him, having no other way of retrieving Siofra. Hannu the liar-thief or Baré the liar-poisoner. Who did she trust least? She was certain of one thing, however. The girl's life, and maybe her own, depended on figuring out the truth.

As they approached the shore, they began to see curious sparks in the air. A few at first, and Mae wondered if they were the embers of another fire. The sparks, adrift on the wind, thickened. They were rainbow-hued and soon swarmed round the lorry, glowing dots bouncing off the windscreen, obscuring the view. Some stuck there and Mae saw they were made of myriad shapes—distorted cubes and skewed spheres. She got lost eyeballing the tiny shapes' astonishing variety. They didn't dim, didn't burn out. Yet sometimes they seemed to vanish suddenly, leaving no trace. This perturbed her.

"Bad for my servos," fretted Hannu.

A bitter dusty taste—the sourness of a past that never stopped pursuing you—filled Mae's mouth. As if the Caul were reaching out to her.

She looked up and, suddenly, there it was, through the drizzle of sparks.

"Well, shit," said Hannu, braking to a halt and staring ahead. Mae, rigid in her seat, hugged herself.

It was a colossal swirling gray funnel reaching down from the sky. It rotated slowly, distinct shaded currents shifting and snaking through it. It stabbed into the shore, piercing the divide between land and Caul, in the exact spot where Main's Facility had stood. Mae blinked. A tornado? A typhoon? But instead of sucking up it seemed to be drawing down, as if tugging at the clouds, as if—was she being fanciful?—draining the sky. The shadowy grayness was hard to focus on. It had the depthlessness of the Caul, and around the funnel those sparks swirled and danced in their millions.

"What is it?" she asked.

"What've they done?" wondered Hannu.

Mae hadn't the slightest idea. Dr. Carlyle had said nothing. Dr. Machalek called it an experiment or an accident. The grayness and the rainbow embers made it difficult to tell if the building was underneath it or simply gone.

She closed her eyes. Took a moment to settle herself. She opened them again. She peered out at the Caul. They were a few kilos away. But the Caul was shining. Lit-up rollers were pushing hard into shore. She felt that habitual tingling in her legs. That burgeoning urge. The familiarity almost a relief.

"Did they do this?" asked Hannu.

Do what? she wondered. Lives were lost, Dr. Machalek had said. Don't interfere, Dr. Caryle had warned Mae. But look at it! That monstrous thing! Who was interfering?

"Take us in," she said.

"Why? The Facility's gone."

"We need to see for ourselves." For myself.

The wind got up as they closed on it. In the gale, sparks pinged hard against the cab. Touchdown was where the Caul met the shore. The Facility was totally gone but much of the compound behind remained intact. The nanomesh fence was down and Hannu drove over it. He parked on a concrete apron that was fractured into a dozen canted slabs. The lorry rocked in the wind. They saw cabins and toppled farm pods. Jeeps—none of them Magellan's—and land cruisers were parked in a tidy line. Sparks swirled chaotically in the air and Mae wondered where they came from. Up close, the gray pouring down was troublingly well-defined. Fifty metres away, and it had a distinct, if roiling, surface. Like water or a wall you might go up to and touch.

Too like the Caul, she thought.

Neither she nor Hannu spoke for a time.

The wind moaned when it wasn't howling at them.

"I'm going out," she said at last. He grunted but followed her.

Mae shielded her eyes with a scarf. Hannu had his goggles.

As they staggered through the compound, the swirling sparks struck hard and sharp and sore as flying grit. They kept their distance from the howling gray vortex. But the gale dragged at them, trying to haul them closer. Walking was a struggle.

"What's that?" called Hannu, pointing beyond one of the cabins.

They struggled over there. She saw a line of them. Five in total. Humps in the pebbles on the far side of the fallen fence. They crossed over the fence. The humps were a couple of metres apart, two metres long and half a metre high. At one end of each hump, a metal pole had been forced into the ground. Names were scrawled on the poles.

"They were the lucky ones," called a hoarse voice. "They died almost instantly."

She and Hannu turned to find Dr. Machalek, leaning on his stick.

o

MAE HAD MET DR. MACHALEK near the end of her first year on Earth.

In his off-duty hours, he'd been running a clinic out of a tent near the Drop Zone. Main did not like it, but he'd got the PA on side by convincing them incinerating out-of-date medicines was immoral when they could be used to help sick wreckers. This was before the PA had got serious about stopping ships illegally coming to Earth. At that time the shore beat to the ebb and flow of trafficked lost souls.

Mae hadn't been sick, but she'd asked this fresh-faced, recently arrived doctor if he'd enquire of his patients if they'd encountered Albert of Mars. A few months later, when they'd met again, he was able to provide her with a couple of suggestive tales.

The first was from Farah, who'd lacked the courage to follow her lover Iqra into the Caul. Their ship had crashed on landing, and an Albert was among those pulling survivors out the wreck. It was a long walk to the Alhaju Mosque, where they'd been due to spend a month cleansing themselves before crossing over. This Albert had led the pair there. Farah had asked why he'd helped. "I want you to find your God," he'd told them. "But what about you?" they'd asked. "Why are *you* here?" Albert's reply had chilled Farah: "I came looking for the devil."

The second came from a teenage boy whose religious fervour had so swept him up he'd abandoned his family and come alone to Earth, only to discover he feared the Caul too much to enter it. The boy, starving after his rations ran out, had been brought back from the brink of death by a man who'd fed and watered him. For days, he had nursed the boy back to health. The boy told the man of his regrets. The man said there was no way to beat the quarantine. But he might find employment near one of the Drop Zones. MainClan handed out defunct or defective supplies in return for gruntwork. The boy had asked the man if that was how he survived. The man had rubbed his head. "I know MainClan of old," he'd said. "They trade in secrets and lies. That's the currency I'm interested in."

Dr. Machalek had seen neither the boy nor Farah again. And there were no further tales of Alberts or unnamed men on a quest to help others along the shore.

○

THE VACANT SLEEVE OF DR. MACHALEK'S COAT whipped back and forth in the wind as he moved stiffly back over the fence towards one of the small cabins in the compound.

Hannu, close behind Mae, muttered loudly that they were wasting time.

"Somewhere else you need be?" she wondered.

The doctor handed Mae the stick and pulled open the door. He took the stick back and they followed him inside. Light came from a small window. Mae saw two cots with sleeping bags, a table with chairs. On the table were dirty dishes, a burner, a dirty saucepan, bottles of water, and several medical kits. On the floor were crates filled with files. Some were open and papers spilled or had been blown over the floor.

Dr. Machalek heaved himself into a chair at the table. He discarded his stick and dug in a coat pocket. He pulled out a handful of vials. He examined this haul, dropping the empties in his lap. He closely examined the remaining three full ones. Two he pocketed, the third he put on the table. He coughed, winced, grunted again.

"Find me a syringe, please," he said to Hannu, pointing at the medical kits.

One-handed, the doctor unbuttoned and shrugged off his coat. He winced.

"Please can I have assistance," he said to Mae. She helped him remove the coat and then the shirt he wore beneath. His left shoulder, she saw, was heavily bandaged. She froze as understanding dawned. She'd known something was wrong with his arm and shoulder. Now it was obvious. He'd lost his left arm.

With his right hand, the doctor carefully peeled off the bandages around the shoulder. They were clean. He paused and said to her, "You might want to look away."

Mae could hear Hannu poking around behind her. She shook her head.

When the bandages were off, she saw that the skin on and around his shoulder had turned gray. Black tendrils were spreading across his chest. She stared in dumb incomprehension. There was no stump. He had no wound. No folded or sutured skin. She was looking at . . . nothing. Just a fuzzy grayness, a not-quite emptiness where an arm should have been attached. It resembled a migraine halo. She felt nauseous. She blinked at it as if her eyes were faulty and the arm might reappear any second.

Dr. Machalek was right. She didn't want to look at it.

"What happened?" she asked.

"Same thing as happened to my colleagues outside," he said. "Their suffering was at least mercifully short," he added, wincing again. "I'm afraid it's spreading rather fast."

Mae said nothing, considering him. They'd known each other a long time. Such longevity was to be respected. It wasn't friendship. Neither sought the other out. It was an awareness of what each must have endured in not surrendering to death or the Caul. An acceptance that every compromise was personal.

He looked back at her, irises faint rings around the pools of his pupils, with a morose vacancy she'd come to recognize, and to fear.

Behind him, Hannu noisily ransacked the medkits. She wondered which drugs the doctor was taking. Thought of her own recent dependency.

At last, Hannu located a syringe. "Good boy," said Dr. Machalek, taking it.

"Where is Dr. Carlyle?" she asked.

He shrugged. "She comes and she goes."

"Where does she go?"

Another shrug. "She's quite stirred up."

"About the deaths?"

"Main will take it all away from her."

"Take what?"

He frowned. "Her work, the surviving samples."

Mae pondered this. "You mean Magellan's berg?"

He didn't appear to have heard her. He stuck the syringe needle in the vial. Then he put the vial in his mouth, bit down on it and one-handed withdrew the vial's clear liquid into the syringe. His hand shook. "She blew it up."

"The berg?" asked Mae, astonished. "Is that what happened here?"

He leaned towards her and said, "You always did ask a lot of questions."

And you avoid answering them, she thought.

"I've got a question," barked Hannu. "Where're Baré and the girl?"

Dr. Machalek ignored him. "Dr. Carlyle called it a runaway reaction. She used a shielded fusion pump to fire a vast multiple of teravolts into the samples. She wanted to dilate space itself." He fell silent. "Destroyed the lab. Then the Facility. That took a few hours. She says it is remarkably stable. She's quite excited by it. She calls it an intrusion of interdimensional foam."

The doctor fell silent, the effort of speaking clearly tiring him. He held up the syringe. "Please, will you do the honours. My coordination's shot."

"What is it?" she asked as neutrally as she could.

"A little cocktail to ease the pain."

Mae picked up the vial, but her eyes couldn't read the label. She turned back to the doctor and examined the coarse skin of his arm, found a faint gray vein. Carefully, she inserted the needle. She hesitated a moment, fearing she was hurting him. He'd closed his eyes. Finally, she thumbed the plunger.

When he opened them again, he looked relieved. "Dr. Carlyle says it's a miracle."

"Main don't know?"

"She says I should leave. They'll figure something's up. They'll send people to ask questions." He smiled at her, eyes filming up with some strong emotion. "Like you."

Nothing like me, thought Mae.

He shook his head. "But by then it'll be too late."

"What about Baré?" asked Hannu. "The child. Did Baré bring her here?"

Dr. Machalek wiped his brow. "Jean Baré was lucky to get out when she did."

Mae couldn't tell if these side-step responses to their questions were further signs of his intoxication, evidence of a deteriorating mind or outright evasions. Her money was on all three.

"Magellan thought Jean still worked for Main," she said.

The doctor shrugged.

Mae felt her heart sink. "She's a spy, isn't she."

"A spy?"

"For Main." Why not push him further? She licked her lips and speculated aloud: "A spy like you."

He didn't deny it.

The cabin shook in a violent, howling gust. A shower of sparks out the window.

"What do Main want with Siofra?" she asked.

"They know what she is."

Hannu was still: arms crossed, jaw tense, watching closely.

"What is she?" she asked, dry-mouthed. The sense that everybody but her knew the truth about Siofra had been haunting Mae for days. The child was the key to actions—from murder to arson to kidnapping—playing out here. Yet she had a fear that even if she figured out Siofra's importance, it wouldn't be quite graspable. As if the world as it now existed was beyond the comprehension of someone like her.

Dr. Machalek looked morose. He nodded at the nearest cot. His breathing had grown laboured. "Under there," he said to Mae. She went over and found a battered journal. Written in block capitals on the journal's cover: YEAR FIVE. Mae flicked through it and saw Magellan's cramped, dense writing.

"We're wasting time, Mae," complained Hannu. "She's not here."

"Baré gave you this?" she asked, ignoring him.

"She wanted you to have it. She said you needed to understand."

Baré had taken the journals and left them with the Twins. Now the missing one had turned up here. She's leaving me breadcrumbs, thought Mae. But leading where? "So Jean and Siofra did come here," she said.

"Baré's orders were to bring the girl here if anything happened." He scratched his beard vaguely. "I told them to run, to hide. Main can't be trusted. Not now."

Hannu was suddenly crouching by the doctor, gripping his arm. "Doc, where did you tell them to go? We're trying to help here."

"*Help?* Who do you imagine you're helping?" Those morose black eyes were mocking. "Baré isn't stupid. She knows she's on her own now."

"He doesn't know where they are," concluded Mae.

Hannu rose and snatched the journal right out of her hands.

This stunned her—as did the cold fury she saw in his eyes—yet a moment later he was blinking at her as if he was as surprised as she. The journal, however, remained clutched possessively against his chest.

"Hannu . . ." she said.

"I'll . . . I'll be waiting in the lorry," he mumbled and fled from the cabin.

She couldn't let him go. She didn't trust him not to drive away without her and she needed that journal. She made to follow the mechanic.

"Mae," said Dr. Machalek, a catch in his voice. "Stay a moment. *Please.*"

She halted, guilty and wary. Was this yet another trap? Ever since she'd found the girl, she'd felt pushed and pulled around by others' actions and expectations. Yet she also sensed they were puppets themselves, tugged this way and that by forces or beliefs they but dimly understood. What was it Albert said? *True power is never seen, only the shadow it casts.* And the inevitable corollary: *You can't fight shadows.*

"It won't be long," said the doctor, his words slurring. "I promise."

In that moment, it came to her. "What did I give you?"

"Muscle relaxant." He swallowed, then explained: "My cardiovascular system is gradually shutting down. Lungs first. I'll slowly asphyxiate, but to me it'll feel just like going to sleep. Unless I've got the dose all wrong, of course." He laughed, coughed.

The urge to chase after Hannu was still in her legs. I came here for the girl, she thought, not this. But the doctor gazed at her, those eyes dark pools of need.

"Will you hold my hand?" he asked.

Mae exhaled slowly. She wanted it clear that she was staying under duress. I've been tricked into killing a man, she thought. She refused to sit, instead standing beside him. Took his hand in hers. She kept her eyes away from his headache-inducing shoulder. "You didn't do anything, Mae," he said. "I didn't have long left. Necrosis. Whatever happened to my arm, it is slowly killing me."

The skin was dry, unexpectedly soft. She could feel the beat of his heart: slow, slightly erratic. He talked to her. Spoke of his life before Earth. The mistakes he'd made. She knew the story already yet in this telling there was neither bitterness nor regret.

"Why come here, Mae?" he said quietly. "Even as a scientist, why come here? There is no hope. Earth is dead. Even Dr. Carlyle understands that. Only the damned end up on Earth. We've all transgressed. You come here because you've got no other options. That gives Main leverage. My job was to keep the staff alive and operational. Then a few years ago I was secretly ordered to spy on Magellan. Behind Hastings' back. Ever been the servant of two masters?"

Two masters? thought Mae. Weren't they all on the same side? "Who . . ."

"Impossible to do it alone," he continued.

"So you recruited Baré."

“She’d already left us. She was lonely out there.” He sniffed. “Aren’t we all?”

He squeezed Mae’s hand. The intimate gesture made her shiver. Not since Albert had another person clung to her like this.

“I accepted years ago that Earth can’t redeem us,” he said, the words slow now, coming sparingly. “For too long . . . we’ve hoped to rescue this planet, despite being the ones to ravage it. And when it turned against us . . . we thought we could figure out the problem and solve it. We’d save Earth and in doing so save ourselves. That’s always been our mistake. Maybe Earth can’t be saved . . . So where does that leave us?”

Mae said nothing. She wondered what belief would consume her when her time came. She could feel his pulse in her hand. Steady, but faint.

She closed her eyes. The itch to leave had passed. She held his hand even as his grip on hers weakened. She was here for him. This soul who’d been on Earth for as long as she. One of the damned, he’d said. And why not? It certainly felt like it. They were ghosts haunting a world that had long ceased to notice them.

Yet the longer she held his hand, the more she imagined it was another’s.

She knew Albert was long dead. She’d always known. But that had never stopped her dreaming of what might have been.

Minutes passed. His breaths grew shallower. Got longer, more drawn out.

She expected his pulse to quicken as the end neared, but it didn’t. Time slowed down. Albert an old man now. Old as her. His heart fading.

His soft hand in hers. How he had once held her on Mars.

His breathing quiet now. The pulse stilling. The wind so loud.

The shadow of all those empty years falling away.

IT HAD BEEN DR. MACHALEK HIMSELF who put an end to Mae's search for Albert.

After following up his tales, she'd returned and made camp nearby. They'd got to know one another. He was candid, telling of the charges of medical negligence that had caused him to end up here. A wrong dosage had been prescribed, and six people had died. The forty hours' unrelieved duty on a ward in the middle of an influenza epidemic was considered irrelevant by the court. Hours before he was to be sentenced and stripped of his licence to practise, Main had made their offer. He was in no position to refuse.

Though Dr. Machalek had resigned himself to his fate—"Welcome to my personal purgatory"—he was sympathetic to Mae's quest. He told her of the Twins. "They take in waifs and strays," he'd said. "Their home is open to everyone. You must go to them."

She had learned caution in her year on Earth. She spent three months learning all she could about the Twins before approaching Kansas. They were hospitable, friendly, generous. They knew everyone. It was inconceivable Albert wouldn't have sought them out. It was as if his meandering trail had been leading her this way all along.

She'd been astonished to see the house rising out of the ground. A piece of history standing erect on the pebbled plain. It wasn't assembled out of scavenged parts. It was whole, perfect. Like coming home. She didn't quite believe in it. Never had.

They'd welcomed Mae with open arms. Two other penitents were already there, helping in the garden: It was bigger back then. You weren't invited into the house. They shared food with you and in return you toiled among the extensive beds and planters. An elaborate system of traps, pipes, and tanks collected sparse fallings of rain. There was a shed to sleep in if you wished to stay. Mae slept out in the open in the tent she'd brought with her. She'd been growing less comfortable around people.

The church's allotments on Mars meant Mae needed little instruction. When the others had moved on, Mae was alone with the Twins. Soon they knew all her secrets. They were so open that Mae let her guard down. They asked lots of questions about Albert and did not seem surprised that he had abandoned her like he had. They wanted to know why she'd followed. "Because he lied to me," she'd answered without thinking. She'd wondered if that were true.

The Twins, however, accepted it, as they accepted all who came. They were sorry they couldn't help her. Albert, they told her, had not visited them.

Finally, a year and three months after she'd arrived, she accepted Albert's trail had gone cold.

O

BY THE TIME SHE MADE IT BACK OUTSIDE, the lorry was gone.

But Hannu had left her a message.

She stared at the vehicles, unsure at first what she was seeing.

Slashed tyres. Shattered windscreens. Bonnets up, wires cut. Puddles under holed fuel tanks. The fuel in the punctured reservoir still leaking into the ground. The air reeking. He was taking no chances. The message abundantly clear: Don't follow.

Over by where they'd parked, she found her pack. He'd emptied it, chucked its contents on the ground for the wind to scatter. Gathering it up, she gasped at finding Year Five among the journals. Forgotten, or discarded? she wondered. He must believe he'd found what he was looking for, she thought. Certainly, he no longer needed her.

She couldn't return to the cabin. Colour embers swirled around her. In her ears the gale howled, and the Caul bashed itself against the shore. She sheltered in a fallen farm pod, insects, both grubs and imagoes, crawling out of the wreck. She ate and drank from her rations. Opened Year Five and read it from cover to cover twice.

It was twilight before she'd finished. She'd cross-checked what she'd read with the other journals. Enough answers were there to make her feel sick with dread.

The multi-hued sparks—bluettes, Magellan called them—left glittering trails across the darkening sky. Now she had a name for them, they seemed to take on a new significance. She watched as some winked into and out of existence. There, not there. It was as if the very air was coming alive above her.

She wondered what she could do. Hannu was hours ahead. She'd no means of following, except by foot. She was still considering the walk when she saw a light in the sky.

It was high, big, and fast approaching.

YEAR FIVE

Day 8, Month 4

I see it: the heart of the Topologie—the attractor. A fuzzy gray space nested in a knot of tangled geometry. Yet whenever I approach, every twist and turn of the surrounding space leads me astray. I get lost in the thick, sulphurous fog as if it refuses to grant me access. Kept out, I feel teased, taunted even.

The inner Topologie is a maze of dumbfounding geometry that reorients itself twice a day. This complicated architecture of headache-inducing shapes is completely fog-smothered so the microsats are no help. On foot, I stumble among inside-out angles and inverted corners, folding curves and exploded spheres, carrying my annotated map. I can barely see more than a few metres. Around me formless shadows loom in the gray. The rope slows me, but I dare not continue untethered. To think I have had to resort to this again. From the start, my exploration of the Topologie has been two steps forward and one back. It feels too often like a game. Teased by glimpses of wonders, I overcome obstacles to reach them only to be offered a glimpse of some new, out-of-reach marvel.

The Cauldron has also turned nasty.

I daren't admit this to Gemma, but its effects are particularly insidious around the attractor. The urge to bolt headlong through the tangled structures until I find the Cauldron is like a thirst I must urgently slake. I know that if I surrender for even a second, it will have me.

I miss having Gemma at my side. But she is now too tired to accompany me. She pores over my results the moment I return. I love coming home to her every evening. She talks excitedly about finding the attractor, almost as excitedly as she does about the coming birth. If I can only find it before the baby comes.

Perhaps I am speaking prematurely—I have not told Gemma this—but I can see an end in sight. Once I have found the attractor and uncovered its secrets, we can try to persuade Main to get the PA quarantine lifted. We will have been here five years.

That way I can make it up to Gemma. I brought us here and I must get us out. For our sake and for the life of our unborn child.

Day 10, Month 4

Didn't get into the site. Gemma woke me in the night to say she was bleeding. I drove to the Facility and collected Dr. Machalek. He examined Gemma, doing the best he could with the crude instruments he has at his disposal. He told us everything was fine as far as he could determine. He insisted that Gemma rested.

I have spent the rest of the day attending to Gemma and reviewing my progress through the inner Topologie. It is pitiful. However, a thought struck me: I know what the attractor looks like now. Sometimes I find it and sometimes I don't. But I cannot gain access. I remember when first I tried to enter the Topologie, roped and secured. Only when I freed myself could I enter. I do not trust myself in the inner Topologie. But if I do not, why should the attractor?

[Ten pages cut out]

Day 12, Month 4

It was an effort to return, today. Gemma's calculations pinpoint the attractor's shifts between tides down to fewer than ten metres. I find it every time, but I can't get closer. The miasma hides invisible projections that block my approach. There are gaps and distortions in solid shapes that unfold before my squinting eyes. I suffer headaches and visual disruptions with migraine halos. I feel dizzy and sometimes I vomit. The eternal ringing of the Topologie is so distorted around the attractor that it might be playing backwards. Worse than Leviathan.

Day 13, Month 4

A day of stumbling back and forth like I was intoxicated. At times, my concentration deserted me. Once or twice, I couldn't remember why I was there, even where *there* was. I came to doubt space itself. We occupy it, it surrounds us, yet I realized how ill-defined my conception of space has been until losing my grasp of it. Like an astronaut who can no longer tell up from down, my sense of it has been failing me these last few days. I am left flailing about in proximity to the attractor.

Day 14, Month 4

I feel close.

Day 15, Month 4

During the first low tide, I found the way into the strange attractor.

I do not know how. Bloody-minded persistence? I endured all the usual defences flung at me: dizziness, sickness, disorientation, which I passed through one at a time like the final circles of hell. By then I was crawling, exhausted.

Blindly, I put one hand in front of the other, and I nearly fell inside.

The violent geometry fell away to reveal a large cenote in the ground. It was half-blocked with further geometric projections, vanishing into darkness. I hesitated. For all I knew the Cauldron awaited me below. Besides, I did not have long before the next tide. Reluctantly, I turned and left, re-enduring its defences on my way out.

I am eager to tell Gemma, but daren't excite her. I must first explore and learn what it is. If the attractor proves not to be the key to the Topologie she will be devastated.

Day 16, Month 4

I decided to share my discovery with Gemma, but on my return tonight she was cold and uncommunicative. She barely touched the meal I prepared. At bedtime she told me what was wrong. Dr. Carlyle had visited. The Facility's head of research was intoxicated and in apparent despair, perhaps due to her failure to make progress with the Cauldron. Their conversation had gone badly.

"She demanded to know what progress we'd made," Gemma said. "I decided to come clean and told her we theorised the Topologie is the partial manifestation of higher dimensional mathematics, which suggests the Caul is a kind of activator bridge or portal into hyperspace. She was unimpressed. 'Tell me something I don't already know.' She'd dropped all her materialist pretence. Stunned, I asked her what she wanted. 'Not damned theories, only facts I can touch or manipulate. How far have you penetrated?'" This was my moment to tell Gemma the truth, but she rushed on. "Dr. Carlyle raged at me. She accused us of being Main's unwitting fools! 'What do you think will happen when they figure out you've accessed these higher dimensions?'" Gemma bit back tears. "Then I said something stupid. I accused her of wanting to keep the Caul all to herself. 'You think it can be possessed? You're as small-minded as they are. How long before they take it from us?' After that she left. I don't understand. She seemed angry we'd found something she had not, but also fearful. I see myself in her, Carl. In another fifteen years, the Caul will have driven me quite mad."

I held her until she drifted into a fitful sleep.

Day 17, Month 4

I can now run the gauntlet of the attractor's physical defences in minutes. While the way is never the same twice, I move through as if by instinct or a kind of muscle memory. I don't consciously think about it.

My new troubles begin, however, when I descend. The cenote is a kind of shaft blocked with a geometry of prisms and polyhedra. There is space enough for me to wriggle through. But I am soon overwhelmed by further feelings of nausea as well as dread. I grow convinced death awaits me below.

Day 18, Month 4

Five metres deeper, I estimate. The shaft remains choked with a hyperspatial geometry that changes every tide. How deep does it go? My fear has not eased but I grow accustomed to it. It is no longer paralysing. When I pause to rest, close my eyes, I sense things coming apart. I move carefully for my limbs are never where I expect them, as if my body's proprioception is dysfunctional.

The conviction that if I go deeper, I will die never leaves me. It's Cartier and Yishiha, all over again. They all wrote something similar at difficult points. I fear I'll never return to Gemma and our baby. Yet I keep going. The self-hatred that occasionally afflicts me above crashes down like I'm being crushed by one of those non-Euclidean boulders. Every bad thing I have ever done or thought haunts me: lying to Gemma, tricking her into coming here, giving Main's ambitions a veneer of legitimacy. Sometimes I want to stop and wait for the tide to come and take me. But such tricksy thoughts are not mine. I keep going.

Day 20, Month 4

Today, I reached the bottom of the shaft.

I estimate it is fifty metres below the Topologie surface. Before entering it, as well as during much of my descent, I ran the gauntlet of visual and aural distortions, enduring both headache and sickness. Halfway down, these afflictions lessened. I also stopped needing my headtorch. Light was—how can I describe it?—*creeping up* from below: An eerie illumination tentatively feeling its way upwards. It was accompanied by a faint drone: repetitive escalating harmonic waves, like Shepard tones. The air grew steadily warmer and moister. As I continued to descend, the light and sound grew less diffuse—louder, brighter—their presence more distinct and increasingly hypnotic.

By the time the shaft bottomed out, my eyes and ears felt pummelled by a terrific sensory overload. I could barely see or hear anything else, blinded by a visual cacophony of scintillating brightness and deafened by a blaring harmonic spectrum.

For time out of mind, I crouched at the base of this vertical canal, head tucked protectively into my body: a foetus terrified by the sensory din of the world beyond.

Did it ease, or did I grow acclimatised to it? I cannot say.

My next conscious thought was of observing a slowly rotating kaleidoscope. I blinked at spinning and splitting rainbows of iridescence. Gradually, my visual field resolved into forms that, while not wholly recognisable, I could at least pick out in this shimmering sea of luminescence. Sonorous plainsongs whispered in the air.

On all sides, I was surrounded by a blazing coral reef of clashing colours and jostling polychromatic harmonies. Ahead, I saw a fractal honeycomb of interlocking indigo cubes. Above me, whirlpools of floating red beads spun in shining ruby galaxies. A silvery saddle drifted by, translucent as a jellyfish. Inverted spheres, the size and colour of squashed oranges, fell through the air like curled leaves. A stand of tall, thin tubes with branching emerald tops waved like a wind-swaying forest.

I stared amazed, awed, as multitudes of molten shapes, upon which filigrees of light flamed and danced, winked into or out of existence, expanding or shrinking, as they entered or left this spot in their passage through interdimensional space.

Finally, I plucked up the courage to move deeper inside.

I crept forward across a shimmering carpet of reactive polychromatics, whose fluorescing colours bleached to gray as they became my footprints. Tiny hypercubes tumbled through the air in clouds like drifting grains of pollen. Everywhere were shapes I'd seen on my surface wanderings, but, unlike those hard, unyielding unicoloured objects above, down here all was fluid, bright, vivid. Burgeoning with life.

How can I describe this to Gemma? Looking at these inadequate words, I see how poorly I am conveying what I saw. My wife must see this, and yet, in her condition, how can she? I must hold my tongue.

Day 22, Month 4

The below space teems with animation. A phosphorescing masquerade of living colour and light to which I alone am witness. It *is* vitality incarnate. Above, the Topologie is cold and dead by comparison. Like a crust, a shell. What does it mean?

What are these shapes that are never still? They are liquid. They are light. They float like spectres. They pass by and through one another (and me), knowing neither boundaries of space nor the force of gravity.

I want to name them. They are sparks of life. They whisper, they sing. They are playful. I'm calling them bluettes.

My attempted interactions with the bluettes are failures. When I try to touch a shoal of spinning tori, they pass through my fingers, disappearing into dimensions I can neither reach out to, nor see. I am haunted by how little here is (literally) within my grasp. I am but a pale ghost among such brilliance.

Is this life? It moves. There are clear patterns. What is it made of? Where does it come from? How big is it? It does not respond to my passing, except in one disturbing way. My touch—hands, boots, skin—leaches all colour from the shapes and the floor. They turn instantly back to the pale-yellow ceramic. I can see my passage in footprints that look like bleached coral. Thankfully, they are gone when I next return.

I tried to speak to Gemma about the attractor, but doing so felt like admitting a betrayal. I should have told her I'd found it long ago. I was tongue-tied, my mouth unable to shape the words like they were as mutable as the structures I find it impossible to describe. I shut up. When did silence become the biggest lie of all?

Day 23, Month 4

I had an idea and took some of the shards and sand from above down below with me. In seconds they were glistening, then glittering, vibrant patterns shifting over their surfaces. They moved, rising from the ground and drifting away. The inanimate now animate. I chased after but quickly lost them.

Gemma tells me I talk a mixture of biology and geometry in my sleep. Does it make any sense or is it just gibberish? I asked her, worriedly. She patted my hand. "To you, or to me?"

Day 25, Month 4

Visited during both tides, today. During the second, I was struck by a realization. The Topologie at high tide, when the fog and Cauldron conceal it, is a soft place. At that time a metamorphosis occurs. Down here: The transformations occur constantly. It means the Caul is not required for fluidity. Is something else driving it?

Day 26, Month 4

I stare around me at this, a cornucopia of shape, flow, and branch. I am reminded of docs telescoping a billion years of old Earth's once abundant wildlife into hours of vivid footage. In the attractor, I watch myriad forms explode across multiple dimensions.

All below the surface.

We had no idea.

We stood, unseeing, upon a vast hyperobject.

Day 28, Month 4

This planet is neither dead nor dying—as Gemma has long believed. It is alive. Perhaps more alive than it ever was when we proliferated over its surface.

Day 29, Month 4

Above, I trudge through bleached coral. Down below, I bathe in beauty.

Day 2, Month 5

Some days, I'm fit to burst with wanting to tell Gemma. But I know I must wait. I must not overexcite her. When our child has come, we can visit together. We three.

Day 3, Month 5

The attractor dazzles me. It confounds my senses. It is Bifröst, the bridge to Asgard. Beneath the Topologie, Earth is startlingly alive. There are hundreds of Topologies. Each must have its own attractor. Are they individual or joined below the surface, forming a huge web of animation? Or perhaps the whole planet is like this below the surface. An intricate hyperobject, a vibrant Gaia in which the unwary and semi-blind might lose themselves.

Day 5, Month 5

We talk of Earth being transformed. Gemma and I catalogue our hyperdimensions. Resources and lives are expended on trying to understand what ails the planet. We seek an explanation of what happened, of how Earth's nature was fundamentally changed. But maybe these hyperdimensions were always here, we just couldn't see them. Earth didn't change. We did. The doors of perception opened—and, fearful, we fled.

Day 7, Month 5

Some days, I feel as if I have fallen down a rabbit hole and into a dream. I glimpse mathematical wonders, but always I am aware that I don't belong here. This is not my home. I am an unwelcome guest. A mortal treading in Elysium.

Day 10, Month 5

I have heard it said humanity changed when we left Earth. Some argue we stopped being human altogether. But that is wrong, I think. What if, instead, we grew more human? And in being *more human* that meant being *less of Earth*. Down here I am a wandering explorer seeking pathways back to old Earth. Perhaps there aren't any. Earth and humanity have diverged, going their separate ways. We are no longer of Earth. We don't belong here. In old spacefaring stories (before we *were* spacefarers) we called ourselves Earthlings. What if we are not Earthlings, after all? What if we never were?

Day 12, Month 5

Gemma complained of abdominal pains but refused to get in the jeep when I proposed we visit Machalek. I said I would get him, but she swore and told me that if I went, she wouldn't be here when I got back.

Day 13, Month 5

Another day in the camp. I daren't leave Gemma, much as I am eager to get back to the attractor. She lay in bed all day and would barely say a word.

Day 17, Month 5

I don't know what I've done. There will be consequences and yet I'd do it all over again. I have betrayed the person I love but I did it all *for* love. I pray she will understand when I find the courage to tell her. Whatever happens, I know I was compelled to act this way. I could not bear to see her hurt further. I could do nothing else.

Gemma woke me yesterday morning to tell me that her waters had broken. My immediate feeling was panic. Gemma herself was calm but worried. Her contractions had already started. Machalek had told us that the baby was not due for another month. We had not planned to have the baby here. We needed help. I moved the jeep. But just as Gemma was leaving the caravan, she doubled over in pain. "It's coming," she gasped.

I didn't dare leave her to summon help. I got her back into the caravan and made such preparations as I could while trying to comfort her. The contractions were already just minutes apart. Within an hour they were under thirty seconds. She lay on our bed, squirming as each wave of agony struck. I offered painkillers but she knocked them out my hand. I repeatedly washed and scrubbed my hands, readying myself for the final labour. Yet I waited in vain. The next eight hours are a horrid blur of screams and howls, not all of them Gemma's. The bed was fouled. There was much blood. We cursed one another. Finally, between her legs I glimpsed a small miracle: the crowning.

It was over an hour after the baby's head became visible before the rest of her emerged. Gemma pushed and pushed and screeched and roared while I carefully pulled and twisted and at last hauled this fragile little life out into the world. By this time, it was late afternoon. Gemma lay on her back, exhausted. Between ragged panting breaths, she asked for the little girl she'd fought so hard to bring into existence. She grew impatient with me. In my hands I was holding this warm wet bundle, tears in my eyes. She was so small. So perfect. I couldn't speak. I simply handed the silent little thing to my wife. Gemma cradled her baby in her arms. She kissed her, then mercifully passed into unconsciousness.

I stared at the faint smile on her sleeping face, aghast. I wept, cursing myself.

The baby was dead: too small, too early. Without medical support, she'd had no chance. My wife, shattered by her exertions, was deeply asleep. When I told her she would be broken, perhaps beyond repair. Why had I said nothing?

I felt a hole open up inside. It threatened to swallow me.

I stared at the contented smile on Gemma's lips in mounting panic. Killing that smile would break my heart. I didn't dare think what it would do to Gemma. I wanted to make it better. I wanted to turn back time and fix this. Then a wild, crazy thought came to me. I couldn't fix this but perhaps I could make amends. I checked the time. I did not have long. Very carefully, I removed the still warm body of our daughter from Gemma's arms. She woke briefly. I said I was settling her. I gave her a pill—a sedative—telling her it would help her rest. I wrapped the baby in a blanket, left the caravan, and ran to the jeep. I drove like a madman, knowing I had so little time.

When I entered the Topologie the tide had already turned. I drove pell-mell through a landscape of unnerving geometry. Thankfully, the fog was light, little more than a mist, allowing me to race down routes I knew well. Four years after our arrival I no longer needed maps to navigate my way to the Topologie's heart. The main arteries are fixed, and I know where they lead. By the time I abandoned the jeep and was running through the tangled structures of the inner Topologie, I had but minutes left. By instinct alone I found the nest holding the attractor. I plunged into the fuzzy miasma. I heard the Cauldron waves breaking metres away. At the entrance, I paused, taking a deep breath, suddenly overcome by the recklessness of my intentions. Would anyone understand? I was here now, I told myself. I was committed.

I descended into the darkness. I climbed down by touch alone, my little bundle strapped to my chest. I reached the bottom, enveloped in light. The tumbling bluettes, which ordinarily ignore me, separated, giving me space as if my precious burden was known to them. Surrounded by this multidimensional kaleidoscope, I made an offering of my dead child. I remember chanting words, over and over. I do not remember what. Then I thought of Gemma. I wrenched myself away from the body. I fled, emerging just as the Cauldron spilled into the hole. Somehow, I reached the jeep, drove like the devil back to the camp.

Gemma was still sleeping when I returned. I cleaned up the caravan as best I could. Some sheets and towels were so dirtied and bloody that I burnt them. I briefly thought of erasing all evidence of the birth. A mad, half-formed thought I quickly dismissed. Gemma surfaced briefly, gummy and stupid with sleep. I gave her another pill. I was not ready to speak to her. I was having regrets. I knew what I had done was wrong. Yet had I not sensed a force or intelligence among those shifting, transforming structures? Whatever was down there was alive. I felt it in my bones. Matter was its plaything. The inanimate could be made animate by will alone. Was I wrong to want to give my child a second chance? I do not believe in ghosts but perhaps the attractor could imbue her stilled pattern. Yet as the hours passed the regrets multiplied. I tried explaining it to Gemma in my head, but even to my ears I sounded insane. She'd never understand. Would she even believe me? She thought our child was alive. When she learned the truth she'd hate me—if she even believed me.

Before I knew it, I was checking she was still sleeping and then driving back to the Topologie. I was determined to undo this stupid mistake. I followed the tide out, metre by metre. The rhythm of the waves was like the beat of a pulse. The shadow-dappled surface was a cobbled coat that never stopped moving. I drummed my fingers on the wheel. I did not know what I was going to find when I got to the attractor. Or, more properly, I was sure I would find nothing.

No trace of our child. Yet I hoped my offering would be rejected and I could take the body back to Gemma, explain, and apologise.

I waited a half hour in the jeep outside the tangled inner Topologie, not trusting myself to follow the retreating Cauldron. Finally, I plucked up my courage and stood above the cenote. Minutes passed. I almost walked away before I heard a faint sound. Quickly, I struggled down through the confounding shapes, projections, and turns. I heard it still. A sort of gurgling. In my haste, I almost tumbled down the shaft.

Finally, I reached the bottom. Silence. The brightness dimmed to a mere glow. No movement. The bustling shapes were still. I heard that sound again. I could see a passage before me. Down it, I saw only darkness stretching interminably towards my future. I felt my throat closing up. I had to follow it. I did not care if I died there. I'd welcome it. I would stay with my child, always and forever.

That sound again: urgent, demanding, loud now. Echoing down the tunnel I stumbled through.

The dim light brightened and there she was.

Lying in her blanket, our baby, crying out lustily.

I gathered her up. Only later did I realize I never had any sense of the oppressive attractor. But what does that matter. I'm never returning here.

I drove home slowly and carefully, our little girl crying out in hunger. When I arrived back at the camp, Gemma was stirring. I slipped our little girl into bed, beside her. She stretched, blinking. She put our baby to her breast and gave me a smile that put steel rods in my fatigued legs.

I didn't know what to say. Exhausted, I smiled back.

DAY EIGHT CONTINUED

DR. CARLYLE, BENT AGAINST THE GALE, walking rapidly away from the copter she'd just landed, halted with a start on discovering Mae blocking her path. A patch covered her left eye. Recovering fast, she said, "This is a Main Facility. You're trespassing. Get out."

Mae, meeting her dismissive one-eyed glare levelly, said: "This isn't a Main anything. It belongs to the Caul now."

Dr. Carlyle looked away, gaze drawn to the wrecked vehicle pool. "Who did this?" she asked, clearly not believing Mae capable of such wanton destruction.

Try me, thought Mae, saying nothing.

The wind moaned around them, bluettes pricking their age-scoured faces. She watched, astonished, as one spark passed through her hand as if it wasn't there. She shivered. I'm a ghost, she thought.

Dr. Carlyle said, "Is Doc Machalek—"

"Dead," whispered Mae. "In the cabin."

"He said he didn't have long," returned the doctor, a statement whose indifference would have been chilling had her face not looked so stricken. "I asked him to come with me, but he refused."

"Where've you been?" Mae asked.

Dr. Carlyle ignored that. "Why are you here, Mae?"

She explained about Baré taking the girl. "They've been and gone," she said.

"I told you to keep your nose out of Main business."

"So Siofra is Main business, after all?"

Dr. Carlyle grinned, shook her head in resignation. "Help me, Mae. We should bury the doc."

Mae didn't trust Dr. Carlyle. But she had a copter, which could travel the fifty kilos to the Topologie in less than an hour. And didn't she owe Dr. Machalek?

They didn't dig a hole. Together they dragged the doctor's body from the cabin and lay it alongside the other mounds. Then they piled pebbles on it until they couldn't see him anymore. Stone to stone, thought Mae. They found a marker, put his name on it. They stood at opposite ends of the grave in silence. The wind spoke for them.

Bluettes hissed by like blazing confetti.

Finally, Mae could take it no longer. "I need to find the girl," she said.

"I'm sure you do."

"Just drop me there."

"It's not safe to fly after dark."

"But Hannu—"

"Mae, if I get involved, I'm making trouble for myself."

Mae had no polite answer to that, so she gave none.

"You told me Magellan had been murdered. Do you still think that?"

Mae nodded. "I believe it was because of the girl."

"Why?"

Mae shrugged. "She's . . . different." Had Dr. Carlyle read Magellan's journals? Did she know about Baré and Dr. Machalek? "I think Main want to study her and Magellan wouldn't let them."

"You're being careful, Mae. You don't trust me. That's sensible." She delicately touched her patch, as if it itched. "I don't trust you, either. You were very quick to involve yourself in Magellan's death, as well as take charge of his daughter."

Mae bristled. "Someone—"

"But you're right to worry about the child." She fiddled with her necklace. "What about Hannu? Why's he interested?"

"I think he was offered a deal. The girl in exchange for getting off Earth."

"Whose deal?"

"Too many people on this shore know about Siofra," she said evasively, thinking of Rawat and Kozlov's alliance. How many other allegiances might an opportunity like the girl create? And was she seriously contemplating making one with Dr. Carlyle?

"You don't know, Mae, or are you just not telling?"

Mae the detective had never liked being questioned herself. "Where did you go in the copter?" she shot back.

"You are persistent. I had to see how far the change had spread."

"What change?"

It was the first time Mae had ever seen her look uncertain of anything. "You've been here long as I have, Mae. You must have noticed. The increase in berg numbers. The Caul has been gradually changing. We were taught it had usurped the oceans. No one understood this transformation was just the beginning."

"The beginning of what?" The Magellans had speculated that the Caul was an in-between stage, she recalled.

"I don't know. It appears to be a phase transition. A sudden critical mass—"

"Caused by your experiment—"

"Experiments don't cause things, they confirm theories," said Dr. Carlyle. "This one was based on the Magellans' ideas and our work here with the berg fragments."

Which you also got from the Magellans, thought Mae. The science might stretch her understanding but not the baser behaviour of the humans trying to uncover it.

"What happened to your eye?"

"Same thing as happened to the doc's arm. Same as what killed the others." She touched her patch again. "I got too close. We opened up . . . an inter-dimensional foam. It came through but a part of us was taken in return."

"Taken?"

She shivered. "Folded away. It's . . . I see things with this eye."

"See?"

"Shadows," she said, hands clutching one another. "Shades."

"Why haven't you asked Main for help?"

Dr. Carlyle froze. "How do you know I haven't?"

"They'd be here." It didn't add up to Mae. "Why haven't you told Main?" she repeated.

Had Dr. Carlyle turned against Main? she wondered. No, that didn't feel quite right. She wasn't the sort to quit. Not after thirty years. She was committed to her work, she'd fight. She thought of the Magellans, living by their Topologie all those years. And where was her remorse? Her staff were all dead. She saw ghosts, she said. Yet it didn't seem to bother her. Cover it over, like a dead eye. Another fact just to be accepted.

Such insouciance reminded Mae of something from long ago.

"I was raised in a church," Mae said. "From an early age, their beliefs are instilled in you. Even when you come to reject them, as many of us do, they still shape you. Whenever I think of the past or look into the future, I do so with the eyes of a former member of the Church of Venerable Light's congregation. The past, they taught us, was the key to the future." She shrugged. "Maybe it is, and maybe it isn't."

Dr. Carlyle looked ardently bored.

"On Mars, the churches held an ecumenical council every few years. I was taken to one when I was ten. I remember being astonished by the range of beliefs. All those different religions in one chamber. Everyone believed in a different future, but we were united in our belief in the past and its consequences—Earth was humankind's fall, and we were in need of redemption. We all agreed on the problem, just not the solution."

The doctor moved away, heading back to the cabin. Mae followed, still talking.

"So many different faiths, dressed up in their individual livery. I was particularly taken by the symbols of allegiance. Not the common crosses, crescents, ouroboroses and stars. But the peculiar ones. The Earths and suns. Ours was rather mundane: a telescope. I remember one symbol: a lemniscate ouroboros. A lazy-eight snake eating its tail. I always thought it rather bold. It belonged to the Church of the Axion who believe in the necessity of the Earth's demise. That without our exodus we cannot achieve our destiny, which is to be out among the infinite stars. They push for a second exodus. They believe the dead are a part of the bargain. A sacrifice required for what is to come."

Dr. Carlyle stopped at the cabin door, her back to Mae.

"The Magellans mistook it for a symbol of scientific observance. I know different. I recognised what your necklace meant the first time I met you. The question is, do you wear it for sentimental reasons, or does it still have meaning for you?"

Dr. Carlyle turned, fingering the necklace. "Mae, I've been working here over half my life. I'm a scientist through and through."

"Belief can be a crutch or an inspiration." Pure Sister Ursula. "You could be Axion's first and Main's second."

"All this speculation because I haven't told Main?" She shook her head. "Mae, that suspicious mind of yours is getting paranoid. If Axion seek the stars, what business would they have down here on Earth?"

Mae came closer. "You're the scientist, you tell me."

Dr. Carlyle ruminated, staring not at Mae but into some far-off, unreachable place. A place of shades, of ghosts.

"Get some sleep," she said. "We'll leave at first light."

Mae lay in the doctor's cot, but sleep eluded her. The window was lit up with Caul-glow, throwing a milky patina on every surface. Bluettes flitted.

As the night wore on, she turned over in her mind what Dr. Carlyle had told her. None of it stacked up. She didn't think Dr. Carlyle had told her many lies, but omissions were just as deceptive. The doctor's sudden capitulation over going after Siofra particularly concerned her. Everything she knew about Dr. Carlyle indicated the last thing she'd do would be to help Mae. Which meant Dr. Carlyle had her own reasons for doing so. Might she be Dr. Machalek's second master?

Mae sighed. Her mind was not going to let this rest. She rose, took her bag, and looked at Dr. Carlyle, who'd taken a handful of pills before she'd slept and was dead to the world. Piled under her cot were files and handwritten papers.

More notes to join the Magellans' notes. Spiders industriously producing thick webs of information and speculation. She silently took a small pile of papers and sat by the window to read by the light of the Caul.

All these entangling webs, she thought, and here am I.

A lonely fly.

DAY NINE

THEY ROSE AND FLEW towards a fiery orange eye, low and glowering in the east.

Towering behind them, the shadowy funnel continued to drag down the sky. Electric bluettes danced in the wind, leaving a million glittering trails in the air. To the south, the Caul stretched away—not gray, but white—a shimmering, palely shining sea.

"It's apocalyptic," yelled Mae.

"All ends are beginnings," Dr. Carlyle yelled back.

The copter was deafening, roaring its passage across the pebble plain. Dr. Carlyle said they'd enough fuel to get there and back. Strapped in her seat, Mae worried. They were sixteen hours behind Hannu. If he'd followed Baré and Siofra to the Topologie, whatever he'd intended had likely played out by now. The chances of the girl still being there were diminishing by the hour.

Dr. Carlyle did not pilot them along the shore. Instead, they curved inland. "Gray or white, the Caul still plays merry hell with this bird's instruments."

Mae gasped when she looked north. The Caul had flooded so much more of the pebble plain. Huge parts were under the pale-glowing milky liquid, while snaking rivers carved up the rest, icy white seams slicing through the ground. Most rivers came from the Caul, having breached the pebble ridges. Others fountained out of the ground in tumbling geysers. The land was sinking, the Caul exultant.

Mae feared for her hut. She thought of Rawat and Kozlov and the Twins. Had it taken their homes? Had it got them? All these years, they'd resisted, never giving in. But now, as if tired of waiting, the Caul had come for them.

"You sure your experiment didn't cause this?" called Mae.

"It was always coming," replied Dr. Carlyle.

Was it? she wondered. The Caul invading. The Topologie transforming. So what? They were not her real concern. It's people, she thought, always damned people. Baré had drugged her. Hannu had destructively marooned her. Now she depended on Dr. Carlyle—the highest-ranking Main official on this stretch of shore—who answered questions evasively and had never had time for penitents, or Siofra.

Until now.

They needed to have a conversation about that before landing. She'd put it off until they were in the air because she expected it to go badly.

Eventually, she said, "Last night, I couldn't sleep."

"I offered you pills."

"You've got a lot of notebooks. Same kind as Magellan's journals."

"Were you looking for something to read?"

"It was the handwriting," she said. Reaching into her pack, she removed a sheet of paper that she carefully unfolded. "When I found Siofra, she gave me this."

Dr. Carlyle glanced over.

"The numbers are orbital coordinates," said Mae. "At first, I thought it Magellan's writing, but it doesn't match his journals. Nor is it Gemma's."

Dr. Carlyle frowned but said nothing.

Mae reached into her pack again and took out another sheet covered in writing. "I took this from the notebooks. They're yours, I think."

Dr. Carlyle didn't glance over this time. "Snooping, Mae? We spoke about this."

"It's the same handwriting," said Mae, holding the sheets side by side. "Microsat orbital coordinates, written by you. Why, I asked myself, would Siofra have those?"

Her question hung in the air. Dr. Carlyle's eyes were fixed on the burning sun, rising to meet them. Between breaths, Mae took the faintest of sniffs.

"What do you want, Mae?" Dr. Carlyle asked.

"I don't believe my finding Siofra was an accident," said Mae. "Magellan sent her to me, carrying coordinates you wrote down."

For a time, she feared Dr. Carlyle wasn't going to respond.

Finally, the doctor said, "Mae, I keep telling you, but you refuse to listen. You stick your nose where it is not wanted, you'll come to regret it."

"I'm a penitent. Regrets are all I've got."

Dr. Carlyle ruminated a long moment before speaking again: "Main are about to be extremely upset. They will send people in numbers, and they will have questions for anyone they find here. They will be merciless in their search for answers."

Outside, strings of bluettes, their colours burned gold by the rising sun, trailed across the sky.

Mae sniffed again. When she'd got into the copter, she'd detected a strong odour she couldn't help but recognise. She'd first noticed it in the cabin last night, but faintly. She said, "Is this all about your experiment?"

"You've seen the bergs," said Dr. Carlyle. "They're the most obvious sign the Caul has been changing. They are everywhere. Growing more numerous, ever larger, each year. Some are kilos across. We long suspected the bergs might hold the key to the Caul. What we didn't know, until Gemma told me, is that the Magellans had retrieved one from the Topologie. It took a year to convince her to hand it over."

The Magellans and Dr. Carlyle, thought Mae, caught up in their scientific back and forth along the shore. But was it a conversation, or an argument?

"We called them bergs because we thought they were like crystals precipitating out of a liquid. A solidifying, like ice from water. But studying a berg was to learn it wasn't like any matter we'd seen before. Gemma warned me the patterning was hypnotic. Look into it, and you feel it looking into you. We are drawn to it. Like our compulsion to enter the Caul itself. We see the surface, but we feel the deeps."

Mae nodded. She'd experienced it herself. Magellan had called it Janus—a doorway. But to where exactly?

"You need to understand how Main works. Research is siloed. You have your task, and you stick to it. It allows them complete control of any discoveries made here. Long ago, they had decided the clusters were a curious but dangerous epiphenomenon of the Caul. They'd lost too many staff and resources probing them. They weren't worth the candle."

"So, the PA sending the Magellans—"

"They were seen as an irritation at first. Main knew about the hyperdimensions already. What could two theoretical mathematicians learn that decades of field research had failed to find? Main paid them no heed. They were an irrelevance. That was their mistake. Because, year after year, the Magellans quietly proved hyperdimensions lay at the heart of everything."

"You were paying attention."

Dr. Carlyle's visor glowed orange, reflecting the fiery orb rising ahead. "Main will be furious when they discover the truth was under their nose all along. But by then it will be too late."

Mae said nothing, thinking: She's gone rogue.

They curved south, heading back to shore.

Mae sniffed, wincing at the threadlike odour of smoke. Insidious signature of fire. Of the burning of Magellan's camp.

Hadn't Rawat claimed he'd heard thunder? The copter had been there.

She'd believed Hannu had been responsible, but what if it was Dr. Carlyle?

By then it will be too late. Suddenly, it was clear to Mae.

Dr. Machalek had indicated that Main were distrustful, spying on their staff. Comms would of course be monitored. So how to get a message off Earth without Main knowing? Magellan's microsats surveyed the Topologie. If Main believed him a crank, they'd pay little attention to any launches from his camp. But put one in the right orbit—an orbit that someone was told to watch—and it'd be as good as sending up a flare.

Had Dr. Carlyle gone to the camp to see if Magellan had launched the microsat? And, on finding the spent launcher, had she burned the camp to destroy any remaining evidence? She kept saying: Don't upset Main. She meant: I already have.

"You're running and taking your discoveries with you," Mae said.

But Dr. Carlyle, never one for being candid, only said: "I'm telling you, Mae, so you understand what is at stake. I'll take you to Siofra because I owe the Magellans. But Main are coming. They'll cut a swathe across this shore to learn the truth. You don't want to be in their way."

Mae said nothing. She thought of the mounds next to the compound. Of Gemma, who'd vanished. Hastings too. And, finally, murdered Magellan. Dr. Carlyle had been closely involved in some manner with each one of them and now they were all gone.

They'll cut a swathe across this shore.

Wasn't Dr. Carlyle—her destructive experiment, covering her tracks—cutting her own swathe? *What must we do for our beliefs, for our church?* Sister Ursula had once asked.

Everywhere she turned, Mae was seeing ghosts.

○

A CITY. A REEF. A NEST. A HIVE. A vibrant, teeming body. Electric with light, colour, and animation, the Topologie grew brighter as they approached. It dazzled in its arrays of wild polychromatics. Mae stared and stared and stared some more. Lit-up domes like those on Mars. Curved lustrous towers tall as rockets. Effulgent rings suspended above it all like sections of orbitals. It was astonishing. It was numbing. A miracle and an abomination. Between those weird towers and domes, a million bluettes flew or swam or drifted. Swarming. Shoaling. Flocking. Like insects. Like fish. Like birds. Like nothing she'd ever seen. A shining, bristling, seething monster.

Mae's first glimpse of the Topologie up close was just as Magellan had described the attractor below the surface. A living, pulsing system. Something animated. And lapping its far shores was the Caul in its radiant white coat. Revealing a clean, freshly scrubbed face. But no new look could disguise its raw hunger. Its need.

It was still the adversary.

The copter made two sweeps of the shore in front of the Topologie. Mae breathed a sigh of relief. It didn't appear overrun by the Caul. "Low tide," confirmed Dr. Carlyle.

But of Baré and Siofra there was no immediate sign. Perhaps they'd instead returned to Magellan's camp?

"Would they have gone inside?" asked Dr. Carlyle.

Mae was too busy scanning the shore to answer. "There!" she said, pointing.

Dr. Carlyle brought them down low. Mae had spotted a tent and a few Main crates belonging to the Facility compound. No vehicle. "Someone's been here."

"And they planned on coming back."

"Or they left in a hurry."

Mae wanted Dr. Carlyle to land but she took them back up. They flew around the camp in circles. "What are we . . ." Dr. Carlyle held up a warning finger.

A minute later Mae could see them. "Wheel marks," she said. Faint trails in the pebbles leading to or from the camp. Some running parallel with the shore. Some heading to the Topologie. "Two sets. One set wider than the other."

Hannu. That settled it.

Dr. Carlyle brought them down close to the camp. While she shut the bird down, Mae was out making a rapid examination of what had been left. Two sleeping bags. A water container. A burner set up for cooking. Clean pans and plates. Everything was neat and tidy. All suggestive of Baré but no obvious evidence of Siofra, or Hannu.

Dr. Carlyle emerged from the copter and watched Mae's inspection. "The tide has turned," she said. "It will overrun the Topologie in a couple of hours. If you're not out by then, I'm leaving."

"You think they're still in there?"

Dr. Carlyle shrugged. "The girl isn't my priority, Mae."

Mae put down her pack. Her canteen of water went in her coat pocket. She rose and found Dr. Carlyle holding out her sunglasses. "You'll need these," she said.

Dark lines feathered the skin around the eyepatch, Mae noticed. Just like Dr. Machalek had had across his chest. Necrosis. *The girl isn't my priority.*

She took the glasses with a nod, turned, and walked quickly away.

It was about a kilo to the Topologie. There was no fog obscuring it. Instead, the air thrummed with vibrant, scintillating bluettes. They seemed to whisper in the wind. In the distance she could see the Caul crashing on the shore. She looked back to see Dr. Carlyle checking the copter. Did she trust her to stay? Did she have a choice?

Twenty minutes later, she was out of breath and following wheel marks into the outer edges of the Topologie. Around her geometric shapes big as boulders had erupted from the sandy ground. Sandy ground that glowed in rainbow hues except where the wheel marks had sunk into it. There, the sand was a dull, gray-brown colour. She bent and gathered a handful of the coruscating sand. It was made of tiny glowing and glittering shell-like fragments. But the moment she touched any the light drained out of it. She was left holding plain old sand. She looked back and could see her footsteps, a dull, gray-brown trail in the chromatic hues. Like her passing was poison.

The air was thick with bluettes. Some tiny as pollen grains, others the size of her thumb. The air whispered with their flitting passage. Sometimes they struck her. Any that collided fell, rapidly turning gray and crumbling to dust.

My grayness is catching, she thought. Gray as the Caul. I am toxic. I am death.

Ahead, reared a storm of shape and light. A migraine of impossible, contorted geometry. Sprays of curves. Scattered angles. Atomised surfaces. Bluettes flickered and darted, shapeshifting restlessly in the air. Her stomach yawned, the space around her feeling like it was shifting—expanding and contracting, like a many-folded concertina. Mae's heart raced. Her hands trembled. Overcome by intimations of infinity, she stopped. Closed her eyes. Shut it out. Get a grip, old woman.

Opened her eyes. Such light. Such unstill ugliness. She dismissed the structures rising ahead. She'd ignore them. They disgusted her.

○

TIME STRETCHED, and some unknown number of minutes later, Mae was inside, carefully picking her way among—and lost within—the Topologie's towering and shining shape. She walked a kind of canyon, following the wheel tracks: one narrow, one wide. The fluid maelstrom of bluettes danced and whispered and dazzled.

Finally, up ahead, she spotted Hannu's lorry. It had got stuck, its cab buried in a gray cuboid crumbling to sand. She walked slowly around it and found his footprints dulling the ground, as if they'd deadened it. Still wearing Magellan's boots. They followed the jeep tracks.

She paused a moment. She examined both boot prints and jeep tracks. Then she looked at her own prints. Hers were matte, dull. But the older tracks had faint flecks of colour in them, had a little lustre. As if they were sparking to life.

Sunglasses on, eyes down, avoiding the tumble of headache-inducing shapes, Mae thought only of the girl. Siofra was everything now. With a lurch of her labouring heart, she realized she'd willingly lay down her own life so the girl could live. Only two other individuals had previously driven her to such depths of feeling. But learning the limits of your selfishness was an awareness as frightening as it was freeing.

And Mae had always feared what she might be capable of when cornered.

Perhaps a hundred metres further on—space as difficult to estimate as time—she found the jeep. It was hemmed in by iridescent coral-coloured cuboids and spheroids. The ground beneath and around the jeep was gray death. A tube ran from the open fuel hatch to the ground. A hydrocarbon stink of fuel. She peered inside. No Baré. No Siofra.

Finding the doors unlocked, she got in, sat in the driver's seat, considered her next move. Took off Dr. Carlyle's sunglasses. Squeezed shut her eyes. Banish the Topologie. Those restless, unstill shapes.

Eyes open. Seeing bluettes buzz carelessly around the jeep cabin. They passed through glass like there was nothing there. They were beginning to annoy her.

She rifled the jeep, seeking a clue, something useful. Gave up. Put on the glasses and stepped outside. Two footprint trails—one small set, one big set. The bigger on top of the smaller. Hannu following Baré. No sign of Siofra.

She tracked the meandering footprint trails into the heart of the Topologie. The luminous tumble of shapes grew more tightly packed and harder to navigate.

For years, Magellan had explored a hypergeometry of supple ceramic that induced dizziness and nausea. The sensory disorientation Mae endured was a visual assault, an almost-blinding colour-storm. Shapes pulsed and shifted, inflated or deflated, grew corners or sides—or lost them. She sensed that these solid forms were mere shadows, 3D silhouettes of structures whose true depth was beyond her grasp. When, she wondered despairingly, did I start thinking like the Magellans?

She paused and drank some water. How long had she been here? How long did she have before the tide swept in? She looked up and the air above was a teeming murmuration of bluettes whose movements pulsed and shifted in synchronicity.

Just as Magellan had described below. Only now above.

What did it mean? Mae neither knew, nor cared. The only thing clear to her was that she was no scientist.

Eyes down, she reminded herself. Follow the trail.

A few metres further on the footprints entered a small opening stained entirely gray. She took off the sunglasses, and bent, gasping, to examine the ground. Something had happened here. Footprints entered it. No footprints left. Instead, there was a trail of unbroken gray. Mae stared at it. She spotted a boot print just outside it, crisp and clear.

Something—or someone—had been dragged.

She followed the trail round several corners. Ducked under a drooping saddle. Circumnavigated a deflated, wrinkled dome. She came to a sudden halt.

Lying, wedged in a corner between an engorged gray cone and a slant-faced cuboid, was Jean Baré. She lay on her side. Her ankles were bound with wire. Hands were tied behind her back.

"Mae!" she gasped in a croaky voice.

Mae didn't move. "Jean, where's Siofra?"

"Siofra? Have you seen her?"

"No. I asked where she is."

"I don't know. She ran in here last night and never came out."

Mae said nothing.

"Hannu showed up at our camp. I told her to hide." She coughed.

Mae came over. Got down on her knees. Out came the canteen. Baré gulped greedily at the water. Mae dug out her knife to cut the wires. She hesitated.

Baré had poisoned her. Looted her kit. Put Siofra at risk. Done Dr. Machalek's bidding. "Why'd you come here?" she asked Baré.

"It's the only place she might be safe."

"From who?"

Baré sobbed but said nothing. "Mae—"

"Dr. Machalek told me about you."

"I was never going to go through with it, Mae."

"So they sent Hannu."

"He never said anything. Never asked about her. Just sat with me, like he was waiting. I don't think he slept all night. I know I didn't. In the morning when the tide was down, I was going to pack up and leave, hoping he'd go too. He shook his head. He told me to go get Siofra. If I didn't, he'd go and get her himself. I drove in, as he said. Halfway there, I looked back and he was following."

Mae gave her some more water.

"I think she's in the attractor. It's somewhere close, but I can't find it. He told me to tell him where it was. When I told him I didn't know, he tied me up. Then he dragged me here, shouting for Siofra, making threats. She's a smart girl and never showed herself."

"Where's he now?" asked Mae.

"He ran off when he heard the copter. Mae, why haven't you untied me?"

It was a good question. Mae didn't have a good answer.

"Baré!" It was Hannu. The shout coming from the direction Mae had come.

She moved fast. She put the knife in Baré's trouser pocket. She got to her feet. "Don't let him know," she hissed.

Baré's eyes were wide with alarm, but Mae was already turning away, placing her feet in Hannu's boot steps. Walking away from him, following his trail that followed Baré's earlier footprints, which, Mae had no doubt, led towards the attractor.

The woman's lies, like her footprints, left a distinct trail.

It wasn't far. Hannu's and Baré's colour-leaching footprints circled a particularly tangled area of erupted bright structures. It looked impenetrable. Mae knew she wasn't getting in there. Just as she was never heading underground to find the damn attractor.

Instead, she rested on a torus. She gazed at the structures above her, shimmering in their emerald, ruby, sapphire hues. Was it her imagination, or were they all leaning towards that tangled eruption of geometry? The bluettes were twinkling dust darting in the air, their soft whistling a faint but mournful chorus.

Mae closed her eyes and listened.

Distantly, she could hear the tide. The insistent wash and shush of approaching waves. But there was something more. A deeper echo of the bluette's whistling. A kind of repetitive droning. It sounded close.

Mae's eyes snapped open.

She carefully stepped away from Hannu and Baré's prints, concentrating on the faint up-and-down droning. Every moment her ears grew more attuned to what was clearly now a faint wailing. In her way, a litter of impossible, scintillating shapes.

Duck under. Climb over. Step around. Bat aside the distracting bluettes.

At first, she didn't appreciate that she'd found the child.

At her feet, a mass of bluettes gathered in a huge ball-like swarm: A coruscating cluster that hurt her eyes. She crouched down, and slowly, gently, brushed them away. New ones kept arriving. She swatted them aside. Her touch left a dull, ashen dust on the ground. But she kept at it—brushing, swatting—removing layers of them. Strata.

Until there she was.

Siofra, curled up on the ground. She looked like she was sleeping, but she was still emitting that faint keening from her open mouth. Mae leaned close. "Siofra," she whispered, knowing Hannu might be close. That she'd left a dead-footprint trail.

The girl stirred. Snuffled. Was she sleeping? The ground around the girl was gray now with dust where Mae had removed the bluettes. Her touch was death, but not the girl's, not even in her red coat.

Above them, spiralling clouds of bluettes twitched and stirred.

"Siofra . . ." The girl moved and Mae saw that she was holding something. One of her toys, perhaps. The girl opened her eyes, saw Mae and smiled. She stretched. She wiggled the toes of her bare feet. The gray bundle in her arms was small and wrinkled like a sack. Siofra looked into Mae's eyes and held out what she was holding.

Mae took off the dark glasses to see it better.

Tiny, wrinkled, leathery. In a compacted face, slits for eyes, mouth, nostrils. Four stubby limbs. Mae had no doubt what it was. She gasped and shrank back.

The girl stared at her, eyes hurt. Mae returned her gaze, revolted, feeling sick and dizzy. "S-Siofra," she said accusingly, looking at the tiny thing.

It was marbit-sized. New-born. A shrunken, desiccated husk.

The knowledge of the crime Magellan had committed here all those years ago was still fresh in Mae's mind. Yet the possibility that Siofra was not even Siofra had never occurred to her. Even as she tried to make full sense of what the girl held, she wondered if the girl had any inkling of what she'd found down in the attractor. This changes everything, Mae thought. But did it? What was Siofra? Until moments ago, she was a child. An orphan. Someone who people wanted and who Mae wanted to protect. Now, she was not even human. Had never been.

So what is she? Mae asked herself again. What isn't she? And why did it matter? And the obvious answer came to her. It mattered very much to those who sought her.

The Magellans had speculated the clusters were changeling cities—the Caul crudely imitating or aping human forms. But the girl . . . Mae shook her head. How could this be?

With one hand, Siofra reached out and took Mae's hand. Mae resisted. She wasn't going to touch the body. But the girl simply held her hand in a tight grasp. The child's skin was warm and soft. She was frowning unhappily at Mae.

Mae talked to the girl—the words coming easily—about her missing mother and her dead father. About the body Siofra was holding. She would not touch it, she explained and said that Siofra should not either. Siofra shook her head violently.

The bluettes, merrily droning in brilliant leafy yellow and green crescents, circled round them. A dizzying living geometry. Magellan had declared its vibrancy beautiful. Yet, in its midst, Mae had found death.

"It belongs here," she told the girl. "We must leave it here."

The girl again shook her head fiercely.

Mae could hear the approaching tide. It was close. Siofra might survive the Caul, but Mae had no illusions what would happen to her. They had to leave.

"It's time to go, Siofra. We must leave it behind. Jean needs us."

But Siofra was peering past Mae, suddenly alert.

Mae heard his footsteps. Quick, clumping, nearby. She put her finger to her lips. The girl nodded, got to her feet, still holding the little bundle.

But Mae knew they couldn't hide. She'd left a trail for him to follow.

She caught a whiff of him, the foul reek of fuel carrying on the air. She took Siofra's hand, to lead her away. They were in more open space when she turned and there he was. Hannu's face broke into a sour smile.

"Mae! You've found her for me. I knew you would."

○

AT SOME POINT in the last thirty years, Mae had died inside.

It was easier to tell herself that than admit she'd forgotten how to be human.

Nevertheless, she'd had to go on living. Here on a cursed Earth, she'd fashioned an existence for herself out of the detritus of other lives. A patchwork assemblage of being. It had been lonely. Months might go by between contact with another penitent. Yet company, tormenting you with all you'd lost, had to be avoided.

Ghosts haunted no one more than themselves.

The struggle for existence was a purgatory. It stopped you feeling. Made you animal. A machine. Everything a simple matter of inputs and outputs. When you no longer cared about anyone, especially yourself, you could stop making any effort to be human. With no one to love and no one to love you, nothing you did mattered. There were no consequences.

She'd felt nothing but the persistent ache of the Caul, year after year.

Tirelessly washing back and forth, the Caul was utterly indifferent to the human life drawn to its shores. Yet Mae had told herself she hated the Caul because she blamed it for everything. She called it her adversary. It was a lie. A pretence to maintain the fiction that she could still feel things. That, despite everything, she remained human.

Her hatred had been no more a part of her than the ragged, threadbare clothing she wore day and night.

Only the arrival of the girl had revealed the truth.

In the last eight days, Mae had been unable not to care for Siofra. She hadn't wanted this, but, for good or ill, the girl had brought something in Mae back to life.

And now she was terrified of what would happen next.

Because losing the girl would mean losing forever what she'd regained.

○

IN THE SILENCE, Mae could hear the approaching waves. They were too close.

Hannu stood in their way, raising a gray, cross-shaped object in his right hand. A tool or a weapon, she thought. He was staring at Siofra. Mae dug in her coat pocket, put her hand around the jeep's flare gun. Shouldn't have given up her knife.

"That's close enough, Hannu," she said. She felt slightly dislocated, not entirely present. Was it the proximity to the Caul? Snagging at her thoughts.

The girl was leaning against Mae's leg.

Mae caught another strong whiff of fuel. The object he held appeared to be a home-made crossbow. A rusty metal bolt was held in a groove along its top. It was an ugly thing, but Mae had no doubt it was well made.

"Hannu." It was hard speaking. She realized she was scared.

She gripped the flare gun tight. Pins and needles in her fingers.

"Mae," he said, "step away from Siofra."

He angled the crossbow until it pointed at Mae. "Now!"

She didn't move. He swung the weapon, pointing it at Siofra. "Send her to me."

Mae's mouth was dry. "What are you going to do?" she croaked.

"You won't get away again," he said, still aiming at Siofra. "Coming with me."

"The Caul," she said. "We need to get out of here."

"When she gets to me."

"Disappear, Siofra," she whispered. "Hide."

"I heard that!"

But Siofra hadn't heard, or was ignoring Mae. She still clung to the little body.

Mae came to a decision. "We're walking out of here. You can come with us or stay here. But Siofra and I are walking out together."

Mae let go the flare gun, taking Siofra's hand. They would have to be fast. The Caul was coming in quick. She turned, putting the sound of the tide behind them, and led them away. An image of Baré, lying tied up, flashed briefly in her mind, but she squashed it down. She'd done what she could.

She didn't check if Hannu was following.

Over. Under. Around. Through. Navigating an absurd regurgitated geometry.

Stumbling through blazing blizzards of tumbling, choking bluettes.

Hannu was always just a step behind.

"Magellan," she said thickly. "That was you."

It was a full minute before he replied. "Didn't want to . . . wasn't going to. Bastard left me no choice."

"The choice . . . was all yours, Hannu."

"Mae"—it came out as a cry—"I'm no killer . . . Really."

He stank of fuel. She remembered the rubber hose. He liked scavenging, she recalled. He couldn't help it. This was a man who'd put himself together from whatever junk he could lay his hands on, like one of his machines. Like all of us, she thought.

Mae was tiring. Siofra was tugging her along, maintaining a steady but unremitting pace. She was not used to this. The coruscating shapes swam before her eyes. She was seeing black dots. Stay focused, old woman, keep him talking.

"What was the deal, Hannu?" she asked. "Take the girl and you get off Earth?"

He said nothing.

"Penitents don't get off Earth," she said. "They lied to you."

He growled. "Magellan was leaving. He'd cut a deal."

"Who told you that?"

"Dr. Carlyle arranged it . . ."

Mae stopped, turned. "Dr. Carlyle?"

He looked at her defiantly. It was what he believed, she saw. Was it true?

She felt a tug on her arm. She turned and shuddered. There was the Caul, straight ahead, streaming across the ground. But she could hear waves behind her.

They were going to be cut off.

Siofra tugged her hand again, leading Mae to their right. They rounded a pillar that over their heads repeatedly branched in multiple, radial symmetries.

Mae knew she couldn't keep this up. She let go Siofra's hand. Pushed the child. "Run!" she hissed. "Run!"

She turned and took two steps back, yanking the flare gun from her pocket. Hannu stopped, open-mouthed. Point blank, she fired. He cried out just as his fuel-soaked clothes burst into a fountain of flame.

Mae dropped the gun, turned again and lurched after the child.

Just ahead, the girl was waiting in a clearing, clutching her bundle. Mae was gasping, out of breath. She could hear the Caul. The roar of the crashing waves echoing among the towering structures around them.

She took the girl's hand, but the girl was looking wild-eyed behind her. Mae turned. He was back. Clothes slightly charred, smoking. Hair singed. Unharmed.

But angry now.

"That's enough." He grabbed Mae's arm, held it tight. He swung his weapon up.

Siofra was backing away.

"No," said Mae. "Hannu—"

He pulled the trigger.

The girl's red coat, pierced by the bolt, was pinned to the ground. Next to it, the dropped mummified little body.

Mae, staring dumbly at where the girl had been standing a moment before, struggled to believe what her eyes weren't seeing. "Siofra?"

Siofra, however, had vanished.

"Damn it!" Hannu cursed her. He let go of Mae's arm. "Little witch . . . likes its vanishing tricks." Stiffly, he turned, peering suspiciously around. "Where's she gone?"

Mae's lungs burned. Her head ached like it would split. But finally, she knew. Like Magellan had known, and Baré knew, and Rawat and Hannu and heaven knew who else living beside the Caul. Siofra had vanished into that place others couldn't go. Inside those curled-up dimensions denied to humans.

But if the child isn't human, her throbbing head puzzled, what is she?

"Wasting time," he muttered. He was fitting another bolt in his crossbow. He stepped back and pointed it at Mae. She knew she couldn't move. Even if the Caul was sweeping in, she couldn't take another step. Let it claim her.

"Come out!" he yelled. "Come out, or she's next."

The girl suddenly appeared behind Hannu, like she'd popped out from behind an invisible wall. She was bare and she stared at them both with an eerie, otherworldly stillness that scared Mae. Hannu must have seen her look, for he turned. Before he could aim, the girl seemed to shrink suddenly, vanishing altogether.

"Shit! Shit!" Hannu was sweating, his face had gone chalk white. "If she gets away again . . . Should have kept your nose out of it."

She heard a swashing and whooshing, and there was the milky Caul. Just metres away, rushing in, flooding the clearing.

"Hannu," said Mae, paralysed with horror. "The Caul . . ."

"Shh," he hissed, looking and listening for what his senses couldn't grasp.

"Siofra!" he yelled. "Remember your father! It'll happen again."

He pointed his weapon vaguely at Mae. He wasn't wrong about himself, she thought. Killing didn't come easy. She could see the horror in his eyes. The suffering it brought him. She wondered if he'd slept since killing Magellan.

A breath of air and Mae felt a wrench as if her perceptions were yanked into the perpendicular. Astonishingly, a small body had materialised in her arms.

A stunned Mae somehow caught the falling girl.

She heard a sharp crack, followed by a shriek.

Mae stared at the metal bolt skewering the child's arm. Blood-splattered white skin. The girl cried out, struggling in Mae's arms, moving but not moving. A flickering figure, there and not there, an octopus of legs and arm flailing into and out of space. But Mae clung to this insubstantial creature, clung to Siofra like she'd never clung so tightly to anything in her life, turning, hunching over, shielding the girl's body from Hannu. You didn't have to understand what something was to know the world was better for its existence. That protecting it somehow made you a better person.

"Now she ain't going anywhere," he growled, discarding his weapon. "She's stuck here with the rest of us."

"Stuck?" gasped Mae.

"She can't disappear, not with that in her. Like a bug pinned to a board."

Mae's grip on the girl was slackening. Her head was pounding. Fire in her blood. Eyes snagged by the Caul. A hand's depth, only metres away. A rush of urgent need swelling inside her. Just a few steps. Don't think. Move. Meet the advancing tide. Her torments over.

Hannu came in close and bellowed, "Get out my way, old woman."

He didn't sound like the Hannu she knew. Must be someone else, she thought vaguely. But he looked so like Hannu. Hadn't he a brother somewhere?

"She's the Caul's monster. You hate the Caul. It took your Albert."

Mae shook her head. "It didn't," she said. "I know it didn't."

That, she knew, was a fact.

"Then you've been lying to yourself all these years."

Had she? She could see the Caul creeping closer. She welcomed it.

"Hannu!" Not her. Someone else's voice.

Mae looked up as Baré careened past her. Running, a glint of light in her hand. Hannu let out an explosive oof as she hit him. He stumbled backwards. Mae's knife stuck out of his side. He stared at it a moment. Then, in movements that came one after the other in rapid succession, he opened his mouth, vomited an arc of blood and fell back, landing on his backside with a splash of radiant white light.

Mae saw him look down stupidly as a ripple of Caul wavelets washed over his legs. His eyes were tarnished silver. Suddenly, the mechanic shifted violently as if wrenched by some invisible force. He seemed to crumple up—limbs swivelling, torso folding and doubling over—in a sickening way that Mae could never afterwards get out of her head. Like a sheet of paper crushed into a ball. And then he was gone.

Baré, turning, lifted Siofra out of Mae's arms. She hugged the child tight, then she retrieved the coat before the Caul got it and wrapped her in it.

Mae stared at the little gray husk lying on the ground. Another advancing rush of bright milky foam surrounded and floated it. Lifted up, like Magellan at his funeral, it retreated on the ebb.

Mae was spellbound, unable to take her eyes from the body.

Baré took her hand, gently tugged her away. "Mae," she said.

"Leave me," said Mae. The darting bluettes were whispering. The waves echoing through the geometry were calling her name. There was a ringing on the wind, a faint tolling. An elegy as old as time. She hadn't surrendered herself to the Caul. But, at long last, it was coming for her. It was before her. She didn't have to do anything.

She watched the little body, being swept away on its last journey. She wanted more than anything to follow it.

In that moment, her adversary, the terrible hyperobject that had usurped Earth, swelled in her senses. She smelled dust, so thick she tasted it on her tongue. The Caul's light so blinded her she felt those endless multidimensions unravelling, beckoning.

Dust—the Caul's scent: musty, old stone. The observatory walls of her childhood. A church-claimed orphan. A lost child unwillingly homed. The smell of difficult Sister Ursula—the only woman she'd ever dreamed of calling mother.

Dust in her heart, in her head. Lives ground down by endless, marching time. So much dust.

It was how the Caul got to you, reaching inside you and finding your weakness. Unravelling you. Revealing your own deep time, the dust within you. The dead past the grit around which the pearl of the future accumulated. Death at the heart of life.

Mae was stepping forward, welcoming her dissolution, when Baré carefully steered her sideways and together, carrying the child, they walked out of the Topologie and away from the Caul.

And that tiny husk? No one ever spoke of it again.

○

LATER, THUNDER RUMBLES, RISING TO A SCREAM. Every living soul along the shore looks to the sky. Sees the heavens defiled by a rocket, engines flaring as it searches for a place to land.

YEAR NINE

[Pages torn out throughout.]

Day 16, Month 4

Visited the tree, and who did I find? Mae Jameson, kneeling before it like a penitent before her God. Half a dozen marbits hung from her belt. We looked at one another in embarrassed silence. She asked after Siofra. Detecting no chiding, I explained she was back at the camp. "She doesn't like coming here." I spoke of Gemma's love for this tree and how, since there was no other marker of her life, I often came here. "To talk?" To apologise, I confessed. She nodded, saying, "I talk to Albert." She visits, she told me, because "here I don't feel the Caul." You choose to live by it, I said. "I came to find Albert and I won't abandon him." I didn't point out he'd abandoned her. I came to make my name and lost my wife, I said. We both looked at the bare, dead tree, contemplating our follies. To think I once dismissed Mae for her reticence. It is a strength, I realize. A refusal to compromise, to bend to the Cauldron's will. "Its existence corrupts us," she said. I nodded, thinking of sacrifices that had not been mine to make. "This tree reminds me," she said, staring at the gnarled trunk and broken branches, "that death ought to be a state of grace." We parted soon after.

Day 19, Month 4

Encountered Dr. Carlyle at the Twins'. Had the most peculiar conversation on our own at the back of the house. She spoke quietly, as if there were ears other than the Twins' nearby. She told me her experiments had reached a critical juncture. If she was right—"If Gemma's calculations aren't off," she added—then "we'll unfold space." Astonished, as well as horrified at her audacity, I said: At the Facility? But that's dangerous. "It's daring. And it will put Main's nose out of joint," she replied. "You must be prepared." For what? I asked, suddenly fearful. She leaned towards me. "My work is based on your wife's. When Main figure out the implications, they'll come calling, and their tolerance of you and the child may come to a sudden end."

Was this a threat? Is Dr. Carlyle in league with Jean? I shrugged, but inside I was terrified for Siofra. What does she know? What has Jean told her?

"I'm trying to help you," she said.

I told her Gemma had paid a terrible price for the knowledge she gained.

Dr. Carlyle's smile was pointed. "Her sacrifice was not in vain."

We stood in silence. I told her I didn't care what she did as long as she left Siofra and me out of it.

"You misunderstand me," she said.

On the contrary, I told her, I think I understand you all too well.

Day 26, Month 4

It is most peculiar. I never know from day to day whether I will visit the attractor, but Siofra always does. I wake and if I find she's sitting in the jeep I know it is a day we will go there. If not, I know it is a day of camp study. Anyone reading this will think I am allowing her to lead me, but I assure you that is not the case. If she is in the jeep, then it is simply a good day to visit the Topologie.

Later

We are watched. I don't see them clearly or very often. They are careful. But I know they are there. I feel it. Watching can't tell them much, not when they don't follow us into the Topologie. I am now convinced Hastings wasn't behind my troubles. I showed him the truth and they got rid of him. Dr. Carlyle, then? I don't know. But someone is spying on us again.

The changes continue, spreading out from the attractor. The fog, which once hid and protected, grows thinner by the day. The Topologie sparks to life. I see more and more bluettes outside. Siofra is delighted . . .

[rest of entry torn out]

Day 5, Month 5

I have been trying to decipher the mathematics in Gemma's pain journal. It is like having a conversation with my lost wife: she racing ahead, me stumbling after. These ideas came to her when she was lost to her pain. Were they a kind of relief, a refuge or a distraction? Or did the pain of her body turning against her somehow put her in an elevated state of mind? From agony to ecstasy?

In her final entries (all are undated) Gemma wonders if the attractor is a surface response to a deeper hypocentre or zero point deep in the planet. If so, she speculates, then the Caul must originate here on Earth. She calls the Topologies doppelganger cities, claims they are a geomathematical response. To what? She is unclear. She imagines alterations to the planet's biosignature, writing:

WHAT IF THE FUNDAMENTALS OF LIFE HERE ON EARTH HAVE BEEN REWRITTEN? WHAT IF WE'RE THE ALIENS NOW? PERHAPS WE ALWAYS WERE . . .

Day 19, Month 5

Today was our strangest visit yet to the attractor. Normally, inside the inner Topologie, Siofra runs ahead, and I don't see her until I'm down below, but today she waited. It was bright, sparkling with life. Bluettes paraded around us in a patterned spectrum. Before we entered, she took my hand and squeezed.

Down below, in the Shape Garden, I watched Siofra communing with the brilliant chiaroscuro. It is a kind of dance or play. The bluettes, these mini-hyperobjects, revolve around her in glittering arrays. She vanishes and appears. I wonder what she sees, where she goes. How far down does this extend? Turtles all the way. Yet we both know this can't last. It is changing. Siofra is bright down here. She shines. Sometimes so bright I can't look at her. But the Shape Garden grows less bright, just as the Topologie above is lighting up, tide by tide. My footsteps, my touch, kill the light, as if I am toxic. I watch as Siofra rotates and slides away from me. My daughter comes apart in pieces, parts of her literally disappearing in stages, one after the other like she is being dismantled or erased, and I fear for . . .

[two pages torn out]

—been hours. I frantically checked my watch. Then I saw movement, that familiar stir of shapes, and she emerged. I saw her from multiple angles at once. The back of an ear, alongside her left eye. An elbow segueing into her lips. A calf and neck congruent. And glistening, maroon sacks suggestive of internal organs pulsing and beating. I was cross-eyed trying to make sense of it. I turned away and mercifully when I looked back Siofra was whole, no longer a Cubist nightmare. She stood naked before me, smiling. I think, today, for the first time, I truly saw her for what she is. There seemed to be more of her than usual, my eyes and head aching as if I could not take it all in. I sensed angles and curves I couldn't grasp, realizing there were literally sides to Siofra I had never seen. Like one of

Gemma's higher dimensional shapes, I see only the 3D shadow she casts in our narrow universe. I see but a fraction of what she really is, of what she is capable of. With a horrid lurch in my gut, I understood she is no more my daughter than Earth is or ever was ours. It holds multitudes we have never seen. Any sense of true belonging is misplaced. A nostalgia for something that never truly existed.

Gemma, in her journal, claims Earth is being reborn or remade:

AKIN TO A LARVA DISSOLVING ITS CHRYSALIS TO SOON EMERGE AS AN IMAGO. EARTH REJECTS US BECAUSE WE NO LONGER FIT. WHY CAN'T WE APPRECIATE THAT?

Siofra took my hand and led me out of the attractor and, as she did so, I knew we were leaving for the last time. Not just the attractor but also the Topologie—Siofra's yolk or nursery. I looked at her and I saw clearly that, one way or another, our days here are numbered.

Day 28, Month 5

We drove to Hannu's. The jeep has been playing up. Took him seconds to identify the problem but hours to make a new part. (The Facility has spares, but he wasn't sure we'd make it. I was relieved as I am wary of going there.) Hannu spent most of his time in his workshop but kept coming out and checking up on Siofra, who was exploring, examining everything in sight. "She's just curious," I told him. "Didn't you hear, Siofra?" he called out. "Curiosity killed the cat."

Day 5, Month 6

Woke to find Rawat prowling the camp. I told him he was trespassing—a mistake. He said I had no rights here, the whole planet belongs to the Cauldron, accusing *me* of being the trespasser. "Only your academic arrogance prevents you seeing it." A year ago, I wouldn't have listened to a word but now I appreciate he has a point. I asked him what he wanted and saw the yearning in his eyes. A need. "I cannot help you," I told him. "She can," he whispered. Siofra, sleepyheaded, stood at the door. She and Rawat stared at one another. "She is a messenger," he said. "A seed out of which the future will grow." I stared at him. What do you mean? I asked, but I was thinking of the Topologie above, sparking to life—and Siofra's brightness below. He wanted to approach but I would not let him. He left, cursing me. Our need to leave is more urgent than ever.

Day 12, Month 6

Drove alone to Jean's cottage. Told her I knew she spied for Main. She didn't deny it. I said Siofra and I had to leave. I said I was prepared to cut a deal. I'd hand over all our notes in return. If I didn't get an answer within the week, I'd burn everything. She began to cry. She shook her head. "You can't trust them," she sobbed. Tell them, I told her impatiently. "No," she said. Don't you want to help Siofra? I asked. "It would only make things worse for both of you," she said. She asked me in, but I had to get away.

Day 19, Month 6

I do not know what to do. Too many people know or have guessed the truth. I feel watched. Sometimes I fear everyone is against us. Should I worry more about those in the Facility or my fellow penitents? Who can we trust?

Day 2, Month 7

A pleasantly diverting day at the Twins'. They are wise in many ways and in others so hidebound. Over tea, surrounded by their sculptures, I asked what they would do if everything changed. They looked at me uncomprehendingly. What if the Cauldron stopped being the Cauldron? I explained. They laughed. "Did you think the Caul drew us here?" Serpa asked. Didn't it? "No," said Sousa. "We came for the space. For solitude." "Speak for yourself, silly moo," demurred Serpa. But the Cauldron inspires you, I protested. Serpa smiled: "Art is seeing what others do not." And you're so sociable, I persisted. "We like our solitude, but I hope we are not rude," said Sousa. If Siofra and I manage to leave, they are going to think us very rude. Felt terribly unwell when we returned. Headache. Feverish. I seemed to see Siofra in all her hyperdimensionality. Whenever I am ill, I worry what will happen to her. I slept and when I woke, feeling much better, Siofra was holding my hand. For now, we look out for each other.

Day 19, Month 7

Dr. Carlyle visited. Normally she wanders the camp, and I feel we're being inspected. Today, she was agitated and came straight to the point: "It'll soon be over." You've finished your experiments? I asked. "One last one." She looked away and then back at me, clutching her ridiculous necklace. "Carl. We must leave." Main's abandoning the Facility? I asked. She shook her head. "You and me. I told you, when they figure out the truth, Main will want answers. We cannot be here." Why? I asked, despair yawning inside me. How will I protect Siofra? "You must come with me," she said. What? How? Where? I was babbling, trying to make sense of this. Baré said leaving was impossible, I told her. "I have the means," said Dr. Carlyle. "You must be the way." She explained. You don't have to do this, I told her. My arguments were dismissed. "If something happens to me . . ." She didn't finish, shrugging fatalistically. What she asks is so little, but in agreeing to it, I will be throwing in my lot with her. What would Gemma say?

Day 26, Month 7

I didn't agree to anything, yet why do I wake every day dreading the next visit?

Day 3, Month 8

Still no word. Perhaps it was a lie, a test?

The Topologie blazes like a city at night and the Caul is brightening too.

Day 8, Month 8

I've told Siofra to hide if anyone should come. It is our game.

Day 7, Month 9

Middle of the night: A knocking at the caravan door. Dr. Machalek, with instructions. Firstly, a sheet of paper with sat launch coordinates on it. "That's the signal," he told me. "It'll mean waiting eight days." His eyes were bloodshot, empty. He looked like he'd been up for a week. What's happened? I asked, thinking of Dr. Carlyle's experiment. "I don't know what she's up to. It's that berg stuff. But she keeps saying that when Main find out they will be murderous. She's been lying to them for years. They will be after you too. After all of us." He walked back to his land cruiser. No different to the ones that used to watch us from afar. He lifted out two crates of journals. "Dr. Carlyle's notes," he explained. "For safekeeping, in case . . ." He shrugged. "You'll know what to do with them." In case? I wondered aloud. He put his hand on my shoulder and said, "There's no stopping her. She believes she's the Good Shepherd."

I didn't ask for this. I didn't want to be a part of it.

But there is Siofra.

Day 8, Month 9

The microsat is out. Half a dozen times I almost launched it this morning as instructed, but something held me back. Now it is too late. Our watcher has returned. I feel under siege. Eight days, said

Dr. Machalek. A dangerous eternity of waiting, of being watched. I would risk myself for Siofra, but not Dr. Carlyle.

Gemma was right all along. We should never have returned to Earth. We were cast out. Not because we were reckless stewards or an alien entity usurped us. But because we behaved like it was ours to do with as we pleased. It was never ours. We couldn't see the world as it truly was. Beguiled by surfaces, we never saw its depths.

It has taken nine years to see the truth. It took Siofra. I have made so many mistakes. I thought I knew what I was doing, but I never understood the breadth and depth of my own ignorance. I trusted the wrong people. Those I asked to help me have suffered. I am a poor excuse for a human being, putting my needs before anyone else's. I've failed Siofra.

I have given her Dr. Carlyle's paper. If something happens to me, I've told her who to find. I don't trust anyone else—including myself—to do the right thing. Our responsibility always must be to others before ourselves. Gemma knew it in her heart. That is the truest love. It was a love I didn't understand enough to properly return. It is too late for me. They are watching. They will be coming. But I will be waiting.

[No more entries]

DAY TEN

MAE WALKED THE LAST KILO TO KANSAS. She leaned on the stick handed her by the medics. Making her into the old woman she felt. Pebbles trembled beneath her moccasins. She hobbled through the garden. Trees in planters dropped brown leaves. In every breath, she tasted mulch and rot. Autumnal sweetness. A redolence of ghosts.

Visiting the Twins had always felt too much like coming home. Kansas disarmed you. You let your guard down. But, by God, you wanted to. No one could healthily live their whole life clinging to an edge. Even those who believed they had chosen to do so.

She waited. Sculptures tinkled and moaned in the stiff breeze. Further tremors.

Nobody came out of the house to greet her.

She gingerly climbed the steps up to the veranda feeling a distinct twinge in her ankle. Yesterday, they'd pumped her full of drugs, yanking her back after the walk out of the Topologie had almost killed her. Today, an accelerated-healing hangover had her feeling woozy as hell. Not so much born again, she thought, as dying postponed.

She knocked hard on the door.

The wind gusted. Leaves whirled from the trees. Timbers creaked. No answer.

She knocked again. Gave it another minute. She called out. Nothing.

She let herself in.

Inside, everything was still. She passed through the hall and reception rooms like a spectre, staring at the gifted, scavenged, and made furniture and ornaments. A half century of acquired junk. Stuff given away or to which the Twins had offered a home. Here lay the accumulated detritus of an untold number of lives, relics passed down or looted from generations of ancestors. It was the cosiest of mausoleums.

In the kitchen she found piles of days-old dirty dishes. Jars of herbs had been taken down from shelves and lay open on the table.

"Sousa?" she called. "Serpa?"

She climbed the stairs. The wood groaned mournfully with each step.

She'd been upstairs just three days ago. It was light and airy, less cluttered. She couldn't at first work out what had changed. Then it came to her. The house felt empty, deserted. She feared they had fled, that she was too late.

At the top, she turned to her right, the bedroom.

She paused in the doorway. Sousa was sitting in a wicker chair, in the far corner of the room. The red cheeks of her lined face were streaked with long-dried tears. She didn't look at Mae, just continued staring unwaveringly at the bed. Mae followed her wooden gaze. In the middle of the bed, covered by a few thin sheets, lay a sprawled figure. The head lay under a pillow, which had been forcefully pressed flat.

"It hurt so much," croaked Sousa. "She begged. She begged and begged me."

○

MAE WAITED ON THE VERANDA while Sousa made tea. She listened to the older woman clatter about in the kitchen. Pouring water. The whistle of the kettle. Clinking china. Finally, Sousa appeared carrying a tray with a teapot and a pair of mismatched cups and saucers. She set the tray on the low table and sat gratefully.

"We'll let it stew a minute," she said, a catch in her voice.

Sousa had needed coaxing down the stairs. When asked, she told Mae she'd been there a day, unable to think of a reason to move. In the kitchen she'd drunk three cups of water in quick succession, gasping between each one like she was coming up for air.

"Something's happened," said Sousa, looking south through her garden.

"The Caul has invaded the shore. It shines now, all day."

"I can smell it."

"Dr. Carlyle says it's a new phase."

Mae's feelings were ambivalent. All her life she'd existed in the adversary's shadow, told it had rendered Earth uninhabitable. Living beside it, she'd hated it, convinced of its role in luring away the person she'd loved. Now, if the scientists were to be believed—big if—the adversary was less a threat to life on Earth than a newly emerging stage of that life. In the wake of so much unquantifiable death, this almost religious idea of rebirth felt incongruous, even indecent.

"You found Jean and Siofra?" asked Sousa.

Mae didn't answer.

"Well, here *you* are, anyway." Sousa picked up the teapot and swirled the liquid inside. She carefully poured the tea and passed a full cup, on a saucer, to Mae. She placed her own cup and saucer in her lap.

"You make a nice family, the three of you." Sousa's smile was unusually forced. "It suits you. We never liked seeing you on your own."

Mae looked at the tea, licked dry lips. "I've been on my own for thirty years."

Sousa nodded thoughtfully, as if this explained much.

They were quiet again.

"There was a rocket," said Sousa suddenly. "I heard it, yesterday."

"Soon be leaving."

Sousa's eyes were bright. "An orbiter? Not a drop, then."

"Summoned by Dr. Carlyle. Siofra and Baré will be on it." Mae looked down at the steaming acid-green liquid. She sniffed. A bitter, almost acrid smell. The Twins were partial to astringent concoctions.

"And you?" asked Sousa in a whisper.

Mae swallowed. She didn't have an answer to that yet.

She looked at the garden. She'd often thought of it as a makeshift Eden, in defiance of the Caul. The first garden reborn as the last. Life cheating death.

The silence between them stretched awkwardly.

Sousa, finally, broke it. "I hoped you'd come back."

The cup was warming Mae's hands. "All paths return us to Kansas," she said.

Sousa lifted her cup, said nothing.

Mae raised her cup too, blew lightly on the tea's surface. "The other day you told me Serpa said she'd met Albert. Was that true?"

A breeze whipped through the garden, sending leaves spinning. Sousa stared at the view before turning back to Mae. "Did I believe her?"

"I'm asking if you lied to me."

"Ah. I see." She lowered her cup. "Well, I'm afraid that was very underhand of me. I wanted to distract you."

"Why?"

"I could see you wondering what Hannu and Serpa were talking about in the garden."

"I suspected they were talking about the girl."

"They were discussing what to do with you."

Mae said nothing.

"You coming across Siofra rather messed things up."

I didn't come across her, she thought. Magellan sent her to me.

"It made my other half rather cross and conflicted."

The veranda was shaken by another tremor.

"Hannu's gone," said Mae. She meant dead. Why can I never say what I mean to the Twins?

Sousa seemed to understand. "Right. Well, that's probably for the best, all things considered."

"Best for who?"

"He turned very bitter and angry. As if what happened was our fault."

"He admitted killing Magellan." Just before you flared him, she reminded herself.

"Did he?" She shook her head irritably. "I told Serpa he was too highly strung."

"He hurt the child." The medic who'd treated Siofra was baffled by the bolt's disappearance from his hands the instant he'd removed it from her arm. Siofra's look of innocence had not helped any.

"She's okay now?"

"She'll live." As will I, she thought, knowing that was down to Jean Baré.

"I'm glad. We always liked her."

Mae gave her a sceptical frown.

"I told you, my other half was conflicted."

"And you?"

Sousa stared into the middle distance. "You are not so different from Serpa and I, Mae. We are penitents. All we've ever been looking for is redemption."

Mae considered this. "Is escaping Earth redemption?" she asked.

Sousa narrowed her eyes. "You know," she said.

Mae nodded. "Yes, I know."

"H-how long?"

"You've been telling me for years," said Mae. "I only had to listen."

Looking for Albert, she'd come to Earth armed only with her knowledge of what drove the man she'd loved: A campaigning journalist seeking stories of injustice, who never saw a conspiracy he didn't want to take to pieces to see what made it tick. But she'd found scant evidence of her husband, and fewer real clues concerning what might have lured him here. Over the years, however, her restless, enquiring mind had noted curious parallels between what she saw and heard at the Twins' and Albert's Big Lies. Albert accused Main of concealing the truth about Earth. The Twins questioned the Facility's true purpose. Albert suspected Main secretly stationed agents on Earth. The Twins hinted they were in hiding. Albert believed there'd been a secret war for control of Main. The Twins told tales of betrayal by a hated family. At some point, Mae found Albert's MainClan conspiracies and the hints the Twins dropped about themselves getting muddled in her head. What if these stories were one and the same? Identical events viewed from very different angles. A confusion of perspectives.

"I also opened my eyes," Mae said. She tapped her foot on the veranda. "Someone built this house for you."

A sharp intake of breath from Sousa, as if she'd been hurt. They regarded one another for a long moment. Finally, Sousa spoke. "Earth was my idea. If the family were to never hear from us again, then being marooned was preferrable to prison. Serpa had to be persuaded not to fight. A public trial had to be avoided. Everyone would have been brought down: Main, our family, us. Quarantine guaranteed our silence."

"What had you done?" asked Mae.

"There's only one crime in the clans," said Sousa dismissively.

Mae nodded. "Getting caught."

"At first, Serpa suffered terribly. Being so disconnected, she said, was like losing a limb. For several years, she obsessed over leaving. I had to remind her of the terms of our deal. Over time, however, she saw how I was thriving away from the family's petty rivalries, our clan battles, the scheming and backstabbing for a bigger share or more control. Here, no one watches our every move. We live an unobserved life. We do not compete, one against another. To survive, we each have to be our best selves. Taking only what we need. For long decades we were happy together."

Sousa pursed her lips. "Then the Magellans arrived. Right from the start, they were a problem. We were drawn to them. They weren't Main. They were so different to the others we met. Both determined and purposeful. Serpa was sure they'd solve the riddle of the Caul. They awoke the want in her. First, she began to court Hastings. He didn't know about us. She dropped hints about our links to Main. Soon he was giving us reports on Dr. Carlyle and the Magellans." She shook her head. "She's always been very persuasive. When the Magellans had the child, everything went up a notch. Siofra, she told me, is our ticket off Earth. She recruited Dr. Machalek to act as spy."

Sousa paused. "You aren't drinking your tea, Mae."

"Neither are you."

She nodded. "Where was I? The child. I knew I couldn't allow it. But Serpa had Hastings wrapped around her finger. She was going to use him and the Magellans to make her play to Main, to the family. I had to intervene."

"Hastings disappeared."

A moment's hesitation. "She was furious with me."

"What did you do?"

"I think you already know." She sniffed. "Not that it did any good. She moved on to Hannu, making promises to him she could never keep. I warned her it would be impossible. Even if Main believed her, came for the girl, saw what we saw, and the clan in their gratitude pardoned us—four highly unlikely occurrences—I couldn't go back. You won't have forgotten what it's like off Earth, Mae. Living in tin cans. Breathing fetid air. Cheek by jowl. We've been prisoners, captives ever since we left Earth. We belong here. Solid rock beneath our feet. Under a free sky. This is our one and only home." She shivered. "I warned her, but by then she was sick and desperate."

"You said she begged you. Begged you to what?"

"She had to be stopped, Mae. Don't you understood that? I had to do the right thing for both of us. For the child too."

Mae looked at the garden. Dying annuals. Withered leaves. Planters in their coffin rows. An oasis in a desert, she'd once thought. It had been a mirage, a lie.

There was a lump in her throat. This was as good a confession as she could have hoped for, she supposed. More than she'd ever expected to get, if she was honest. Yet she didn't feel anything. Just numbness. That same sense of emptiness she'd carried with her all these years. There was no Main conspiracy. Magellan had died because he'd been caught in the competing ambitions of two spoiled, cast-out sisters.

Sousa's smile rallied. "I made the tea for us both, Mae." She lifted her cup. "We're both seeking redemption. Well, here it is. Drink your fill."

The idea didn't repel her. "What if I don't want to drink?"

Sousa said nothing.

"Albert," Mae said quietly. "I think he came looking for you. Perhaps he believed you were guiding Main's activities from here." She swallowed, thinking how the stories we tell ourselves make fools of us. "Did you offer him tea? Like you did Hastings. And Magellan: He left here sick, not long ago."

There was a tremor. Beneath the surface, according to Dr. Carlyle, Earth churned. The Magellans had called the process of transformation a hyperobject. A structure of such colossal scale it was impossible to properly grasp its entirety, its significance.

Sousa shook her head. "Truth is never the consolation we hope it will be."

"I have to know. Please." Begging, she thought disgustedly, now I'm begging.

Sousa raised the cup to her lips, waited a moment, eyes meeting Mae's. "Drink your tea." She took a delicate sip. "Then I'll tell you."

Here it was. The invitation. A devil's bargain. Mae stared at her cup and the promise it held. Was it any different to the one offered by the Caul? Each an ending. Wasn't that what she sought, why she was here? "Just tell me," she said tiredly.

Sousa sipped again.

"You're a stubborn old woman, Mae." She stared out across her garden. "This was our paradise, for a short time." Her smile bitter now. "But that's all we get."

She finished her tea, closed her eyes. Time seemed to stand still.

Mae considered the Earth and the innumerable multitudes that had been here before them. All the living and dying they had done.

All that endless possibility and variety, the good and the bad, rolled up inside each of us at birth and continuously unspooling until the day we are gone. So many brief lives.

Eventually, Mae put down the cup of now cold tea. She wanted to say a final word but couldn't think what. She eased herself to her feet. She limped across the veranda and through the garden. A hundred metres away, she turned. Sousa was a tiny figure dwarfed by the grotesque house built for her on the plain.

The ground beneath Mae's feet shivered. The Caul on the move. A bluette, a tumbling, shining scarlet tetrahedron, carelessly drifted by on the breeze.

Mae thought then of Albert, the man she had loved and lost, had known and not known. A ghost haunting her all these years. But wasn't this a world of ghosts?

She walked north. The rocket, carrying the girl, would be taking off soon.

Yet for her there was only the last tree on Earth.

Mother Earth had cast off her children.

But some of us came home, thought Mae.

To die a penitent was not to die an orphan.

ADDENDUM

HAZARD BUOY:

Earth L2 Orbit

From Sol 3039.03.01.13.00

Continuous broadcast, all channels:

WARNING!

Imminent planetary collapse.

Volatile gravitational and geomagnetic fields.

High probability of thermonuclear fusion.

Cardinal light buoys in place.

Approach no closer than 0.1 AU.

WARNING ENDS.

P.A.

First Report of Investigation into Earth Catasterism

Prepared by Office of System Affairs, Planetary Authority Secretariat
Date Sol standard 3040.02.07.00.00

For the eyes of General Assembly Heads only.

Contents:

BULLETIN:

Casting on all Sol system channels.

From Axion of the Seven Churches of Revelation.

Sol 3043.05.01.12.00

DEATH NOTICE

Begin message: *** Sister Superior Dr. Jane Carlyle ***

Sister Superior Carlyle has passed away after many years resisting an aggressive, debilitating cancer. Over a life of considerable achievements, she will be primarily remembered for her long stint as one of the last scientists on Earth, witnessing its final ecdysis, and for her theoretical insights, which led directly to the development and (ongoing) testing of the Carlyle-Magellan-Alcubierre Hyperspatial Warp Drive. With the opportunity to escape the Sol system within reach, no one did more to bring about the prophesised Second Exodus. Conferral of sainthood is pending.**:message ends.**

SERVICE RAID REPORT 572/AB/94X

Port Olympus Station, Mars

Sol 3055.09.25.18.47

Ranking Officer: Deputy Director K. Skarbek
Arrests: 46 (31 adults, 15 children)
Reasons for Raid: Intelligence gathered of an illegal assembly of worshippers to be led by the wanted radical and seditionist known as Starchild
Summary of Raid: Unresisted arrest of 46 congregation participants. Despite confirming Starchild's presence, securing all exits to the assembly hall prior to commencing raid, and mounting an extensive search, Starchild eluded arrest.
Further actions: Continue to follow up leads regarding Starchild's whereabouts and activities. Share intelligence with other Service stations. Immediate release of congregation participants without charge.

www.ingramcontent.com/pod-product-compliance
Lightning Source LLC
LaVergne TN
LVHW031741191125
825924LV00004B/154
* 9 7 9 8 8 9 5 1 5 0 5 2 8 *